The Abinger Edition
of E. M. Forster

Edited by
OLIVER STALLYBRASS

Volume 11

E. M. Forster dedicated
"Two Cheers for Democracy"

To
Jack Sprott
of The University
of Nottingham, England
and
Bill Roehrich
of Lost Farm,
Tyringham, Massachusetts

Two Cheers
for Democracy

E. M. Forster

Edward Arnold

First published 1951
First published in the Abinger Edition 1972 by
Edward Arnold (Publishers) Ltd
25 Hill Street, London W1X 8LL

ISBN 0 7131 5658 9

Printed in Great Britain by
Richard Clay (The Chaucer Press) Ltd
Bungay, Suffolk

Contents

v

Editor's Introduction

Winding up his diary for 1950, E. M. Forster notes: "My book of articles now ready for casting. Not ill-content when thinking of it—pains will start with reading it for revision." The book is *Two Cheers for Democracy*, and by "casting" Forster probably means "casting off"—publishers' and printers' jargon for the process of calculating how big a book a given typescript or equivalent will make. In the case of a miscellany submitted, of necessity, in a wide variety of printed and typescript formats, the process is a pernickety one requiring more patience and a higher degree of numeracy than many authors possess; and the plan, no doubt, was for the British publisher, Edward Arnold, to make sure that the book was of suitable length before Forster began the detailed work of revision. For a miscellany, *Two Cheers for Democracy* is in fact, like its predecessor *Abinger Harvest*, a very substantial book. Yet we can safely assume that no omissions were requested of Forster for this (or any other) reason, since on the contrary he was able, over the next six months, to insert four additional items as they were written.

Two Cheers for Democracy was published, by Edward Arnold in London and Harcourt, Brace in New York, on 1 November 1951. Of the seventy or so essays, talks and reviews which it contains, three—"Anonymity" (1925), "A Letter to Madan Blanchard" (1931) and "The Stratford Jubilee of 1769" (1932) —are pieces which for some reason had been excluded from *Abinger Harvest* (1936). The remainder represent, in quantitative terms, rather more than half of Forster's occasional writings between the autumn of 1935 and the summer of 1951. Details of their first publication are given in the notes at the end of this volume, and Forster himself, in his Acknowledgements, has mentioned some of the periodicals involved; the others are the *Atlantic Monthly*, the *Calendar of Modern Letters*, *Harper's Magazine*, *London Calling*, the *London Mercury*, the *Nation* (New York), the *New York Times Book Review* and *Tribune*.

Of the various publications to which Forster contributed in the 1930s and 1940s two stand pre-eminent: the *Listener*, with thirty-one items reprinted in the present volume, and the *New Statesman*, with fourteen, all of them written between 1939 and 1944. The high figure for the *Listener* stems largely (twenty-one items) from Forster's success as a broadcaster; but it is not surprising to find that the literary editor of each of these journals during the years in question was a personal friend of Forster's: Raymond Mortimer of the *New Statesman* and, more particularly, J. R. Ackerley of the *Listener*.

In an interview recorded in 1965 and broadcast after Forster's death in 1970,[1] Joe Ackerley talked about his editorial relationship with Forster:

> Morgan Forster was the greatest journalist catch during my twenty-five years as literary editor of the *Listener*, and became increasingly so during that period. If you could land him for an article, or a book review, you landed the whale and were the envy of every other literary editor in London. The *Listener* was fortunate. . . . Morgan did a lot for me during my literary-editorship. He always helped his friends. . . . He always did for the *Listener* whatever I asked him to do, if he was interested. "Send the book along," he'd say, "and I'll see if I like it." Even when he could have got better paid elsewhere.

And even though, until 1958, reviews in the Book Chronicle section were unsigned. On this Ackerley—who in that year helped me to identify Forster's anonymous contributions—comments:

> Now, that was something! Our greatest living English novelist doing unsigned reviews. Moreover, he disapproved of anonymity. . . . I believe I am right in saying that he thought anonymous reviewing "sheer funk".

One is reminded of Forster's approving reference (page 214) to the high Ydgrunites' view of ideals: "they were always willing to drop a couple to oblige a friend."

Apart from the broadcast talks, at least seven of the longer pieces—on anonymity, art for art's sake, criticism, Skelton, Crabbe, Virginia Woolf and English prose between the wars—originated as lectures. Of Forster's craftsmanship in the medium of the spoken word, and more particularly the broadcast talk, John Arlott, who for several years produced his monthly book-talks to India, has written perceptively and with authority.[2] Forster's sensitiveness to his audience emerges also—as, *pace* his own modest Prefatory Note, do his skill and judgement in revising for publication—from the comparison of surviving scripts with the versions published in the *Listener* (or *London Calling*) and in *Two Cheers for Democracy*. Rough edges left by the revision process

[1] The transcript has been made available to me by the kindness of Mr Neville Braybrooke, and is here quoted, with permission, from an appendix to his edition of *The Letters of J. R. Ackerley* (London, Duckworth, 1973).

[2] In *Aspects of E. M. Forster*, edited by Oliver Stallybrass (London, Arnold, and New York, Harcourt, Brace, 1969), pp. 87–92.

are rare indeed;[3] much more typical are such tiny felicities as that represented by the word "cloister" at the end of the fourth paragraph of "Gide and George" (page 221), where Forster first wrote "the study and the cloister", then changed "cloister" to "platform" for his Indian audience, but reverted to "cloister" for successive published versions.

This piece, indeed, illustrates well not only the changes specific to talks or lectures, but those that are just as likely to occur anywhere: the elimination of topicalities, the removal or insertion of a qualification, more rarely an apparent change of view—as when *The Immoralist*, described in 1943 as Gide's "best and most disquieting work", becomes in 1951 merely his "most disquieting work". Here, to illustrate the neat excision of ephemera, is the opening paragraph of "Gide and George":

Two modern writers of European reputation, the Frenchman André Gide and the German Stefan George, offer contrasted reactions to the present chaos. I will begin with Gide.

This has been distilled from the following:

This talk is about two modern writers of European reputation. They are not well known in England, nor I suppose in India, but they are great names on the Continent, the tormented Continent, and in different ways they illustrate its tragedy. One of them is André Gide, the French novelist and man of letters. The other is a fine German poet, Stefan George. You may jump to hear me referring politely to a German poet on the British radio, and you will jump still higher when I add that the Nazis approve of this particular poet and have constituted him their national bard. If Dr Goebbels happened to be listening now, he would certainly be surprised at my praising Stefan George, who is his own speciality, and he would wonder what I was up to. I am up to something. I won't reveal what it is just yet. Let us leave Dr Goebbels in suspense for a little, and begin by discussing André Gide.

Towards the end of the talk Forster—who, by the way, was on the Nazi black list—put Goebbels out of his suspense; and at the very end came "There is also a third reaction—the saint's—about which you may know more than I do"—followed by a few

---

[3] In "Romain Rolland and the Hero" the third paragraph originally ended: ". . . was awarded the Nobel Prize for literature in 1916. I must now repeat that date—1916. Romain Rolland has entered the first world-war." And the next paragraph opens: "He was shattered by it to an extent which we can scarcely comprehend." In revising, Forster has removed the sentence repeating "1916" and changed "has" to "had", thereby producing a slightly pointless sentence whose one fact could have been neatly absorbed into the opening of the next paragraph. See page 227.

references to translations of Gide and George, and to commentaries on the latter.

So much for the "pains" of revision. But the preparation of *Two Cheers for Democracy* involved not only sensitive and judicious attention to each of its component parts, but, as with *Abinger Harvest*,[4] much thought about its shaping into an artistic whole:

> A chronological arrangement would have been simplest. But I was anxious to produce a book rather than a time-string . . .[5]

As in *Abinger Harvest*, too, Forster opens with what pretends to be a random set of notes, proceeds via political and social concerns to the arts, glances at the past, and invokes the sense of place: now a sub-continent, now a house, and finally a particularly well-loved corner of England.

Long before 1951, Forster was widely regarded as, at the very least, one of the five major English novelists of the twentieth century. Now, with *Two Cheers for Democracy* to set beside and complement *Abinger Harvest*, he was established also as an outstanding essayist, and as the spokesman *par excellence* for the liberal humane values represented, in Forster's view, by such men as Erasmus, Montaigne, Voltaire and André Gide: tolerance, sensitiveness, the capacity both to enjoy and to endure, scepticism over panaceas, distrust of authority, love of truth, and an unwavering belief in personal relationships, as well as in a personal culture that need involve neither aloofness nor mateyness. "The desire to know more, the desire to feel more, and, accompanying these but not strangling them, the desire to help others: here, briefly, is the human aim" (pp. 299–300)—and *Two Cheers for Democracy*, to adapt Forster's conclusion, exists partly to further it.

To emphasize this aspect of the collection seems natural: Forster himself offers "as a key to the book" the famous essay "What I Believe", and there are some half-dozen other essays, all in the first 120 pages, which are central to an understanding of his ideas on society and art. Even in the book reviews and literary essays—one or two of which, like "*Julius Caesar*", are on the slight or superficial side—he seems happiest when he is able to glance beyond the book to the ideas and values it stands for. *Two Cheers for Democracy*, in short, is a more consistently serious book than *Abinger Harvest*.

---

[4] On this aspect of which see David I. Joseph, *The Art of Rearrangement: E. M. Forster's* Abinger Harvest (New Haven and London, Yale University Press, 1964).

[5] Forster's firm rejection of chronology, here and in *Abinger Harvest*, is one reason why, in an edition likely to include six volumes of essays and the like, it was decided not to merge collected and uncollected items into a single chronological sequence (as has been well done with Orwell).

It is also a tougher one, the toughness being all the more effective for the deceptively playful spirit in which, so often, battle is engaged. "Jew-Consciousness" provides a good example: after an extremely amusing account of two preparatory schools where it was a disgrace to have, respectively, a sister and a mother, Forster suddenly pounces:

> Those preparatory schools prepared me for life better than I realized, for having passed through two imbecile societies, a sister-conscious and a mother-conscious, I am now invited to enter a third. I am asked to consider whether the people I meet and talk about are or are not Jews, and to form no opinion on them until this fundamental point has been settled. What revolting tosh! Neither science nor religion nor common sense has one word to say in its favour.

And there follows a devastating indictment of antisemitism. Or take "A Duke Remembers", where, reviewing what is clearly an inane, complacent book, Forster contents himself with mild badinage ("a tremendously aristocratic shoot . . . great names hurtle through the air") until the last paragraph. This concerns a veteran who, about to be decorated by Lord Roberts, "opened his coat, and out popped the head of a kitten". Forster points the moral and adorns the tale:

> All must deplore the veteran's conduct, yet the public is bound to pop out a kitten occasionally, or it would burst. It has, every now and then, to remind the governing classes that they must not take themselves and their awards too seriously, and if it is ever afraid to do this England will cease to be England.

Then, as a cunningly placed variation on the same theme, he turns his attention, in the next essay, to the egregious Mrs Miniver—whom, like antisemitism, he approaches obliquely:

> A working-class man I know—he grew up in a Gloucestershire village—has told me of the reactions of the villagers there to the parson thirty years back. The parson was not disliked, he was a kindly, friendly fellow, who had the right word for every occasion. But when the right word was spoken and he passed out of earshot, swinging his stick and looking right and left at the sky, the villagers came into their own for a moment, and used foul language about him. They had to, to clear their chests and to get rid of their feeling of incompetence. To preserve their manhood and their self-respect, they had to splutter a little smut.

A pleasant quotation, that, with which to conclude; not least because the psychological subtlety ("feeling of *incompetence*") and the eye for the telling detail ("swinging his stick and looking right and left at the sky") are among the hallmarks of a novelist— one who for valid private reasons had stopped writing novels.

In preparing this edition of *Two Cheers for Democracy* I have received generous and valuable help of one kind or another from the following individuals and organizations: Mr Stanley Adamson; Mrs Sylvia Anthony; Mr Neville Braybrooke; the British Museum (Department of Printed Books, especially Mr Ian Willison); Mr Benjamin Britten; Cambridge University Library; Mr John Davey (Edward Arnold Ltd); Mr Angus Davidson; Mr P. N. Furbank; Mrs Martha Hartley; Mr Colin Haycraft (Gerald Duckworth & Co. Ltd); Mr Peter Hoare (formerly Brynmor Jones Library, University of Hull; Miss Joan Houlgate (Reference Librarian, B.B.C.); the Humanities Research Center, University of Texas (Mr F. W. Roberts, Director, and Mrs June Moll, Librarian); Mr Christopher Isherwood; Miss Christine Jackson (National Council for Civil Liberties); Mr Bernard Jones; Miss B. J. Kirkpatrick; the London Library, especially Dr Martin Schor and Miss Barbara Tarrant; Mrs Sylvia McGeachie; Mr T. S. Matthews; Mr G. T. Mitchell (London School of Economics); Miss Patricia Parkin; Mr C. W. Roberts; Professor Mark Roskill (University of Massachusetts); Professor C. R. Sanders (Duke University); Mrs Gunvor Stallybrass; Miss Rita Vaughan (Harcourt Brace Jovanovich, Inc.); Mrs Valerie Weston (India Office Library and Records); and, at King's College, Cambridge, Dr Donald Parry, Vice-Provost; Dr A. N. L. Munby, Librarian, Mr Donald Loukes, Assistant Librarian, and other members of the Library staff; Miss Elizabeth Ellem and Mrs Penelope Bulloch, successive custodians of the Forster archive; Mr Christopher Prendergast; Mr Philip Radcliffe; and Mr George Rylands. (See p. 409.) Certain outstanding and continuing debts have been more fully acknowledged elsewhere in this edition; on this occasion I hope that my thanks to all concerned will not seem the less warm for being so summarily expressed.

OLIVER STALLYBRASS

Earlier British editions of *Two Cheers for Democracy* were dedicated "to Jack Sprott, of the University of Nottingham, England, and to Bill Roehrich, of Lost Farm, Tyringham, Massachusetts". In American editions, Bill Roerick (*sic*) was named first. W. J. H. Sprott (1897–1971) was Professor of, successively, Philosophy and Psychology at Nottingham; William Roehrich or Roerick is an actor.

Prefatory Note

These essays, articles, broadcasts, etc., were nearly all of them composed after the publication of *Abinger Harvest*, that is to say after 1936. A title for the collection has been difficult to find. One of my younger friends suggested *Two Cheers for Democracy* as a joke, and I have decided to adopt it seriously.

Arrangement has been still more difficult. A chronological arrangement would have been simplest. But I was anxious to produce a book rather than a time-string, and to impose some sort of order upon the occupations and preoccupations, the appointments and disappointments, of the past fifteen years. Division into two sections proved helpful. The opening section, "The Second Darkness", concentrates on the war which began for Great Britain in 1939, though earlier elsewhere, and which is still going on. Subjects such as Antisemitism, the Nazis, Liberty, the Censorship are here discussed. The climate is political, and the conclusion suggested is that, though we cannot expect to love one another, we must learn to put up with one another. Otherwise we shall all of us perish.

The second section, "What I Believe", covers the same period as the first and sometimes the same subjects, but its climate is ethical and aesthetic. It opens with an essay which may be regarded as a key to the book. Then come the arts. I have found by experience that the arts act as an antidote against our present troubles and also as a support to our common humanity, and I am glad to emphasize this at a time when they are being belittled and starved. Theories of art are followed by the arts in action— literature particularly: Skelton and Shakespeare to Forrest Reid, Voltaire to Proust and Iqbal, together with items less easily accommodated, such as Mrs Miniver, the Duke of Portland, my own grandfather, and my own library. Then places: in them also I believe. Beginning with the Pelew Islands, which I have only visited vicariously, I flit via India and South Africa to the United States, to Europe, to England, and finally spiral down upon Abinger, the village in Surrey which was for many years my home.

That ends the miscellany. I hope it may reveal some unity of outlook, for it certainly lacks unity of atmosphere; some of the items being expository in tone and others allusive. The broadcasts have been troublesome. There is something cajoling and ingratiating about them which cannot be exorcised by editing, and they have been the devil to reproduce. I have not been consistent over broadcasts. In some cases I have taken the microphone by the horns and printed the script as it stood. Elsewhere I have attempted concealments which the reader will probably detect.

Until livelier counsels prevailed "The Last of Abinger" was to have been the book's general title. But I do not really want to record the last of anything and am glad to change. Human life is still active, still carrying about with it unexplored riches and unused methods of release. The darkness that troubles us and tries to degrade us may thin out. We may still contrive to raise three cheers for democracy, although at present she only deserves two.

Cambridge, England, 1951   E.M.F.

Acknowledgements

My thanks for permission kindly given to reprint previously published material are due, in the first place, to the Syndics of the Cambridge University Press for *Virginia Woolf*; the University Board of the University of Glasgow for *English Prose between 1918 and 1939*—and for the quotations within it from T. E. Lawrence's *The Seven Pillars of Wisdom* (Jonathan Cape Ltd) and Lytton Strachey's *Queen Victoria* (Chatto and Windus Ltd) to the respective authors' executors and publishers; the Harvard University Press for *The Raison d'Être of Criticism*; and the Hogarth Press for *Anonymity* and *A Letter to Madan Blanchard*.

Also to the following: the *Abinger Chronicle*, the British Broadcasting Corporation (and more particularly the *Listener*), *Horizon*, *Reynolds News*, the *New Statesman and Nation*, *New Writing*, the *Spectator*, *Time and Tide*, and Anjuman-e-Taraqqi-e-Urdu.

The essays on Crabbe and on Skelton have not been published before; nor has the meditation with which the miscellany closes.

E.M.F.

Part One
The Second Darkness

The Last Parade

Paris Exhibition, 1937: Palace of Discovery, Astronomical Section: model of the Earth in space. Yes, here is a model of this intimate object. It is a tidy size—so large that Europe or even France should be visible on it—and it revolves at a suitable rate. It does not take twenty-four hours to go round as in fact, nor does it whizz as in poetry. It considers the convenience of the observer, as an exhibit should. Staged in a solemn alcove, against a background of lamp-super-black, it preens its contours eternally, that is to say from opening to closing time, and allows us to see our home as others would see it, were there others who could see. Its colouring, its general appearance, accord with the latest deductions. The result is surprising. For not France, not even Europe, is visible. There are great marks on the surface of the model, but they represent clouds and snows, not continents and seas. No doubt the skilled observer could detect some underlying fussiness, and infer our civilization, but the average voyager through space would only notice our clouds and our snows; they strike the eye best. Natural boundaries, guns in action, beautiful women, pipe-lines—at a little distance they all wear the same veil. Sir Malcolm Campbell beats his own records till he sees his own back, Mr Jack Hulbert cracks still cleaner jokes, forty thousand monkeys are born in Brazil and fifty thousand Italians in Abyssinia, the Palace of the Soviets rises even higher than had been planned, Lord Baden-Powell holds a yet larger jamboree, but all these exercises and the areas where they occur remain hidden away under an external shimmer. The moon—she shows her face. Throned in an adjacent room, the moon exhibits her pockmarks nakedly. But the Earth, because she still has atmosphere and life, is a blur.

Paris Exhibition: the Spanish Pavilion, the Italian Pavilion. The other pavilions. The Palaces of Glass and of Peace. The Eiffel Tower. The last-named occasionally sings. Moved by an emission of Roman candles from its flanks, it will break of an evening into a dulcet and commanding melody. When this happens the pavilions fold their hands to listen, and are steeped for a little in shadow, so that the aniline fountains may play more brightly in the Seine. The melody swells, inciting the fireworks as they the melody, and both of them swell the crowd. O synchronization! O splendour unequalled! Splendour ever to be surpassed? Probably never to be surpassed. The German and Russian Pavilions, the Chinese and Japanese Pavilions, the British and Italian Pavilions, any and all of the pavilions, will see to that. The Eiffel Tower sings louder, a scientific swan. Rosy chemicals stimulate her spine, she can scarcely bear the voltage, the joy, the pain. . . . The emotion goes to her tiny head, it turns crimson and vomits fiery serpents. All Paris sees them. They astonish the Panthéon and Montmartre. Even the Institut de France notices, heavy-browed, dreaming of cardinals, laurels, and *réclame* in the past. O inspired giraffe! Whatever will the old thing turn into next? Listen and see. The crisis is coming. The melody rises by slight and sure gradations, *à la* César Franck, spiralling easily upward upon the celestial roundabout. Bell pop popple crack, is the crisis, bell pop popple crack, the senses reel, music and light, lusic and might, the Eiffel Tower becomes a plesiosaurus, flings out her arms in flame, and brings them back smartly to her vibrating sides, as one who should say "Là!" Bell pop crack pop popple bell. The carillon dies away, the rockets fall, the senses disentangle. There is silence, there are various types of silences, and during one of them the Angel of the Laboratory speaks. "Au revoir, mes enfants," she says. "I hope you have enjoyed yourselves. We shall meet again shortly, and in different conditions." The children applaud these well-chosen words. The German Pavilion, the Russian Pavilion, confront one another again, and a small star shines out on the top of the Column of Peace.

Paris Exhibition: van Gogh. When the day breaks, van Gogh can be found if wanted. He is housed in the corner of another palace between maps of Paris and intellectual hopes for the future, and the space suffices him. Well content with his half-dozen rooms, he displays his oddness and his misery to tired feet. "Sorrow is better than joy," he writes up upon the white walls of his cell. Here are pictures of potatoes and of miners who have eaten potatoes until their faces are tuberous and dented and their skins grimed and unpeeled. They are hopeless and humble, so he loves them. He has his little say, and he understands what he is saying, and he cuts off his own ear with a knife. The gaily painted boats

4

of Saintes Maries sail away into the Mediterranean at last, and the Alpilles rise over St Rémy for ever, but nevertheless "sorrow is better than joy", for van Gogh. What would the Eiffel Tower make of such a conclusion? Spinning in its alcove for millions of years, the Earth brings a great artist to this. Is he just dotty, or is he failing to put across what is in his mind? Neither, if we may accept historical parallels. Every now and then people have preferred sorrow to joy, and asserted that wisdom and creation can only result from suffering. Half a mile off, Picasso has done a terrifying fresco in the Spanish Pavilion, a huge black and white thing called *Guernica*. Bombs split bull's skull, woman's trunk, man's shins. The fresco is indignant, and so it is less disquieting than the potato-feeders of van Gogh. Picasso is grotesquely angry, and those who are angry still hope. He is not yet wise, and perhaps he is not yet a creator. Nevertheless, he too succeeds in saying something about injustice and pain. Can one look through pain or get round it? And can anything be done against money? On the subject of money, van Gogh becomes comprehensible and sound. He has got round money because he has sought suffering and renounced happiness. In the sizzle surrounding him, his voice stays uncommercial, unscientific, pure. He sees the colour "blue", observes that the colour "yellow" always occurs in it, and writes this preposterous postulate up upon the white walls. He has a home beyond comfort and common sense with the saints, and perhaps he sees God.

The Soviet Pavilion. This, bold and gleaming, hopes to solve such problems for the ordinary man. And for the ordinary woman too, who, of enormous size, leans forward on the roof beside her gigantic mate. Seen from the side, they and the building upon which they stand describe a hyperbola. They shoot into space, following their hammer and sickle, and followed by the workers' world state. The conception is satisfying, but a hyperbola is a mathematical line, not necessarily an aesthetic one, and the solid and ardent pair do not group well when viewed from the banks of the bourgeois Seine. Challenging injustice, they ignore good taste, indeed they declare in their sterner moments that injustice and good taste are inseparable. Their aims are moral, their methods disciplinary. Passing beneath their sealed-up petticoats and trousers, we enter a realm which is earnest, cheerful, instructive, constructive and consistent, but which has had to blunt some of the vagrant sensibilities of mankind and is consequently not wholly alive. Statistics, maps and graphs preach a numerical triumph, but the art-stuff on the walls might just as well hang on the walls of the German Pavilion opposite: the incidents and the uniforms in the pictures are different but the mentality of the artists is the same, and is as tame. Only after a little thinking does one get over one's disappointment and see the matter in perspective. For the Soviet Pavilion is a nudge to the blind. It is trying, like van Gogh, to dodge money and to wipe away the film of coins and notes which keeps forming on the human retina. One of the evils of money is that it tempts us to look at it rather than at the things that it buys. They are dimmed because of the metal and the paper through which we receive them. That is the fundamental deceitfulness of riches, which kept worrying Christ. That is the treachery of the purse, the wallet and the bank-balance, even from the capitalist point of view. They were invented as a convenience to the flesh, they have become a chain for the spirit. Surely they can be cut out, like some sorts of pain. Though deprived of them the human mind might surely still keep its delicacy unimpaired, and the human body eat, drink and make love. And that is why every bourgeois ought to reverence the Soviet Pavilion. Even if he is scared at Marxism he ought to realize that Russia has tried to put men into touch with things. She has come along with a handkerchief and wiped. And she has wiped close to the exhibition turnstiles and amid the chaos and carnage of international finance.

Park of Attractions. I did enjoy myself here, I must say. That is the difficulty of considering the Exhibition: it is in so many pieces and so is oneself. After seeing the German Pavilion, which presents Valhalla as a telephone-box, and the Belgian Pavilion, which is very lovely, and many other sacred and serious objects, I sought the Park of Attractions and went up to space in a pretence-balloon. A crane lifted me into the void while another crane lowered another balloon, which filled with people when my balloon was up. Then my balloon came down and the other balloon went up. So I got out and walked over the surface of the Earth to the Dervish Theatre. Then I watched other people play a game called "Déshabiller vos vedettes". I thought a vedette was a boat. Here it was a tin lady, naked except for a cincture of green feathers which the entrants tried to shoot off. Then I went to a booth advertising "Perversités. Images Troublantes". The entrance fee was a franc, which helped me to keep my head. Inside were some distorting mirrors, a little black savage who kept lashing herself or himself with a bunch of boot-laces, and some holes through which improper photographs should have been seen, but I got muddled and missed them. Oh, the French, the French! Well pleased, I came out. It was a lovely evening. The moon, which had been trying various styles from Neon to Panthéon, now imitated a pretence-balloon. The Park of Attractions, which is extremely clever and pretty, was girt with a scenic railway, and at intervals the shrieks of voyagers through space rent the night. There was plenty to spend money on. Money, money, money! The crowd was what journalists call "good-humoured"; and I, a journalist, was part of it. Tunisians and Moroccans strolled about and sometimes kissed one another. Oh, the French! Why are they so good at organizing these lighter happinesses? The English admire them, and themselves produce the suety dreariness, the puffed pretentiousness, of Wembley.

Satan. Unexpected but unmistakable, he appears in the great entrance court of the Italian Pavilion, amongst the fragments of the lovely Italian past. These fragments are bent to his service—Garibaldi, St Francis, Ravenna mosaics, Pompeian doves. He is to the left as one comes in, clothed all in black, and he dominates a large feeble picture of carnage. He is weakness triumphant—that is his role in the modern world. He presses a button and a bull bursts. He sprays savages with scent. He tilts his head back till his chin sticks out like a tongue and his eyeballs stare into his brain. Decent people take no notice of him or make fun of him, but presently something goes wrong with their lives: certain islands are inaccessible, a letter is unanswered, bonds confiscated, a friend takes a trip over the frontier and never returns. Elsewhere in this same pavilion are his instruments: things easily let off. He has only one remark to make: "I, I, I". He uses the symbols of the sacred and solemn past, but they only mean "I". Here, among superficial splendours of marble, he holds his court, and no one can withstand him except van Gogh, and van Gogh has nothing to lose. The rest of us are vulnerable, science is doing us in, the Angel of the Laboratory switches off the fire-works, and burns up the crowd without flame.

Meanwhile, and all the while, the Earth revolves in her alcove, veiled in wool. She has sent samples of her hopes and lusts to Paris; that they will again be collected there, or anywhere, is unlikely, but she herself will look much the same as soon as one stands a little back in space. Even if the Mediterranean empties into the Sahara it will not make much difference. It is our clouds and our snows that show.

[1937]

The Menace to Freedom

The menace to freedom is usually conceived in terms of political or social interference—Communism, Fascism, Grundyism, bureaucratic encroachment, censorship, conscription and so forth. And it is usually personified as a tyrant who has escaped from the bottomless pit, his proper home, and is stalking the earth by some mysterious dispensation, in order to persecute God's elect, the electorate. But this is too lively a view of our present troubles, and too shallow a one. We must peer deeper if we want to understand them, deep into the abyss of our own characters. For politics are based on human nature; even a tyrant is a man, and our freedom is really menaced today because a million years ago Man was born in chains.

That unfortunate event lies too far back for retrospective legislation; no declarations of independence touch it; no League of Nations can abolish it. Man grew out of other forms of life; he has evolved among taboos; he has been a coward for centuries, afraid of the universe outside him and of the herd wherein he took refuge. So he cannot, even if he wishes it, be free today. In recent centuries—Greece saw the first attempt—he tried to become an individual, an entity which thinks for itself, says what it thinks, and acts according to its own considered standards; and there has been much applause for this attempt in art and literature, but it is abortive morally because of those primeval chains. The ghosts of chains, the chains of ghosts, but they are strong enough, literally stronger than death, generation after generation hands them on. More recently still, Man has dallied with the idea of a social conscience, and has disguised the fear of the herd as loyalty towards the group, and has persuaded himself that when he sacrifices himself to the State he is accomplishing a deed far more satisfying than anything which can be accomplished alone. Alone? As if he had ever been alone! He has never had the opportunity. Only Heaven knows what Man might accomplish alone! The service that is perfect freedom, perhaps. As things are, the poor creature presents a sorry spectacle to the philosopher—or, rather, he would do so if philosophers existed,

9

but we have realized since the days of Voltaire and Rousseau that they do not exist. There is no such person as a philosopher; no one is detached; the observer, like the observed, is in chains.

To the best minds of the eighteenth and nineteenth centuries freedom appeared as a blessing which had to be recovered. They believed that a little energy and intelligence would accomplish this. The chains had only to be broken violently, the conventions patiently unloosed, and either by revolutionary or by constitutional methods Man would re-enter his heritage and the tyrant sink back into his pit. The twentieth century knows more history than that and more psychology, and has suffered more; its disillusion over peace in 1914 has been swiftly followed by its disillusion over democracy today. The tyrant no longer appears as a freak from the pit, he is becoming the norm, country after country throws him up, he springs from any class of society with an ease which once seemed admirable; requiring only opportunity and ruthlessness, he supersedes parliaments and kings. And consequently many people do not believe in freedom any more, and the few who do regard it as something that must be discovered, not recovered. They think that it is a blessing which we have never possessed up to now. They hope for a revelation in the human make-up which will allow it to emerge. And there is this to be said for such optimism: the human make-up is certainly changing; we alter ourselves merely by knowing more about ourselves, and we know more about ourselves yearly. Perhaps, under the inrush of scientific inventions, the change will proceed still quicker. Perhaps, after the storms have swept by and the aeroplanes crashed into one another and wireless jammed wireless, a new creature may appear on this globe, a creature who, we pretend, is here already: the individual.

How the globe would get on, if entirely peopled with individuals, it is impossible to foresee. However, Man has another wish, besides the wish to be free, and that is the wish to love, and perhaps something may be born from the union of the two. Love sometimes leads to an obedience which is not servile—the obedience referred to in the Christian epigram above quoted. Love, after a dreadful period of inflation, is perhaps coming back to its proper level and may steady civilization; up-to-date social workers believe in it. It is difficult not to get mushy as soon as one mentions love, but it is a tendency that must be reckoned with, and it takes as many forms as fear. The desire to devote oneself to another person or persons seems to be as innate as the desire for personal liberty. If the two desires could combine, the menace to freedom from within, the fundamental menace, might disappear, and the political evils now filling all the foreground of our lives would be deprived of the poison which nourishes them. They will not wilt in our time, we can hope for no immediate relief. But it is a good thing, once in a way, to speculate on the remoter future. It is a good thing, when freedom is discussed, not always to be wondering what ought to be done about Hitler, or whether the decisions of the Milk Marketing Board are unduly arbitrary. There is the Beloved Republic to dream about and to work for through our dreams; the better polity which once seemed to be approaching on greased wheels; the City of God.

[1935]

Jew-Consciousness

Long, long ago, while Queen Victoria reigned, I attended two preparatory schools. At the first of these, it was held to be a disgrace to have a sister. Any little boy who possessed one was liable to get teased. The word would go round: "Oh, you men, have you seen the Picktoes' sister?" The men would then reel about with sideway motions, uttering cries of "Sucks" and pretending to faint with horror, while the Picktoes, who had hitherto held their own socially in spite of their name, found themselves banished into the wilderness, where they mourned, Major with Minor, in common shame. Naturally anyone who had a sister hid her as far as possible, and forbade her to sit with him at a Prizegiving or to speak to him except in passing and in a very formal manner. Public opinion was not bitter on the point, but it was quite definite. Sisters were disgraceful. I got through all right myself, because my conscience was clear, and though charges were brought against me from time to time they always fell through.

It was a very different story at my second school. Here, sisters were negligible, but it was a disgrace to have a mother. Crabbe's mother, Gob's mother, eeugh! No words were too strong, no sounds too shrill. And since mothers at that time of life are commoner than sisters, and also less biddable, the atmosphere of this school was less pleasant, and the sense of guilt stronger. Nearly every little boy had a mother in a cupboard, and dreadful revelations occurred. A boy would fall ill and a mother would swoop and drive him away in a cab. A parcel would arrive with "From Mummy for her darling" branded upon it. Many tried to divert suspicion by being aggressive and fastening female parents upon the weak. One or two, who were good at games and had a large popularity-surplus, took up a really heroic line, acknowledged their mother brazenly, and would even be seen walking with her across the playing-field, like King Carol with Madame Lupescu. We admired such boys and envied them, but durst not imitate them. The margin of safety was too narrow. The convention was established that a mother spelled disgrace, and no individual triumph could reverse this.

12

Those preparatory schools prepared me for life better than I realized, for having passed through two imbecile societies, a sister-conscious and a mother-conscious, I am now invited to enter a third. I am asked to consider whether the people I meet and talk about are or are not Jews, and to form no opinion on them until this fundamental point has been settled. What revolting tosh! Neither science nor religion nor common sense has one word to say in its favour. All the same, Jew-consciousness is in the air, and it remains to be seen how far it will succeed in poisoning it. I don't think we shall ever reintroduce ghettos into England; I wouldn't say for certain, since no one knows what wickedness may not develop in his country or in himself if circumstances change. I don't think we shall go savage. But I do think we shall go silly. Many people have gone so already. Today, the average man suspects the people he dislikes of being Jews, and is surprised when the people he likes are Jews. Having been a Gentile at my first preparatory school and a Jew at my second, I know what I am talking about. I know how the poison works, and I know too that if the average man is anyone in particular he is a preparatory-school boy. On the surface, things do not look too bad. Labour and Liberalism behave with their expected decency and denounce persecution, and respectability generally follows suit. But beneath the surface things are not so good, and anyone who keeps his ears open in railway carriages or pubs or country lanes can hear a very different story. A nasty side of our nation's character has been scratched up—the sniggering side. People who would not ill-treat Jews themselves, or even be rude to them, enjoy tittering over their misfortunes; they giggle when pogroms are instituted by someone else and synagogues defiled vicariously. "Serve them right really, Jews." This makes unpleasant reading, but anyone who cares to move out of his own enlightened little corner will discover that it is true. The grand Nordic argument, "He's a bloody capitalist so he must be a Jew, and as he's a Jew he must be a Red," has already taken root in our filling-stations and farms. Men employ it more frequently than women, and young men more frequently than old ones. The best way of confuting it is to say sneeringly, "That's propaganda." When "That's propaganda" has been repeated several times, the sniggering stops, for no goose likes to think that he has been got at. There is another reply which is more intellectual but which requires more courage. It is to say, "Are you sure you're not a Jew yourself? Do you know who your eight great-grandparents were? Can you swear that all the eight are Aryan?" Cool reasonableness would be best of all, of course, but it does not work in the world of today any better than in my preparatory schools. The only effective check to silliness is silliness of a cleverer type.

Jew-mania was the one evil which no one foretold at the close of the last war. All sorts of troubles were discerned and discernable—nationalism, class-warfare, the split between the haves and the have-nots, the general lowering of cultural values. But no prophet, so far as I know, had foreseen this anti-Jew horror, whereas today no one can see the end of it. There had been warnings, of course, but they seemed no more ominous than a poem by Hilaire Belloc. Back in India, in 1921, a colonel lent me the *Protocols of the Elders of Zion*, and it was such an obvious fake that I did not worry. I had forgotten my preparatory schools, and did not see that they were about to come into their own. To me, antisemitism is now the most shocking of all things. It is destroying much more than the Jews; it is assailing the human mind at its source, and inviting it to create false categories before exercising judgement. I am sure we shall win through. But it will take a long time. Perhaps a hundred years must pass before men can think back to the mentality of 1918, or can say with the Prophet Malachi, "Have we not all one father? Hath not one God created us?" For the moment, all that we can do is to dig in our heels, and prevent silliness from sliding into insanity.

[1939]

Our Deputation

Our deputation straggled across Whitehall in the sleet, harried by taxis upon either flank. It jumped a bank of slush, slid upon the pavement, caught hands, upsa! and finally entered the Government Office of its choice. We took off our hats in the vestibule, then realized that we had done so too soon and were being despised by the commissionaires, so we put them on again. Dinginess and warmth surrounded us; it was like being in the belly of a not very healthy monster. At the top of a huge and enormous stairway (both adjectives are needed to describe the architecture) stretched the huge and enormous room where the Minister had consented to receive us and to hear our prayer. Away at the end of it loomed the picture of some statesman or royalty, huge and enormous, and only partially visible through the spume. Our hats came off for good now. Having hung them and our greatcoats and mufflers upon the branches of a metallic tree, we placed ourselves at a table which may justly be called gigantic. The chairs seemed miles apart. Honoured but isolated, we could no longer hold one another's hands. After a minute or two, which were spent in dreamily looking at papers, a door near the picture opened, and the Minister popped in.

All rose to their feet. The Minister recoiled as if horror-struck by the commotion he had created. "Sit sit down, do please sit sit sit," he said. We obeyed. The Minister sat too, supported on either side by important permanencies belonging to his department.... He heard our prayer, which was tersely phrased so as not to waste his time. He thanked us and announced that even now he was attempting to grant it, and to find a statutory form in which to embody our wishes and his own. This sounded splendid. But he was finding it difficult to do this, he went on, very, very difficult difficult. His manner now became bewildered and almost childlike; he seemed baffled by the intricacies of drafting and began to hint that the task of doing as he liked might prove to be beyond his power. "If you can can can help me," he pleaded, "if you can can can can ..." and before we knew where we were he was giving us a good dressing-down. He said that if

15

we—not that he meant us personally or any of the organizations that we represented—still, if we could check certain undesirable tendencies and ensure that certain contraventions of the law were not repeated in the future we should greatly facilitate his task. The deputation bowed its head like a flower in a frost, and, gazing at my particular bit of the table, I reflected upon the technique which is employed by those in high authority when they desire to administer a snub. They carry on like this: they begin a sentence deeply, gruffly, gently; it moves along like a large friendly animal; then it twitters, turns acid and thin and passes right overhead with a sort of whistling sound. An awed pause followed. However, one of the deputation pulled himself together and gave, I thought, an excellent performance in the same key. We entirely agreed with the Minister, he said, his voice still deep. We felt exactly as the Minister felt. No one could deplore more than we did the tendencies, the manifestations that had been mentioned. But (and here his voice grew thinner) there was surely an Act of Parliament already in existence which dealt with such matters, and this being so (voice now well overhead) the deputation did not quite appreciate why they should be raised here. There was now a pause at the ministerial end of the table, and it was conveyed to us, by shiftings of pince-nez and bleakness of cheeks, that our champion had not contributed anything constructive. Next, one of the important permanencies spoke, and his voice too went up in the air at the end in a bitter whistle. Was the interview going to be an unfriendly one? No, no, nothing as definite as that. Civilities were re-exchanged, time was up, we thanked and were counter-thanked, our opinions were to be given their full weight, and, performing a final can-can, the Minister slipped from the room. He had performed his duty, and we ours. We went to the tree which had all the time supported our greatcoats, we unwound our mufflers from its branches and placed our hats upon our heads, and we passed down the stairway back into the snow and the dirt outside, and resolved into our component parts.

[1939]

Racial Exercise

Let us do some easy exercises in Racial Purity.

And let me offer myself for dissection purposes.

If I go the right way about it, I come of an old English family, but the right way is unfortunately a crooked one. It is far from easy going in the branches of my genealogical tree. I have to proceed via my father to his mother, thence to her mother, and thence to her father. If I follow this zigzag course I arrive in the satisfactory bosom of a family called Sykes, and have a clear run back through several centuries. The Sykeses go right away ever so far, right back to a certain Richard of Sykes Dyke who flourished somewhere about the year 1400. Whether inside their dyke, which lay in Cumberland, or outside it, which was Yorkshire, this family never did anything earth-shaking, still they did keep going in the documentary sense, they made money and married into it, they became mayors of Pontefract or Hull, they employed Miss Anna Seward as a governess, and, in the seventeenth century, one of them, a Quaker, was imprisoned on account of his opinions in York Castle, and died there. I come of an old English family, and am proud of it.

Unfortunately in other directions the prospect is less extensive. If I take a wrong turning and miss the Sykeses, darkness descends on my origins almost at once. Mrs James is a case in point, and a very mortifying one. Mrs James was a widow who not so very long ago married one of my great-grandfathers. I am directly descended from her, know nothing whatever about her, and should like at all events to discover her maiden name. Vain quest. She disappears in the mists of antiquity, like Richard of Sykes Dyke, but much too soon. She might be anyone, she may not even have been Aryan. When her shadow crosses my mind, I do not feel to belong to an old family at all.

After that dissection, let us proceed to do our easy Racial Exercise.

It is this: Can you give the names of your eight great-grandparents?

The betting is at least eight to one against. The Royal Family could, some aristocrats could, and so could a few yeomen who have lived undisturbed in a quiet corner of England for a couple of hundred years. But most of the people I know (and probably most of the people who read these words) will fail. We can often get six or seven, seldom the whole eight. And the human mind is so dishonest and so snobby that we instinctively reject the eighth as not mattering, and as playing no part in our biological make-up. As each of us looks back into his or her past, doors open upon darkness. Two doors at first—the father and the mother— through each of these two more, then the eight great-grand-parents, the sixteen great-greats, then thirty-two ancestors . . . sixty-four . . . one hundred and twenty-eight . . . until the re-searcher reels. Even if the stocks producing us interbred, and so reduced the total of our progenitors by using some of them up on us twice, even if they practised the strict domestic economy of the Ptolemies, the total soon becomes enormous, and the Sykeses in it are nothing beside the Mrs Jameses. On such a shady past as this—our common past—do we erect the ridiculous doctrine of Racial Purity.

In the future the situation will be slightly less ridiculous. Registers of marriage and birth will be kept more carefully, bastardy more cunningly detected, so that in a couple of hundred years millions of people will belong to Old Families. This should be a great comfort to them. It may also be a convenience, if governments continue to impose racial tests. Citizens will be in a position to point to an Aryan ancestry if their government is Aryan, to a Cretinist ancestry if it is Cretin, and so on, and if they cannot point in the direction required they will be sterilized. This should be a great discomfort to them. Nor will the steriliza-tion help, for the mischief has already been done in our own day, the mess has been made, miscegenation has already taken place. Whether there ever was such an entity as a "pure race" is debatable, but there certainly is not one in Europe today—the internationalisms of the Roman Empire and of the Middle Ages have seen to that. Consequently there never can be a pure race in the future. Europe is mongrel for ever, and so is America.

How extraordinary it is that governments which claim to be realistic should try to base themselves on anything so shadowy and romantic as race! A common language, a common religion, a common culture all belong to the present, evidence about them is available, they can be tested. But race belongs to the unknown and unknowable past. It depends upon who went to bed with whom in the year 1400, not to mention Mrs James, and what historian will ever discover that? Community of race is an illusion. Yet belief in race is a growing psychological force, and we must reckon with it. People like to feel that they are all of a piece, and one of the ways of inducing that feeling is to tell them that they come of pure stock. That explains the ease with which the dictators are putting their pseudo-science across. No doubt they are not cynical about it, and take themselves in by what they say. But they have very cleverly hit on a weak spot in the human equipment—the desire to feel a hundred per cent, no matter what the percentage is in.

A German professor was holding forth the other day on the subject of the origins of the German people. His attitude was that the purity of the Nordic stock is not yet proved and should not be spoken of as proved. But it should be spoken of as a fact, because it is one, and the proofs of its existence will be forthcoming as soon as scholars are sufficiently energetic and brave. He spoke of "courage" in research. According to his own lights, he was a disinterested researcher, for he refused to support what he knew to be true by arguments which he held to be false. The truth, being *a priori*, could afford to wait on its mountain top until the right path to it was found: the truth of Nordic purity which every German holds by instinct in his blood. In India I had friends who said they were descended from the Sun and looked down on those who merely came from the Moon, but they were not tense about it and seemed to forget about it between times, nor did they make it a basis for political violence and cruelty; it takes the West to do that.

Behind our problem of the eight great-grandparents stands the civilizing figure of Mendel. I wish that Mendel's name was mentioned in current journalism as often as Freud's or Einstein's. He embodies a salutary principle, and even when we are superficial about him he helps to impress it in our minds. He suggests that no stock is pure, and that it may at any moment throw up forms which are unexpected, and which it inherits from the past. His best-known experiments were with the seeds of the pea. It is impossible that human beings can be studied as precisely as peas —too many factors are involved. But they too keep throwing up recessive characteristics, and cause us to question the creed of racial purity. Mendel did not want to prove anything. He was not a "courageous" researcher, he was merely a researcher. Yet he has unwittingly put a valuable weapon into the hands of civilized people. We don't know what our ancestors were like or what our descendants will be like. We only know that we are all of us mongrels, dark-haired and light-haired, who must learn not to bite one another. Thanks to Mendel and to a few simple exercises we can see comparatively clearly into the problem of race, if we choose to look, and can do a little to combat the pompous and pernicious rubbish that is at present being prescribed in the high places of the earth.

[1939]

Post-Munich

During the present decade thousands and thousands of innocent people have been killed, robbed, mutilated, insulted, imprisoned. We, the fortunate exceptions, learn of this from the newspapers and from refugees, we realize that it may be our turn next, and we know that all these private miseries may be the prelude to an incalculable catastrophe, in which the whole of western civilization and half oriental civilization may go down. Perhaps history will point to these years as the moment when man's inventiveness finally outbalanced his moral growth, and toppled him downhill.

The decade being tragic, should not our way of living correspond? How can we justify trivialities and hesitations? Ought we not to rise to the great dramatic conception which we see developing around us? The situation is tremendous; it has never been equalled, because the world has never before been so closely interlocked. The pillars of the twenty-thousand-year-old house are crumbling, the human experiment totters, other forms of life watch. Ought we not, at such a moment, to act as Wagnerian heroes and heroines, who are raised above themselves by the conviction that all is lost or that all can be saved, and stride singing into the flames?

To ask such a question is to answer it. No one who debates whether he shall behave tragically can possibly be a tragic character. He may have a just sense of the stage; he may discern the scene darkening and the powers of evil marching and the ravens gathering; he may feel the first breath of the tempest as it lifts him off his feet and whirls him backwards. But he is not properly cast as an actor; there will be something petty in him—perhaps something recalcitrant—which mars the aesthetic unity. He will not even pay the tribute of unalloyed terror. He will be half frightened and half thinking about something else on the very steps of the altar, and when the sacrificial knife falls he will perish an unworthy victim, a blemished and inferior lamb, of little esteem at the banquet of the gods.

The state of being half frightened and half thinking about something else at the same time is the state of many English people today. It is worth examining, partly because it is interesting, partly because, like all mixed states, it can be improved by thought. Only Heaven and Hell are stable. It is a 1939 state. In 1938 we were fresher and less complex. War was promised or threatened us for a certainty; we went inspired or demented according to our quality, and our actions bore some relation to the *Zeitgeist*'s. Exalted in contrary directions, some of us rose above ourselves and others committed suicide. One elderly gentleman, for instance, described in the newspaper as having a great many friends, exclaimed to his housekeeper, "Oh Agnes, Agnes, what will become of us all now?" and jumped out of a top-storey window in his pyjamas. He saw what he could do and he did it, and his conduct when analysed shows parallels with Brünnhilde's. Others saw something else they could do and, like Siegmund, prepared to fight—with what weapons and against what they did not stay to consider. These certainties and heroisms came to their end when Mr Chamberlain paid his first call upon Herr Hitler. I was in London that dark Wednesday night when the news of an agreement between them seeped through. It was good news, and it ought to have brought great joy; it did bring joy to the House of Commons. But unimportant and unpractical people often foresee the future more clearly than do those who are engaged in shaping it, and I knew at once that the news was only good in patches. Peace flapped from the posters, and not upon the wings of angels. I trailed about reading the notices, some of which had already fallen into the gutter. On the Thursday I returned to the country, and found satisfaction there in a chicken-run which I had helped build earlier in the week.

This post-Munich world may not last long, but we are living in it now, and we have not any other life. We have to make the best of an unexplored and equivocal state, and we are more likely to succeed if we give up any hope of simplicity. "Prepare, prepare!" does not do for a slogan. No more does "Business as usual". Both of them are untrue to the spirit of 1939, the spirit which is half afraid and half thinking about something else. We are urged, by bishops and captains of industry, to face facts, and we ought to. But we can only face them by being double-faced. The facts lie in opposite directions, and no exhortation will group them into a single field. No slogan works. All is lost if the totalitarians destroy us. But all is equally lost if we have nothing left to lose. And the imperfect and blemished lamb, as he stands at the foot of the altar, is partly atremble because of the oncoming knife, and partly thinking of other things—of the meadows he has walked in, of the games he has played, of the books he has read, of the friends he has made. Perhaps he will decide to be a brave lamb and not to fear death, and, if he does this, death will certainly become painless for him, and mutilation painless until it occurs. It is common sense to be brave. But bravery and cowardice are only different sides of the same small shield. They do not cover the whole complexity. Apart from them exist the "other things" which riddle the little creature's mind, and make him now stronger and now weaker, now the heir of all of the ages, and now a contemptible failure: the "other things" which are summed up as civilization.

These mixed states are terrible for the nerves. That is the real drawback in them. They give us no chance to feel solid. What with the bravery-cowardice factor, and what with the civilization factor, we are assailed right and left. Sensitive people are having a particularly humiliating time just now. Looking at the international scene, they see, with a clearness denied to politicians, that if Fascism wins we are done for, and that we must become Fascist to win. There seems no escape from this hideous dilemma, and those who face it most honestly often go jumpy. They are vexed by messages from contradictory worlds, so that whatever they do appears to them as a betrayal of something good; they feel that nothing is worth attempting, they drop their hands, break off in the middle with a shriek, smash physical or spiritual crockery. If they could sell themselves, they would find peace; they could, on the one hand, go out hammer and tongs for National Service, pacifism, suicide, etc.; or, on the other hand, they could shut themselves up with their culture and try to hatch something out in isolation, as Remy de Gourmont did in the last war and as Jean Giono hopes to do in the next one. But they are too fine to sell themselves; that is their glory and their trouble. They see through all the slogans. Their grasp on reality paralyses them. Paradoxically, they become more and more negative and ineffective, until leadership passes to their inferiors.

It is not easy to help such people; they are too highly developed to be saved by anyone but themselves. One little tip does occur to me, but it is only applicable to such of them as still have money. Those of them who have money should start spending it at once—spending quiets the nerves—and should spend it as if civilization is permanent; buy books, go to concerts and plays. It is childish to save; thrift was only a virtue so long as it paid, which it has ceased to do. And it is fantastic to spend too much on charity; all the money in England could not stay the world's misery now, or even solve the refugee problem. Spending on art has this advantage, apart from the pleasure to be gained from it: it does maintain an artistic framework which may come in useful in the future; it is connected with a positive hope.

This decade has lasted long enough, and the Crisis in particular has become a' habit, indeed almost a joke. Emotions are no longer deeply stirred by it, and when Germany or Italy destroys an extra country we are upset for a shorter period each time. We are worried rather than frantic. But worry is terribly insidious; besides taking the joy out of life, it prevents the victim from being detached and from observing what is happening to the human experiment. It tempts him to simplify, since through simplification he may find peace. Nagging and stinging night and day, it is the undying worm, the worst of our foes. The only satisfactory release is to be found in the direction of complexity. The world won't work out, and the person who can realize this, and not just say it and lament it, has done as well as can be expected of him in the present year.

[1939]

Gerald Heard

While the noise of the conflict grows nearer, it is curious to listen to another sound, which bids us hope. Curious, and disturbing; for we are reluctant to hope when we have once settled comfortably down to despair. Some spiritual retreat seems the best that remains for a decent person at this moment of general collapse, this moment when the governments kill and the churches have nothing to say. Spiritual! Such a comfortable word! Mr Gerald Heard would agree that salvation lies in its direction, but, differing from the rest of our monitors, he would say that the spirit is not a dug-out but a bomb. It explodes. It attacks by leaping forward inside the individual. Such leaps have occurred in the past, and much of his latest book, *Pain, Sex and Time*, is engaged in examining them. They have been made unconsciously; today man is conscious of himself, and must advance consciously. He has to learn how to let himself off. Where is the trigger? And how shall he pull it?

Of these two questions, the first is easier to answer than the second. Mr Heard can point—and most people will agree with him—to unused energy inside the human animal. Man has not specialized; he did not go in for wings like the birds, or armour-plating like the crocodiles. He kept himself free, with the result that he has created aeroplanes and tanks, and with the still more important result that he is free to develop psychologically. Man's physical evolution is at an end; his evolution through the psyche can, if he chooses, continue. His capacity for pain and his capacity for sex (in both of which he surpasses his fellow animals) are both symptoms of unused energy. If he can detonate his powers, he will blow away the economic and political horrors now surrounding him—horrors which do not merely destroy his body but work inward and destroy his power to understand.

We have here the old doctrine of the Change of Heart, but in a violent and earthly form. Mr Heard dislikes otherworldliness; he thinks it is one of the three mistakes that the human race must rectify, the other two mistakes being belief in an anthropomorphic God, and belief in reason. He dislikes the Quaker ineffectiveness which, after a quiet sit, goes back to money-making and meals, and opposes Armageddon with philanthropy. A Change of Heart in the explosive sense does, however, appeal to him, and if any tricks, gadgets or drugs are likely to induce it he is willing to try them. They have been practised in the past—the Fakirs and the Shakti Yogins have both tried, by experimenting with pain and with sex, to enhance normal consciousness. And though we need not, and probably should not, copy the past, we can learn from it.

Now one of these gadgets has been the Group. He has always invested heavily in the Group. The Group could, in his judgement, pull the trigger and detonate the bomb. "Where two or three are gathered together" an accession of power is felt. He thinks that all who believe in Man's unused powers should gather into what he calls "Colleges". We should there train scientifically the development of our consciousness, which has hitherto been allowed to sprout haphazard. And the Colleges would contain three grades of inmates, roughly corresponding to the three first grades of the Hindu caste-system. The highest grade, the "Neo-Brahmin", would be indifferent to amusement and to possessions, and so have the authority and the integrity out of which an International Police Force could be created.

Here we come up against the third, and the most difficult, of his problems. Find the trigger—that is not difficult; most of us can find it; most of us know that there are unexplored forces in the human heart, which could be used for good. Pull the trigger and release the bomb—that is more difficult, still it may be possible; it may be possible, through group work and scientific technique, to produce the Neo-Brahmin. But hit the mark? Ah, that is more difficult still! In other words: Would the least notice be taken, by any existing political authority, of Mr Heard's Colleges?

He faces this, he faces everything. His International Police Force is, of course, psychological; it would not work by scolding people into good behaviour but by helping them to understand themselves. It would, in particular, have a Mission to Dictators. But how would they receive such a mission? Here, as always, his analysis is admirable. He draws a convincing picture of the Dictator's misery, and we can endorse it. Our horror and disgust at Hitler are mixed up with pity for a fellow creature who has so completely missed the boat. Never, to his dying day, can such a man enjoy the joys of which he deprives others. He has cut him-

self off for ever from the beauty and the glory of the civilized
world. Mr Heard would, however, argue that, at certain
moments, a Hitler can be "got at" by the Neo-Brahmin, the
trained psychologist, and be brought round; he *can* be made to
catch the boat. And he quotes a few examples from history.
But the examples are unconvincing and meagre. Tyrants have
seldom listened to sages for more than a minute or two, and they
have seldom done more than listen. The bomb of the spirit can
explode, but its direct action seems no stronger than a paper
bag's. Mr Heard's analysis works. His remedy would fail.

[1939]

They Hold Their Tongues

Some day, some intellectual day, when Satire revisits our mad-house, an entertaining book could be written around this war. Its title might be *They Hold Their Tongues*, and it would be a ballet rather than a book. The scene will be laid in the Ministry of Decontamination, in the Announcer's Parlour, and at the signs of the Walls Have Ears and the No Bird Sings. The enemy will also be shown, listening to us listening to him listening to us listening to him in an infinite series of sandbags, and the strain will become so great that the military mind will collapse and be unable to distinguish objective from base. Truth and falsehood will be disintegrated into particles which are so small as to be equally useless, and action will become so indirect as to be indirigible. Armies march in the correct direction in order to deceive their generals, airmen drop lethal messages wrapped round dud bombs, clergymen pray for evil lest their congregations be led into it, donkeys bark, dogs mew, cats mew too because cats are subtler than dogs. Enter the experts, for the military mind is conscious today of the existence of the mind. Enter the Science of Psychology. Officially installed in a cellar, it abolishes the art of knowing what people are like, and ensures that they are incomprehensible to themselves as well as to others. Frankness is as fatal as kindness, so all hold their tongues. Yes—it might be an amusing entertainment. But it will not be a genial one, and it will not end with an all-round laugh and a kindly apotheosis of the average man. It will have a touch of the rancid flatness which is a part of true satire—for Satire does not merely bite the victim, it lets down the reader too. A few grim survivors, aristocrats, may appreciate it. Swift might contribute. Blake even:

> I was buried near this dyke,
> That my friends may weep as much as they like.

Dante too. Dante the fantasist—how wickedly he would have described the folk who have held their tongues so well that their tongues come off in their hands. There, beyond Phlegethon, he would place them, and at the base of each tongue would nestle an atrophied brain. Their enormous ears are sewn against their scalps, so that they listen in with a vengeance. Virgil points at the horrible posies, gathers his mantle around him, and registers historical disgust. "Here," says Virgil, "is the recompense of those who have gagged their countrymen for their country's sake, instead of praising their God. Here are the chiefs of police and the card-indexers, and the takers of fingerprints, and Creon, King of Thebes, who issued the fatal edict, and the silencers of Lorca. Look at them, take warning from those dribbling gullets and, while speech is yours, speak." Far away, beyond the other bank of the river, in Paradise, Beatrice, who is the divine wisdom, echoes the secular warning: "Speak, speak," she cries, "for in the beginning was the Word."

The light shineth in the darkness, and the light comprehendeth not the darkness. It was the true light, which lighteth every man that cometh into the world, but it has had to be put out. There is no place in a modern war for spontaneity, and never before has the spirit of man been so menaced and insulted. The cloud of his inventions has thickened, descended upon him, blacked him out. He is dazed by darkness. Night is right, and if he holds up so much as a candle to the naughty world the air-warden reports him for beckoning to death. One natural gesture, and he may destroy himself and his friends. If indeed he still has any friends. Old intimacies may survive the censorship, but what new ones can grow up under it? In this scientific mist, this skilful and deliberate disintegration, what place can be found for the camaraderie and love that have sweetened wars in the past? Blood used to get warm before it was shed. Now—coldness, depression, suspicion, loneliness. Courage—abundance of courage, but it is the courage that dares not be neighbourly, lest the enemy smell out the place. "Where two or three are gathered together...." As if by the intervention of Satan, all the old religious and moral tags work out wrong. Where two or three are gathered together, they are more readily detected by hostile aircraft, so they must be prohibited.

Those of us who were brought up in the old order, when Fate advanced slowly, and tragedies were manageable, and human dignity possible, know that that order has vanished from the earth. We are not so foolish as to suppose that fragments of it can be salvaged on some desert island. But since it is the best thing we knew or are capable of knowing, it has become a habit which no facts can alter, it has gone underground like the subterranean Nile in the Book of the Dead. Love, peace, speech, light—these four are the columns of the Temple of Osiris, which no longer stands upon earth. Descending with Dante and the old Egyptians, we seek subterranean streams, we adjust in some spiritual region the balance which has been upset for ever here, we rejoin our friends, we punish our victorious foes, and—most important of all—we see face to face, and know even as we are known. This is sometimes called faith. The honester word for it is habit. It is no more than remembering a tune, it is carrying a rhythm in one's head after the instruments have stopped.

We hope, of course, that a new tune, inaudible to ourselves, is now being played to the young, and that one day it will re-echo and give them the strength which certainly keeps us going now. But on that point we can get no evidence, and never shall get any. We do expect, though, that those who chronicle this age and its silliness, and look back from their intellectual day upon us, the tongue-holders, will accord us not only pity, which we fully deserve, but disdain.

[1939]

Three Anti-Nazi Broadcasts

1 Culture and Freedom

By profession, I am a writer. I know nothing about economics or politics, but I am deeply interested in what is conveniently called culture, and I want it to prosper all over the world. My belief is that, if the Nazis won, culture would be destroyed in England and the Empire. In the Kaiser's war, Germany was just a hostile country. She and England were enemies, but they both belonged to the same civilization. In Hitler's war Germany is not a hostile country, she is a hostile principle. She stands for a new and a bad way of life and, if she won, would be bound to destroy our ways. There is not room in the same world for Nazi Germany and for people who don't think as she does. She says so herself, and if any Nazi should honour me by listening to my remarks I do not think he will disagree with them.

Now, Germany is not against culture. She does believe in literature and art. But she has made a disastrous mistake: she has allowed her culture to become governmental, and from this mistake proceed all kinds of evils. In England our culture is not governmental. It is national: it springs naturally out of our way of looking at things, and out of the way we have looked at things in the past. It has developed slowly, easily, lazily; the English love of freedom, the English countryside, English prudishness and hypocrisy, English freakishness, our mild idealism and good-humoured reasonableness have all combined to make something which is certainly not perfect, but which may claim to be unusual. Our great achievement has been in literature: here we rank high, both as regards prose and verse. We have not done much in painting or music, and patriots who pretend that we have only make us look silly. We have made a respectable, though not a sublime, contribution to philosophy. That—so far as it can be summed up in a few words—is the English achievement.

But before going on to the German achievement, which was also an important one, I want to say something about freedom,

31

because, to my mind, freedom is bound up with the whole question of culture. The Nazis condemn it, in practice and theory, and assert that civilization will flourish without it. Individualists like myself believe that it is necessary. As a writer, I have three reasons for believing in freedom.

Firstly, the writer himself must feel free, or he may find it difficult to fall into the creative mood and do good work. If he feels free, sure of himself, unafraid, easy inside, he is in a favourable condition for the act of creation.

The second reason also concerns the writer—and indeed the artist generally. It is not enough to feel free; that is only the start. To feel free may be enough for the mystic, who can function alone and concentrate even in a concentration camp. The writer, the artist, needs something more—namely freedom to tell other people what he is feeling. Otherwise, he is bottled up and what is inside him may go bad. And here is where the trouble starts. The Nazis step forward and say: "One moment, please. Allow me, the Government, first to hear what you are wanting to say. If I decide it is convenient, you may say it, but not otherwise." The Nazis do not and cannot prevent freedom to think and to feel—though they would no doubt condemn it from the National-Socialist point of view as a selfish waste of time. They cannot interfere there, but they can and do prevent freedom to communicate. They do step in and say: "Before you publish your book, before you show your picture, before you sing your song, I must read, I must look, I must listen." And the knowledge that they can do this reacts disastrously upon the artist. He is not like the mystic; he cannot function in a vacuum, he cannot spin tales in his head or paint pictures in the air, or hum tunes under his breath. He must have an audience, he must express his feelings, and if he knows he may be forbidden to express himself he becomes afraid to feel. Officials, even when they are well-meaning, do not realize this. Their make-up is so different. They assume that when a book is censored only the book in question is affected. They do not realize that they may have impaired the creative machinery of the writer's mind, and prevented him from writing good books in the future.

So here are two of my reasons for believing that freedom is necessary for culture. The third reason concerns the general public. The public, on its side, must be free to read, to listen, to look. If it is prevented from receiving the communications which the artist sends, it becomes inhibited, like him, though in a different way: it remains immature. And immaturity is a great characteristic of the public in Nazi Germany. If you look at a photograph of our enemies they may strike you as able and brave and formidable, even heroic. But they will not strike you as grown-up. They have not been allowed to hear, to listen or to look. Only people who have been allowed to practise freedom can have the grown-up look in their eyes.

I do not want to exaggerate the claims of freedom. It does not guarantee the production of masterpieces, and masterpieces have been produced under conditions far from free—the *Aeneid*, for instance, or the plays of Racine. Freedom is only a favourable step—or, let us say, three little steps. When writers (and artists generally) feel easy, when they can express themselves openly, when their public is allowed to receive their communications, there is a chance of the general level of civilization rising. Before the war, it was rising a little in England, it was rising a great deal in France, it was rising in Czechoslovakia, Scandinavia, the Netherlands. In Germany it was falling. During the last ten years her achievements in art, in literature, in speculation, in unapplied science, were contemptible. But she was perfecting her instruments of destruction and she now hopes by their aid to reduce neighbouring cultures to the same level as her own.

When a culture is genuinely national, it is capable, when the hour strikes, of becoming super-national, and contributing to the general good of humanity. It gives and takes. It wants to give and take. It has generosity and modesty, it is not confined by political and geographic boundaries, it does not fidget about purity of race or worry about survival, but, living in the present and sustained by the desire to create, it expands wherever human beings are to be found. Our civilization was ready to do this when the hour struck, and the civilization of France, our lost leader, was ready, too. We did not want England to be England for ever; it seemed to us a meagre destiny. We hoped for a world to which, when it had been made one by science, England could contribute. Science has duly unified the world. The hour has struck. We cannot contribute. And why?

The historian of the future, and he alone, will be able to answer this question authoritatively. He will see the true perspective of this 1940 crisis, and it may appear as small to him as the crisis of 1914 already appears to us. Our present troubles may be the prelude to a vast upheaval which we cannot hope to understand.

We have to answer out of our ignorance, and as well as we can. And to my limited outlook Hitler's Germany is the villain, it is she who, when the hour struck, ruined the golden moment and ordered an age of bloodshed.

Germany also has a great national culture. She was supreme in music, eminent in philosophy, weak (like England) in the visual arts, and highly gifted though not supremely gifted in literature. That, put in a sentence, was her achievement, and all the world was wanting to share it with her, and to profit by it, and to give and take. The Nazis willed otherwise. A national culture did not suit them. It had to be governmental. It can therefore never become super-national or contribute to the general good of humanity. Germany is to be German for ever, and more German with each generation. "What is 'to be German'?" asked Hitler, in a speech he made a few years ago at Munich, and he replied: "The best answer to this question does not define, it lays down a law." Did you ever hear such an extraordinary reply? To be German is—to be German. Thus labelled, Germany presses on to a goal which can be described in exalted language, but which is the goal of a fool. For, all the time she shouts and bullies her neighbours, the clock of the world moves on, and science makes the world one. "Gangsterdom for ever" is a possibility and the democracies are fighting against it. "Germany for ever" is an uneducated official's dream.

When a national culture becomes governmental, it is always falsified. For it never quite suits the official book. The words and the images that have come down to us through the centuries are often contradictory, they represent a bewildering wealth of human experience, which it is our privilege to enjoy, to examine and to build on. A free country allows its citizens this privilege. A totalitarian country cannot, because it fears diversity of opinion. The heritage of the past has to be overhauled so that the output of the present may be standardized, and the output of the present has to be standardized or Germany would cease to be German. Nothing could be more logical than the dreary blind-alley down which the Nazis advance, and down which they want to herd the whole human family. It leads nowhere, not even into Germany. They have got into it because they have worshipped the State. And they cannot feel safe until the rest of the world is in it too. Wherever they see variety, spontaneity, anything different from themselves, they are doomed to attack it. Germany's very gifts, her own high cultural achievement, must be recompounded and turned to poison, so that the achievements of others may perish.

2 *What Has Germany Done to the Germans?*

It is most important to remember that Germany had to make war on her own people before she could attack Europe. So much has been happening lately that we sometimes forget that during the past seven years she robbed and tortured and interned and expelled and killed thousands and thousands of her own citizens. When she had got rid of them, and not until then, she was in a position to transfer operations, and start against France and England. The 1914 war was not preceded by all this cruelty inside Germany, nor by these floods of unhappy and innocent refugees.

So here are a few instances of Germany's treatment of Germans. I shall not be so much concerned with physical bullying as with the attempts of the Nazis to bully and twist the mind. They are no fools—it is a great mistake to keep on making fun of them—and a good deal of what they say sounds at first sensible and even noble. For instance, they say that instinct is superior to reason, and character better than book-learning. I agree. Baldur von Schirach, who was until lately one of their youth-leaders, says: "The Nazi revolution is and always has been a revolution of the soul. It reveals that power which the intellectual will deny, since it is as inconceivable to him as is the God who gave it: the power of the soul and sentiment."

This sounds all right, but why does the soul always require a machine-gun? Why can the character only cope with the intellect when it has got it inside a concentration camp, and is armed with a whip? Why does the instinct instinctively persecute? Why does sentiment mean insensitiveness? On the surface, the Nazi creed seems not too bad; scratch the surface, and you will find intolerance and cruelty. I cannot go through the list of German writers and painters and sculptors and architects and musicians and philosophers and scientists and theologians who have been persecuted by Germany in the past seven years. It would take too long. But think of Einstein, the greatest scientist living, who gave us a new view of the universe: he is in exile. Think of Freud, the psychologist: he has died in exile. Think of Thomas Mann: he only wanted to write his novels and live in

35

peace, but he had to write them in his own way, he had to be independent, and he is in exile. Think of the smaller people, friends of my own: I know a writer who escaped from Vienna, a charming fellow, whose crime it was to be a Jew, and another writer, a pure-blooded Aryan from Berlin, whose crime it was to think. I see my own sort of person being downed and insulted, and when I am told that the Nazi revolution is a revolution of the soul—well, I wonder.

Not long ago, at Munich, Hitler made a speech about art. He began by complaining that the Jews, with their so-called artistic criticism, had muddled the public, and put art on the level of fashion, which changes yearly. Art, he said, was not fashionable, not international, but eternal, like the national spirit of Germany, and the artist must set up a monument to his country, not to himself. You may not object to this; indeed, when Hitler distinguishes art from fashion, you may quite well agree. But he goes on: "As for the degenerate artists, I forbid them to force their so-called experiences upon the public. If they do see fields blue, they are deranged, and should go to an asylum. If they only pretend to see them blue, they are criminals, and should go to prison. I will purge the nation of them, and let no one take part in their corruption—his day of punishment will come."

Just as the scientist may not settle what experiments to make, so the artist may not settle how to express himself. In both cases an official intervenes. The official has never seen a field blue, and that decides for all time the colour of fields. The speech ends with the crack of a whip; the audience has been transported from the art-gallery to the concentration camp, where it will remain unless it mends its ways and enjoys what Hitler says is beautiful. This threat of a purge runs through all Nazi culture; the idea that one person may like one thing and another another is intolerable to it; it cannot be happy unless it bullies. I do not myself see fields blue, but I do not get upset about it, and when a great artist like van Gogh does see them blue I am thankful to look for a moment through his eyes.

Now for literature. Let me recall that famous Burning of the Books, for it illustrates better than any single event can the way in which Germany has been behaving to Germans. The Nazis wished it to symbolize their cultural outlook, and it will. It took place on 13 May 1933. That night twenty-five thousand volumes were destroyed outside the University of Berlin, in the presence of forty thousand people. Most people enjoy a blaze, and we are told that the applause was tremendous. Some of the books were by Jews, others Communist, others liberal, others "unscientific", and all of them were "un-German". It was for the Government to decide what was un-German. There was an elaborate ritual. Nine heralds came forward in turn, and consigned an author with incantations to the flames. For example, the fourth herald said: "Condemning the corrosion of the soul by the exaggeration of the dangers of war! Upholding the nobility of the human spirit! I consign to the flames the writings of Sigmund Freud." The seventh herald said: "Condemning the literary betrayal of the World War soldier! Upholding the education of our people in the spirit of reality! I consign to the flames the writings of Erich Marie Remarque", the author of the novel *All Quiet on the Western Front*. There were holocausts in the provinces too, and students were instructed to erect "pillars of infamy" outside their universities; the pillar should be "a thick tree-trunk, somewhat above the height of a man", to which were to be nailed "the utterances of those who, by their participation in activities defamatory of character, have forfeited their membership in the German nation". Note the reference to "character", it is significant. "Character", like the "soul", is always an opportunity for brutality. The Burning of the Books was followed by a systematic control of literature. A bureau was created to look after public libraries, second-hand shops were purged, books may not be published without licence, and a licence is also required for commenting.

Unfortunately for the Nazis, not all books are modern books. Germany has had a great literature in the past, and they have had to do something about that. They have been especially troubled by Goethe and Heine. Over Heine they have taken a strong line, since he was a Jew; they have denounced him as "the most baneful fellow that has ever passed through German life, soul-devastating, soul-poisoning" (notice again the "soul"), and have banned his works. Goethe had to be treated with more respect— so far as I know, they have not banned Goethe. But they rightly consider him their arch-enemy. For Goethe believed in toleration, he was the nationalist who is ripe for super-nationalism, he was the German who was wanting Germany's genius to enrich the whole world. His spirit will re-arise when this madness and cruelty have passed.

I could give more examples, but I have said enough to show how Germany has behaved to her own people. When she had

37

finished with them, she turned against us. It is all part of a single movement, which has as its aim the fettering of the writer, the scientist, the artist and the general public all over the world.

3 What Would Germany Do to Us?

What would the Nazis do to civilization in these islands and in the Empire if they won?

I don't suggest that conditions over here are perfect. During the present century, the writer and the artist generally have worked under growing disabilities; the law of libel hits them unfairly, so does the dramatic censorship. And since last September things have got worse, owing to regulations necessary for the Defence of the Realm; publishers and printers are frightened of handling anything which may be thought disloyal, with the result that much original work and valuable comment are being stifled. This cannot be helped; a war is on, so it is no use whining. But it is as well to remember that as soon as the war is won people who care about civilization in England will have to begin another war, for the restoration and extension of cultural freedom.

But, although cultural conditions are not perfect in this country (and it would be cant to pretend that they are), they are paradise compared with the conditions in Germany, and heaven compared with the conditions which Germany would impose on us if she beat us. I want to describe what she would do to us if she got the chance.

You may say: "Oh, but how do you know? No doubt the Nazis would impose appalling peace terms on us if they won, but why should they interfere with our culture?" My answer to that is: "I do know, because I have the record of what they have done to other countries, particularly to Czechoslovakia and to Poland." Destruction of national culture is part of their programme of conquest. In Czechoslovakia, for instance, they have banned the operas of Smetana and the plays of Čapek. They have revised schoolbooks, falsified Czech history, forbidden the singing of Czech national songs, and subsidized German educational institutions, for which the Czechs have to pay. In Poland the fate of culture has been still more tragic, since Poland is a conquered country: their conduct in Poland is the model which the Nazis would follow if they got over here. Listen, for instance, how they have treated the University of Cracow—and then put for "Cracow" "Oxford" or any other university which you know. Last November, 170 professors and teachers at Cracow were summoned by the chief of the Gestapo to the hall of the university and placed under arrest on the grounds that they were continuing their work without Nazi permission. They were sent straight off to concentration camps in Germany, where sixteen of them died, and their places were filled by Nazi nominees. I know Cracow. I had friends in the university there of whom I can get no news. They have welcomed me to their charming little flat overlooking the green boulevards; they have shown me their noble city with its great Catholic churches and its marvellous fortress. Owing to their kindness and hospitality, it has happened that Cracow has become for me a symbol of Nazi bullying on the Continent, and I can hardly see its name without trembling with rage. I mention it now—that lost and lovely place—because one needs to visualize in these terrible times. It does not convey much if I say, "The Nazis would reorganize and re-staff our educational system." It does convey something if I say, "They would treat Oxford as they have treated Cracow." They are stamping out culture everywhere in Poland, so far as they can. They consider it their mission to do so, on the ground that the Poles are naturally inferior to Germans. "A Pole is a Pole," writes a Nazi journalist, "and any attempt at familiarity must be rebuffed."

Let us now consider the effect of a Nazi victory upon our civilization.

Our press, our publishing and printing trades, our universities and the rest of our educational system would be instantly controlled. So would theatres, cinemas and the wireless. The British Government (assuming that one remained) would be held responsible for their conduct, and have to punish them if they did anything which annoyed Berlin. There would be complete remodelling. In these respects, the methods adopted in Czechoslovakia and Poland would be followed, and with the maximum of brutality; the joy of baiting Englishmen in England would be intoxicating. Germanization would probably not be attempted. But the Gestapo and the rest of the occupying force would, of course, import such Nazi culture as was necessary for their spiritual sustenance, and we should have to pay for German libraries and German schools, into which, as members of an inferior race, we should not be allowed to go.

What about our literature? The fate of individual writers would be hard. Those of any eminence would probably be

39

interned and shot. This, however painful to themselves, would not, it is true, be a great blow to literature, for by the time writers have become eminent they have usually done their best work. What would matter, what would be disastrous, is the intimidation of our younger writers—men and women in their twenties and thirties, who have not yet had the chance to express themselves. The invaders would take good care to frighten or cajole them. Forbidden to criticize their conquerors, forbidden to recall the past glories of their country, or to indulge that free movement of the mind which is necessary to the creative act, they would be confined to trivialities, or to spreading their masters' opinions. A bureau would be established, and licences to create or to comment would be issued, as in Germany by Dr Goebbels, and withdrawn if independence were shown. Rebelliousness might mean death. I don't think this is a fancy picture. It is only what is happening in Europe, and why should we get special terms? And I am not accusing our enemies of any general hatred of culture. They like culture. They are human beings, who enjoy reading books or going to plays and films, just as we do. They too want to be happy. The Germans don't hate culture, but they are doomed to oppose it because it is mixed up with thought and action, because it is mixed up with the individual; just as it is their doom to oppose science and religion.

Would they try to burn English books too? I don't think so. It would mean too big a blaze. We should probably be left with our existing libraries and allowed to read our classics in such spare time as we possessed. I do think, though, that a different interpretation of English literature would be attempted in our schools. They would put it to our young people that our best writers were Nazis at heart, and so try to warp their minds. It is interesting, in this connection, to read what Nazi critics have been saying lately about Shakespeare and Carlyle. They have not got a bad case over Carlyle—he had something of the Nazi about him: he despised individualism and liberty and worshipped the dictator-hero. However, Carlyle also said, "Thought is stronger than artillery-parks," and this side of him the Nazis don't mention. The case of Shakespeare is more complicated. The Germans have, for several generations, invested so heavily in Shakespeare that they dare not, even under the present regime, sell out; and they are worried because we like Shakespeare too—we even maintain that he was an Englishman. So they have had to make him into "the special case of a poet who is not affected by a war with England", and they brandish him at us for our castigation, and to our shame. You may think this foolish, but it shows their mentality: it shows how they twist things and how they would twist our minds through our own national literature if they got into our country.

Those seem to me the chief cultural points in a Nazi conquest —and you will remember that I am keeping to this particular aspect, and not talking about politics and economics. They want our land, it is true; they want our money—sure. But they also want to alter our civilization until it is in line with their own. If my view of them is right, they cannot *help* doing this: it is, so to speak, their fate. They have identified civilization with the State, and the National Socialist state cannot be secure until no civilization exists except the particular one which it approves.

This being so, I think we have got to go on with this hideous fight. I cannot see how we are to make terms with Hitler, much as I long for peace. For one thing, he never keeps his word; for another, he tolerates no way of looking at life except his own way. A peace which was the result of a Nazi victory would surely not differ much from a Nazi war. Germans would no longer be killed, but they would go on killing others until no one survived to criticize them. In the end, they might achieve world-domination and institute a culture. But what sort of culture would it be? What would they have to work with? For you cannot go on destroying lives and living processes without destroying your own life. If you continue to be greedy and dense, if you make power and not understanding your aim, if, as a French friend of mine puts it, you erect "a pyramid of appetites on a foundation of stupidity", you kill the impulse to create. Creation is disinterested. Creation means passionate understanding. Creation lies at the heart of civilization like fire in the heart of the earth. Around it are gathered its cooler allies, criticism, the calm use of the intellect, informing the mass and moulding it into shape. The intellect is not everything—the Nazis are quite right there. But no one can insult the intellect as they do without becoming sterile and cruel. We know their cruelty. We should see their sterility if this orgy of destruction were to stop, and they turned at their Führer's command to the production of masterpieces.

In this difficult day when so many of us are afraid, in this day when so many brave plans have gone wrong and so many devices have jammed, it is a comfort to remember that violence has so far never worked. Even when it seems to conquer, it fails in the long run. This failure may be due to the Divine Will. It can also be ascribed to the strange nature of Man, who refuses to live by bread alone, and is the only animal who has attempted to understand his surroundings.

[1940]

Tolerance

Everybody is talking about reconstruction. Our enemies have their schemes for a new order in Europe, maintained by their secret police, and we on our side talk of rebuilding London or England, or western civilization, and we make plans how this is to be done. Which is all very well, but when I hear such talk, and see the architects sharpening their pencils and the contractors getting out their estimates, and the statesmen marking out their spheres of influence, and everyone getting down to the job, a very famous text occurs to me: "Except the Lord build the house, they labour in vain that build it." Beneath the poetic imagery of these words lies a hard scientific truth, namely, unless you have a sound attitude of mind, a right psychology, you cannot construct or reconstruct anything that will endure. The text is true, not only for religious people, but for workers whatever their outlook, and it is significant that one of our historians, Dr Arnold Toynbee, should have chosen it to preface his great study of the growth and decay of civilizations. Surely the only sound foundation for a civilization is a sound state of mind. Architects, contractors, international commissioners, marketing boards, broadcasting corporations will never, by themselves, build a new world. They must be inspired by the proper spirit, and there must be the proper spirit in the people for whom they are working. For instance, we shall never have a beautiful new London until people refuse to live in ugly houses. At present, they don't mind; they demand more comfort, but are indifferent to civic beauty; indeed they have no taste. I live myself in a hideous block of flats, but I can't say it worries me, and until we are worried all schemes for reconstructing London beautifully must automatically fail.

What, though, is the proper spirit? We agree that the basic problem is psychological, that the Lord must build if the work is to stand, that there must be a sound state of mind before diplomacy or economics or trade conferences can function. But what state of mind is sound? Here we may differ. Most people, when asked what spiritual quality is needed to rebuild civilization, will reply "Love". Men must love one another, they say; nations must do likewise, and then the series of cataclysms which is threatening to destroy us will be checked.

Respectfully but firmly, I disagree. Love is a great force in private life; it is indeed the greatest of all things; but love in public affairs does not work. It has been tried again and again: by the Christian civilizations of the Middle Ages, and also by the French Revolution, a secular movement which reasserted the Brotherhood of Man. And it has always failed. The idea that nations should love one another, or that business concerns or marketing boards should love one another, or that a man in Portugal should love a man in Peru of whom he has never heard— it is absurd, unreal, dangerous. It leads us into perilous and vague sentimentalism. "Love is what is needed," we chant, and then sit back and the world goes on as before. The fact is, we can only love what we know personally. And we cannot know much. In public affairs, in the rebuilding of civilization, something much less dramatic and emotional is needed, namely tolerance. Tolerance is a very dull virtue. It is boring. Unlike love, it has always had a bad press. It is negative. It merely means putting up with people, being able to stand things. No one has ever written an ode to tolerance, or raised a statue to her. Yet this is the quality which will be most needed after the war. This is the sound state of mind which we are looking for. This is the only force which will enable different races and classes and interests to settle down together to the work of reconstruction.

The world is very full of people—appallingly full; it has never been so full before—and they are all tumbling over each other. Most of these people one doesn't know and some of them one doesn't like; doesn't like the colour of their skins, say, or the shapes of their noses, or the way they blow them or don't blow them, or the way they talk, or their smell, or their clothes, or their fondness for jazz or their dislike of jazz, and so on. Well, what is one to do? There are two solutions. One of them is the Nazi solution. If you don't like people, kill them, banish them, segregate them, and then strut up and down proclaiming that you are the salt of the earth. The other way is much less thrilling, but it is on the whole the way of the democracies, and I prefer it. If you don't like people, put up with them as well as you can. Don't try to love them; you can't, you'll only strain yourself. But try to tolerate them. On the basis of that tolerance a civilized future may be built. Certainly I can see no other foundation for the post-war world.

For what it will most need is the negative virtues: not being huffy, touchy, irritable, revengeful. I have lost all faith in positive militant ideals; they can so seldom be carried out without thousands of human beings getting maimed or imprisoned. Phrases like "I will purge this nation", "I will clean up this city", terrify and disgust me. They might not have mattered when the world was emptier; they are horrifying now, when one nation is mixed up with another, when one city cannot be organically separated from its neighbours. And another point: reconstruction is unlikely to be rapid. I do not believe that we are psychologically fit for it, plan the architects never so wisely. In the long run, yes, perhaps; the history of our race justifies that hope. But civilization has its mysterious regressions, and it seems to me that we are fated now to be in one of them, and must recognize this and behave accordingly. Tolerance, I believe, will be imperative after the establishment of peace. It's always useful to take a concrete instance; and I have been asking myself how I should behave if, after peace was signed, I met Germans who had been fighting against us. I shouldn't try to love them; I shouldn't feel inclined. They have broken a window in my little ugly flat for one thing. But I shall try to tolerate them, because it is common sense, because in the post-war world we shall have to live with Germans. We can't exterminate them, any more than they have succeeded in exterminating the Jews. We shall have to put up with them, not for any lofty reason, but because it is the next thing that will have to be done.

I don't, then, regard tolerance as a great eternally established divine principle, though I might perhaps quote "In my Father's house are many mansions" in support of such a view. It is just a makeshift, suitable for an overcrowded and overheated planet. It carries on when love gives out, and love generally gives out as soon as we move away from our home and our friends, and stand among strangers in a queue for potatoes. Tolerance is wanted in the queue; otherwise we think, "Why will people be so slow?"; it is wanted in the tube, or "Why will people be so fat?"; it is wanted at the telephone, or "Why are they so deaf?" or, conversely, "Why do they mumble?" It is wanted in the street, in the office, at the factory, and it is wanted above all between classes, races and nations. It's dull. And yet it entails imagination. For you have all the time to be putting yourself in someone else's place. Which is a desirable spiritual exercise.

This ceaseless effort to put up with other people seems tame, almost ignoble, so that it sometimes repels generous natures, and I don't recall many great men who have recommended tolerance. St Paul certainly did not. Nor did Dante. However, a few names occur. Going back over two thousand years, and to India, there is the great Buddhist Emperor Asoka, who set up inscriptions recording not his own exploits but the need for mercy and mutual understanding and peace. Going back about four hundred years, to Holland, there is the Dutch scholar Erasmus, who stood apart from the religious fanaticism of the Reformation and was abused by both parties in consequence. In the same century there was the Frenchman Montaigne, subtle, intelligent, witty, who lived in his quiet country house and wrote essays which still delight and confirm the civilized. And England: there was John Locke, the philosopher; there was Sydney Smith, the Liberal and liberalizing divine; there was Lowes Dickinson, writer of *A Modern Symposium*, which might be called the Bible of Tolerance. And Germany—yes, Germany: there was Goethe. All these men testify to the creed which I have been trying to express: a negative creed, but necessary for the salvation of this crowded jostling modern world.

Two more remarks. First, it is very easy to see fanaticism in other people, but difficult to spot in oneself. Take the evil of racial prejudice. We can easily detect it in the Nazis; their conduct has been infamous ever since they rose to power. But we ourselves—are we guiltless? We are far less guilty than they are. Yet is there no racial prejudice in the British Empire? Is there no colour question? I ask you to consider that, those of you to whom tolerance is more than a pious word. My other remark is to forestall a criticism. Tolerance is not the same as weakness. Putting up with people does not mean giving in to them. This complicates the problem. But the rebuilding of civilization is bound to be complicated. I only feel certain that unless the Lord builds the house they will labour in vain who build it. Perhaps, when the house is completed, love will enter it, and the greatest force in our private lives will also rule in public life.

[1941]

Ronald Kidd

An address delivered at his funeral

"Und eine Freiheit macht uns alle frei."

In the past few months the Council for Civil Liberties has lost both its President, Henry Nevinson, and its first Secretary. It is the President who should be speaking now, but as he is no longer with us I have been asked to give a short address. I do so reluctantly; but I see that an address is necessary, for Ronald Kidd was a public figure, and it is seemly that there should be some public discourse here, however inadequate.

Those who knew him best, better than I did, will agree with me, I think, that the public side in him, the civic side, the side that serves humanity, was superbly developed. Of course he had his personal life, like the rest of us, but it is this altruistic activity that so impressed, this service of the elusive principle which we call liberty; which we can none of us define, but in which we all believe. I suppose he must have had an enthusiasm for liberty all his life, but it became noticeable in 1934, when he called together a few others who shared his hopes and his anxieties, and founded this Council. I was not one of the original group, but I joined soon afterwards, and I well remember our original offices. They were in a mews. The staircase was so narrow that one could scarcely get up it, and the room at the top was so small that one could scarcely turn round. There was no organization and no staff. And from that room Kidd hired a great hall down in Westminster, and convened there the great meeting of protest against the Sedition Bill which first brought our Council into general notice. From that moment he never looked back; he moved from enterprise to enterprise, and he not only achieved himself: he left foundations upon which others are building and will build. The little room has become a suite of offices, the reaching out of individual to individual has become a great national organization with branches and affiliations all over the British Isles, and indeed outside them. That Sedition Bill I mentioned—the B.B.C. would not report it, but when Ronald Kidd died this week accounts of his life and work were broadcast over the Continent and the Empire as well as at home.

That is fame. That is success. But there is something more to

47

remember. He gave to that work all his strength, and he did, literally, die that we might be free. If he had cared for our freedom less, if he had worked less, if he had nursed his health and considered his own comfort, he could have been alive now, though it could not have been a life he valued. I know the political and philosophical difficulties inherent in this idea of freedom: freedom for what; freedom to do what; freedom at whose expense, and so on. As a conception it is negative; but as a faith it is positive, and Ronald Kidd upheld it till his dying day.

When during his last illness I went down to see him in his private residence and later in the hospital, I found him still concentrated on the Council and its work, on our annual general meeting which he could not attend, on his pamphlet *The Fight for a Free Press*, which has just appeared. He knew he was ill and he could discuss his symptoms, but they never held the first rank, as they do with ordinary invalids.

This is not the place, nor have I the ability, to discuss his outlook, or to illustrate the various methods through which he worked: pamphlets, speeches, interviews with Cabinet Ministers, visits to police stations and police courts, street watchings—all played their part. One thing strikes me, though, and that is why I quoted that line from Schiller: he knew that freedom is not the perquisite of any one section of the community; neither the employing classes nor the working classes nor the artistic and literary classes can be truly free unless all are free. That—unformulated perhaps—was his belief, and perhaps that was why such contradictory judgements were passed on him by those who had not worked with him. I have heard him accused in different quarters of being a Communist, a Gladstonian Liberal, a secret agent, the wrong sort of Irishman and a hopeless John Bull. Happy the man who is accused of so much, for it proves that his mind is alive. Kidd was active, whenever he saw the possibility of promoting and extending civil liberty. He was tethered to no other formula.

When a man dies, he becomes part of history and one thinks of historical parallels, and it occurs to me today—I don't know whether you will agree—that there was in our friend something of the Ancient Roman, the Tribune of the People, who contends that the *Res Publica* should be the possession of all. Even in his outward habit I see something of this; in his gravity, his courtesy, his eloquence. I see it still more in his selflessness, his stubborn courage, his loyalty, his refusal to admit defeat, his adherence to principles. There is here something that suggests the grandeur and the sternness of certain heroes of the ancient world, and their strife for an individual liberty compatible with civic righteousness. May his example remain with us! May we continue the fight that is never done!

[1942]

The Tercentenary of the
Areopagitica

Milton's *Areopagitica* was published exactly three hundred years ago. The Parliament was fighting the King. Milton upheld Parliament, but it had just given him a very unpleasant shock. It had passed a defence regulation for the control of literature, and had placed all printed matter under a censorship. "No book etc. shall from henceforward be printed or exposed for sale unless the same be first approved of and licensed by such persons" as Parliament shall appoint.

There are usually two motives behind any censorship—good, and bad. The good motive is the desire of the authorities to safeguard and strengthen the community, particularly in times of stress. The bad motive is the desire of the authorities to suppress criticism, particularly of themselves. Both these motives existed in 1644, as they do in 1944, and, in Milton's judgement, the bad then predominated over the good. He was profoundly shocked that Parliament, which fought for liberty, should be suppressing it, and he issued his *Areopagitica* as a protest. It is the most famous of his prose works—partly because it is well written, but mainly because it strikes a blow for British freedom. It has been much praised, and sometimes by people who do not realize what they are praising and what they are letting themselves in for. In celebrating its tercentenary let us do so with open eyes.

To begin with one of Milton's smaller points: the inconvenience of a censorship to a creative or scholarly writer. All that he says here is true, though not of prime importance. It is intolerable, he exclaims, that "serious and elaborate writings, as if they were no more than the theme of a Grammar-lad . . . must not be uttered without the cursory eyes of a temporizing and extemporizing licenser". It is being treated like a schoolboy after one is grown up. The censor is probably some overworked and dim little official who knows nothing about literature and is scared of anything new. Yet the writer has to "trudge" to him to get his script passed, and if he makes any alteration afterwards he must make application again. "I hate a pupil teacher, I endure not an instructor," proud Milton cries, and, when he is reminded that the censor does after all represent the State, he hits back fiercely with "The State shall be my governors, but not my critics". All this is very much what a scholar or a creative artist might charge against a censor today: the big mind having to apply for permission to the fidgety small mind, and the small mind being supported by the authority of the State. It is all quite true; though why should not distinguished writers be put to trouble if it is to the general good? Why should they not submit to censorship if the national welfare requires it?

But there is much more to the problem, and the bulk of the *Areopagitica* is occupied with larger questions. Censorship means uniformity and monotony; and they mean spiritual death. "Where there is much desire to learn, there of necessity will be much arguing, much writing, many opinions; for opinion in good men is but knowledge in the making." And he apostrophizes London at war in words we might gladly use today:

> Behold now this vast City; a City of refuge, the mansion-house of liberty, encompassed and surrounded with his [God's] protection; the shop of war hath not there more anvils and hammers waking . . . than there be pens and heads there, sitting by their studious lamps, musing, searching, revolving new notions and ideas . . . others as fast reading, trying all things, assenting to the force of reason and convincement.

All this free writing and reading will pass with the institution of the censorship, and its disappearance means the spiritual impoverishment of us all, whether we write and study or not. Intellectuals, in Milton's opinion, are not and cannot be apart from the community, and are essential to its health.

And then he tackles the problem of bad or harmful books. Might it not be well to prohibit them? He answers, No. It is preferable that bad books should be published rather than that all books should be submitted before publication to a government official. What is bad will be forgotten, and free choice in reading is as important as it is in action. Truth is "a perpetual progression". Also who is to settle what is bad? Who indeed! I recall in this connection an argument I had with an acquaintance during the first war. He was for prohibiting bad books, and when I asked him which books he answered "Conrad's novels". He did not care for them. He was an able public-spirited fellow, and later on he became an M.P.

C   51

If there is no censorship, is the writer or the newspaper editor to be above the law? Not at all. That is not Milton's position. If a book or pamphlet or newspaper is illegal it can, after publication, be prosecuted. The grounds of prosecution in his day were two—blasphemy and libel—and they hold good in our day, prosecutions for blasphemy now being very rare and prosecutions for libel very frequent. Milton did not set writers above the law. He did insist on punishment afterwards rather than censorship beforehand. Let a man say what he likes and then suffer if it is illegal. This seems to me the only course appropriate to a democracy. It is for the courts, and for no one else, to decide whether a book shall be suppressed.

Milton, wouldst thou be living at this hour? "Yes and No," Milton would answer. He would certainly be heart and soul with us in our fight against Germany and Japan, for they stand for all that he most detested. And he would note with approval that there is no direct censorship of books. But he would disapprove of the indirect censorship operating on them through the paper control. At the present moment, most of the paper available goes to government departments, the publication of new books gets cut down, and most of our great English classics have gone out of print. Nor would he have approved of any attempt of publishers to combine and decide what books should be published. Would he have liked the wireless? Yes and No. He would have been enthusiastic over the possibilities of broadcasting, and have endorsed much it does, but he would not approve of the "agreed script" from which broadcasters are obliged to read for security reasons. He believed in free expression and in punishment afterwards if the expression turned out to be illegal; but never, never supervision beforehand, and whether the supervision was called censorship or licensing or "agreed script" would have made no difference to him. You can argue that the present supervision of broadcasters is necessary and reasonable, and that a silly or cranky speaker might do endless harm on the air. But if you feel like that you must modify your approval of the *Areopagitica*. You cannot have it both ways. And do not say, "Oh, it's different today—there's a war on." There was equally a war on in 1644. The fact is, we are willing enough to praise freedom when she is safely tucked away in the past and cannot be a nuisance. In the present, amidst dangers whose outcome we cannot foresee, we get nervous about her, and admit censorship. Yet the past was once the present, the seventeenth century was once "now", with an unknown future, and Milton, who lived in his "now" as we do in ours, believed in taking risks.

In places, then, the *Areopagitica* is a disturbance to our self-complacency. But in other places it is an encouragement, for Milton exalts our national character in splendid words. He was intensely patriotic—on the grounds that, when France was a tyranny and Germany a muddle, we were insisting on freedom of speech and being admired for it by European scholars. He had travelled on the Continent before the Civil War, and sat among her learned men, and, he goes on,

> been counted happy to be born in such a place of Philosophic freedom, as they supposed England was, while themselves did nothing but bemoan the servile condition into which learning amongst them was brought. . . . I took it as a pledge of future happiness, that other Nations were so persuaded of her liberty.

And he is proud—and how justly—of the variety of opinion incidental to our democracy, of "this flowery crop of knowledge and new light" as opposed to that "stark and dead congealment of wood and hay and stubble" engendered by the pressure of totalitarianism. Our enemies, he notes, mistake our variety for weakness—exactly the mistakes the Germans were to make about us both in 1914 and in 1939.

> The adversary again applauds, and waits the hour, when they have branched themselves out, saith he, small enough into parties and partitions, then will be our time. Fool! he sees not the firm root, out of which we all grow, though into branches: nor will beware until he see our small divided maniples cutting through at every angle of his ill-united and unwieldy brigade.

"Ill united and unwieldy brigade"—could there be a phrase more prophetic of the Axis? But we must not dwell on the phrase too much, for the subject of the *Areopagitica* is not tyranny abroad but the need, even in wartime, of liberty at home. Not the beam in Dr Goebbels's eye, but the mote in our own eye. Can we take it out? Is there as much freedom of expression and publication in this country as there might be? That is the question which, on its tercentenary, this explosive little pamphlet propounds.

[1944]

53

The Challenge of our Time[1]

Temperamentally, I am an individualist. Professionally, I am a writer, and my books emphasize the importance of personal relationships and the private life, for I believe in them. What can a man with such an equipment, and with no technical knowledge, say about the Challenge of our Time? Like everyone else, I can see that our world is in a terrible mess, and having been to India last winter I know that starvation and frustration can reach proportions unknown to these islands. Wherever I look, I can see, in the striking phrase of Robert Bridges, "the almighty cosmic Will fidgeting in a trap". But who set the trap, and how was it sprung? If I knew, I might be able to unfasten it. I do not know. How can I answer a challenge which I cannot interpret? It is like shouting defiance at a big black cloud. Some of the other speakers share my diffidence here, I think. Professor Bernal does not. He perceives very precisely what the Challenge of our Time is and what is the answer to it. Professor Bernal's perceptions are probably stronger than mine. They are certainly more selective, and many things which interest or upset me do not enter his mind at all—or enter it in the form of cards to be filed for future use.

I belong to the fag-end of Victorian liberalism, and can look back to an age whose challenges were moderate in their tone, and the cloud on whose horizon was no bigger than a man's hand. In many ways it was an admirable age. It practised benevolence and philanthropy, was humane and intellectually curious, upheld free speech, had little colour-prejudice, believed that individuals are and should be different, and entertained a sincere faith in the progress of society. The world was to become better and better, chiefly through the spread of parliamentary institutions. The education I received in those far-off and fantastic days made me soft, and I am very glad it did, for I have seen plenty of hardness since, and I know it does not even pay. Think of the end of Mussolini—the hard man, hanging upside-down

[1] From a broadcast series; Professor Bernal had been one of the previous speakers.

54

THE CHALLENGE OF OUR TIME

like a turkey, with his dead mistress swinging beside him. But though the education was humane it was imperfect, inasmuch as we none of us realized our economic position. In came the nice fat dividends, up rose the lofty thoughts, and we did not realize that all the time we were exploiting the poor of our own country and the backward races abroad, and getting bigger profits from our investments than we should. We refused to face this unpalatable truth. I remember being told as a small boy, "Dear, don't talk about money, it's ugly"—a good example, that, of Victorian defence mechanism.

All that has changed in the present century. The dividends have shrunk to decent proportions and have in some cases disappeared. The poor have kicked. The backward races are kicking—and more power to their boots. Which means that life has become less comfortable for the Victorian liberal, and that our outlook, which seems to me admirable, has lost the basis of golden sovereigns upon which it originally rose, and now hangs over the abyss. I indulge in these reminiscences because they lead to the point I want to make.

If we are to answer the Challenge of our Time successfully, we must manage to combine the new economy and the old morality. The doctrine of *laissez-faire* will not work in the material world. It has led to the black market and the capitalist jungle. We must have planning and ration-books and controls, or millions of people will have nowhere to live and nothing to eat. On the other hand, the doctrine of *laissez-faire* is the only one that seems to work in the world of the spirit; if you plan and control men's minds you stunt them, you get the censorship, the secret police, the road to serfdom, the community of slaves. Our economic planners sometimes laugh at us when we are afraid of totalitarian tyranny resulting from their efforts—or rather they sneer at us, for there is some deep connection between planning and sneering which psychologists should explore. But the danger they brush aside is a real one. They assure us that the new economy will evolve an appropriate morality, and that when all people are properly fed and housed they will have an outlook which will be right, because they are the people. I cannot swallow that. I have no mystic faith in the people. I have in the individual. He seems to me a divine achievement and I mistrust any view which belittles him. If anyone calls you a wretched little individual—and I've been called that—don't you take it lying down. You are important because everyone else is an individual too—

55

including the person who criticizes you. In asserting your personality you are playing for your side.

That, then, is the slogan with which I would answer, or partially answer, the Challenge of our Time. We want the New Economy with the Old Morality. We want planning for the body and not for the spirit. But the difficulty is this: where does the body stop and the spirit start? In the Middle Ages a hard-and-fast line was drawn between them, and according to the medieval theory of the Holy Roman Empire men rendered their bodies to Caesar and their souls to God. But the theory did not work. The Emperor, who represented Caesar, collided in practice with the Pope, who represented Christ. And we find ourselves in a similar dilemma today. Suppose you are planning the world distribution of food. You can't do that without planning world population. You can't do that without regulating the number of births and interfering with family life. You must supervise parenthood. You are meddling with the realms of the spirit, of personal relationships, although you may not have intended to do so. And you are brought back again to that inescapable arbiter, your own temperament. When there is a collision of principles would you favour the individual at the expense of the community, as I would? Or would you prefer economic justice for all at the expense of personal freedom?

In a time of upheaval like the present, this collision of principles, this split in one's loyalties, is always occurring. It has just occurred in my own life. I was brought up as a boy in one of the home counties, in a district which I still think the loveliest in England. There is nothing special about it—it is agricultural land, and could not be described in terms of beauty spots. It must always have looked much the same. I have kept in touch with it, going back to it as to an abiding city and still visiting the house which was once my home, for it is occupied by friends. A farm is through the hedge, and when the farmer there was eight years old and I was nine we used to jump up and down on his grandfather's straw ricks and spoil them. Today he is a grandfather himself, so that I have the sense of five generations continuing in one place. Life went on there as usual until this spring. Then someone who was applying for a permit to lay a water-pipe was casually informed that it would not be granted since the whole area had been commandeered. Commandeered for what? Had not the war ended? Appropriate officials of the Ministry of Town and Country Planning now arrived from

London and announced that a satellite town for sixty thousand people is to be built. The people now living and working there are doomed; it is death in life for them and they move in a nightmare. The best agricultural land has been taken, they assert; the poor land down by the railway has been left; compensation is inadequate. Anyhow, the satellite town has finished them off as completely as it will obliterate the ancient and delicate scenery. Meteorite town would be a better name. It has fallen out of a blue sky.

"Well," says the voice of planning and progress, "why this sentimentality? People must have houses." They must, and I think of working-class friends in north London who have to bring up four children in two rooms, and many are even worse off than that. But I cannot equate the problem. It is a collision of loyalties. I cannot free myself from the conviction that something irreplaceable has been destroyed, and that a little piece of England has died as surely as if a bomb had hit it. I wonder what compensation there is in the world of the spirit for the destruction of the life here, the life of tradition.

These are personal reminiscences and I am really supposed to be speaking from the standpoint of the creative artist. But you will gather what a writer who also cares for men and women and for the countryside must be feeling in the world today. Uncomfortable, of course. Sometimes miserable and indignant. But convinced that a planned change must take place if the world is not to disintegrate, and hopeful that in the new economy there may be a sphere both for human relationships and for the despised activity known as art. What ought the writer, the artist, to do when faced by the Challenge of our Time? Briefly, he ought to express what he wants and not what he is told to express by the planning authorities. He ought to impose a discipline on himself rather than accept one from outside. And that discipline may be aesthetic, rather than social or moral: he may wish to practise art for art's sake. That phrase has been foolishly used and often raises a giggle. But it is a profound phrase. It indicates that art is a self-contained harmony. Art is valuable not because it is educational (though it may be), not because it is recreative (though it may be), not because everyone enjoys it (for everybody does not), not even because it has to do with beauty. It is valuable because it has to do with order, and creates little worlds of its own, possessing internal harmony, in the bosom of this disordered planet. It is needed at once and now. It is needed before it is appreciated and independent of appreciation. The idea that it should not be permitted until it receives communal acclaim, and unless it is for all, is perfectly absurd. It is the activity which brought man out of original darkness and differentiates him from the beasts, and we must continue to practise and respect it through the darkness of today.

I am speaking like an intellectual, but the intellectual, to my mind, is more in touch with humanity than is the confident scientist, who patronizes the past, over-simplifies the present, and envisages a future where his leadership will be accepted. Owing to the political needs of the moment, the scientist occupies an abnormal position, which he tends to forget. He is subsidized by the terrified governments who need his aid, pampered and sheltered as long as he is obedient, and prosecuted under Official Secrets Acts when he has been naughty. All this separates him from ordinary men and women and makes him unfit to enter into their feelings. It is high time he came out of his ivory laboratory. We want him to plan for our bodies. We do not want him to plan for our minds, and we cannot accept, so far, his assurance that he will not.

[1946]

George Orwell

George Orwell's originality has been recognized in this country; his peculiar blend of gaiety and grimness has been appreciated, but there is still a tendency to shy away from him. This appeared in our reception of his most ambitious work, *1984*. America clasped it to her uneasy heart, but we, less anxious or less prescient, have eluded it for a variety of reasons. It is too bourgeois, we say, or too much to the left, or it has taken the wrong left turn, it is neither a novel nor a treatise, and so negligible, it is negligible because the author was tuberculous, like Keats; anyhow, we can't bear it. This last reason is certainly a respectable one. We all of us have the right to shirk unpleasantness, and we must sometimes exercise it. It may be our only defence against the right to nag. And that Orwell was a bit of a nagger cannot be denied. He found much to discomfort him in his world and desired to transmit it, and in *1984* he extended discomfort into agony. There is not a monster in that hateful apocalypse which does not exist in embryo today. Behind the United Nations lurks Oceania, one of his three world-states. Behind Stalin lurks Big Brother, which seems appropriate, but Big Brother also lurks behind Churchill, Truman, Gandhi, and any leader whom propaganda utilizes or invents. Behind the North Koreans, who are so wicked, and the South Koreans, who are such heroes, lurk the wicked South Koreans and the heroic North Koreans, into which, at a turn of the kaleidoscope, they may be transformed. Orwell spent his life in foreseeing transformations and in stamping upon embryos. His strength went that way. *1984* crowned his work, and it is understandably a crown of thorns.

While he stamped he looked around him, and tried to ameliorate a world which is bound to be unhappy. A true liberal, he hoped to help through small things. Programmes mean pogroms. Look to the rose or the toad or, if you think them more significant, look to art or literature. There, in the useless, lies our scrap of salvation.

If a man cannot enjoy the return of spring, why should he be happy in a labour-saving Utopia ? . . . I think that by retaining one's childhood love of such things as trees, fishes, butterflies and . . . toads, one makes a peaceful and decent future a little more probable, and that by preaching the doctrine that nothing is to be admired except steel and concrete, one merely makes it a little surer that human beings will have no outlet for their surplus energy except in hatred and leader worship.

The above is a quotation from *Shooting an Elephant*, his post-humous volume of essays. Here is another quotation from it:

If you wanted to add to the vast fund of ill-will existing in the world at this moment, you could hardly do it better than by a series of football matches between Jews and Arabs, Germans and Czechs . . . each match to be watched by a mixed audience of 100,000 spectators.

Games are harmless, even when played unfairly, provided they are played privately. It is international sport that helps to kick the world downhill. Started by foolish athletes, who thought it would promote "understanding", it is supported today by the desire for political prestige and by the interests involved in the gate-moneys. It is completely harmful. And elsewhere he considers the problem of nationalism generally. British imperialism, bad as he found it in Burma, is better than the newer imperialisms that are ousting it. All nations are odious but some are less odious than others, and by this stony, unlovely path he reaches patriotism. To some of us, this seems the cleanest way to reach it. We believe in the roses and the toads and the arts, and know that salvation, or a scrap of it, is to be found only in them. In the world of politics we see no salvation, we are not to be diddled, but we prefer the less bad to the more bad, and so become patriots, while keeping our brains and hearts intact.

This is an uneasy solution, and no one can embrace Orwell's works who hopes for ease. Just as one is nestling against them, they prickle. They encourage no slovenly trust in a future where all will come right, dear comrades, though we shall not be there to see. They do not even provide a mystic vision. No wonder that he could not hit it off with H. G. Wells. What he does provide, what does commend him to some temperaments, is his belief in little immediate things and in kindness, good temper and accuracy. He also believes in "the people", who, with their beefy arms akimbo and their cabbage-stalk soup, may survive when higher growths are cut down. He does not explain how "the people" are to make good, and perhaps he is here confusing belief with compassion.

He was passionate over the purity of prose, and in another essay he tears to bits some passages of contemporary writing. It is a dangerous game—the contemporaries can always retort—but it ought to be played, for, if prose decays, thought decays and all the finer roads of communication are broken. Liberty, he argues, is connected with prose, and bureaucrats who want to destroy liberty tend to write and speak badly, and to use pompous or woolly or portmanteau phrases in which their true meaning or any meaning disappears. It is the duty of the citizen, and particularly of the practising journalist, to be on the lookout for such phrases or words and to rend them to pieces. This was successfully done a few years ago in the case of "bottleneck". After "a vicious circle of interdependent bottlenecks" had been smashed in *The Times*, no bottleneck has dared to lift its head again. Many critics besides Orwell are fighting for the purity of prose and deriding officialese, but they usually do so in a joking offhand way, and from the aesthetic standpoint. He is unique in being immensely serious, and in connecting good prose with liberty. Like most of us, he does not define liberty, but being a liberal he thinks that there is more of it here than in Stalin's Russia or Franco's Spain, and that we need still more of it, rather than even less, if our national tradition is to continue. If we write and speak clearly, we are likelier to think clearly and to remain comparatively free. He gives six rules for clear writing, and they are not bad ones.

Posthumous sweepings seldom cohere, and *Shooting an Elephant* is really a collection of footnotes to Orwell's other work. Readers can trace in it affinities with *Animal Farm* or *1984* or *The Road to Wigan Pier* or *Burmese Days*. They can also trace his development. The earlier writing (e.g. the title-essay) is forceful but flat. There are no reverberations. In the later work—despite his preoccupation with politics—more imaginative notes are sounded. We part company with a man who has been determined to see what he can of this contradictory and disquieting world and to follow its implications into the unseen—or anyhow to follow them round the corner.

[1950]

Part Two
What I Believe

What I Believe

I do not believe in Belief. But this is an Age of Faith, and there are so many militant creeds that, in self-defence, one has to formulate a creed of one's own. Tolerance, good temper and sympathy are no longer enough in a world which is rent by religious and racial persecution, in a world where ignorance rules, and Science, who ought to have ruled, plays the subservient pimp. Tolerance, good temper and sympathy—they are what matter really, and if the human race is not to collapse they must come to the front before long. But for the moment they are not enough, their action is no stronger than a flower, battered beneath a military jackboot. They want stiffening, even if the process coarsens them. Faith, to my mind, is a stiffening process, a sort of mental starch, which ought to be applied as sparingly as possible. I dislike the stuff. I do not believe in it, for its own sake, at all. Herein I probably differ from most people, who believe in Belief, and are only sorry they cannot swallow even more than they do. My law-givers are Erasmus and Montaigne, not Moses and St Paul. My temple stands not upon Mount Moriah but in that Elysian Field where even the immoral are admitted. My motto is: "Lord, I disbelieve—help thou my unbelief."

I have, however, to live in an Age of Faith—the sort of epoch I used to hear praised when I was a boy. It is extremely unpleasant really. It is bloody in every sense of the word. And I have to keep my end up in it. Where do I start?

With personal relationships. Here is something comparatively solid in a world full of violence and cruelty. Not absolutely solid, for Psychology has split and shattered the idea of a "Person", and has shown that there is something incalculable in each of us, which may at any moment rise to the surface and destroy our normal balance. We don't know what we are like. We can't know what other people are like. How, then, can we put any trust in personal relationships, or cling to them in the gathering political storm? In theory we cannot. But in practice we can and do. Though A is not unchangeably A, or B unchangeably B, there can still be love and loyalty between the two. For the purpose of

65

living one has to assume that the personality is solid, and the "self" is an entity, and to ignore all contrary evidence. And since to ignore evidence is one of the characteristics of faith, I certainly can proclaim that I believe in personal relationships.

Starting from them, I get a little order into the contemporary chaos. One must be fond of people and trust them if one is not to make a mess of life, and it is therefore essential that they should not let one down. They often do. The moral of which is that I must, myself, be as reliable as possible, and this I try to be. But reliability is not a matter of contract—that is the main difference between the world of personal relationships and the world of business relationships. It is a matter for the heart, which signs no documents. In other words, reliability is impossible unless there is a natural warmth. Most men possess this warmth, though they often have bad luck and get chilled. Most of them, even when they are politicians, *want* to keep faith. And one can, at all events, show one's own little light here, one's own poor little trembling flame, with the knowledge that it is not the only light that is shining in the darkness, and not the only one which the darkness does not comprehend. Personal relations are despised today. They are regarded as bourgeois luxuries, as products of a time of fair weather which is now past, and we are urged to get rid of them, and to dedicate ourselves to some movement or cause instead. I hate the idea of causes, and if I had to choose between betraying my country and betraying my friend I hope I should have the guts to betray my country. Such a choice may scandalize the modern reader, and he may stretch out his patriotic hand to the telephone at once and ring up the police. It would not have shocked Dante, though. Dante places Brutus and Cassius in the lowest circle of Hell because they had chosen to betray their friend Julius Caesar rather than their country Rome. Probably one will not be asked to make such an agonizing choice. Still, there lies at the back of every creed something terrible and hard for which the worshipper may one day be required to suffer, and there is even a terror and a hardness in this creed of personal relationships, urbane and mild though it sounds. Love and loyalty to an individual can run counter to the claims of the State. When they do—down with the State, say I, which means that the State would down me.

This brings me along to Democracy, "Even love, the beloved Republic, That feeds upon freedom and lives". Democracy is not a beloved Republic really, and never will be. But it is less hateful than other contemporary forms of government, and to that extent it deserves our support. It does start from the assumption that the individual is important, and that all types are needed to make a civilization. It does not divide its citizens into the bossers and the bossed—as an efficiency-regime tends to do. The people I admire most are those who are sensitive and want to create something or discover something, and do not see life in terms of power, and such people get more of a chance under a democracy than elsewhere. They found religions, great or small, or they produce literature and art, or they do disinterested scientific research, or they may be what is called "ordinary people", who are creative in their private lives, bring up their children decently, for instance, or help their neighbours. All these people need to express themselves; they cannot do so unless society allows them liberty to do so, and the society which allows them most liberty is a democracy.

Democracy has another merit. It allows criticism, and if there is not public criticism there are bound to be hushed-up scandals. That is why I believe in the press, despite all its lies and vulgarity, and why I believe in Parliament. Parliament is often sneered at because it is a Talking Shop. I believe in it *because* it is a talking shop. I believe in the Private Member who makes himself a nuisance. He gets snubbed and is told that he is cranky or ill-informed, but he does expose abuses which would otherwise never have been mentioned, and very often an abuse gets put right just by being mentioned. Occasionally, too, a well-meaning public official starts losing his head in the cause of efficiency, and thinks himself God Almighty. Such officials are particularly frequent in the Home Office. Well, there will be questions about them in Parliament sooner or later, and then they will have to mind their steps. Whether Parliament is either a representative body or an efficient one is questionable, but I value it because it criticizes and talks, and because its chatter gets widely reported.

So two cheers for Democracy: one because it admits variety and two because it permits criticism. Two cheers are quite enough: there is no occasion to give three. Only Love the Beloved Republic deserves that.

What about Force, though? While we are trying to be sensitive and advanced and affectionate and tolerant, an unpleasant question pops up: does not all society rest upon force? If a government cannot count upon the police and the army, how can it hope to rule? And if an individual gets knocked on the head or sent to a labour camp, of what significance are his opinions?

This dilemma does not worry me as much as it does some. I realize that all society rests upon force. But all the great creative actions, all the decent human relations, occur during the intervals when force has not managed to come to the front. These intervals are what matter. I want them to be as frequent and as lengthy as possible, and I call them "civilization". Some people idealize force and pull it into the foreground and worship it, instead of keeping it in the background as long as possible. I think they make a mistake, and I think that their opposites, the mystics, err even more when they declare that force does not exist. I believe that it exists, and that one of our jobs is to prevent it from getting out of its box. It gets out sooner or later, and then it destroys us and all the lovely things which we have made. But it is not out all the time, for the fortunate reason that the strong are so stupid. Consider their conduct for a moment in *The Nibelung's Ring*. The giants there have the guns, or in other words the gold; but they do nothing with it, they do not realize that they are all-powerful, with the result that the catastrophe is delayed and the castle of Valhalla, insecure but glorious, fronts the storms. Fafnir, coiled round his hoard, grumbles and grunts; we can hear him under Europe today; the leaves of the wood already tremble, and the Bird calls its warnings uselessly. Fafnir will destroy us, but by a blessed dispensation he is stupid and slow, and creation goes on just outside the poisonous blast of his breath. The Nietzschean would hurry the monster up, the mystic would say he did not exist, but Wotan, wiser than either, hastens to create warriors before doom declares itself. The Valkyries are symbols not only of courage but of intelligence; they represent the human spirit snatching its opportunity while the going is good, and one of them even finds time to love. Brünnhilde's last song hymns the recurrence of love, and since it is the privilege of art to exaggerate she goes even further, and proclaims the love which is eternally triumphant, and feeds upon freedom and lives.

So that is what I feel about force and violence. It is, alas! the ultimate reality on this earth, but it does not always get to the front. Some people call its absences "decadence"; I call them "civilization" and find in such interludes the chief justification for the human experiment. I look the other way until fate strikes me. Whether this is due to courage or to cowardice in my own case I cannot be sure. But I know that, if men had not

---

looked the other way in the past, nothing of any value would survive. The people I respect most behave as if they were immortal and as if society was eternal. Both assumptions are false: both of them must be accepted as true if we are to go on eating and working and loving, and are to keep open a few breathing-holes for the human spirit. No millennium seems likely to descend upon humanity; no better and stronger League of Nations will be instituted; no form of Christianity and no alternative to Christianity will bring peace to the world or integrity to the individual; no "change of heart" will occur. And yet we need not despair, indeed, we cannot despair; the evidence of history shows us that men have always insisted on behaving creatively under the shadow of the sword; that they have done their artistic and scientific and domestic stuff for the sake of doing it, and that we had better follow their example under the shadow of the aeroplanes. Others, with more vision or courage than myself, see the salvation of humanity ahead, and will dismiss my conception of civilization as paltry, a sort of tip-and-run game. Certainly it is presumptuous to say that we *cannot* improve, and that Man, who has only been in power for a few thousand years, will never learn to make use of his power. All I mean is that, if people continue to kill one another as they do, the world cannot get better than it is, and that, since there are more people than formerly, and their means for destroying one another superior, the world may well get worse. What is good in people—and consequently in the world—is their insistence on creation, their belief in friendship and loyalty for their own sakes; and, though Violence remains and is, indeed, the major partner in this muddled establishment, I believe that creativeness remains too, and will always assume direction when violence sleeps. So, though I am not an optimist, I cannot agree with Sophocles that it were better never to have been born. And although, like Horace, I see no evidence that each batch of births is superior to the last, I leave the field open for the more complacent view. This is such a difficult moment to live in, one cannot help getting gloomy and also a bit rattled, and perhaps short-sighted.

In search of a refuge, we may perhaps turn to hero-worship. But here we shall get no help, in my opinion. Hero-worship is a dangerous vice, and one of the minor merits of a democracy is that it does not encourage it, or produce that unmanageable type of citizen known as the Great Man. It produces instead different kinds of small men—a much finer achievement. But people who

69

cannot get interested in the variety of life, and cannot make up their own minds, get discontented over this, and they long for a hero to bow down before and to follow blindly. It is significant that a hero is an integral part of the authoritarian stock-in-trade today. An efficiency-regime cannot be run without a few heroes stuck about it to carry off the dullness—much as plums have to be put into a bad pudding to make it palatable. One hero at the top and a smaller one each side of him is a favourite arrangement, and the timid and the bored are comforted by the trinity, and, bowing down, feel exalted and strengthened.

No, I distrust Great Men. They produce a desert of uniformity around them and often a pool of blood too, and I always feel a little man's pleasure when they come a cropper. Every now and then one reads in the newspapers some such statement as: "The *coup d'état* appears to have failed, and Admiral Toma's whereabouts is at present unknown." Admiral Toma had probably every qualification for being a Great Man—an iron will, personal magnetism, dash, flair, sexlessness—but fate was against him, so he retires to unknown whereabouts instead of parading history with his peers. He fails with a completeness which no artist and no lover can experience, because with them the process of creation is itself an achievement, whereas with him the only possible achievement is success.

I believe in aristocracy, though—if that is the right word, and if a democrat may use it. Not an aristocracy of power, based upon rank and influence, but an aristocracy of the sensitive, the considerate and the plucky. Its members are to be found in all nations and classes, and all through the ages, and there is a secret understanding between them when they meet. They represent the true human tradition, the one permanent victory of our queer race over cruelty and chaos. Thousands of them perish in obscurity, a few are great names. They are sensitive for others as well as for themselves, they are considerate without being fussy, their pluck is not swankiness but the power to endure, and they can take a joke. I give no examples—it is risky to do that—but the reader may as well consider whether this is the type of person he would like to meet and to be, and whether (going further with me) he would prefer that this type should *not* be an ascetic one. I am against asceticism myself. I am with the old Scotsman who wanted less chastity and more delicacy. I do not feel that my aristocrats are a real aristocracy if they thwart their bodies, since bodies are the instruments through which we

WHAT I BELIEVE

register and enjoy the world. Still, I do not insist. This is not a
major point. It is clearly possible to be sensitive, considerate and
plucky and yet be an ascetic too, and if anyone possesses the first
three qualities I will let him in! On they go—an invincible army,
yet not a victorious one. The aristocrats, the elect, the chosen,
the Best People—all the words that describe them are false, and
all attempts to organize them fail. Again and again Authority,
seeing their value, has tried to net them and to utilize them as the
Egyptian Priesthood or the Christian Church or the Chinese
Civil Service or the Group Movement, or some other worthy
stunt. But they slip through the net and are gone; when the door
is shut, they are no longer in the room; their temple, as one of
them remarked, is the holiness of the Heart's affections, and their
kingdom, though they never possess it, is the wide-open world.

With this type of person knocking about, and constantly crossing one's path if one has eyes to see or hands to feel, the experiment of earthly life cannot be dismissed as a failure. But it may
well be hailed as a tragedy, the tragedy being that no device has
been found by which these private decencies can be transmitted
to public affairs. As soon as people have power they go crooked
and sometimes dotty as well, because the possession of power
lifts them into a region where normal honesty never pays. For
instance, the man who is selling newspapers outside the Houses
of Parliament can safely leave his papers to go for a drink, and
his cap beside them: anyone who takes a paper is sure to drop a
copper into the cap. But the men who are inside the Houses of
Parliament—they cannot trust one another like that, still less can
the Government they compose trust other governments. No
caps upon the pavement here, but suspicion, treachery and
armaments. The more highly public life is organized the lower
does its morality sink; the nations of today behave to each other
worse than they ever did in the past, they cheat, rob, bully and
bluff, make war without notice, and kill as many women and
children as possible; whereas primitive tribes were at all events
restrained by taboos. It is a humiliating outlook—though the
greater the darkness, the brighter shine the little lights, reassuring
one another, signalling: "Well, at all events, I'm still here. I
don't like it very much, but how are you?" Unquenchable lights
of my aristocracy! Signals of the invincible army! "Come along
—anyway, let's have a good time while we can." I think they
signal that too.

The Saviour of the future—if ever he comes—will not preach

71

a new Gospel. He will merely utilize my aristocracy, he will make effective the goodwill and the good temper which are already existing. In other words, he will introduce a new technique. In economics, we are told that if there was a new technique of distribution there need be no poverty, and people would not starve in one place while crops were being ploughed under in another. A similar change is needed in the sphere of morals and politics. The desire for it is by no means new; it was expressed, for example, in theological terms by Jacopone da Todi over six hundred years ago. "Ordena questo amore, tu che m'ami," he said; "O thou who lovest me—set this love in order." His prayer was not granted, and I do not myself believe that it ever will be, but here, and not through a change of heart, is our probable route. Not by becoming better, but by ordering and distributing his native goodness, will Man shut up Force into its box, and so gain time to explore the universe and to set his mark upon it worthily. At present he only explores it at odd moments, when Force is looking the other way, and his divine creativeness appears as a trivial by-product, to be scrapped as soon as the drums beat and the bombers hum.

Such a change, claim the orthodox, can only be made by Christianity, and will be made by it in God's good time: man always has failed and always will fail to organize his own goodness, and it is presumptuous of him to try. This claim—solemn as it is—leaves me cold. I cannot believe that Christianity will ever cope with the present world-wide mess, and I think that such influence as it retains in modern society is due to the money behind it, rather than to its spiritual appeal. It was a spiritual force once, but the indwelling spirit will have to be restated if it is to calm the waters again, and probably restated in a non-Christian form. Naturally a lot of people, and people who are not only good but able and intelligent, will disagree here; they will vehemently deny that Christianity has failed, or they will argue that its failure proceeds from the wickedness of men, and really proves its ultimate success. They have Faith, with a large F. My faith has a very small one, and I only intrude it because these are strenuous and serious days, and one likes to say what one thinks while speech is comparatively free; it may not be free much longer.

The above are the reflections of an individualist and a liberal who has found liberalism crumbling beneath him and at first felt ashamed. Then, looking around, he decided there was no special

72

reason for shame, since other people, whatever they felt, were equally insecure. And as for individualism—there seems no way of getting off this, even if one wanted to. The dictator-hero can grind down his citizens till they are all alike, but he cannot melt them into a single man. That is beyond his power. He can order them to merge, he can incite them to mass-antics, but they are obliged to be born separately, and to die separately, and, owing to these unavoidable termini, will always be running off the totalitarian rails. The memory of birth and the expectation of death always lurk within the human being, making him separate from his fellows and consequently capable of intercourse with them. Naked I came into the world, naked I shall go out of it! And a very good thing too, for it reminds me that I am naked under my shirt, whatever its colour.

[1938]

Art in General

Anonymity: An Enquiry

Do you like to know who a book's by?

The question is more profound than may appear. A poem, for example: do we gain more or less pleasure from it when we know the name of the poet? The "Ballad of Sir Patrick Spens", for example. No one knows who wrote "Sir Patrick Spens". It comes to us out of the northern void like a breath of ice. Set beside it another ballad whose author is known—"The Rime of the Ancient Mariner". That, too, contains a tragic voyage and the breath of ice, but it is signed by Samuel Taylor Coleridge, and we know a certain amount about this Coleridge. Coleridge signed other poems and knew other poets; he ran away from Cambridge; he enlisted as a dragoon under the name of Trooper Comberbache, but fell so constantly from his horse that it had to be withdrawn from beneath him permanently; he was employed instead upon matters relating to sanitation; he married Southey's sister, and gave lectures; he became stout, pious and dishonest, took opium and died. With such information in our heads, we speak of "The Ancient Mariner" as "a poem by Coleridge", but of "Sir Patrick Spens" as "a poem". What difference, if any, does this difference between them make upon our minds? And in the case of novels and plays—does ignorance or knowledge of their authorship signify? And newspaper articles—do they impress more when they are signed or unsigned? Thus—rather vaguely—let us begin our quest.

Books are composed of words, and words have two functions to perform: they give information or they create an atmosphere. Often they do both, for the two functions are not incompatible, but our enquiry shall keep them distinct. Let us turn for our next example to public notices. There is a word that is sometimes hung up at the edge of a tramline: the word "Stop". Written on a metal label by the side of the line, it means that a tram should stop here presently. It is an example of pure information. It creates no atmosphere—at least, not in my mind. I stand close to the label and wait and wait for the tram. If the tram comes, the information is correct; if it doesn't come, the information is in-

77

correct; but in either case it remains information, and the notice is an excellent instance of one of the uses of words.

Compare it with another public notice which is sometimes exhibited in the darker cities of England: "Beware of pickpockets, male and female." Here, again, there is information. A pickpocket may come along presently, just like a tram, and we take our measures accordingly. But there is something else besides. Atmosphere is created. Who can see those words without a slight sinking feeling at the heart? All the people around look so honest and nice, but they are not, some of them are pickpockets, male or female. They hustle old gentlemen, the old gentleman glances down, his watch is gone. They steal up behind an old lady and cut out the back breadth of her beautiful sealskin jacket with sharp and noiseless pairs of scissors. Observe that happy little child running to buy sweets. Why does he suddenly burst into tears? A pickpocket, male or female, has jerked his halfpenny out of his hand. All this, and perhaps much more, occurs to us when we read the notice in question. We suspect our fellows of dishonesty, we observe them suspecting us. We have been reminded of several disquieting truths, of the general insecurity of life, human frailty, the violence of the poor, and the fatuous trustfulness of the rich, who always expect to be popular without having done anything to deserve it. It is a sort of *memento mori*, set up in the midst of Vanity Fair. By taking the form of a warning it has made us afraid, although nothing is gained by fear; all we need to do is to protect our precious purses, and fear will not help us to do this. Besides conveying information it has created an atmosphere, and to that extent is literature. "Beware of pickpockets, male and female" is not good literature, and it is unconscious. But the words are performing two functions, whereas the word "Stop" only performed one, and this is an important difference, and the first step in our journey.

Next step. Let us now collect together all the printed matter of the world into a single heap: poetry books, exercise books, plays, newspapers, advertisements, street notices, everything. Let us arrange the contents of the heap into a line, with the works that convey pure information at one end, and the works that create pure atmosphere at the other end, and the works that do both in their intermediate positions, the whole line being graded so that we pass from one attitude to another. We shall find that at the end of pure information stands the tramway notice "Stop", and that at the extreme other end is lyric poetry. Lyric poetry is absolutely no use. It is the exact antithesis of a street notice, for it conveys no information of any kind. What's the use of "A slumber did my spirit seal" or "Whether on Ida's shady brow" or "So, we'll go no more a roving" or "Far in a western brookland"? They do not tell us where the tram will stop or even whether it exists. And, passing from lyric poetry to ballad, we are still deprived of information. It is true that "The Ancient Mariner" describes an Antarctic expedition, but in such a muddled way that it is no real help to the explorer, the accounts of the polar currents and winds being hopelessly inaccurate. It is true that the "Ballad of Sir Patrick Spens" refers to the bringing home of the Maid of Norway in the year 1285, but the reference is so vague and confused that the historians turn from it in despair. Lyric poetry is absolutely no use, and poetry generally is almost no use.

But when, proceeding down the line, we leave poetry behind and arrive at the drama, and particularly at those plays that purport to contain normal human beings, we find a change. Uselessness still predominates, but we begin to get information as well. *Julius Caesar* contains some reliable information about Rome. And when we pass from the drama to the novel the change is still more marked. Information abounds. What a lot we learn from *Tom Jones* about the west countryside! And from *Northanger Abbey* about the same countryside fifty years later! In psychology too the novelist teaches us much. How carefully has Henry James explored certain selected recesses of the human mind! What an analysis of a country rectory in *The Way of All Flesh*! The instincts of Emily Brontë—they illuminate passion. And Proust—how amazingly does Proust describe not only French society, not only the working of his characters, but the personal equipment of the reader, so that one keeps stopping with a gasp to say, "Oh! how did he find that out about me? I didn't even know it myself until he informed me, but it is so!" The novel, whatever else it may be, is partly a noticeboard. And that is why many men who do not care for poetry or even for the drama enjoy novels and are well qualified to criticize them.

Beyond the novel we come to works whose avowed aim is information, works of learning, history, sociology, philosophy, psychology, science, etc. Uselessness is now subsidiary, though it still may persist as it does in the *Decline and Fall* or *The Stones of Venice*. And next come those works that give, or profess to give, us information about contemporary events: the newspapers.

79

(Newspapers are so important and so peculiar that I shall return to them later, but mention them here in their place in the procession of printed matter.) And then come advertisements, time-tables, the price list inside a taxi, and public notices: the notice warning us against pickpockets, which incidentally produced an atmosphere though its aim was information, and the pure information contained in the announcement "Stop". It is a long journey from lyric poetry to a placard beside a tramline, but it is a journey in which there are no breaks. Words are all of one family, and do not become different because some are printed in a book and others on a metal disc. It is their functions that differentiate them. They have two functions, and the combination of those functions is infinite. If there is on earth a house with many mansions, it is the house of words.

Looking at this line of printed matter, let us again ask ourselves: Do I want to know who wrote that? Ought it to be signed or not? The question is becoming more interesting. Clearly, in so far as words convey information, they ought to be signed. Information is supposed to be true. That is its only reason for existing, and the man who gives it ought to sign his name, so that he may be called to account if he has told a lie. When I have waited for several hours beneath the notice "Stop", I have the right to suggest that it be taken down, and I cannot do this unless I know who put it up. Make your statement, sign your name. That's common sense. But as we approach the other function of words—the creation of atmosphere—the question of signature surely loses its importance. It does not matter who wrote "A slumber did my spirit steal", because the poem itself does not matter. Ascribe it to Ella Wheeler Wilcox and the trams will run as usual. It does not matter much who wrote *Julius Caesar* and *Tom Jones*. They contain descriptions of ancient Rome and eighteenth-century England, and to that extent we wish them signed, for we can judge from the author's name whether the description is likely to be reliable; but beyond that the guarantee of Shakespeare or Fielding might just as well be Charles Garvice's. So we come to the conclusion, firstly, that what is information ought to be signed; and, secondly, that what is not information need not be signed.

The question can now be carried a step further.

What is this element in words that is not information? I have called it "atmosphere", but it requires stricter definition than that. It resides not in any particular word, but in the order in which words are arranged—that is to say, in style. It is the power that words have to raise our emotions or quicken our blood. It is also something else, and to define that other thing would be to explain the secret of the universe. This "something else" in words is undefinable. It is their power to create not only atmosphere, but a world, which, while it lasts, seems more real and solid than this daily existence of pickpockets and trams. Before we begin to read "The Ancient Mariner" we know that the Polar Seas are not inhabited by spirits, and that if a man shoots an albatross he is not a criminal but a sportsman, and that if he stuffs the albatross afterwards he becomes a naturalist also. All this is common knowledge. But when we are reading "The Ancient Mariner", or remembering it intensely, common knowledge disappears and uncommon knowledge takes its place. We have entered a universe that only answers to its own laws, supports itself, internally coheres, and has a new standard of truth. Information is true if it is accurate. A poem is true if it hangs together. Information points to something else. A poem points to nothing but itself. Information is relative. A poem is absolute. The world created by words exists neither in space nor time though it has semblances of both, it is eternal and indestructible, and yet its action is no stronger than a flower; it is adamant, yet it is also what one of its practitioners thought it to be, namely the shadow of a shadow. We can best define it by negations. It is not this world, its laws are not the laws of science or logic, its conclusions not those of common sense. And it causes us to suspend our ordinary judgements.

Now comes the crucial point. While we are reading "The Ancient Mariner" we forget our astronomy and geography and daily ethics. Do we not also forget the author? Does not Samuel Taylor Coleridge, lecturer, opium-eater and dragoon, disappear with the rest of the world of information? We remember him before we begin the poem and after we finish it, but during the poem nothing exists but the poem. Consequently while we read "The Ancient Mariner" a change takes place in it. It becomes anonymous, like the "Ballad of Sir Patrick Spens". And here is the point I would support: that all literature tends towards a condition of anonymity, and that, so far as words are creative, a signature merely distracts us from their true significance. I do not say literature "ought" not to be signed, because literature is alive, and consequently "ought" is the wrong word to use. It wants not to be signed. That puts my point. It is always tugging in that direction and saying in effect: "I, not my author, exist really." So do the trees, flowers and human beings say, "I really exist, not God," and continue to say so despite the admonitions to the contrary addressed to them by clergymen and scientists. To forget its Creator is one of the functions of a Creation. To remember him is to forget the days of one's youth. Literature does not want to remember. It is alive—not in a vague complementary sense—but alive tenaciously, and it is always covering up the tracks that connect it with the laboratory.

It may here be objected that literature expresses personality, that it is the result of the author's individual outlook, that we are right in asking for his name. It is his property—he ought to have the credit.

An important objection; also a modern one, for in the past neither writers nor readers attached the high importance to personality that they do today. It did not trouble Homer or the various people who were Homer. It did not trouble the writers in the Greek Anthology, who would write and rewrite the same poem in almost identical language, their notion being that the poem, not the poet, is the important thing, and that by continuous rehandling the perfect expression natural to the poem may be attained. It did not trouble the medieval balladists, who, like the cathedral-builders, left their works unsigned. It troubled neither the composers nor the translators of the Bible. The Book of Genesis today contains at least three different elements—Jahvist, Elohist and Priestly—which were combined into a single account by a committee who lived under King Josiah at Jerusalem and translated into English by another committee who lived under King James I at London. And yet the Book of Genesis is literature. These earlier writers and readers knew that the words a man writes express him, but they did not make a cult of expression as we do today. Surely they were right, and modern critics go too far in their insistence on personality.

They go too far because they do not reflect what personality is. Just as words have two functions—information and creation—so each human mind has two personalities, one on the surface, one deeper down. The upper personality has a name. It is called S. T. Coleridge, or William Shakespeare, or Mrs Humphry Ward. It is conscious and alert, it does things like dining out, answering letters, etc., and it differs vividly and amusingly from other personalities. The lower personality is a very queer affair. In many ways it is a perfect fool, but without it there is no literature, because unless a man dips a bucket down into it occasionally he cannot produce first-class work. There is something general about it. Although it is inside S. T. Coleridge, it cannot be labelled with his name. It has something in common with all other deeper personalities, and the mystic will assert that the common quality is God, and that here, in the obscure recesses of our being, we near the gates of the Divine. It is in any case the force that makes for anonymity. As it came from the depths, so it soars to the heights, out of local questionings; as it is general to all men, so the works it inspires have something general about them, namely beauty. The poet wrote the poem, no doubt, but he forgot himself while he wrote it, and we forget him while we read. What is so wonderful about great literature is that it transforms the man who reads it towards the condition of the man who wrote, and brings to birth in us also the creative impulse. Lost in the beauty where he was lost, we find more than we ever threw away, we reach what seems to be our spiritual home, and remember that it was not the speaker who was in the beginning but the Word.

If we glance at one or two writers who are not first-class this point will be illustrated. Charles Lamb and R. L. Stevenson will serve. Here are two gifted, sensitive, fanciful, tolerant, humorous fellows, but they always write with their surface-personalities and never let down buckets into their underworld. Lamb did not try: bbbbuckets, he would have said, are bbeyond me, and he is the pleasanter writer in consequence. Stevenson was always trying oh ever so hard, but the bucket either stuck or else came up again full of the R.L.S. who let it down, full of the mannerisms, the self-consciousness, the sentimentality, the quaintness which he was hoping to avoid. He and Lamb append their names in full to every sentence they write. They pursue us page after page, always to the exclusion of higher joy. They are letter-writers, not creative artists, and it is no coincidence that each of them did write charming letters. A letter comes off the surface: it deals with the events of the day or with plans: it is naturally signed. Literature tries to be unsigned. And the proof is that, whereas we are always exclaiming "How like Lamb!" or "How typical of Stevenson!" we never say "How like Shake-speare!" or "How typical of Dante!" We are conscious only of the world they have created, and we are in a sense co-partners in it. Coleridge, in his smaller domain, makes us co-partners too. We forget for ten minutes his name and our own, and I contend that this temporary forgetfulness, this momentary and mutual anonymity, is sure evidence of good stuff. The demand that literature should express personality is far too insistent in these days, and I look back with longing to the earlier modes of criticism where a poem was not an expression but a discovery, and was sometimes supposed to have been shown to the poet by God.

The personality of a writer does become important after we have read his book and begin to study it. When the glamour of creation ceases, when the leaves of the divine tree are silent, when the co-partnership is over, then a book changes its nature, and we can ask ourselves questions about it such as "What is the author's name?", "Where did he live?", "Was he married?" and "Which was his favourite flower?" Then we are no longer reading the book, we are studying it and making it subserve our desire for information. "Study" has a very solemn sound. "I am studying Dante" sounds much more than "I am reading Dante". It is really much less. Study is only a serious form of gossip. It teaches us everything about the book except the central thing, and between that and us it raises a circular barrier which only the wings of the spirit can cross. The study of science, history, etc., is necessary and proper, for they are subjects that belong to the domain of information, but a creative subject like literature— to study that is excessively dangerous, and should never be attempted by the immature. Modern education promotes the unmitigated study of literature and concentrates our attention on the relation between a writer's life—his surface life—and his work. That is one reason why it is such a curse. There are no questions to be asked about literature while we read it because "la paix succède à la pensée", in the words of Paul Claudel. An examination paper could not be set on "The Ancient Mariner" as it speaks to the heart of the reader, and it was to speak to the heart that it was written, and otherwise it would not have been written. Questions only occur when we cease to realize what it was about and become inquisitive and methodical.

A word in conclusion on the newspapers—for they raise an interesting contributory issue. We have already defined a newspaper as something which conveys, or is supposed to convey, information about passing events. It is true, not to itself like a poem, but to the facts it purports to relate—like the tram notice. When the morning paper arrives it lies upon the breakfast table simply steaming with truth in regard to something else. Truth, truth, and nothing but truth. Unsated by the banquet, we sally forth in the afternoon to buy an evening paper, which is published at midday as the name implies, and feast anew. At the end of the week we buy a weekly, or a Sunday paper, which as the name implies has been written on the Saturday, and at the end of the month we buy a monthly. Thus do we keep in touch with the world of events as practical men should.

And who is keeping us in touch? Who gives us this information upon which our judgements depend, and which must ultimately influence our characters? Curious to relate, we seldom know. Newspapers are for the most part anonymous. Statements are made and no signature appended. Suppose we read in a paper that the Emperor of Guatemala is dead. Our first feeling is one of mild consternation; out of snobbery we regret what has happened, although the Emperor didn't play much part in our lives, and if ladies we say to one another, "I feel so sorry for the poor Empress." But presently we learn that the Emperor cannot have died, because Guatemala is a Republic, and the Empress cannot be a widow, because she does not exist. If the statement was signed, and we know the name of the goose who made it, we shall discount anything he tells us in the future. If—which is more probable—it is unsigned or signed "Our Special Correspondent", we remain defenceless against future misstatements. The Guatemala lad may be turned on to write about the Fall of the Franc and mislead us over that.

It seems paradoxical that an article should impress us more if it is unsigned than if it is signed. But it does, owing to the weakness of our psychology. Anonymous statements have, as we have seen, a universal air about them. Absolute truth, the collected wisdom of the universe, seems to be speaking, not the feeble voice of a man. The modern newspaper has taken advantage of this. It is a pernicious caricature of literature. It has usurped that divine tendency towards anonymity. It has claimed for information what only belongs to creation. And it will claim it as long as we allow it to claim it, and to exploit the defects of our psychology. "The High Mission of the Press." Poor Press! As if it were in a position to have a mission! It is we who have a mission to it. To cure a man through the newspapers or through propaganda of any sort is impossible; you merely alter the symptoms of his disease. We shall only be cured by purging our minds of confusion. The papers trick us not so much by their lies as by their exploitation of our weakness. They are always confusing the two functions of words and insinuating that "The Emperor of

Guatemala is dead" and "A slumber did my spirit seal" belong to the same category. They are always usurping the privileges that only uselessness may claim, and they will do this as long as we allow them to do it.

This ends our enquiry. The question "Ought things to be signed?" seemed, if not an easy question, at all events an isolated one, but we could not answer it without considering what words are, and disentangling the two functions they perform. We decided pretty easily that information ought to be signed; common sense leads to this conclusion, and newspapers which are largely unsigned have gained by that device their undesirable influence over civilization. Creation—that we found a more difficult matter. "Literature wants not to be signed," I suggested. Creation comes from the depths—the mystic will say from God. The signature, the name, belongs to the surface-personality, and pertains to the world of information, it is a ticket, not the spirit of life. While the author wrote he forgot his name; while we read him we forget both his name and our own. When we have finished reading we begin to ask questions, and to study the book and the author, we drag them into the realm of information. Now we learn a thousand things, but we have lost the pearl of great price, and in the chatter of question and answer, in the torrents of gossip and examination papers, we forget the purpose for which creation was performed. I am not asking for reverence. Reverence is fatal to literature. My plea is for something more vital: imagination. "Imagination is as the immortal God which should assume flesh for the redemption of mortal passion" (Shelley). Imagination is our only guide into the world created by words. Whether those words are signed or unsigned becomes, as soon as the imagination redeems us, a matter of no importance, because we have approximated to the state in which they were written, and there are no names down there, no personality as we understand personality, no marrying or giving in marriage. What there is down there—ah, that is another enquiry, and may the clergymen and the scientists pursue it more successfully in the future than they have in the past.

[1925]

Art for Art's Sake

An address delivered before the American
Academy and the National Institute of
Arts and Letters in New York

I believe in art for art's sake. It is an unfashionable belief, and
some of my statements must be of the nature of an apology.
Sixty years ago I should have faced you with more confidence. A
writer or a speaker who chose "Art for Art's Sake" for his theme
sixty years ago could be sure of being in the swim, and could feel
so confident of success that he sometimes dressed himself in
aesthetic costumes suitable to the occasion—in an embroidered
dressing-gown, perhaps, or a blue velvet suit with a Lord Fauntle-
roy collar; or a toga, or a kimono, and carried a poppy or a lily or
a long peacock's feather in his medieval hand. Times have
changed. Not thus can I present either myself or my theme
today. My aim rather is to ask you quietly to reconsider for a
few minutes a phrase which has been much misused and much
abused, but which has, I believe, great importance for us—has,
indeed, eternal importance.

Now we can easily dismiss those peacock's feathers and other
affectations—they are but trifles—but I want also to dismiss a
more dangerous heresy, namely the silly idea that only art matters, an idea which has somehow got mixed up with the idea of art
for art's sake, and has helped to discredit it. Many things, besides
art, matter. It is merely one of the things that matter, and, high
though the claims are that I make for it, I want to keep them in
proportion. No one can spend his or her life entirely in the
creation or the appreciation of masterpieces. Man lives, and
ought to live, in a complex world, full of conflicting claims, and
if we simplified them down into the aesthetic he would be
sterilized. Art for art's sake does not mean that only art matters,
and I would also like to rule out such phrases as "The Life of
Art", "Living for Art" and "Art's High Mission". They confuse and mislead.

What does the phrase mean? Instead of generalizing, let us
take a specific instance—Shakespeare's *Macbeth*, for example, and
pronounce the words, "*Macbeth* for *Macbeth*'s sake". What does
that mean? Well, the play has several aspects—it is educational,
it teaches us something about legendary Scotland, something

about Jacobean England, and a good deal about human nature and its perils. We can study its origins, and study and enjoy its dramatic technique and the music of its diction. All that is true. But *Macbeth* is furthermore a world of its own, created by Shakespeare and existing in virtue of its own poetry. It is in this aspect *Macbeth* for *Macbeth*'s sake, and that is what I intend by the phrase "art for art's sake". A work of art—whatever else it may be—is a self-contained entity, with a life of its own imposed on it by its creator. It has internal order. It may have external form. That is how we recognize it.

Take for another example that picture of Seurat's which I saw two years ago in Chicago—*La Grande Jatte*. Here again there is much to study and to enjoy: the pointillism, the charming face of the seated girl, the nineteenth-century Parisian Sunday sunlight, the sense of motion in immobility. But here again there is something more; *La Grande Jatte* forms a world of its own, created by Seurat and existing by virtue of its own poetry: *La Grande Jatte pour La Grande Jatte: l'art pour l'art.* Like *Macbeth* it has internal order and internal life.

It is to the conception of order that I would now turn. This is important to my argument, and I want to make a digression, and glance at order in daily life, before I come to order in art.

In the world of daily life, the world which we perforce inhabit, there is much talk about order, particularly from statesmen and politicians. They tend, however, to confuse order with orders, just as they confuse creation with regulations. Order, I suggest, is something evolved from within, not something imposed from without; it is an internal stability, a vital harmony, and in the social and political category it has never existed except for the convenience of historians. Viewed realistically, the past is really a series of *dis*orders, succeeding one another by discoverable laws, no doubt, and certainly marked by an increasing growth of human interference, but disorders all the same. So that, speaking as a writer, what I hope for today is a disorder which will be more favourable to artists than is the present one, and which will provide them with fuller inspirations and better material conditions. It will not last—nothing lasts—but there have been some advantageous disorders in the past—for instance, in ancient Athens, in Renaissance Italy, eighteenth-century France, periods in China and Persia—and we may do something to accelerate the next one. But let us not again fix our hearts where true joys are not to be found. We were promised a new order after the First

World War through the League of Nations. It did not come, nor have I faith in present promises, by whomsoever endorsed. The implacable offensive of Science forbids. We cannot reach social and political stability, for the reason that we continue to make scientific discoveries and to apply them, and thus to destroy the arrangements which were based on more elementary discoveries. If Science would discover rather than apply—if, in other words, men were more interested in knowledge than in power—mankind would be in a far safer position, the stability statesmen talk about would be a possibility, there could be a new order based on vital harmony, and the earthly millennium might approach. But Science shows no signs of doing this: she gave us the internal combustion engine, and before we had digested and assimilated it with terrible pains into our social system she harnessed the atom, and destroyed any new order that seemed to be evolving. How can man get into harmony with his surroundings when he is constantly altering them? The future of our race is, in this direction, more unpleasant than we care to admit, and it has sometimes seemed to me that its best chance lies through apathy, uninventiveness and inertia. Universal exhaustion might promote that Change of Heart which is at present so briskly recommended from a thousand pulpits. Universal exhaustion would certainly be a new experience. The human race has never undergone it, and is still too perky to admit that it may be coming and might result in a sprouting of new growth through the decay.

I must not pursue these speculations any further—they lead me too far from my terms of reference and maybe from yours. But I do want to emphasize that order in daily life and in history, order in the social and political category, is unattainable under our present psychology.

Where is it attainable? Not in the astronomical category, where it was for many years enthroned. The heavens and the earth have become terribly alike since Einstein. No longer can we find a reassuring contrast to chaos in the night sky and look up with George Meredith to the stars, the army of unalterable law, or listen for the music of the spheres. Order is not there. In the entire universe there seem to be only two possibilities for it. The first of them—which again lies outside my terms of reference —is the divine order, the mystic harmony, which according to all religions is available for those who can contemplate it. We must admit its possibility, on the evidence of the adepts, and we must believe them when they say that it is attained, if attainable, by prayer. "O Thou, who changest not, abide with me," said one of its poets. "Ordena questo amore, tu che m'ami," said another: "Set love in order, thou who lovest me." The existence of a divine order, though it cannot be tested, has never been disproved.

The second possibility for order lies in the aesthetic category, which is my subject here: the order which an artist can create in his own work, and to that we must now return. A work of art, we are all agreed, is a unique product. But why? It is unique not because it is clever or noble or beautiful or enlightened or original or sincere or idealistic or useful or educational—it may embody any of those qualities—but because it is the only material object in the universe which may possess internal harmony. All the others have been pressed into shape from outside, and when their mould is removed they collapse. The work of art stands up by itself, and nothing else does. It achieves something which has often been promised by society, but always delusively. Ancient Athens made a mess—but the *Antigone* stands up. Renaissance Rome made a mess—but the ceiling of the Sistine got painted. James I made a mess—but there was *Macbeth*. Louis XIV—but there was *Phèdre*. Art for art's sake? I should just think so, and more so than ever at the present time. It is the one orderly product which our muddling race has produced. It is the cry of a thousand sentinels, the echo from a thousand labyrinths; it is the lighthouse which cannot be hidden; *c'est le meilleur témoignage que nous puissions donner de notre dignité. Antigone* for *Antigone*'s sake, *Macbeth* for *Macbeth*'s, *La Grande Jatte pour La Grande Jatte.*

If this line of argument is correct, it follows that the artist will tend to be an outsider in the society to which he has been born, and that the nineteenth-century conception of him as a bohemian was not inaccurate. The conception erred in three particulars: it postulated an economic system where art could be a full-time job, it introduced the fallacy that only art matters, and it over-stressed idiosyncrasy and waywardness—the peacock-feather aspect—rather than order. But it is a truer conception than the one which prevails in official circles on my side of the Atlantic—I don't know about yours: the conception which treats the artist as if he were a particularly bright government advertiser and encourages him to be friendly and matey with his fellow citizens, and not to give himself airs.

Estimable is mateyness, and the man who achieves it gives many a pleasant little drink to himself and to others. But it has

no traceable connection with the creative impulse, and probably
acts as an inhibition on it. The artist who is seduced by mateyness may stop himself from doing the one thing which he, and he
alone, can do—the making of something out of words or sounds or
paint or clay or marble or steel or film which has internal harmony and presents order to a permanently disarranged planet.
This seems to be worth doing, even at the risk of being called
uppish by journalists. I have in mind an article which was published some years ago in the London *Times*, an article called "The
Eclipse of the Highbrow", in which the "Average Man" was
exalted, and all contemporary literature was censured if it did not
toe the line, the precise position of the line being naturally known
to the writer of the article. Sir Kenneth Clark, who was at that
time director of our National Gallery, commented on this
pernicious doctrine in a letter which cannot be too often quoted.
"The poet and the artist," wrote Clark, "are important precisely
because they are not average men; because in sensibility, intelligence, and power of invention they far exceed the average."
These memorable words, and particularly the words "power of
invention", are the bohemian's passport. Furnished with it, he
slinks about society, saluted now by a brickbat and now by a
penny, and accepting either of them with equanimity. He does
not consider too anxiously what his relations with society may be,
for he is aware of something more important than that—namely
the invitation to invent, to create order, and he believes he will
be better placed for doing this if he attempts detachment. So
round and round he slouches, with his hat pulled over his eyes,
and maybe with a louse in his beard, and—if he really wants one—
with a peacock's feather in his hand.

If our present society should disintegrate—and who dare
prophesy that it won't?—this old-fashioned and démodé figure
will become clearer: the bohemian, the outsider, the parasite,
the rat—one of those figures which have at present no function
either in a warring or a peaceful world. It may not be dignified
to be a rat, but many of the ships are sinking, which is not dignified either—the officials did not build them properly. Myself, I
would sooner be a swimming rat than a sinking ship—at all
events I can look around me for a little longer—and I remember
how one of us, a rat with particularly bright eyes called Shelley,
squeaked out, "Poets are the unacknowledged legislators of the
world," before he vanished into the waters of the Mediterranean.

What laws did Shelley propose to pass? None. The legislation of the artist is never formulated at the time, though it is some-times discerned by future generations. He legislates through creating. And he creates through his sensitiveness and his power to impose form. Without form the sensitiveness vanishes. And form is as important today, when the human race is trying to ride the whirlwind, as it ever was in those less agitating days of the past, when the earth seemed solid and the stars fixed, and the dis-coveries of science were made slowly, slowly. Form is not tradi-tion. It alters from generation to generation. Artists always seek a new technique, and will continue to do so as long as their work excites them. But form of some kind is imperative. It is the surface crust of the internal harmony, it is the outward evidence of order.

My remarks about society may have seemed too pessimistic, but I believe that society can only represent a fragment of the human spirit, and that another fragment can only get expressed through art. And I wanted to take this opportunity, this vantage-ground, to assert not only the existence of art, but its pertinacity. Looking back into the past, it seems to me that that is all there has ever been: vantage-grounds for discussion and creation, little vantage-grounds in the changing chaos, where bubbles have been blown and webs spun, and the desire to create order has found temporary gratification, and the sentinels have managed to utter their challenges, and the huntsmen, though lost individually, have heard each other's calls through the impenetrable wood, and the lighthouses have never ceased sweeping the thankless seas. In this pertinacity there seems to me, as I grow older, something more and more profound, something which does in fact concern people who do not care about art at all.

In conclusion, let me summarize the various categories that have laid claim to the possession of order.

(1) The social and political category. Claim disallowed on the evidence of history and of our own experience. If man altered psychologically, order here might be attainable; not otherwise.

(2) The astronomical category. Claim allowed up to the present century, but now disallowed on the evidence of the physicists.

(3) The religious category. Claim allowed on the evidence of the mystics.

(4) The aesthetic category. Claim allowed on the evidence of various works of art, and on the evidence of our own creative

impulses, however weak these may be, or however imperfectly they may function. Works of art, in my opinion, are the only objects in the material universe to possess internal order, and that is why, though I don't believe that only art matters, I do believe in Art for Art's Sake.

[1949]

The Duty of Society
to the Artist

A great deal has been said about the duty of the artist to society. It is argued that the poet, the novelist, the painter, the musician, has a duty to the community; he is a citizen like everyone else; he must pull his weight, he must not give himself airs, or ask for special terms, he must pay his taxes honourably, and keep the laws which have been made for the general good. That is the argument and it is a reasonable one. But there is another side: what is the duty of society to the artist? Society certainly has a duty to its members; it has a duty to the engineer who serves it loyally and competently: it must provide him with the necessary tools and not allow him to starve; it has a duty to the stock-broker who is a competent dealer in stocks: since he is part of a financial system which it has accepted, it must support him and ensure him his due percentage. This is obvious enough. So what is its duty to the artist? If he contributes loyally and competently, ought not society to reward him like any other professional man?

Unfortunately the matter is not so simple. Art is a profession; that is quite true. The novelist or the musician has to learn his job just as the engineer or stockbroker has to learn his, and he too has to make both ends meet and needs to be paid or other-wise supported. But it's such a queer job. I will come back to it in a moment. I want first to consider society, the society we may expect to have after this war. We may expect a society that is highly centralized. It may be organized for peace; we hope it will. It may have to be organized against future wars, and if so, so much the worse. But in either case it will be very tightly knit; it will be planned; and it will be bureaucratic. Bureaucracy, in a technical age like ours, is inevitable. The advance of science means the growth of bureaucracy and the reign of the expert. And, as a result, society and the State will be the same thing.

This has never happened in the past. Society used to be much more diffuse. The government was there, making laws and wars, but it could not interfere so much with the individual; it had not the means. When I was a boy there was no wireless, no motor-cars; at an earlier date there were no telegrams, no railways;

earlier still, no posts. You cannot interfere with people unless you can communicate with them easily. Society was diffuse, and in the midst of the diffusion the artist flourished. If he was a painter he painted for the king and the courtiers, who probably had some individual ideas about painting, or for the great aristocrats, or for the local squire, or for the Church, which was not an individual but which knew what it wanted as regards subject-matter. He lived in a society which was broken up into groups and he had the chance of picking the group which suited him. That society, after lasting for thousands of years, has suddenly hardened and become centralized, and in the future the only effective patron will be the State. The State is in a position to commission pictures, statues, symphonies, novels, epics, films, hot jazz—anything. It has the money, and it commands the available talent. It can and it will encourage the efficient engineer or stockbroker or butcher. What encouragement will it give to an artist?

I am going to imagine an interview between an artist—a painter of genius, I will suppose—and the appropriate state official, whom I will call Mr Bumble. The artist says, "I want to paint the new police station; can I have the job?" Mr Bumble is not interested in painting and he has no reason to suppose that the police care for it either; still, he does his duty, he looks up his instructions, and sees that though police stations are usually left plain there is no regulation against their being coloured. "Yes, that would certainly be in order," he says. "I'm instructed to encourage art and I could give you the job, and I note you have suitable credentials. What sort of picture do you propose to paint?"

"I shall see when I start," replies the artist airily.

"See when you start? Is not that a little vague? I suppose that anyhow you will paint something which is edifying and inspiring?—a figure of Justice, for instance."

"I can't promise to do that. Indeed I don't feel inclined to edify or inspire. No doubt this State of ours is admirable, no doubt our police are a fine body of men—but no: I don't want to paint anything instructive."

"Well, well," says Mr Bumble, and thinks how much easier it is to deal with a stockbroker. "Well, you know about art and I don't, but I always assumed that art existed to make men into better citizens."

"It does sometimes do that," replies the artist, "but not always, and I don't feel inclined to paint that type of picture just now. Sorry."

Mr Bumble, who is a thoroughly decent fellow, is sorry too, and then he has a good idea.

"Still, there's light art, isn't there," he says heavily, "art which amuses and entertains. Provided the requirements of propriety are observed, there's no objection whatever to your painting something popular."

"Yes, art does sometimes entertain," replies the artist. "But not always. And I don't feel inclined to paint that type of picture either."

"May I ask what you do want to do?"

"I want to experiment."

"Experiment? The walls of the new police station are no place for experiments."

"I want to experiment. I want to extend human sensitiveness through paint. That's all that interests me. Perhaps, when I've finished, the picture will instruct and inspire people. Perhaps it will amuse them. I don't know and I don't really care. I want to paint something which will be understood when this society of ours is forgotten and the police station a ruin."

"The new police station a ruin when it has just cost thousands of pounds? How preposterous!"

"Yes, a ruin in the desert like Palmyra and Angkor or Zimbabwe, a ruin like Borobudur or Ajanta; which are remembered today not for their original purposes, but because of the experiments, the discoveries made by artists upon their walls. A ruin like . . ."

But here Mr Bumble holds up his hand. His patience is exhausted, he really cannot waste more time over this flibbertigibbet.

"I can do nothing for you," he says. "You don't fit in. And if you won't fit into the State how can you expect to be employed by the State?"

The artist retorts: "I know I don't fit in. And it's part of my duty not to fit in. It's part of my duty to humanity. I feel things, I express things, that haven't yet been felt and expressed, and that is my justification. And I ask the State to employ me on trust and pay me without understanding what I am up to."

There my dialogue ends. Mr Bumble refuses to give the commission, for it is a pretty tall order to be asked to pay for something which you do not understand; he who pays the piper naturally hopes to call the tune.

I have made that conversation up in order to emphasize the fundamental difficulty which confronts the modern centralized State when it tries to encourage art. The State believes in education. But does art educate? "Sometimes, but not always" is the answer; an unsatisfactory one. The State believes in recreation. But does art amuse? "Sometimes, but not always" is the answer again. The State does *not* believe in experiments, in the development of human sensitiveness in directions away from the average citizen. The artist *does*, and consequently he and the State—who will soon be his sole employer—must disagree.

So that is why there is a problem in the case of the artist which does not arise in the case of the butcher or the engineer. He never quite fits in. This did not matter in the loosely organized societies of the past, but it will matter in the future, where the community will be the only employer, and there is a danger and indeed a probability that art will disappear.

Perhaps I shall make this clearer if I quote from another dialogue, written by Plato. Plato, all through his life, was interested in the relation between the artist and the State, and was worried because the artist never quite fits in. He had himself the artistic temperament. In one of his earlier dialogues, the *Phaedrus*, he calls poetry

a madness . . . the madness of those who are possessed of the Muses; which enters into a delicate mind, and there inspires frenzy. . . . But he who, having no touch of the Muses' madness in his soul, comes to the door and thinks he will get into the temple—he, I say, and his poems are not admitted; the sane man is nowhere at all when he enters into competition with a madman.

The sane man, whom Mr Bumble represents, is certainly not inclined to subsidize madness: the State exists for the sane who have learned to fit in. Plato himself realized this, and in his later life he became enthusiastic about the State, and was obliged to change his attitude towards poetry and art. Personally he loved them as much as ever, but he saw they were disruptive, and he ended by banishing poets from the ideal community, on the ground that they upset people and that you never know what they will say next. He came round to Mr Bumble's view.

Not sharing Plato's totalitarianism, I believe that Mr Bumble ought to have given that commission. I see his difficulties. How, in the first place, was he to know that the applicant was not a fraud? (He would have to rely on some advisory body here.) And in the second place, even if he felt convinced that the artist was genuine as artists go, how should he feel justified in wasting public money on someone so useless? (The answer here is that he must be educated, educated not so much to appreciate art as to respect it. Our officials, when they take up their posts, ought to be instructed in soothing words that there is something in this queer art business which they cannot understand and must try not to resent.)

By the way, I've assumed above that we shall have a stable future after the war. If the future were chaotic, the artist would become a bohemian and an outsider, and the whole problem would alter.

[1942]

Does Culture Matter?

Culture is a forbidding word. I have to use it, knowing of none better, to describe the various beautiful and interesting objects which men have made in the past, and handed down to us, and which some of us are hoping to hand on. Many people despise them. They argue with force that cultural stuff takes up a great deal of room and time, and had better be scrapped, and they argue with less force that we live in a new world which has been wiped clean by science and cannot profit by tradition. Science will wipe us clean constantly, they hope, and at decreasing intervals. Broadcasting and the cinema have wiped out the drama, and quite soon we may hope for some new invention which will wipe out the cinema industry and Broadcasting House. In this constant scrubbing, what place can there be for the Brandenburg Concertos, or for solitary readings of Dante, or for the mosaics of Santa Sophia, or for photographs of them? We shall all rush forward doing our work and amusing ourselves during the recreation hour with whatever gives least bother.

This prospect seems to me so awful that I want to do what I can against it, without too much attempt at fair-mindedness. It is impossible to be fair-minded when one has faith—religious creeds have shown this—and I have so much faith in cultural stuff that I believe it must mean something to other people, and anyhow want it left lying about. Faith makes one unkind: I am pleased when culture scores a neat hit. For instance, Sir Richard Terry, the organist of Westminster Cathedral, once made a remark which gave me unholy joy: speaking to some young musicians at Blackpool, he told them that they could be either men or crooners when they grew up, but not both. A storm in a cocktail resulted. The bands of Mr Jack Payne and Mr Henry Hall fizzed to their depths, and the less prudent members in them accorded interviews to the press. One crooner said that he and his friends could knock down Sir Richard and his friends any day, so they must be men. Another crooner said that he and his friends made more money than Sir Richard's friends, so they must be musicians. The pretentiousness and conceit of these amusement-mongers came out very strikingly. They appeared to be living in an eternal *thé dansant* which they mistook for the universe, and they couldn't bear being teased. For my own part, I don't mind an occasional croon or a blast in passing from a Wurlitzer organ, and Sir Richard Terry's speciality, madrigals, bore me; nevertheless, the music represented by him and his peers is the real thing; it ought to be defended and it has the right occasionally to attack. As a rule, it is in retreat, for there is a hostility to cultural stuff today which is disquieting.

Of course, most people never have cared for the classics, in music or elsewhere, but up to now they have been indifferent or ribald, and good-tempered, and have not bothered to denounce. "Not my sort, bit tame," or "Sounds like the cat being sick, miaou pussy," or "Coo, he must have felt bad to paint them apples blue"—these were their typical reactions when confronted with Racine, Stravinsky, Cézanne. There was no to-do—just "Not my sort". But now the good humour is vanishing, the guffaw is organized into a sneer, and the typical reaction is "How dare these so-called art-chaps do it? *I'll* give them something to do." This hostility has been well analysed by Mrs Leavis, in her study of the English novel. She shows that, though fiction of the best-seller type has been turned out for the last two hundred years, it has only lately realized its power, and that the popular novelist of today tends to be venomous and aggressive towards his more artistic brethren—an attitude in which he is supported by most of the press, and by the cheap libraries. Her attitude leads to priggishness; but it is better to be superior than to kow-tow. There was once a curious incident, which occupied several inches on a prominent page of *The Times*. A popular comedian had been faded out on the air, and the B.B.C., generally so stiff-necked, were grovelling low in apology, and going into all kinds of detail in extenuation of their grave offence. When they had done, the comedian's comment was printed; he professed himself appeased and consented to broadcast in the future. I wonder how much fuss a poet or a philosopher would have made if his talk had been cut short, and how many inches of regret he would have been given.

Incidents like this, so trivial in themselves, suggest that the past, and the creations that derive from the past, are losing their honour and on their way to being jettisoned. We have, in this age of unrest, to ferry much old stuff across the river, and the old stuff is not merely books, pictures and music, but the power to enjoy and understand them. If the power is lost the books, etc., will sink down into museums and die, or only survive in some fantastic caricature. The power was acquired through tradition. Sinclair Lewis, in *Babbitt*, describes a civilization which had no tradition and could consequently only work, or amuse itself with rubbish; it had heard of the past, but lacked the power to enjoy it or understand. There is a grim moment at a medium-istic séance, when Dante is invoked. The company knew of Dante as the guy who got singed, so he duly appears in this capacity and returns to his gridiron after a little banter, with a pleased smirk. He has become a proper comic. And it would seem that he is having a similar if less extreme experience in Soviet Russia. He has been ferried across there, but he is con-demned as a sadist; that is to say, the power to understand him has been left behind. Certainly Dante wrote over the gates of Hell that they were made by the power, wisdom and love of God:

> Fecemi la divina Potestate,
> La somma Sapienza e il primo Amore,

and neither the Middle West nor the Soviets nor ourselves can be expected to agree with that. But there is no reason why we should not understand it, and stretch our minds against his, although they have a different shape. The past is often uncon-genial as far as its statements are concerned, but the trained imagination can surmount them and reach the essential. Dante seems to me a test case. If people are giving him up it is a sign that they are throwing culture overboard, owing to the rough-ness of the water, and will reach the further bank sans Dante, sans Shakespeare and sans everything.

Life on that further bank, as I conceive it, is by no means a nightmare. There will be work for all and play for all. But the work and the play will be split; the work will be mechanical and the play frivolous. If you drop tradition and culture you lose your chance of connecting work and play and creating a life which is all of a piece. The past did not succeed in doing that, but it can help us to do it, and that is why it is so useful. Crooners, best-sellers, electrical-organists, funny-faces, dream-girls and mickey-mice cannot do it—they throw the weight all to one side and increase the split. They are all right when they don't take themselves seriously. But when they begin to talk big and claim the front row of the dress circle, and even get to it, something is wrong. Life on that further bank might not be a nightmare, but some of us would prefer the sleep that has no dreams.

2

Cultivated people are a drop of ink in the ocean. They mix easily and even genially with other drops, for those exclusive days are over when cultivated people made only cultivated friends, and became tongue-tied or terror-struck in the presence of anyone whose make-up was different from their own. Culture, thank goodness, is no longer a social asset, it can no longer be employed either as a barrier against the mob or as a ladder into the aristocracy. This is one of the few improvements that have occurred in England since the last war. The change has been excellently shown in Mrs Woolf's biography of Roger Fry; here we can trace the decay of smartness and fashion as factors, and the growth of the idea of enjoyment.

All the same, we are a drop in the ocean. Few people share our enjoyment so far. Strictly between ourselves, and keeping our limited circulation in mind, let us put our heads together and consider for a moment our special problem, our special blessings, our special woes. No one need listen to us who does not want to. We whisper in the corner of a world which is full of other noises, and louder ones.

Come closer. Our problem, as I see it, is this: is what we have got worth passing on? What we have got is (roughly speaking) a little knowledge about books, pictures, tunes, runes, and a little skill in their interpretation. Seated beside our gas fires, and beneath our electric bulbs, we inherit a tradition which has lasted for about three thousand years. The tradition was partly popular, but mainly dependent upon aristocratic patronage. In the past, culture has been paid for by the ruling classes; they often did not know why they paid, but they paid, much as they went to church; it was the proper thing to do, it was a form of social snobbery, and so the artists sneaked a meal, the author got a sinecure, and the work of creation went on. Today, people are coming to the top who are, in some ways, more clear-sighted and honest than the ruling classes of the past, and they refuse to pay for what they don't want; judging by the noises through the floor, our neighbour in the flat above doesn't want books, pictures, tunes, runes, anyhow doesn't want the sorts which we recommend. Ought we to bother him? When he is hurrying to lead his own life, ought we to get in his way like a maiden aunt, our arms, as it were, full of parcels, and say to him: "I was given these specially to hand on to you ... Sophocles, Velasquez, Henry James. ... I'm afraid they're a little heavy, but you'll get to love them in time, and if you don't take them off my hands I don't know who will ... please ... please ... they're really important, they're culture."

His reply is unlikely to be favourable, but, snubbing or no snubbing, what ought we to do? That's our problem, that's what we are whispering about, while he and his friends argue and argue and argue over the trade-price of batteries, or the quickest way to get from Balham to Ealing. He doesn't really want the stuff. That clamour for art and literature which Ruskin and Morris thought they detected has died down. He won't take the parcel unless we do some ingenious touting. He is an average modern. People today are either indifferent to the aesthetic products of the past (that is the position both of the industrial magnate and of the trade unionist) or else (the Communist position) they are suspicious of them, and decline to receive them until they have been disinfected in Moscow. In England, still the abode of private enterprise, indifference predominates. I know a few working-class people who enjoy culture, but as a rule I am afraid to bore them with it lest I lose the pleasure of their acquaintance. So what is to be done?

It is tempting to do nothing. Don't recommend culture. Assume that the future will have none, or will work out some form of it which we cannot expect to understand. Auntie had better keep her parcels for herself, in fact, and stop fidgeting. This attitude is dignified, and it further commends itself to me because I can reconcile it with respect for the people arguing upstairs. Who am I that I should worry them? Out-of-date myself, I like out-of-date things, and am willing to pass out of focus in that company, inheritor of a mode of life which is wanted no more. Do you agree? Without bitterness, let us sit upon the ground and tell sad stories of the death of kings, ourselves the last of their hangers-on. Drink the wine—no one wants it, though it came from the vineyards of Greece, the gardens of Persia. Break the glass—no one admires it, no one cares any more about quality or form. Without bitterness and without conceit take your leave. Time happens to have tripped you up, and this is a matter neither for shame nor for pride.

The difficulty here is that the higher pleasures are not really wines or glasses at all. They rather resemble religion, and it is impossible to enjoy them without trying to hand them on. The appreciator of an aesthetic achievement becomes in his minor way an artist; he cannot rest without communicating what has been communicated to him. This "passing on" impulse takes various forms, some of them merely educational, others merely critical; but it is essentially a glow derived from the central fire, and to extinguish it is to forbid the spread of the Gospel. It is therefore impossible to sit alone with one's books and prints, or to sit only with friends like oneself, and never to testify outside. Dogmatism is of course a mistake, and even tolerance and tact have too much of the missionary spirit to work satisfactorily. What is needed in the cultural Gospel is to let one's light so shine that men's curiosity is aroused, and they ask why Sophocles, Velasquez, Henry James should cause such disproportionate pleasure. Bring out the enjoyment. If "the classics" are advertised as something dolorous and astringent, no one will sample them. But if the cultured person, like the late Roger Fry, is obviously having a good time, those who come across him will be tempted to share it and to find out how.

That seems to be as far as we can get with our problem, as we whisper together in our unobtrusive flat, while our neighbours, who possess voices more powerful than our own, argue about Balham and Ealing over our heads. Remember, by the way, that we are not creative artists. The creative artist might take another line. He would certainly have more urgent duties. Our chief job is to enjoy ourselves and not to lose heart, and to spread culture not because we love our fellow men, but because certain things seem to us unique and priceless, and, as it were, push us out into the world on their service. It is a Gospel, and not altogether a benign one; it is the zest to communicate what has been communicated. Works of art do have this peculiar pushful quality; the excitement that attended their creation hangs about them, and makes minor artists out of those who have felt their power.

[1935; 1940]

The *Raison d'Être* of Criticism

An address delivered at a Symposium on Music at Harvard University

Believing as I do that music is the deepest of the arts and deep beneath the arts, I venture to emphasize music in this brief survey of the *raison d'être* of criticism. I have no authority here. I am an amateur whose inadequacy will become all too obvious as he proceeds. Perhaps, though, it may be remembered in charity that the word amateur implies love. I love music. Just to love it, or just to love anything or anybody, is not enough. Love has to be clarified and controlled to give full value, and here is where criticism may help. But one has to start with love; one has, in the case of music, to want to hear the notes. If one has no initial desire to listen and no sympathy after listening, the notes will signify nothing, sound and fury, whatever their intellectual content.

The case *against* criticism is alarmingly strong, and much of my survey is bound to be a brief drawn up by the Devil's Advocate. I will postpone the evil day, and begin by indicating the case *for* criticism.

Most of us will agree, I think, that previous training is desirable before we approach the arts. We mistrust untrained appreciation, believing that it often defeats its own ends. Appreciation ought to be enough. But, unless we learn by example and by failure and by comparison, appreciation will not bite. We shall tend to slip about on the surface of masterpieces, exclaiming with joy, but never penetrating. "Oh, I do like Bach," cries one appreciator, and the other cries, "Do you? I don't. I like Chopin." Exit in opposite directions chanting Bach and Chopin respectively, and hearing less the composers than their own voices. They resemble investors who proclaim the soundness of their financial assets. The Bach shares must not fall, the Chopin not fall further, or one would have been proved a fool on the aesthetic stock exchange. The objection to untrained appreciation is not its naïveté but its tendency to lead to the appreciation of no one but oneself. Against such fatuity the critical spirit is a valuable corrective.

Except at the actual moment of contact—and I shall have much to say on the subject of that difficult moment—it is desirable to know why we like a work, and to be able to defend our preferences by argument. Our judgement has been strengthened and if all goes well the contacts will be intensified and increased and become more valuable.

I add the proviso "if all goes well" because success lies on the knees of an unknown god. There is always the contrary danger: the danger that training may sterilize the sensitiveness that is being trained; that education may lead to knowledge instead of wisdom, and criticism to nothing but criticism; that spontaneous enjoyment, like the Progress of Poesy in Matthew Arnold's poem, may be checked because too much care has been taken to direct it into the right channel. Still, it is a risk to be faced, and if no care had been taken the stream might have vanished even sooner. We hope criticism will help. We have faith in it as a respectable human activity, as an item in the larger heritage which differentiates us from the beasts.

How best can this activity be employed? One must allow it to construct aesthetic theories, though to the irreverent eyes of some of us they appear as travelling laboratories, beds of Procrustes whereon Milton is too long and Keats too short. In an age which is respectful to theory—as for instance the seventeenth century was respectful to Aristotle's theory of the dramatic unities —a theory may be helpful and stimulating, particularly to the sense of form. French tragedy could culminate in Racine because certain leading-strings had been so willingly accepted that they were scarcely felt. Corneille and Tasso were less happy. Corneille, having produced the *Cid*, wasted much time trying to justify its deviations from Aristotle's rules; and Tasso wasted even more, for he published his theory of Christian Epic Poetry before he wrote the *Gerusalemme Liberata* which was to illustrate it. His epic was attacked by the critics because it deviated from what Aristotle said and also from what Tasso thought he might have said. Tasso was upset, became involved in three volumes of controversy which not even Professor Saintsbury has read, tried to write a second epic which should not deviate, failed, and went mad. Except in Russia, where the deviations of Shostakovich invite a parallel, a theory in the modern world

has little power over the fine arts, for good or evil. We have no
atmosphere where it can flourish, and the attempts of certain
governments to generate such an atmosphere in bureaus are
unlikely to succeed. The construction of aesthetic theories and
their comparison are desirable cultural exercises; the theories
themselves are unlikely to spread far or to hinder or help.

A more practical activity for criticism is the sensitive dissection
of particular works of art. What did the artist hope to do?
What means did he employ, subconscious or conscious? Did
he succeed, and if his success was partial where did he fail?
In such a dissection the tools should break as soon as they encounter any living tissue. The apparatus is nothing, the specimen
all. Whether expert critics will agree with so extreme a statement is doubtful, but I do enjoy following particular examina-
tions so far as an amateur can. It is delightful and profitable to
enter into technicalities to the limit of one's poor ability, to continue as far as one can in the wake of an expert mind, to pursue
an argument till it passes out of one's grasp. And to have, while
this is going on, a particular work of art before one can be a
great help. Besides learning about the work one increases one's
powers. Criticism's central job seems to be education through
precision.

A third activity, less important, remains to be listed, and since
it lies more within my sphere than precision I will discuss it at
greater length. Criticism can stimulate. Few of us are sufficiently awake to the beauty and wonder of the world, and when
art intervenes to reveal them it sometimes acts in reverse, and
lowers a veil instead of raising one. This deadening effect can
often be dispersed by a well-chosen word. We can be awakened
by a remark which need not be profound or even true, and can
be sent scurrying after the beauties and wonders we were ignor-
ing. Journalism and broadcasting have their big opportunity
here. Unsuited for synthesis or analysis, they can send
out the winged word that carries us off to examine the
original.

There is in fact a type of criticism which has no interpretative
value, yet it should not be condemned offhand. Much has been
written about music, for instance, which has nothing to do with
music and must make musicians smile. It usually describes the
state into which the hearer was thrown as he sat on his chair
at the concert, and the visual images which occurred to him in
that sedentary position. Here is an example, and a very lovely

one, from Walt Whitman. Whitman has heard "one of Beethoven's master septets" performed at Philadelphia (there is only one Beethoven septet, but this the old boy did not know), and the rendering of it on a "small band of well-chosen and perfectly combined instruments" quite carries him away.

> Dainty abandon, sometimes as if Nature laughing on a hillside in the sunshine; serious and firm monotonies, as of winds; a horn sounding through the tangle of the forest, and the dying echoes; soothing floating of waves, but presently rising in surges, angrily lashing, muttering, heavy; piercing peals of laughter, for interstices; now and then weird, as Nature herself is in certain moods—but mainly spontaneous, easy, careless—often the sentiment of the postures of naked children playing or sleeping. It did me good even to watch the violinists drawing their bows so masterly—every motion a study. I allow'd myself, as I sometimes do, to wander out of myself. The conceit came to me of a copious grove of singing birds, and in their midst a simple harmonic duo, two human souls, steadily asserting their own pensiveness, joyousness.

Here is adorable literature, but what has it to do with Op. 20? A poet's imagination has been kindled. He has allowed himself to wander out of himself, but not into Beethoven's self, his presumable goal. He has evoked the visual images congenial to him, and though in the closing phrase there is a concert it is not the one he attended, for it took place in the Garden of Eden.

Another example of such criticism is to be found in Proust. Proust is what Walt Whitman is not—sophisticated, soigné, rusé, maladif. But he too listens to a septet and reacts to it visually, he is carried off his seat into a region which has nothing to do with the concert. It is the septet of Vinteuil, whom we have hitherto known as the composer of a violin sonata. Vinteuil himself, an obscure and unhappy provincial organist, has scarcely appeared; but his sonata, and particularly a phrase in it, la petite phrase, has been an actor in the long-drawn inaction of the novel. Character after character has listened to it, and has felt hope, jealousy, despair, peace, according to the circumstances into which la petite phrase has entered. We do not know what it sounds like, but its arrival always means emotional heightening.

Towards the end of the novel, the hero goes to a musical reception in Paris where a new work is to be performed. He does not bother to look at the programme, being occupied by social trifles. It is a septet—the opening bars are sombre, glacial, as if dawn had not yet risen over the sea. He finds himself in an unknown world, where he understands nothing. Suddenly into this bewilderment there falls—*la petite phrase*, a reference to the sonata. He is listening to a posthumous work of Vinteuil, of whose existence he was unaware. Everything falls into shape. It is as if he has walked in an unknown region and come across the little gate which belongs to the garden of a friend. The septet expands its immensities, now comprehensible. The dawn rises crimson out of the sea, harsh midday rejoicings give way to more images, and the little phrase of the sonata, once virginal and shy, is august, quivering with colours, final, mature.

Now these visual wanderings are not entirely to my taste. Whitman's has its own naïve merit, but in the case of Proust, who is pretentious culturally, we feel uneasy. Shall we then say that they do not and cannot help us musically at all? I think this is too severe. The septets of Beethoven and of Vinteuil have come no nearer to us, but we have been excited, we have been disposed to listen to sounds, we have been challenged to test the descriptions and to decide whether we agree with them. This general sharpening of interest is desirable. It can be effected in various ways: by a legitimate critic like Donald Tovey, by a grand old boy at Philadelphia, or by a snobby Frenchman in the Faubourg St Germain. Not all ways are equally good. Those who hear music will always interpret it best. But those who don't hear it after the first few notes have also their use. Their wanderings, their visual images, their dreams, help to sharpen us. They recall us to the importance of sounds, and, their inferior in other ways, we may perhaps manage to listen to the sounds longer than they did.

Examples of higher musical value are to be found in the early journalism of Bernard Shaw. Though Shaw is a man of letters, like Whitman and Proust, and readily runs after his own thoughts and pictorial images, he does manage to remember the music. He can interpret as well as stimulate. He can say for instance of Haydn: "Haydn would have been among the greatest had he been driven to that terrible eminence; but we are fortunate enough in having had at least one man of genius who was happy enough in the Valley of Humiliation to feel no compulsion to struggle on through the Valley of the Shadow of Death." What a sensitive and just reflection! How admirably it expresses that turning away from the tragic so often displayed by Haydn—for instance in the opening of the C Major Symphony, Op. 97! He has turned to gaiety not because he is afraid of tragedy, which would discompose the listener, but because he prefers not to be tragic. This is an essential in Haydn, and, apprehending it, Shaw convinces us that he is inside music and could have criticized it more deeply, had his career and his inclinations allowed.

I like, in this connection, jokes about music, the irresponsible folly which sometimes kicks a door open as it flies. They too may incline us to listen to sounds. When our English humorist, Beachcomber, says "Wagner is the Puccini of music," he says rather more than he says. Besides guying a well-worn formula, he pierces Grand Opera itself, and reveals Brünnhilde and Butterfly transfixed on the same mischievous pin. I like, too, the remark of an uncle of mine, a huntin', fishin', shootin', sportin' sort of uncle, whose aversion to the arts was very genuine. "They tell me," he said one day thoughtfully, "they tell me music's like a gun: it hurts less when you let it off yourself." Besides getting in a well-directed gibe, and discomposing my aunt, who adored Mendelssohn, he indicated very neatly the gulf between artist on the one hand and critic on the other. Those who are involved and those who appraise are never hurt in the same way. This is, as a matter of fact, going to be our chief problem here, and perhaps it will come the fresher because my uncle hit at it in his slapdash fashion before striding back to his dogs.

For now our trouble starts. We can readily agree that criticism has educational and cultural value; the critic helps to civilize the community, builds up standards, forms theories, stimulates, dissects, encourages the individual to enjoy the world into which he has been born; and on the destructive side he exposes fraud and pretentiousness and checks conceit. These are substantial achievements. But I would like if I could to establish the *raison d'être* of criticism on a higher basis than that of public utility. I would like to discover some spiritual parity between it and the objects it criticizes, and this is going to be difficult. The difficulty has been variously expressed. One writer—Mr F. L. Lucas —has called criticism a charming parasite; another—Chekhov— complains it is a gadfly which hinders the oxen from ploughing; a third—the eighteenth-century philosopher Lord Kames— compares it to an imp which distracts critics from their objective and incites them to criticize each other. My own trouble is not so much that it is a parasite, a gadfly or an imp, but that there is a basic difference between the critical and creative states of mind, and to the consideration of that difference I would now invite your attention.

What about the creative state? In it a man is taken out of himself. He lets down as it were a bucket into his subconscious, and draws up something which is normally beyond his reach. He mixes this thing with his normal experiences, and out of the mixture he makes a work of art. It may be a good work of art or a bad one—we are not here examining the question of quality —but whether it is good or bad it will have been compounded in this unusual way, and he will wonder afterwards how he did it. Such seems to be the creative process. It may employ much technical ingenuity and worldly knowledge, it may profit by critical standards, but mixed up with it is this stuff from the bucket, this subconscious stuff, which is not procurable on demand. And when the process is over, when the picture or symphony or lyric or novel (or whatever it is) is complete, the artist, looking back on it, will wonder how on earth he did it. And indeed he did not do it on earth.

A perfect example of the creative process is to be found in "Kubla Khan". Assisted by opium, Coleridge had his famous dream, and dipped deep into the subconscious. Waking up, he started to transcribe it, and was proceeding successfully when that person from Porlock unfortunately called on business.

> Weave a circle round him thrice,
> And close your eyes with holy dread,
> For he on honey-dew hath fed,
> And drunk the milk of Paradise—

and in came the person from Porlock. Coleridge could not resume. His connection with the subconscious had snapped. He had created and did not know how he had done it. As Professor John Livingston Lowes has shown, many fragments of Coleridge's day-to-day reading are embedded in "Kubla Khan", but the poem itself belongs to another world, which he was seldom to record.

The creative state of mind is akin to a dream. In Coleridge's case it was a dream. In other cases—Jane Austen's for instance —the dream is remote or sedate. But even Jane Austen, looking back upon *Emma*, could have thought: "Dear me, how came I to write that? It is not ill-contrived." There is always, even with the most realistic artist, the sense of withdrawal from his own creation, the sense of surprise.

The French writer, Paul Claudel, gives the best description known to me of the creative state. It occurs in *La Ville*. A poet is speaking. He has been asked whence his inspiration comes, and how is it that when he speaks everything becomes explicable although he explains nothing. He replies:

> I do not speak what I wish, but I conceive in sleep,
> And I cannot explain whence I draw my breath, for it is
>   my breath which is drawn out of me.
> I expand the emptiness within me, I open my mouth, I
>   breathe in the air, I breathe it out.
> I restore it in the form of an intelligible word,
> And having spoken I know what I have said.

There is a further idea in the passage, which my brief English paraphrase has not attempted to convey: the idea that if the breathing in is *in*spiration the breathing out is *ex*piration, a prefiguring of death, when the life of a man will be drawn out of him by the unknown force for the last time. Creation and death are closely connected for Claudel. I'm confining myself, though, to his description of the creative act. How precisely it describes what happened in "Kubla Khan"! There is conception in sleep, there is the connection between the subconscious and the conscious, which has to be effected before the work of art can be born, and there is the surprise of the creator at his own creation.

> Je restitue une parole intelligible.
> Et, l'ayant dite, je sais ce que j'ai dit.

Which is exactly what happened to Coleridge. He spoke and then knew what he had said, but as soon as inspiration was interrupted he could not say any more.

After this glance at the creative state, let us glance at the critical. The critical state has many merits, and employs some of the highest and subtlest faculties of man. But it is grotesquely remote from the state responsible for the works it affects to expound. It does not let down buckets into the subconscious. It does not conceive in sleep, or know what it has said after it has said it. Think before you speak is criticism's motto; speak before you think creation's. Nor is criticism disconcerted by people arriving from Porlock; in fact it sometimes comes from Porlock itself. While not excluding imagination and sympathy, it keeps them and all the faculties under control, and only employs them when they promise to be helpful.

Thus equipped, it advances on its object. It has two aims. The first and the more important is aesthetic. It considers the object in itself, as an entity, and tells us what it can about its life. The second aim is subsidiary: the relation of the object to the rest of the world. Problems of less relevance are considered, such as the conditions under which the work of art was composed, the influences which formed it (criticism adores influences), the influence it has exercised on subsequent works, the artist's life, the lives of the artist's father and mother, prenatal possibilities and so on, straying this way into psychology and that way into history. Much of the above is valuable. But if we wheel up an aesthetic theory—the best obtainable, and there are some excellent ones—if we wheel it up and apply it with its measuring rods and pliers and forceps, its calipers and catheters, to a particular work of art, we are visited at once, if we are sensitive, by a sense of the grotesque. It doesn't work, two universes have not even collided, they have been juxtaposed. There is no spiritual parity. And, if criticism strays from her central aesthetic quest to influences and psychological and historical considerations, something does happen then, contact is established. But no longer with a work of art.

A work of art is a curious object. Isn't it infectious? Unlike machinery, hasn't it the power of transforming the person who encounters it towards the condition of the person who created it? (I use the clumsy phrase "towards the condition" on purpose.) We—we the beholders or listeners or whatever we are—undergo a change analogous to creation. We are rapt into a region near to that where the artist worked, and, like him, when we return to earth we feel surprised. To claim we actually entered his state and became co-creators with him there is presumptuous. However much excited I am by Brahms's Fourth Symphony, I cannot suppose I feel Brahms's excitement, and probably what he felt is not what I understand as excitement. But there has been an infection from Brahms through his music to myself. Something has passed. I have been transformed towards his condition, he has called me out of myself, he has thrown me into a subsidiary dream; and when the passacaglia is trodden out, and the transformation closed, I too feel surprise.

Unfortunately this infection, this sense of cooperation with a creator, which is the supremely important step in our pilgrimage through the fine arts, is the one step over which criticism cannot help. She can prepare us for it generally, and educate us to keep our senses open, but she has to withdraw when reality approaches, like Virgil from Dante on the summit of Purgatory. With the coming of love, we have to rely on Beatrice, whom we have loved all along, and if we have never loved Beatrice we are lost. We shall remain pottering about with theories and influences and psychological and historical considerations—supports useful in their time, but they must be left behind at the entry of Heaven. I would not suggest that our comprehension of the fine arts is or should be of the nature of a mystic union. But, as in mysticism, we enter an unusual state, and we can only enter it through love. Putting it more prosaically, we cannot understand music unless we desire to hear it. And so we return to the earth.

Let us reconsider that troublesome object, the work of art, and observe another way in which it is recalcitrant to criticism. I am thinking of its freshness. So far as it is authentic, it presents itself as eternally virgin. It expects always to be heard or read or seen for the first time, always to cause surprise. It does not expect to be studied, still less does it present itself as a crossword puzzle, only to be solved after much re-examination. If it does that, if it parades a mystifying element, it is, to that extent, not a work of art, not an immortal Muse, but a Sphinx who dies as soon as her riddles are answered. The work of art assumes the existence of the perfect recipient, and is indifferent to the fact that no such person exists. It does not allow for our ignorance and it does not cater for our knowledge.

This eternal freshness in creation presents a difficulty to the critic, who when he hears or reads or sees a work a second time rightly profits by what he has heard or read or seen of it the first time, and studies and compares, remembers and analyses, and often has to reject his original impressions as trivial. He may thus in the end gain a just and true opinion of the work, but he ought to remain startled, and this is usually beyond him. Take Beethoven's Ninth Symphony, the one in A. Isn't it in A? The opening bars announce that key as explicitly as fifths can, leaving us only in doubt as to whether the movement will decide on the major or minor mode. In the fifteenth bar comes the terrifying surprise, the pounce into D minor, which tethers the music, however far it wanders, right down to the ineluctable close. Can one hope to feel that terror and surprise twice?

Can one avoid hearing the opening bars as a preparation for the pounce—and thus miss the life of the pounce? Can we combine experience and innocence? I think we can. The willing suspension of experience is possible, it is possible to become like a child who says "Oh!" each time the ball bounces, although he has seen it bounce before and knows it must bounce.

It is possible but it is rare. The critic who is thoroughly versed in the score of the Ninth Symphony and can yet hear the opening bars as a trembling introduction in A to the unknown has reached the highest rank in his profession. Most of us are content to remain well-informed. It is so restful to be well-informed. We forget that Beethoven intended his symphony to be heard always for the first time. We forget with still greater ease that Tchaikovsky intended the same for his Piano Concerto in B flat minor. Dubious for good reasons of that thumping affair, we sometimes scold it for being "stale"—a ridiculous accusation, for it too was created as an eternal virgin, it too should startle each time it galumphs down the waltz. No doubt the concerto, and much music, has been too often performed, just as some pictures have been too often looked at. Freshness of reception is exhausted more rapidly by a small or imperfect object than by a great one. Nevertheless the objects themselves are eternally new, it is the recipient who may wither. At the opening of Goethe's *Faust*, Mephistopheles, being stale himself, found the world stale, and reported it as such to the Almighty. The archangels took no notice of him and continued to sing of eternal freshness. The critic ought to combine Mephistopheles with the archangels, experience with innocence. He ought to know everything inside out, and yet be surprised. Virginia Woolf—who was both a creative artist and a great critic—believed in reading a book twice. The first time she was an archangel: she abandoned herself to the author unreservedly. The second time she was Mephistopheles: she treated him with severity and allowed him to get away with nothing he could not justify. After these two readings she felt qualified to discuss the book. Here is good rule-of-thumb advice. But it does not take us to the heart of our problem, which is super-rational. For we ought really to read the book in two ways at once. (And we ought to look at a picture in two ways at once, and to listen to music similarly.) We ought to perform a miracle the nature of which was hinted at by the Almighty when he said he was always glad to receive Mephistopheles in Heaven and hear him chat.

I would speak tentatively, but it seems to me that we are most likely to perform that miracle in the case of music. Music, more than the other arts, postulates a double existence. It exists in time, and also exists outside time, instantaneously. With no philosophic training, I cannot put my belief clearly, but I can conceive myself hearing a piece as it goes by and also when it has finished. In the latter case I should hear it as an entity, as a piece of sound-architecture, not as a sound-sequence, not as something divisible into bars. Yet it would be organically connected with the concert-hall performance. Architecture and sequence would, in my apprehension, be more closely fused than the two separate readings of a book in Virginia Woolf's.

The claim of criticism to take us to the heart of the arts must therefore be disallowed. Another claim has been made for it, a more precise one. It has been suggested that criticism can help an artist to improve his work. If that be true, a *raison d'être* is established at once. Criticism becomes an important figure, a handmaid to beauty, holding out the sacred lamp in whose light creation proceeds, feeding the lamp with oil, trimming the wick when it flares or smokes. It would be interesting to know whether criticism has helped musicians in their work today, and if so how. Has she held up the lamp? No doubt she illuminates past mistakes or merits, that certainly is within her power, but has the better knowledge of them any practical value?

A remark of Mr C. Day Lewis is interesting in this connection. It comes at the opening of *The Poetic Image*.

> There is always something formidable for the poet in the idea of criticism—something, dare I say it? almost unreal. He writes a poem; then he moves on to the new experience, the next poem: and when a critic comes along and tells him what is right or wrong with that first poem, he has a feeling of irrelevance.

Something almost unreal. That is a just remark. The poet is always developing and moving on, and when his creative state is broken into by comments on something he has just put behind him he feels bewildered. His reaction is, "What are you talking about? Must you?" Once again, and in its purest form, the division between the critical and creative states, the absence of spiritual parity, becomes manifest. In its purest form because poetry is an extreme form of art, and is a convenient field for experiment. My own art, the mixed art of fiction, is less suitable, yet I can truly say with Mr Day Lewis that I have nearly always found criticism irrelevant. When I am praised, I am pleased; when I am blamed, I am displeased; when I am told I am elusive, I am surprised—but neither the pleasure nor the sorrow nor the astonishment makes any difference when next I enter the creative state. One can eliminate a particular defect perhaps; to substitute merit is the difficulty. I remember that in one of my earlier novels I was blamed for the number of sudden deaths in it, which were said to amount to forty-four per cent of the fictional population. I took heed, and arranged that characters in subsequent novels should die less frequently and give previous notice where possible by means of illness or some other acceptable device. But I was not inspired to put anything vital in the place of the sudden deaths. The only remedy for a defect is inspiration, the subconscious stuff that comes up in the bucket. A piece of contemporary music, to my ear, has a good many sudden deaths in it; the phrases expire as rapidly as the characters in my novel, the chords cut each other's throats, the arpeggio has a heart attack, the fugue gets into a nose-dive. But these defects—if defects they be—are vital to the general conception. They are not to be remedied by substituting sweetness. And the musician would do well to ignore the critic even when he admits the justice of the particular criticism.

Only in two ways can criticism help the artist a little with his work. The first is general. He ought—if he keeps company at all—to keep good company. To be alone may be best—to be alone was what Fate reserved for Beethoven. But if he wishes to consort with ideas and standards and the works of his fellows —and he usually has to in the modern world—he must beware of the second-rate. It means a relaxation of fibre, a temptation to rest on his own superiority. I do not desire to use the words "superior" and "inferior" about human individuals; in an individual so many factors are present that one cannot grade him. But one can legitimately apply them to cultural standards, and the artist should be critical here, and alive in particular to the risks of the clique. The clique is a valuable social device, which only a fanatic would condemn; it can protect and encourage the artist. It is the artist's duty, if he needs to be in a clique, to choose a good one, and to take care it doesn't make him bumptious or sterile or silly. The lowering of critical standards in what one may call daily studio life, their corruption by adulation or jealousy, may lead to inferior work. Good standards may lead to good work. That is all that there seems to be to say about this vague assistance, and maybe it was not worth saying.

The second way in which criticism can help the artist is more specific. It can help him over details, niggling details, minutiae of style. To refer to my own work again, I have certainly benefited by being advised not to use the word "but" so often. I have had a university education, you see, and it disposes one to overwork that particular conjunction. It is the strength of the academic mind to be fair and see both sides of a question. It is its weakness to be timid and to suffer from that fear-of-giving-oneself-away disease of which Samuel Butler speaks. Both its strength and its weakness incline it to the immoderate use of "but". A good many "but"s have occurred today, but not as many as if I had not been warned. The writer of the opposed type, the extrovert, the man who knows what he knows, and likes what he likes, and doesn't care who knows it—he should doubtless be subject to the opposite discipline; he should be criticized because he never uses "but"; he should be tempted to employ the qualifying clause. The man who has a legal mind should probably go easy on his "if"s. Fiddling little matters. Yes, I know. The sort of trifling help which criticism can give the artist. She cannot help him in great matters.

With these random considerations my paper must close. The latter part of it has been overshadowed and perhaps obsessed by my consciousness of the gulf between the creative and critical states. Perhaps the gulf does not exist, perhaps it does not signify, perhaps I have been making a gulf out of a molehill. But in my view it does prevent the establishment of a first-class *raison d'être* for criticism in the arts. The only activity which can establish such a *raison d'être* is love. However cautiously, or with whatever reservations, after whatsoever purifications, we must come back to love. That alone raises us to the cooperation with the artist which is the sole reason for our aesthetic pilgrimage. That alone promises spiritual parity. My main conclusion on criticism has therefore to be unfavourable; it does not and cannot go to the heart of things, nor have I succeeded in finding that it has given substantial help to the artists.   [1947]

The C Minor of that Life

Does "Three Blind Mice" sound different when it is played in different keys? I ask for first aid on this problem. Of course if it is played high up it will sound different from when it is played low down: the Mice will squeak more shrilly. But that is not my problem. And, of course, if it is played first in one key and then in another, it will sound different the second time, owing to the relation between the keys: the Mice will seem increasingly insolent, or increasingly pathetic. But that again is not my problem. What I am muddling after is this: is there any *absolute* difference between keys—a difference that is inherent, not relative? Have they special qualities, and, if they have, can the qualities be named, and is there any key which is particularly suitable for "Three Blind Mice"?

I have battered my head against this for years—a head untrained musically, and unacquainted with any instrument beyond the piano. Perhaps, like many amateur's problems, it is no problem, but one of those solemn mystifications which are erected by ignorance, and which would disappear under proper instruction. I continue to wonder whether keys have colours, or something analogous to colour (as the scales in Indian music have), whether they tint the tunes which are played in them, and which key would be most suitable for the Mice. C Major? And D major for "Pop Goes the Weasel"? Or is it the other way round? Or does it not matter either way?

The problem, if it is one, is connected with our sense of pitch. If we can't tell what note is being sounded, if we don't know what key the Mice are being played in, why then it can't matter to us in which key they are played. What the ear cannot hear, the heart cannot grieve. And I generally can't tell. My sense of pitch—though it does exist—is shaky and feeble and easily foiled by a few chromatics. I think I can tell when a tune is in C major, and I do frankly consider this key the most suitable for the Mice —it is straightforward, nurserified, unassuming. Mice in A flat would greatly overstate their claims, for A flat is a delicate suave gracious intimate refined key. And Mice in E would be presented far too brilliantly. I mention these three keys (C, A flat and E) because I most readily detect them, and am therefore the more ready to ascribe them characteristics. Besides them, I sometimes spot F, which has the lyric quality of A flat, only less marked, and C sharp (D flat), which has the brilliancy of E, only more marked. Outside these five, it is usually guesswork for me.

The above are all major. More easily detected than any, and more interesting than any, because it moved so often through the mind and under the fingers of Beethoven, is the key of C minor. Perhaps because it evokes him, but perhaps because of something inherent in it which attracted him, it appeals very readily to our sense of pitch, and if the Mice deserted their proper mode and put on its immensities they would soon be run down. Beethoven, like myself, had feelings for certain keys, and he makes some quaint remarks about them. For instance, he calls B minor a "black" key: rather odd—it never struck me as "black"; brown is the utmost I would go to. Again he calls A flat "barbaresco, not amoroso", and here he is obviously wrong! I have already defined the character of A flat! Anyhow, if he did think it "barbaresco", why did he choose it for the slow movement of the Pathetic Sonata? C sharp he calls "maestoso". Here he is quite right, and Wagner agrees with us, and has chosen this sparkling yet noble key for the closes both of *Rheingold* and of *Götterdämmerung*; the Gods go up to Valhalla and fall from it in C sharp.

But of C minor, the key he has made his own, Beethoven says nothing, so far as I know. He has invested in it deeply. If we lost everything he wrote except what is in this key, we should still have the essential Beethoven, the Beethoven tragic, the Beethoven so excited at the approach of something enormous that he can only just interpret and subdue it. It would be a pity to lose a Beethoven unbuttoned, a Beethoven yodelling, but this musician excited by immensities is unique in the annals of any art. No one has ever been so thrilled by things so huge, for the vast masses of doom crush the rest of us before we can hope to measure them. Fate knocks at our door; but before the final tap can sound, the flimsy door flies into pieces, and we never learn the sublime rhythm of destruction.

The catalogue of the C minor items is a familiar one. Heading it is the Fifth Symphony. Then there is the great violin sonata—greater than the Kreutzer, many critics think. There is the Third Piano Concerto. There is the Pathetic Sonata, with its opening groan, and the last piano sonata (Op. 111), with its opening dive into the abyss. There is the movement from the third Rasumovsky quartet, there are the Thirty-Two Variations. And there is probably a good deal more, some of it hidden away in works of other key-signatures. It would be absurd to press for similarities in items so different in intention and in date, but one has in all of them the conviction that Beethoven has found himself, that he is where he most wanted to be, that he is engaged in the pursuit of something outside sound—something which has fused the sinister and the triumphant.

There is a proof of this—at least it seems to me to be a proof—"indication" is the wiser word, no doubt—in the earliest of all the piano sonatas (Op. 2, No. 1). The key is F minor, and we go Mozarting ahead until we reach the last movement. This is a scrattling prestissimo, spitting triplets all over the place, and banging out not very amusing chords. After twenty bars, the triplets run down into the earth and re-emerge in the C minor key. Now the excitement begins. Beethoven, for the first time in his life, opens out. He plays with the new key for twelve bars, establishing it more firmly and heating himself up more at each note—and then out of it there soars a new tune, a tune in octaves, not loud, not elaborate, but tearing down the curtains and letting in the unknown light. As it sings itself out, the triplets get something to do which is worth doing, and when it ends, and the banging chords re-enter, they talk sense. This knack of turning dullish stuff into great stuff is characteristic of Beethoven, and incidentally one of the reasons why one ought never to skip the repeats when playing him—for only at the repeat does one hear what the dullish stuff means. But it thrills me that he should have exercised the knack first in the key of C minor, and that from that attitude he should have prospected the wildest and most wonderful land of his empire.

Thus far have our Mice led us. Holding up their tails, let us count them. Firstly, there may be nothing in key. Secondly, there can be nothing in key unless we have the sense of pitch. Thirdly, Beethoven thought, rightly or wrongly, that there was something in a key, and either chose C minor when he was in a particular mood, or was put into a particular mood after choosing it. Mozart's fondness for D major may also be noted, but in this respect, and indeed in others, Mozart did not go so far.

[1941]

Not Listening to Music

Listening to music is such a muddle that one scarcely knows how to start describing it. The first point to get clear in my own case is that during the greater part of every performance I do not attend. The nice sounds make me think of something else. I wool-gather most of the time, and am surprised that others don't. Professional critics can listen to a piece as consistently and as steadily as if they were reading a chapter in a novel. This seems to me an amazing feat, and probably they only achieve it through intellectual training; that is to say, they find in the music the equivalent of a plot; they are following the ground-bass or expecting the theme to re-enter in the dominant, and so on, and this keeps them on the rails. But I fly off every minute: after a bar or two I think how musical I am, or of something smart I might have said in conversation; or I wonder what the composer—dead a couple of centuries—can be feeling as the flames on the altar still flicker up; or how soon an H.E. bomb would extinguish them. Not to mention more obvious distractions: the tilt of the soprano's chin or chins; the antics of the conductor, that impassioned beetle, especially when it is night time and he waves his shards; the affectation of the pianist when he takes a top note with difficulty, as if he too were a soprano; the backs of the chairs; the bumps on the ceiling; the extreme physical ugliness of the audience. A classical audience is surely the plainest collection of people anywhere assembled for any common purpose; contributing my quota, I have the right to point this out. Compare us with a gang of navvies or with an office staff, and you will be appalled. This, too, distracts me.

What do I hear during the intervals when I do attend? Two sorts of music. They melt into each other all the time, and are not easy to christen, but I will call one of them "music that reminds me of something", and the other "music itself". I used to be very fond of music that reminded me of something, and especially fond of Wagner. With Wagner I always knew where

I was; he never let the fancy roam; he ordained that one phrase should recall the ring, another the sword, another the blameless fool and so on; he was as precise in his indications as an oriental dancer. Since he is a great poet, that did not matter, but I accepted his leitmotiv system much too reverently and forced it onto other composers whom it did not suit, such as Beethoven and Franck. I thought that music must be the better for having a meaning. I think so still, but am less clear as to what "a meaning" is. In those days it was either a non-musical object, such as a sword or a blameless fool, or a non-musical emotion, such as fear, lust or resignation. When music reminded me of something which was not music, I supposed it was getting me somewhere. "How like Monet!" I thought when listening to Debussy, and "How like Debussy!" when looking at Monet. I translated sounds into colours, saw the piccolo as apple-green, and the trumpets as scarlet. The arts were to be enriched by taking in one another's washing.

I still listen to some music this way. For instance, the slow start of Beethoven's Seventh Symphony invokes a gray-green tapestry of hunting scenes, and the slow movement of his Fourth Piano Concerto (the dialogue between piano and orchestra) reminds me of the dialogue between Orpheus and the Furies in Gluck. The climax of the first movement of the Appassionata (the "più allegro") seems to me sexual, although I can detect no sex in the Kreutzer, nor have I come across anyone who could, except Tolstoy. That disappointing work, Brahms's Violin Concerto, promises me clear skies at the opening, and only when the violin has squealed up in the air for page after page is the promise falsified. Wolf's "Ganymed" does give me sky— stratosphere beyond stratosphere. In these cases and in many others music reminds me of something non-musical, and I fancy that to do so is part of its job. Only a purist would condemn all visual parallels, all emotional labellings, all programmes.

Yet there is a danger. Music that reminds does open the door to that imp of the concert-hall, inattention. To think of a gray-green tapestry is not very different from thinking of the backs of the chairs. We gather a superior wool from it, still we do wool-gather, and the sounds slip by blurred. The sounds! It is for them that we come, and the closer we can get up against them the better. So I do prefer "music itself" and listen to it and for it as far as possible. In this connection, I will try to analyse a mishap

that has recently overtaken the Coriolanus Overture. I used to
listen to the Coriolanus for "itself", conscious when it passed of
something important and agitating, but not defining further.
Now I learn that Wagner, endorsed by Sir Donald Tovey, has
provided it with a Programme: the opening bars indicate the
hero's decision to destroy the Volsci, then a sweet tune for female
influence, then the dotted-quaver-restlessness of indecision. This
seems indisputable, and there is no doubt that this was, or was
almost, Beethoven's intention. All the same, I have lost my
Coriolanus. Its largeness and freedom have gone. The exquisite sounds have been hardened like a road that has been tarred
for traffic. One has to go somewhere down them, and to pass
through the same domestic crisis to the same military impasse,
each time the overture is played.

Music is so very queer that an amateur is bound to get muddled
when writing about it. It seems to be more "real" than anything,
and to survive when the rest of civilization decays. In these days
I am always thinking of it with relief. It can never be ruined or
nationalized. So that the music which is untrammelled and untainted by reference is obviously the best sort of music to listen to;
we get nearer the centre of reality. Yet though it is untainted it is
never abstract; it is not like mathematics, even when it uses them.
The Goldberg Variations, the last Beethoven sonata, the Franck
Quartet, the Schumann Piano Quintet and the Fourth Symphonies of Tchaikovsky and of Brahms certainly have a message.
Though what on earth is it? I shall get tied up trying to say.
There's an insistence in music—expressed largely through rhythm;
there's a sense that it is trying to push across at us something
which is neither an aesthetic pattern nor a sermon. That's what
I listen for specially.

So music that is itself seems on the whole better than music
that reminds. And now to end with an important point: my
own performances upon the piano. These grow worse yearly, but
never will I give them up. For one thing, they compel me to
attend—no wool-gathering or thinking myself clever here—and
they drain off all non-musical matter. For another thing, they
teach me a little about construction. I see what becomes of a
phrase, how it is transformed or returned, sometimes bottom
upward, and get some notion of the relation of keys. Playing
Beethoven, as I generally do, I grow familiar with his tricks, his
impatience, his sudden softnesses, his dropping of a tragic theme
one semitone, his love, when tragic, for the key of C minor, and

his aversion to the key of B major. This gives me a physical approach to Beethoven which cannot be gained through the slough of "appreciation". Even when people play as badly as I do, they should continue: it will help them to listen.

[1939]

Not Looking at Pictures

Pictures are not easy to look at. They generate private fantasies, they furnish material for jokes, they recall scraps of historical knowledge, they show landscapes where one would like to wander and human beings whom one would like to resemble or adore, but looking at them is another matter, yet they must have been painted to be looked at. They were intended to appeal to the eye, but, almost as if it were gazing at the sun itself, the eye often reacts by closing as soon as it catches sight of them. The mind takes charge instead and goes off on some alien vision. The mind has such a congenial time that it forgets what set it going. Van Gogh and Corot and Michelangelo are three different painters, but if the mind is indisciplined and uncontrolled by the eye they may all three induce the same mood, we may take just the same course through dreamland or funland from them, each time, and never experience anything new.

I am bad at looking at pictures myself, and the late Roger Fry enjoyed going to a gallery with me now and then, for this very reason. He found it an amusing change to be with someone who scarcely ever saw what the painter had painted. "Tell me, why do you like this, why do you prefer it to that?" he would ask, and listen agape for the ridiculous answer. One day we looked at a fifteenth-century Italian predella, where a St George was engaged in spearing a dragon of the plesiosaurus type. I laughed. "Now, *what* is there funny in this?" pounced Fry. I readily explained. The fun was to be found in the expression upon the dragon's face. The spear had gone through its hooped-up neck once, and now startled it by arriving at a second thickness. "Oh dear, here it comes again, I hoped that was all," it was thinking. Fry laughed too, but not at the misfortunes of the dragon. He was amazed that anyone could go so completely off the lines. There was no harm in it—but really, really! He was even more amazed when our enthusiasms coincided: "I fancy we are talking about different things," he would say, and we always were; I liked the mountain-back because it reminded me of a peacock, he because it had some structural significance, though not as much as the sack of potatoes in the foreground.

Long years of wandering down miles of galleries have convinced me that there must be something rare in those coloured slabs called "pictures", something which I am incapable of detecting for myself, though glimpses of it are to be had through the eyes of others. How much am I missing? And what? And are other modern sightseers in the same fix? Ours is an aural rather than a visual age, we do not get so lost in the concert-hall, we seem able to hear music for ourselves, and to hear it as music, but in galleries so many of us go off at once into a laugh or a sigh or an amorous day dream. In vain does the picture recall us. "What have your obsessions got to do with me?" it complains. "I am neither a theatre of varieties nor a spring-mattress, but paint. Look at my paint." Back we go—the picture kindly standing still meanwhile, and being to that extent more obliging than music—and resume the looking business. But something is sure to intervene—a tress of hair, the half-open door of a summer-house, a Crivelli dessert, a Bosch fish-and-fiend salad—and to draw us away.

One of the things that helps us to keep looking is composition. For many years now I have associated composition with a diagonal line, and when I find such a line I imagine I have gutted the picture's secret. Giorgione's *Castelfranco Madonna* has such a line in the lance of the warrior-saint, and Titian's *Entombment* at Venice has a very good one indeed. Five figures contribute to make up the diagonal: beginning high on the left with the statue of Moses, it passes through the heads of the Magdalene, Mary and the dead Christ, and plunges through the body of Joseph of Arimathea into the ground. Making a right angle to it, flits the winged Genius of Burial. And to the right, apart from it, and perpendicular, balancing the Moses, towers the statue of Faith. Titian's *Entombment* is one of my easiest pictures. I look at photographs of it intelligently, and encourage the diagonal and the pathos to reinforce one another. I see, with more than usual vividness, the grim alcove at the back and the sinister tusked pedestals upon which the two statues stand. Stone shuts in flesh; the whole picture is a tomb. I hear sounds of lamentation, though not to the extent of shattering the general scheme; that is held together by the emphatic diagonal, which no emotion breaks. Titian was a very old man when he achieved this masterpiece;

that too I realize, but not immoderately. Composition here really has been a help, and it is a composition which no one can miss: the diagonal slopes as obviously as the band on a threshing-machine, and vibrates with power.

Unfortunately, having no natural aesthetic aptitude, I look for diagonals everywhere, and if I cannot find one think the composition must be at fault. It is a word which I have learnt—a solitary word in a foreign language. For instance, I was completely baffled by Velasquez's *Las Meninas*. Where ever was the diagonal? Then the friend I was with—Charles Mauron, the friend who, after Roger Fry, has helped me with pictures most—set to work on my behalf, and cautiously underlined the themes. There is a wave. There is a half-wave. The wave starts up on the left, with the head of the painter, and curves down and up through the heads of the three girls. The half-wave starts with the head of Isabel de Velasco, and sinks out of the canvas through the dwarfs. Responding to these great curves, or inverting them, are smaller ones on the women's dresses or elsewhere. All these waves are not merely pattern; they are doing other work too— e.g. helping to bring out the effect of depth in the room, and the effect of air. Important too is the pushing forward of objects in the extreme left and right foregrounds, the easel of the painter in the one case, the paws of a placid dog in the other. From these, the composition curves back to the central figure, the lovely child-princess. I put it more crudely than did Charles Mauron, nor do I suppose that his account would have been Velasquez's, or that Velasquez would have given any account at all. But it is an example of the way in which pictures should be tackled for the benefit of us outsiders: coolly and patiently, as if they were designs, so that we are helped at last to the appreciation of something non-mathematical. Here again, as in the case of the *Entombment*, the composition and the action reinforced one another. I viewed with increasing joy that adorable party, which had been surprised not only by myself but by the King and Queen of Spain. There they were in the looking-glass! *Las Meninas* has a snapshot quality. The party might have been taken by Philip IV, if Philip IV had had a Kodak. It is all so casual—and yet it is all so elaborate and sophisticated, and I suppose those curves and the rest of it help to bring this out, and to evoke a vanished civilization.

Besides composition there is colour. I look for that, too, but with even less success. Colour is visible when thrown in my face

—like the two cherries in the great gray Michael Sweerts group in the National Gallery. But as a rule it is only material for dream.

On the whole, I am improving, and after all these years I am learning to get myself out of the way a little, and to be more receptive, and my appreciation of pictures does increase. If I can make any progress at all, the average outsider should do better still. A combination of courage and modesty is what he wants. It is so unenterprising to annihilate everything that's made to a green thought, even when the thought is an exquisite one. Not-looking at art leads to one goal only. Looking at it leads to so many.

[1939]

The Arts in Action

John Skelton

A lecture given at the
Aldeburgh Festival of 1950

John Skelton was an East Anglian; he was a poet, also a clergyman, and he was extremely strange. Partly strange because the
age in which he flourished—that of the early Tudors—is remote
from us, and difficult to interpret. But he was also a strange
creature personally, and whatever you think of him when we've
finished—and you will possibly think badly of him—you will
agree that we have been in contact with someone unusual.

Let us begin with solidity—with the church where he was rector. That still stands; that can be seen and touched, though its
incumbent left it over four hundred years ago. He was rector of
Diss, a market town which lies just in Norfolk, just across the
river Waveney, here quite a small stream, and Diss church is
somewhat of a landmark, for it stands upon a hill. A winding
High Street leads up to it, and the High Street, once very narrow,
passed through an arch in its tower which still remains. The
church is not grand, it is not a great architectural triumph like
Blythburgh or Framlingham. But it is adequate, it is dignified
and commodious, and it successfully asserts its pre-eminence over
its surroundings. Here our poet-clergyman functioned for a time,
and, I may add, carried on.

Not much is known about him, though he was the leading
literary figure of his age. He was born about 1460, probably in
Norfolk, was educated at Cambridge, mastered the voluble inelegant Latin of his day, entered the Church, got in touch with
the court of Henry VII, and became tutor to the future Henry
VIII. He was appointed "Poet Laureate", and this was confirmed by the universities of Cambridge, Oxford and Louvain.
In the early years of Henry VIII he voiced official policy—for
instance, in his poems against the Scots after Flodden. But,
unfortunately for himself, he attacked another and a greater
East Anglian, Cardinal Wolsey of Ipswich, and after that his

THE ARTS IN ACTION

influence declined. He was appointed rector of Diss in 1503, and held the post till his death in 1529. But he only seems to have been in residence during the earlier years. Life couldn't have been congenial for him there. He got across the Bishop of Norwich, perhaps about his marriage or semi-marriage, and he evidently liked London and the court, being a busy contentious fellow, and found plenty to occupy him there. A few bills and documents, a few references in the works of others, a little posthumous gossip, and his own poems, are all that we have when we try to reconstruct him. Beyond doubt he is an extraordinary character, but not one which it is easy to focus. Let us turn to his poems.

I will begin with the East Anglian poems, and with "Philip Sparrow". This is an unusually charming piece of work. It was written while Skelton was at Diss, and revolves round a young lady called Jane, who was at school at a nunnery close to Norwich. Jane had a pet sparrow—a bird which is far from fashionable today, but which once possessed great social prestige. In ancient Rome, Catullus sang of the sparrow of Lesbia, the dingy little things were housed in gilt cages, and tempted with delicious scraps all through the Middle Ages, and they only went out when the canary came in. Jane had a sparrow, round which all her maidenly soul was wrapped. Tragedy followed. There was a cat in the nunnery, by name Gib, who lay in wait for Philip Sparrow, pounced, killed him and ate him. The poor girl was in tears, and her tragedy was taken up and raised into poetry by her sympathetic admirer, the rector of Diss.

He produced a lengthy poem—it seemed difficult at that time to produce a poem that was not long. "Philip Sparrow" swings along easily enough, and can still be read with pleasure by those who will overlook its volubility, its desultoriness and its joky Latin.

It begins, believe it or not, with a parody of the Office for the Dead; Jane herself is supposed to be speaking, and she slings her Latin about well if quaintly. Soon tiring of the church service, she turns to English, and to classical allusions:

> When I remember again
> How my Philip was slain
> Never half the pain
> Was between you twain,
> Pyramus and Thisbe,

As then befell to me;
I wept and I wailéd
The teares down hailéd,
But nothing it availéd
To call Philip again
Whom Gib our cat has slain.
Gib I say our cat
Worrowed him on that
Which I loved best. . . .
I fell down to the ground[1]

Then—in a jumble of Christian and antique allusions, most typical of that age—she thinks of Hell and Pluto and Cerberus —whom she calls Cerebus—and Medusa and the Furies, and alternately prays Jupiter and Jesus to save her sparrow from the infernal powers.

It was so pretty a fool
It would sit upon a stool
And learned after my school. . . .
It had a velvet cap
And would sit upon my lap
And would seek after small wormés
And sometimes white bread crumbés
And many times and oft
Between my breastés soft
It would lie and rest
It was proper and prest!
   Sometimes he would gasp
When he saw a wasp;
A fly or a gnat
He would fly at that
And prettily he would pant
When he saw an ant
Lord how he would pry
After a butterfly
Lord how he would hop
After the grasshop
And when I said "Phip Phip"
Then he would leap and skip
And take me by the lip.
Alas it will me slo
That Philip is gone me fro!

[1] The quotations are not verbally accurate. The text has been simplified for the purpose of reading aloud.

Jane proceeds to record his other merits, which include picking
fleas off her person—this was a sixteenth-century girls' school,
not a twentieth-, vermin were no disgrace, not even a surprise,
and Skelton always manages to introduce the coarseness and
discomfort of his age. She turns upon the cat again, and hopes
the greedy grypes will tear out his tripes.

> Those villainous false cats
> Were made for mice and rats
> And not for birdés small.
> Alas, my face waxeth pale. . . .

She goes back to the sparrow and to the church service, and
draws up an enormous catalogue of birds who shall celebrate his
obsequies:

> Our chanters shall be the cuckoo,
> The culver, the stockdoo,
> The "peewit", the lapwing,
> The Versicles shall sing.

—together with other songsters, unknown in these marshes and
even elsewhere. She now wants to write an epitaph, but is held
up by her diffidence and ignorance; she has read so few books,
though the list of those she has read is formidable; moreover,
she has little enthusiasm for the English language—

> Our natural tongue is rude,
> And hard to be ennewed
> With polished termes lusty
> Our language is so rusty
> So cankered, and so full
> Of froward, and so dull,
> That if I would apply
> To write ornately
> I wot not where to find
> Terms to serve my mind.

Shall she try Latin? Yes, but she will hand over the job to the
Poet Laureate of Britain, Skelton, and, with this neat compliment
to himself, Skelton ends the first part of "Philip Sparrow".

He occupies the second part with praising Jane,

> This most goodly flower,
> This blossom of fresh colour
> So Jupiter me succour
> She flourishes new and new
> In beauty and virtue,

bypasses the sparrow, and enters upon a love poem:

> But wherefore should I note
> How often did I toot
> Upon her pretty foot
> It bruised mine heart-root
> To see her tread the ground
> With heeles short and round.

The rector is in fact losing his head over a schoolgirl, and has to pull himself up. No impropriety is intended, he assures us,

> There was no vice
> Nor yet no villainy,
> But only fantasy. . . .
> It were no gentle guise
> This treatise to despise
> Because I have written and said
> Honour of this fair maide,
> Wherefore shall I be blamed
> That I Jane have named
> And famously proclaimed?
> She is worthy to be enrolled
> In letters of gold.

Then he too slides into Latin and back into the Office of the Dead: *Requiem aeternam dona eis Domine*, he chants.

This poem of Philip Sparrow—the pleasantest Skelton ever wrote—helps to emphasize the difference in taste and in style between the sixteenth century and our own. His world is infinitely remote; not only is it coarse and rough, but there is an uncertainty of touch about it which we find hard to discount. Is he being humorous? Undoubtedly, but where are we supposed to laugh? Is he being serious? If so, where and how much? We don't find the same uncertainty when we read his predecessor Chaucer, or his successor Shakespeare. We know where they stand, even when we cannot reach them. Skelton belongs to an age of break-up, which had just been displayed politically in the Wars of the Roses. He belongs to a period when England was trying to find herself—as indeed do we today, though we have to make a different sort of discovery after a different type of war. He is very much the product of his times—a generalization that can be made of all writers, but not always so aptly. The solidity of the Middle Ages was giving way beneath his feet, and he did not know that the Elizabethan age was coming—any more than we know what is coming. We have not the least idea, whatever the politicians prophesy. It is appropriate, at this point, to quote the wisest and most impressive lines he ever wrote—they are not well known, and probably they are only a fragment. They have a weight and a thoughtfulness which are unusual in him.

> Though ye suppose all jeopardies are passed
>   And all is done that ye lookéd for before,
> Ware yet, I warn you, of Fortune's double cast,
>   For one false point she is wont to keep in store,
>   And under the skin oft festeréd is the sore;
> That when ye think all danger for to pass
> Ware of the lizard lieth lurking in the grass.

It was a curious experience, with these ominous verses in my mind, to go to Diss and to find, carved on the buttress of the church, a lizard. The carving was there in Skelton's day; that he noticed it, that it entered into his mind when he wrote, there is no reason to suppose. But its appearance, combined with the long grass in the churchyard, helped me to connect the present with the past, helped them to establish that common denominator without which neither has any validity.

> That when ye think all danger for to pass
> Ware of the lizard lieth lurking in the grass.

So true of the sixteenth century, so true of today! There are two main answers to the eternal menace of the lizard. One of them is caution, the other courage. Skelton was a brave fellow —his opposition to Cardinal Wolsey proves that—but I don't know which answer he recommends.

But let us leave these serious considerations, and enter Diss church itself, where we shall be met by a fantastic scene and by the oddest poem even Skelton ever wrote: the poem of "Ware the Hawk". Like "Philip Sparrow", it is about a bird, but a bird of prey, and its owner is not the charming Jane, but an ill-behaved curate, who took his hawk into the church, locked all the doors, and proceeded to train it with the help of two live pigeons and a cushion stuffed with feathers to imitate another pigeon. The noise, the mess, the scandal, was terrific. In vain did the rector thump on the door and command the curate to open. The young man—one assumes he was young—took no notice, but continued his unseemly antics. Diss church is well suited to a sporting purpose, since its nave and choir are unusually lofty, and the rood-loft was convenient for the birds to perch on between the statues of the Virgin and St John. Up and down he rushed, uttering the cries of his craft, and even clambering onto the communion table. Feathers flew in all directions and the hawk was sick. At last Skelton found "a privy way" in, and managed to stop him. But he remained impenitent, and threatened that another day he would go fox-hunting there, and bring in a whole pack of hounds.

Now is this an exaggeration, or a joke? And why did Skelton delay making a poem out of it until many years had passed? He does not—which is strange—even mention the name of the curate.

> He shall be as now nameless,
> But he shall not be blameless
> Nor he shall not be shameless.
> For sure he wrought amiss
> To hawk in my church at Diss.

That is moderately put. It was amiss. Winding himself up into a rage, he then calls him a peckish parson and a Domine Dawcock and a frantic falconer and a smeary smith, and scans history in vain for so insolent a parallel; not even the Emperor Julian the Apostate or the Nestorian heretics flew hawks in a church. Nero himself would have hesitated. And the poem ends in a jumble and a splutter, heaps of silly Latin, a cryptogram and a curious impression of gaiety; a good time, one can't help feeling, has been had by all.

How, though, did Skelton get into the church and stop the scandal? Perhaps through the tower. You remember my mentioning that the tower of Diss church has a broad passage-way running through it, once part of the High Street. Today the passage only contains a notice saying "No bicycles to be left here", together with a number of bicycles. Formerly, there was a little door leading up from it into the tower. That (conjectures an American scholar) may have been Skelton's privy entrance. He may have climbed up by it, climbed down the belfry into the nave, and spoiled, at long last, the curate's sport.

There is another poem which comes into this part of Skelton's life. It is entitled "Two Knaves Sometimes of Diss", and attacks two of his parishioners who had displeased him and were now safely dead; John Clerk and Adam Uddersall were their names. Clerk, according to the poet, had raged "like a camel" and now lies "starke dead, Never a tooth in his head, Adieu, Jayberd, adieu," while as for Uddersall, "Belsabub his soule save, who lies here like a knave." The poem is not gentlemanly. Little that Skelton wrote was. Not hit a man when he is down or dead? That's just the moment to wait for. He can't hit back.

The last East Anglian poem to be mentioned is a touching one: to his wife. As a priest, he was not and could not be married, but he regarded his mistress as his legal consort, and the poem deals with a moment when they were parting and she was about to bear a child:

> 'Petually
> Constrained am I
> With weeping eye
>   To mourn and 'plain
> That we so nigh
> Of progeny
> So suddenly
>   Should part in twain.
>
> When ye are gone
> Comfort is none,
> But all alone
>   Endure must I
> With grievely groan
> Making my moan
> As it were one
>   That should needs die.

There is a story about the birth of this child which was written down after Skelton's death, in a collection called *The Merry Tales of Skelton.* According to it, there were complaints to the bishop from the parish, which Skelton determined to quell. So he preached in Diss church on the text *Vos estis,* you are, and suddenly called out, "Wife! Bring my Child." Which the lady did. And he held the naked baby out to the congregation saying: "Is not this child as fair as any of yours? It is not like a pig or a calf, is it? What have you got to complain about to the bishop? The fact is, as I said in my text, *Vos estis,* you be, and have be and will and shall be knaves, to complayne of me without reasonable cause." Historians think that this jest-book story enshrines a tradition. It certainly fits in with what we know of the poet's fearless and abusive character.

Tenderness also entered into that character, though it did not often show itself. Tenderness inspires that poem I have quoted, and is to be found elsewhere in his gentle references to women; for instance, in the charming "Merry Margaret", which often appears in anthologies.

> Merry Margaret
>   As midsummer flower,
> Gentle as falcon
> Or hawk of the tower:
> With solace and gladness
> Much mirth and no madness
> All good and no badness.

And in the less known but still more charming poem "To Mistress Isabel Pennell" which I will quote in full. Isabel was a little girl of eight—even younger than Jane of the sparrow. ("Reflaring", near the beginning of the poem, is "redolent". "Nept" means catmint.)

> By Saint Mary, my Lady,
> Your mammy and your daddy
> Brought forth a goodly baby.
>   My maiden Isabel,
> Reflaring rosabel,
> The fragrant camomel:
>   The ruddy rosary,
> The sovereign rosemary
> The pretty strawberry
>   The columbine, the nept,
> The jelofer well set,
> The proper violet:
>   Ennewed your colour
> Is like the daisy flower
> After the April shower;
>   Star of the morrow gray,
> The blossom on the spray
> The freshest flower of May:
>   Maidenly demure,
> Of womanhood the lure;
> Wherefore I make you sure
>   It were an heavenly health,
> It were an endless wealth,
> A life for God himself
>   To hear this nightingale
> Among the birdés small
> Warbelling in the vale:

> Dug dug,
> Jug jug,
> Good year and good luck,
> With chuck, chuck, chuck, chuck!

Women could touch his violent and rugged heart and make it gentle and smooth for a little time. It is not the dying tradition of chivalry, it is something personal.

But we must leave these personal and local matters, and turn to London and to the political satires. The main group is directed against Cardinal Wolsey. The allusions are often obscure, for, though Skelton sometimes attacks his great adversary openly, at other times he is covering his tracks, and at other times complimentary and even fulsome. The ups and downs of which have furnished many problems for scholars. Two points should be remembered. Firstly, Skelton is not a precursor of the Reformation; he has sometimes been claimed as one by Protestant historians. He attacked the abuses of his Church—as exemplified in Wolsey's luxury, immorality and business. He has nothing to say against its doctrines or organization and was active in the suppression of heresy. He was its loyal if scandalous son.

Secondly, Wolsey appears to have behaved well. When he triumphed, he exacted no vengeance. Perhaps he had too much to think about. The story that Skelton died in sanctuary in St Margaret's, Westminster, fleeing from the Cardinal's wrath, is not true. He did live for the last years of his life in London, but freely and comfortably; bills for his supper parties have been unearthed. And though he was buried in St Margaret's it was honourably, under an alabaster inscription. Bells were pealed, candles were burned. Here again we have the bills.

The chief anti-Wolsey poems are "Speke Parrot", "Colin Clout", "Why come ye not to Court?" and the cumbrous Morality play *Magnificence*.

Speke Parrot—yet another bird; had Skelton a bird complex? Ornithologists must decide—Speke Parrot is one of those convenient devices where Polly is made to say what Polly's master hesitates to say openly. Poor Polly! Still, master is fond of Polly, and introduces him prettily enough.

> Parrot is no churlish chough nor no fleckéd pie,
> Parrot is no penguin that men call a carling,
> Parrot is no woodcock, nor no butterfly,

> Parrot is no stammering stare that men call a starling,
> But Parrot is my own dear heart and my dear darling,
> Melpomene, that fair maid, she burnished his beak:
> I pray you, let Parrot have liberty to speak.

Skelton's genuine if intermittent charm continues into the next stanza:

> Parrot is a fair bird for a lady.
>   God of his goodness him framéd and wrought;
> When parrot is dead, he doth not putrify.
>   Yet all things mortal shall turn unto nought,
>   Except man's soul, that Christ so dearly bought;
> That never may die, nor never die shall—
> Make much of Parrot, the popinjay royal.

The "popinjay royal"—that is to say the bird of King Henry VIII, whose goodness and generosity Wolsey abuses. And parrot, given his beak, says many sharp things against the Cardinal, who "carrieth a king in his sleeve" and plays the Pope's game rather than his liege's. Subtly and obscurely, with detailed attention to his comings and goings, the great man is attacked. It is a London poem, which could not have been written in a Norfolk rectory.

Much more violent is "Why come ye not to Court?" where the son of the Ipswich butcher gets brutally put in his place.

> Why come ye not to Court?
> To which court?
> To the king's court
> Or to Hampton Court?
> The king's court should have the excellence
> But Hampton Court hath the pre-eminence.

And at Hampton Court Wolsey rules, with

> his base progeny
> And his greasy genealogy,
> He came of the sang royall
> That was cast out from a butcher's stall. . . .
> With lewd conditions coated
> As hereafter be noted—
> Presumption and vainglory,
> Envy, wrath and lechery,
> Covertise and gluttony,
> Slothful to do good,
> Now frantic, now stark mad.

As for "Colin Clout". The title is the equivalent of Hodge or the Man in the Street, from whose point of view the poem is supposed to be written. It is a long rambling attack on bishops, friars, monks and the clergy generally, and Wolsey comes in for his share of criticism. I will quote from it not the abusive passages, of which you are getting plenty, but the dignified and devout passage with which it closes. Skelton was, after all, inside the church he criticized, and held its faith, and now and then he reminds us of this.

> Now to withdraw my pen
> And now a while to rest
> Meseemeth it for the best.
>   The forecastle of my ship
> Shall glide and smoothly slip
> Out of the waves wild
> Of the stormy flood
> Shoot anchor and lie at road
> And sail not far abroad
> Till the coast be clear
> And the lode-star appear
> My ship now will I steer
> Towards the port salu
> Of our Saviour Jesu
> Such grace that He us send
> To rectify and amend
> Things that are amiss
> Where that his pleasure is. Amen.

It is a conventional ending, but a sincere one, and reminds us that he had a serious side; his "Prayer to the Father of Heaven" was sung in the church here, to the setting of Vaughan Williams. He can show genuine emotion at moments, both about this world and the next. Here are two verses from "The Manner of the World Nowadays", in which he laments the decay of society.

> Sometimes we sang of mirth and play
> But now our joy is gone away
> For so many fall in decay
>   Saw I never:
> Whither is the wealth of England gone?
> The spiritual saith they have none,
> And so many wrongfully undone
>   Saw I never.

Magnificence, the last of the anti-Wolsey group, is a symbol for Henry VIII, who is seduced by wicked flatterers from his old counsellor (i.e. from Skelton himself). Largess, Counterfeit-Countenance, Crafty - Conveyance, Cloaked - Collusion and Courtly-Abusion are some of the names, and all are aspects of Wolsey. At enormous length and with little dramatic skill they ensnare Magnificence and bring him low. By the time Stage 5, Scene 35 is reached he repents, and recalls his former adviser, and all is well.

Well, so much for the quarrel between Skelton and Wolsey—between the parson from Norfolk and the Cardinal from Suffolk, and Suffolk got the best of it. Skelton may have had right on his side and he had courage and sincerity, but there is no doubt that jealousy came in too. At the beginning of Henry VIII's reign he was a very important person. He had been the King's tutor, he went on a semi-diplomatic mission, and as Poet Laureate he was a mouthpiece for official lampoons. With the advent of Wolsey, who tempted the king with pleasure, his importance declined, and he did not live to see the days when Henry preferred power to pleasure, and Wolsey fell.

The satires against the Scots, next to be mentioned, belong to the more influential period of Skelton's life. They centre round the Battle of Flodden (1513). King Henry's brother-in-law, James IV of Scotland, had challenged him, had invaded England, and been killed at Flodden, with most of his nobility. Skelton celebrates the English victory with caddish joy. In quoting a few lines, I do not desire to ruffle any sensitive friends from over the Border. I can anyhow assure them that our Poet Laureate appears to have got as good as he gave:

> King Jamie, Jemsy, Jocky my jo,
> Ye summoned our king—why did ye so
> To you nothing it did accord
> To summon our king your sovereign lord? . . .
> Thus for your guerdon quit are ye,
> Thanked be God in Trinitie
> And sweet Saint George, our Lady's knight
> Your eye is out: adew, good-night.

And still more abusively does he attack an enemy poet called Dundas who wrote Latin verses against him.

> Gup, Scot,
> Ye blot

Set in better
Thy pentameter
This Dundas
This Scottish ass,
He rhymes and rails
That Englishmen have tails. . . .
Shake thy tail, Scot, like a cur
For thou beggest at every man's door
Tut, Scot, I say
Go shake thee dog, hey. . . .
Dundas,
That drunk ass. . . .
Dundee, Dunbar
Walk Scot,
Walk sot
Rail not so far.

The accusation that Englishmen have tails is still sometimes made,
and is no doubt as true as it ever was. I have not been able to
find out how Dundas made it, since his poem has vanished.
We can assume he was forcible. Nor have I quoted Skelton in
full, out of deference to the twentieth century. He is said to
have written it in his Diss rectory. That is unlikely—not because
of its tone, but because it implies a close contact with affairs
which he could only have maintained at Court.

Our short Skeltonic scamper is nearing its end, but I must
refer to the "Tunning of Elinor Rumming", one of the most
famous of Skelton's poems. Elinor Rumming kept a pub—not
in East Anglia, but down in Surrey, near Leatherhead. The
poem is about her and her clients, who likewise belonged to the
fair sex.

Tell you I will
If that you will
A while be still
Of a comely Jill
That dwelt on a hill:
She is somewhat sage
And well worn in age
For her visage
It would assuage
A man's courage . . .
Comely crinkled
Wondrously wrinkled
Like a roast pig's ear
Bristled with hair.

You catch the tone. You taste the quality of the brew. It is
strong and rumbustious and not too clean. Skelton is going to
enjoy himself thoroughly. Under the guise of a satirist and a
corrector of morals, he is out for a booze. Now the ladies come
tumbling in:

> Early and late
> Thither cometh Kate
> Cisly and Sare
> With their legs bare
> And also their feet
> Fully unsweet
> Their kirtles all to-jagged
> Their smocks all to-ragged,
> With titters and tatters
> Bring dishes and platters
> With all their might running
> To Elinor Rumming
> To have of her tunning.

They get drunk, they tumble down in inelegant attitudes, they
trip over the doorstep, they fight—Margery Milkduck, halting
Joan, Maud Ruggy, drunken Alice, Bely and Sybil, in they come.
Many of them are penniless and are obliged to pay in kind, and
they bring with them gifts often as unsavoury as the drink they
hope to swallow—a rancid side of bacon for example—and they
pawn anything they can lay their hands on, from their husbands'
clothes to the baby's cradle, from a frying-pan to a side-saddle.
Elinor accepts all. It is a most lively and all-embracing poem,
which gets wilder and lewder as it proceeds. Then Skelton
pulls himself up in characteristic fashion.

> My fingers itch
> I have written too mich
> Of this mad mumming
> Of Elinor Rumming.

And remembering that he is a clergyman and a Poet Laureate
he appends some Latin verses saying that he has denounced
drunken, dirty and loquacious women, and trusts they will take
his warning to heart. I wonder. To my mind he has been
thoroughly happy, as he was in the church at Diss when the
naughty curate hawked. I often suspect satirists of happiness—
and I oftener suspect them of envy. Satire is not a straight
trade. Skelton's satires on Wolsey are of the envious type. In

"Elinor Rumming" and "Ware the Hawk" I detect a coarse merry character enjoying itself under the guise of censoriousness.

> Thought is frank and free:
> To think a merry thought
> It cost me little nor nought.

One question that may have occurred to you is this: was Skelton typical of the educated parish priest of his age? My own impression is that he was, and that the men of Henry VIII's reign, parsons and others, were much more unlike ourselves than we suppose, or, if you prefer it, much odder. We cannot unlock their hearts. In the reign of his daughter Elizabeth a key begins to be forged. Shakespeare puts it into our hands, and we recover, on a deeper level, the intimacy promised by Chaucer. Skelton belongs to an age of transition: the silly Wars of the Roses were behind him; he appears even to regret them, and he could not see the profounder struggles ahead. This makes him "difficult", though he did not seem so to himself. His coarseness and irreverence will pain some people and must puzzle everyone. It may help us if we remember that religion is older than decorum.

Of his poetry I have given some typical samples, and you will agree that he is entertaining and not quite like anyone else, that he has a feeling for rhythm, and a copious vocabulary. Sometimes—but not often—he is tender and charming, occasionally he is devout and very occasionally he is wise. On the whole he's a comic—a proper comic, with a love for improper fun, and a talent for abuse. He says of himself, in one of his Latin verses, that he sings the material of laughter in a harsh voice, and the description is apt; the harshness is often more obvious than the laughter, and leaves us with a buzzing in the ears rather than with a smile on the face. Such a row! Such a lot of complaints! He has indeed our national fondness for grumbling—the Government, the country, agriculture, the world, the beer, they are none of them what they ought to be or have been. And, although we must not affix our dry little political labels to the fluidity of the past (there is nothing to tie them on to), it is nevertheless safe to say that temperamentally the rector of Diss was a conservative.

On what note shall we leave him? A musical note commends itself. Let me quote three stanzas from a satire called "Against a Comely Coistroun"—that is to say, against a good-looking kitchen-boy. The boy has been conjectured to be Lambert

Simnel, the pretender to the crown of England. He was silly
as well as seditious, and he fancied himself as a musician and
"curiously chanted and currishly countered and madly in his
musicks mockishly made against the Nine Muses of politic
poems and poets matriculate"—the matriculate being Skelton,
the Poet Laureate. Listen how he gets basted for his incompetence; you may not follow all the words, but you can hear the
blows fall, and that's what matters:

> He cannot find it in rule nor in space,
> He solfas too haute, his treble is too high
> He braggeth of his birth, that born was full base,
> His music without measure, too sharp is his *Mi*,
> He trimmeth in his tenor to counter pirdewy,
> His descant is busy, it is without a mean
> Too fat is his fancy, his wit is too lean.
>
> He rumbleth on a lewd lute "Roty bully joys"
> Rumble down, tumble down, hey go now now!
> He fumbleth in his fingering an ugly good noise,
> It seemeth the sobbing of an old sow!
> He would be made much of, an he wist how;
> Well sped in spindles and turning of tavells;
> A bungler, a brawler, a picker of quarrels.
>
> Comely he clappeth a pair of clavichords
> He whistleth so sweetly, he maketh me to sweat;
> His descant is dashed full of dischords
> A red angry man, but easy to entreat:
> An usher of the hall fain would I get
> To point this proud page a place and a room
> For Jack would be a gentleman, that late was a groom.

Kitchen-boy Simnel, if it be he, was evidently no more a per-
former than he was a prince. Yet I would have liked to have
him here now, red, angry, good-looking, and making a hideous
noise, and to have heard Skelton cursing him as he screeched.
The pair of them might have revived for us that past which is
always too dim, always too muffled, always too refined. With
their raucous cries in your ears, with the cries of the falconer in
Diss church, with the squawkings of Speke Parrot, and the
belchings of Elinor Rumming, I leave you.

[1950]

149

Julius Caesar

While I was considering what to say about *Julius Caesar*, I happened to go to a school entertainment. It was a large primary school, and the boys mostly came from working-class homes; little boys—the eldest couldn't have been fourteen. They acted some scenes out of this very play. They did not act them well—how should they? They had not had the time to rehearse, they forgot their words and said them too fast, also there was not the money to buy properties with: the Roman Senators wore towels and curtains and anything they could scrounge, and a solitary garland of green cardboard was handed from Caesar to Brutus and from Brutus to Antony as the occasion required. The audience were more interested in identifying their offspring than in following the plot. Remarks could be heard such as "There he is, that one's Tom," and there were squeals from babies who were lifted up in their mothers' arms to see better, and seemed critical of what they saw. I was critical myself—yet I had an odd feeling of pleasure and of awe, and certain words of Cassius after the murder came into my mind:

> How many ages hence
> Shall this our lofty scene be acted over,
> In states unborn and accents yet unknown!

If Shakespeare had been present with us in that school, he might not have been flattered but he would not have been surprised, for what he expected to occur has occurred: the play lives.

> O Julius Caesar! thou art mighty yet:
> Thy spirit walks abroad. . . .

It was walking with us as well as circumstances permitted; it was part of the civilization of England and of all who read English.

The general immortality of Shakespeare is too vast a subject. Let us keep to this particular play. Why has it caught on? It is about some old Romans who murdered one of their number and were finally defeated by his friends. The incident was chronicled by a Greek historian, Plutarch, and Shakespeare read a translation of it and turned out a play somewhere about 1600. It seems to have been a success from the first. And we today, though we may not rank it with the Great Four—*Hamlet, Othello, Lear, Macbeth*—always hail it as a typical example of his genius, and are excited when the curtain rises.

It *is* exciting—that is one reason for its popularity. Although it is not carefully constructed like a Greek play or a classical French play, although it is not as cunning in its advance as *Othello* or *Macbeth*, yet it does succeed in startling us and holding us. It effects this by three well-timed explosions. The first of these explosions is of course the murder itself. The preparation for this is masterly—the growth of the conspiracy, omens, storms, apparitions, Portia's forebodings, Calpurnia's dream, the tempting of Caesar to the Senate House, the failure of Artemidorus to save him, the luring away of Antony; and then the deed. And the murder is followed by a second explosion: Antony's funeral speech. The excitement is revived and increased instead of dropping. After that, indeed, there is a lull and a failure to interest, until we come to the plains of Philippi and the third explosion: the quarrel in the tent between Brutus and Cassius. This is so unexpected, so natural psychologically and so touching that it produces a tremendous effect, and after it, his nerves all exhausted, Brutus beholds Caesar's ghost. I do not mean that these three explosions, these three famous scenes, are the only reason for the play's popularity. But they do provide the excitement, and if a drama does not excite the ordinary man it may satisfy its contemporaries, but it has no chance of being acted "in states unborn and accents yet unknown".

The second reason for popularity is the character-drawing, and particularly the character of Brutus. Before I come to it, I am going to risk a generalization about Shakespeare. He was an Elizabethan dramatist, and I do not think the Elizabethans were conscientious over their characters; they would often alter them in the middle in order to get on with the play. Beaumont and Fletcher contain glaring examples of this. Good men become bad and then good again: traitors turn into heroes and vice versa without any internal justification. And Shakespeare sometimes does it too. There is an example—not a glaring one—in this play, in the character of Casca. Casca first appears as extremely polite and indeed servile to Caesar. "Peace ho! Caesar speaks," he cries. Then he shows himself to Brutus and Cassius as a sour blunt contradictious fellow, who snaps them up when they speak and is grumpy when they invite him to supper. You may say this is subtlety on Shakespeare's part, and that he is indicating that Casca is a dark horse. I don't think so. I don't think Shakespeare was bothering about Casca —he is merely concerned to make the action interesting and he alters the character at need. Later on, during the thunderstorm, Casca becomes different again; he walks about with a drawn sword, is deeply moved by the apparitions, and utters exalted poetry. At the murder scene he wounds Caesar in the neck, and then we hear of him no more. His usefulness is over. Contrast Shakespeare here with a modern writer like Tolstoy. Tolstoy is conscientious over his characters, he has a personal responsibility to each of them, he has a vital conception of them, and though they are full of contradictions those contradictions are true to life. Contrast Casca with Dolokhov in *War and Peace*. Shakespeare often doesn't mind about his people. And when I am reading him one of my difficulties is to detect when he does mind and when he doesn't. This may be heresy on my part, but it seems to me that a great deal of Shakespearean criticism is invalid because it assumes that his characters are real people, and are never put in just to make the play go. The play's the thing, I suggest.

It is delightful when the characters are real, when Shakespeare does bother about them. Brutus is real, so is Cassius, so is Antony, so perhaps is Caesar himself. Brutus is an intellectual who can do things, who is not (like Hamlet) hampered by doubts. He can do things—but he always does them wrong: his advice is invariably fatal, from the moment of the murder down to the battle of Philippi. He cannot realize that men seek their own interests, for he has never sought his own, he has lived nobly among noble thoughts, wedded to a noble wife. He is kind to his servant. Everything he does is touched with fineness. Yet Brutus is not frigid. He just avoids being a prig. We are able to take him to our hearts. And with him is associated the worldly but far from contemptible Cassius. Those two speak the same language though they sometimes use different words. And against them is opposed Mark Antony—brilliant, sensuous, devoted to Caesar, but heartless otherwise, and treacherous. These three support the play. The character of Caesar is—difficult: Shakespeare does not present him sympathetically. He makes a few fine remarks like

It seems to me most strange that men should fear:
Seeing that death, a necessary end,
Will come when it will come.

But goes on to talk bombast and to assert that he and Danger

are two lions litter'd in one day
And I the elder and more terrible.

Do you detect a contemporary voice here? I do. It is Mussolini's. His infirmities are insisted on: his epilepsy, his deafness. He is pompous, conceited, showing-off, dictatorial. Indeed, some modern producers have stressed this and have presented *Julius Caesar* as a study in Fascism. But when Caesar is dead his spirit is mighty, and haunts Brutus and wins. I don't know what to make of this. If Shakespeare were a modern writer I should be more clear about his conception. I should be certain that he has planned Caesar to be little in life and great in death. But, being an Elizabethan, is it possible that he may be altering Caesar as he alters Casca, for the sake of the play?

Excitement—and enough real people. Here are two of the reasons why *Julius Caesar* lives, and why, after more than three hundred years, it is acted by primary-school boys. At the end of the performance to which I have referred, after Brutus, aged twelve, had suicided himself, and fallen with rather a thump, another of the children came forward, in his little brown suit, to speak the epilogue. The epilogue was not by Shakespeare. It ran as follows:

I come to say our play is done.
We hope you have enjoyed the fun.

The child then retired. He had spoken briefly but justly. Shakespeare *is* fun. There are murders and ghosts, jealousy, remorse, despair, there is *Othello*, there is *Lear*, there is even *Timon of Athens*—but—how shall I put it? Shakespeare never grumbles. He denounces life but he never complains of it; he presents even its tragedies for our enjoyment.

[1942]

The Stratford Jubilee of 1769

Halfway through the eighteenth century the world of culture was convulsed by the fall of a mulberry tree. A clergyman had cut it down, since it overhung his house, and he could not have supposed that anyone would have objected to such a natural proceeding. But he had reckoned without the *Zeitgeist*. The mulberry tree had been planted by Shakespeare, and the worship of Shakespeare was just ready to begin. A storm of indignation arose, which the clergyman increased by refusing to pay his rates; he was hounded out of Stratford, and it was decreed that no one of his name (which was fortunately Gastrell) should ever be allowed to reside there again. The fallen tree became a sacred object. Relics were made from its wood, and one of these—a casket—was sent up by the Corporation to Garrick, the leading actor of the day. Inside the casket was a flattering address, and the freedom of the town. Now Garrick was already a Shakespeare expert: he had improved the last act of *Hamlet* almost out of recognition, besides transfiguring *Romeo and Juliet*, and he was delighted with the attention. In a letter, still preserved, he thanks the Corporation warmly for the "elegant and inestimable box", and he decided to organize a celebration at Stratford which should place the bard's fame and his own upon a permanent and mutual basis.

It is not the first Shakespeare celebration. The first may have resulted in the death of Shakespeare. Drayton and Jonson, it is said, paid a visit to their friend in 1616, and drank him into his grave. But this only rests on the testimony of another clergyman; nor do we know much about a celebration for which there is historical evidence—the festivities of 1746. These were held in a meadow near the church for the purpose of restoring Shakespeare's monument, and brought in £12 10s., not a large sum, but sufficient to do considerable damage. So Garrick had his precedents. But he worked on a larger scale and in accordance with his own vivid personality. From the stage of Drury Lane he announced that

On Avon's banks where Flowers eternal blow,
Like its full stream, our Gratitude shall flow!

and he planned a three days' Jubilee for the autumn of 1769
which should include almost everything except the performance
of a Shakespeare play—turtles and fireworks, processions, masked
balls and transparencies, all centering round a rotunda on the
model of Ranelagh to be erected on the Bancroft. "Why bring
in Shakespeare?" the purist will murmur. But why not? There
is no reason to suppose that Shakespeare would have minded
being brought in, or that he would have found a rotunda less
congenial than the formidable precipices of red brick which
await him today a few yards down stream.

The graver and grander minds of the epoch held aloof
from "Garrick's Vagary". They suspected frivolity and self-
advertisement. Gray was dubious. Doctor Johnson went to
Brighton. Horace Walpole, over in Paris, announced with concern
that the French were laughing at us. The French were welcome
to laugh at us. Quaffing our mulberry-tree goblets, wearing
our mulberry-tree medals, waving our "Shakespeare Ribbands
in imitation of the Rainbow which unites the colours of all
parties", and singing:

The pride of all Nature was sweet Willy O,
The first of all swains,
He gladden'd the plains,
None ever was like to the sweet Willy O—

—what did we care for the French? And here were the cannons
and guitars to usher in the dawn, and there was *Judith*, an
oratorio by Isaac Bickerstaffe, being performed in the church
to the music of Dr Arne, and there was Boswell dressed as a
Corsican chief with "Corsica Boswell" in his hat, and duchesses
as witches, and Garrick wearing Shakespeare's own gloves, and
the Birthplace in Henley Street illuminated, and the Jubilee
Stakes won by a jockey who admitted that he had no great
taste for reading. All—all was English; so what more did we
want?

Well, one thing more: less English weather.

Ye gods, how it rained! It poured and poured for the whole
three days; the procession had to be given up, the fireworks
would not go off, the Jubilee Stakes were run knee-deep, and
as a final irony the Avon rose during the midnight masquerade
and isolated the rotunda. With great difficulty were the ladies

got out of it in time; screaming and splashing and dressed as witches, Cordelias and what not, they were led over slippery planks to their coaches through darkness and storm. The horses tugged, the wheels sank two feet in water and mud, the Bancroft became a raging sea, and no one in these circumstances paid any attention to Boswell, who tried to recite a poem of his own composition about Corsica, with a mulberry-wood staff in his hand.

Nor was the weather the only disappointment. The citizens of Stratford failed to give satisfaction too. They seem to have been in the grip of two passions—fear and avarice—and the oddest tales about them occur in the contemporary newspapers. Many of them thought that Garrick was the Devil, and barred themselves up in their houses; they were terrified by the decorations, particularly by a transparency of Caliban and Trinculo, and their belief that God's Judgement impended was confirmed by the abnormal floods. Others, more courageous, sallied forth through the sheets of rain to fleece the visitors. Ninepence was charged for washing out a pocket-handkerchief, one-and-sixpence for the Temple of the Graces, and two shillings for telling the time. One of the victims gives details of his expenses. It cost him £49 from London and back for the three days, and he was trying to do things as cheaply as he could. Certainly the cult of Shakespeare starts off with rather a jerk.

However, Garrick managed to recite his Dedication Ode, which was to him and to his patrons the chief item in the Jubilee. He said it with gusto, in spite of a cut chin, caused through the drunkenness of his barber, and he stood in the middle of a line of female singers, who led the choruses. The Ode is an empty piece of writing, but its tone is significant; it blends the exalted and the intimate. The same note is struck in Gainsborough's portrait. There Garrick is depicted with his arm round Shakespeare's waist—if a bust can be said to have a waist. His expression is at once loyal and independent. "Stick to me and I will stick to you," he seems to be saying. It is pleasant to reflect that Shakespeare did not betray him. Although he lost heavily over the fiasco, he got his money back, and more than back, on the stage of Drury Lane, where he presented his "Stratford Jubilee" with enormous success during the following winter.

[1932]

Gibbon and his Autobiography

> It was at Rome, on the 15th of October, 1764, as I sat musing amidst the ruins of the Capitol, while the barefooted friars were singing vespers in the Temple of Jupiter, that the idea of writing the decline and fall of the city first started to my mind.

The sentence is a very famous one, and anyhow the words "decline and fall" give the clue to it. It is written by Edward Gibbon the historian, and he is telling us in his *Autobiography* how he came to write the great history which has made his name immortal. Gibbon has been in my thoughts lately. I often have occasion to go to Putney, now a suburb of London, where he was born. I see the church at the end of Putney Bridge, close to which he resided as a little boy, and the river which he must have contemplated. Resided, contemplated: I use those pompous words on purpose, for even as a little boy Gibbon was not playful or frisky. I cannot imagine him bowling his hoop down Putney High Street, or fishing for sticklebacks in the Thames. But I can imagine him "residing" there, and thus he comes into my thoughts.

I also think of him because I have been rereading the *Decline and Fall* and have been trying to find parallels between the collapse of the Mediterranean civilization which he there describes and the apparent collapse of world civilization today. I have not found many parallels, but I do think it strengthens our outlook occasionally to glance into the past, and to lift our eyes from the wave that threatens to drown us to the great horizons of the sea of history, where personal safety no longer signifies. Gibbon is a great navigator of the sea of history—the greatest whom this country, or perhaps any, has produced—and his work has the majesty, the precision and the reliability of a well-built ship; I had almost added "the poetry and the beauty of a ship", though it is not, strictly speaking, beautiful. Because of my visits to Putney and because of this graver reason I am chatting about him now.

After a sickly childhood at Putney, and an unsatisfactory

term at Oxford, Gibbon led a very happy life as well as a diligent one. His health improved, he made good friends—particularly Lord Sheffield, who edited the *Autobiography*—he worked unceasingly, and after the moment at Rome which he has just described he worked according to a plan. Study and amusement were to him the same thing: he did not split his life into "work" and "recreation", which is what most people do and have to do today; he belonged to the eighteenth century, and he has all the stateliness and the sanity of that limited but admirable age. He died just as the industrial era was starting. I don't think he would have understood it, and it certainly could not have produced him. Later historians, such as Macaulay or Carlyle, are always fussing about something or other—worrying about the underdog or preaching the gospel of work. Gibbon never fusses. He is an aristocrat. The underdog never unduly distresses him, and he never preaches the gospel of work, because work to him was the same as amusement; he often interchanges those two words, which we regard as opposites. In the house of his friend Lord Sheffield, or in his own house in Switzerland, unremitting, unperturbed, he pursued his congenial task, and as the great history went on, and was published volume after volume, he began to realize that to this delightful labour another delight might be added, namely posthumous fame; which has indeed been granted to him. Although the *Decline and Fall* came out nearly two hundred years ago, it is still the leading authority on its period. Macaulay and Carlyle need correcting and supplementing, but the history of Gibbon stands firm. This is an amazing achievement. He is read because of his accuracy to fact and his sound historical judgement; not merely because he is a master of style.

Now this success—this command over his material and over the circumstances of daily life—had to be paid for. Everything has to be paid for, and Gibbon paid by curtailing his passions. He was not an ardent character, he disapproved of enthusiasm, he disliked religion, and the raptures of lovers moved him either to ribaldry or to contempt. Once he, too, had been in love, with a Swiss girl, but his father had disapproved, and sensible young Edward, seeing storms ahead, had given her up without difficulty. "I sighed as a lover, I obeyed as a son" is the famous phrase in which he records this. He could be affectionate and grateful—to Lord Sheffield, to the rather tiresome old aunt who had been good to him when he was a boy at Putney—but he never developed his emotions. For this he has been blamed. But, if you develop your emotions, for that also you have to pay—everything has to be paid for, and he would have impaired the particular qualities that made him great. To me he remains an attractive character, despite his formalism and worldliness. I like to think of him not only writing and reading at his desk, but in society, fashionably dressed, for he was quite the beau, and shaped like a balloon, for he was extremely fond of good food and became plump. The balloon was supported on little legs which twinkled and turned with immense rapidity as Gibbon bowed right and left to the company, and it supported in its turn a face of quite unusual ugliness. Yes! Poor Edward was excessively plain. Once he was taken to see an old French lady who was blind and was accustomed to pass her hands over the faces of visitors, to realize their appearance. When she touched Gibbon's face, the old lady was so startled by what she felt that she exclaimed: "Mais c'est une mauvaise plaisanterie." She could not believe it was a face at all. No doubt Gibbon was sensitive over this—people the shape of balloons often are. But he had many recompenses. He had wisdom, learning, good taste, tolerance, and he lived in an age when those qualities were appreciated, as they are not today. We could not have a Gibbon today. Our conditions forbid it. The war says no. Totalitarianism says no. The social conscience also says no. For good and for evil our faces are turned away from the eighteenth century which he adorned and exemplified. Our historians are either fanatics or scientists, and he was neither. He was a man of letters, equipped for evoking and interpreting the past. The great ship of his genius ploughs seas which, according to theorists, should lie beyond his range, and we can only thank the human star that this is so, that he lived, and lived just when he did.

His *Autobiography* is one of the minor masterpieces of its century. It is a formal, self-conscious work, written to be read, it is intelligent, entertaining, dignified, and often amusing: there is, for instance, a devastating account of contemporary Oxford, which Cambridge at all events has never forgotten. Here's a passage from it where Cambridge also gets involved. He is discussing which is the senior foundation—a question which still agitates their dons. And he calmly remarks:

Perhaps in a separate annotation I may coolly examine the fabulous and real antiquities of our sister universities, a question which has kindled such fierce and foolish disputes among their fanatic sons. In the meanwhile it will be acknowledged that these venerable bodies are sufficiently old to partake of all the prejudices and infirmities of age. The schools of Oxford and Cambridge were founded in a dark age of false and barbarous science [Gibbon was blind to the achievements of medievalism]; and they are still tainted with the vices of their origin. Their primitive discipline was adapted to the education of priests and monks; and the government still remains in the hands of the clergy, an order of men whose manners are remote from the present world, and whose eyes are dazzled by the light of philosophy.

He spent but fourteen months at Oxford, "the most idle and unprofitable of my whole life", and the *Autobiography* goes on to describe his expulsion because he had lapsed into Romanism, his salutary travels on the Continent, the growth of his mental powers, his service in the militia (an invaluable practical training for the future historian), his residences in Switzerland, and the slowly maturing achievement of the *Decline and Fall*. Don't look for gaiety here or for spontaneity, but you will find wit, shrewdness, and the pardonable weightiness of a man who knows that he has genius and has used it properly. The book, by the way, is not Gibbon's own arrangement, but a compilation made by Lord Sheffield out of several separate memoirs which he had left behind him. Sheffield did his work well, so we are quite right, though not quite accurate, in referring to the book as Gibbon's *Autobiography*.

I will conclude with another quotation from it, where he describes how, twenty-three years after its conception in Rome, the colossal enterprise of the *Decline and Fall* is concluded at Lausanne in Switzerland.

I have presumed to mark the moment of conception: I shall now commemorate the hour of my final deliverance. It was on the day, or rather night, of the 27th of June, 1787, between the hours of eleven and twelve, that I wrote the last lines of the last page, in a summer-house in my garden. After laying down my pen, I took several turns in a *berceau*, or covered walk of acacias, which commands a prospect of the country, the lake, and the mountains. The air was temperate, the sky was serene, the silver orb of the moon was reflected from the waters, and all nature was silent. I will not dissemble the first emotions of joy on recovery of my freedom, and, perhaps, the establishment of my fame. But my pride was soon humbled, and a sober melancholy was spread over my mind, by the idea that I had taken an everlasting leave of an old and agreeable companion, and that whatsoever might be the future fate of my *History*, the life of the historian must be short and precarious.

There is great English, and a great rounded life! It is not our English or our life, and it would be useless for us in our twentieth-century circumstances to imitate either the style or the conduct of Gibbon. We have to carry on differently. But he is a land-mark and a signpost—a landmark of human achievement; and a signpost because the social convulsions of the Roman Empire as described by him sometimes prefigure and indicate these convulsions which shake the whole world today.

[1942]

Voltaire and Frederick the Great

Two hundred years ago a Frenchman paid a visit to a German. It is a famous visit. The Frenchman was delighted to come to Germany, his German host delighted to welcome him. They were more than polite to one another, they were enthusiastic, and each thought, "I am sure we are going to be friends for ever." Yet the visit was a disaster. They still talk about it in Germany today, and they say it was the Frenchman's fault. And they still talk about it in France. And I'm going to talk about it now, partly because it makes such a good story, and partly because it contains a lesson for us all, even though it did happen two hundred years back.

The Frenchman was Voltaire. People today sometimes think of Voltaire as a person who sneered at everything, and made improper jokes. He was much more than that, he was the greatest man of his age, indeed he was one of the greatest men whom European civilization has produced. If I had to name two people to speak for Europe at the Last Judgement I should choose Shakespeare and Voltaire—Shakespeare for his creative genius, Voltaire for his critical genius and humanity. Voltaire cared for the truth, he believed in tolerance, he pitied the oppressed, and since he was a forceful character he was able to drive his ideas home. They happen to be my own ideas, and like many other small people I am thankful when a great person comes along and says for me what I can't say properly for myself. Voltaire speaks for the thousands and thousands of us who hate injustice and work for a better world.

What did he do? He wrote enormously: plays (now forgotten); short stories, and some of them are still read—especially that masterpiece, *Candide*. He was a journalist, and a pamphleteer, he dabbled in science and philosophy, he was a good popular historian, he compiled a dictionary, and he wrote hundreds of letters to people all over Europe. He had correspondents everywhere, and he was so witty, so up-to-date, so on-the-spot that kings and emperors were proud to get a letter from Voltaire and hurried to answer it with their own hand. He is not a great creative artist. But he is a great man with a powerful intellect and a warm heart, enlisted in the service of humanity. That is why I rank him with Shakespeare as a spiritual spokesman for Europe. Two hundred years before the Nazis came, he was the complete anti-Nazi.

I am so fond of him that I should like to add he had a perfect character. Alas, he hadn't! He was a bundle of contradictions and nerves. Although he loved truth he often lied. Although he loved humanity he was often malicious. Though generous he was a money-maker. He was a born tease. He had no dignity. And he was no beauty to look at either—a gibbering monkey of a man, very small, very thin, with a long sharp nose, a bad complexion and beady black eyes. He overdressed, as little people sometimes do, and his wig was so large that it seemed to extinguish him.

That is the Frenchman who sets out for Berlin on 25 June 1750; the German whom he is about to visit is Frederick the Great, King of Prussia.

Frederick is one of the founders of modern Germany, and Hitler has made a careful study of him. He plunged Europe into wars to advance his ambitions. He believed in force and fraud and cruelty, and in doing everything himself. He had a genius for organizing, he preferred to employ inferior men, and he despised the human race. That is the dividing line between him and Voltaire. Voltaire believed in humanity. Frederick did not. "You don't know this damned race of men," he once exclaimed. "You don't know them. I do." He was a cynic, and having had a very unhappy childhood he felt till the end of his life that he had not been properly appreciated; and we know how dangerous such men can be, and what miseries they can bring upon themselves and others.

But there was another side to Frederick. He was a cultivated, sensitive gentleman. He was a good musician, he had read widely, and he had made a careful study of French. He even composed a number of French poems—they are not good, still they serve to show that to him German wasn't everything. He was in this way, more civilized than Hitler. There was no Nordic-purity nonsense about him. He did not think that Germany was destined to rule the world: he knew that the world is a very complicated place, and that we have to live and let live in it; he even believed in freedom of speech. "People can say what they like as long as I do what I like" was the way he put it. One day, as he went through Berlin he saw a caricature of himself on a wall, and all he said was: "Oh—hang it down lower so that it can be seen better."

The visit began in a whirl of compliments. Voltaire called Frederick "The Solomon of the North", Frederick declared that of all his victorious titles the most precious was Possessor of Voltaire. He made his guest a court official, housed him royally, gave him a handsome salary, and promised an extra salary to his niece, Madame Denis, if she would care to keep house for him. (We shall hear more of poor Madame Denis in a minute.) Witty conversation, philosophic discussion, delicious food— Frederick liked good food, though he was careful to get it cheap. Everything seemed perfect—but! Not long after his arrival, Voltaire wrote a letter to a friend in France in which the ominous little word "But" keeps occurring.

"The supper parties are delicious. The King is the life of the company. But. I have operas and comedies, reviews and concerts, my studies and books. But, but. Berlin is fine, the princesses charming, the maids of honour handsome. But." We can interpret this But. It is the instinctive protest of the free man who finds himself in the power of a tyrant. Voltaire, for all his faults, was a free man. Frederick had charm and intelligence. But—he was a tyrant.

The visit went wrong shortly. Voltaire did several tiresome things. He got mixed up in a shady financial transaction, he quarrelled with another Frenchman who was in the King's service, he drank too much chocolate, and when the King rationed him he revenged himself by taking the wax candles out of the candlesticks and selling them. All very undignified. And—worst of all—he laughed at the King's French poems. Frederick, like Hitler, fancied himself as an artist, and he had often employed his guest to polish his verses up. Now he was told that the tiresome little monkey was poking fun at him and quoting him all over the place—a serious matter this, for some of the poems were imprudent, and intended for private circulation only. The Solomon of the North was vexed. He thought: "No doubt my visitor is a genius, but he is making more trouble than he's worth, and he's disloyal." And Voltaire thought: "No doubt my host is a mighty monarch, but I would rather worship him from a distance." He left Berlin, after a stay of two years, which had gradually become more and more uncomfortable for both parties.

But that is not the end. The real bust-up was yet to come. It occurred at Frankfurt, where Voltaire was waiting for Madame Denis to join him. Frankfurt did not belong to the King of Prussia. He had no legal authority there at all, but he had his "Gestapo" and he worked through them to interfere with personal liberty. He discovered that Voltaire had taken away from Berlin (it seems by accident) a copy of the wretched French poems, flew into a passion and ordered Voltaire's luggage to be searched. As always, he employed second-rate people and they went too far. They not only searched Voltaire's luggage but they imprisoned him and bullied him night and day in the hope of extracting information which would please their royal master. It is an incredible affair, a real foretaste of Nazi methods. Voltaire tried to escape; he was stopped at the gates of Frankfurt and dragged back, and Madame Denis, who now arrived to join her uncle, was also arrested and ill-treated. Madame Denis was a stout, emotional lady, with some pretensions as an actress. She was not one to suffer in silence, and she soon made Europe ring with her protests. Voltaire's health broke down and he feigned to be more ill than he really was: he ran from his tormentors into an inner room and gasped, "Will you not even allow me to be sick?" His secretary rushed up to assist him, and Voltaire, while making all the motions of vomiting, whispered in his ear, "I am pretending! I am pretending!" He loved fooling people; he could be mischievous even in his misery, and this is to me an endearing trait.

Frederick saw things had gone too far. Voltaire and his niece were released, and in later years the two great men corresponded almost as enthusiastically as before. But they were careful not to meet, and Voltaire at all events had learned a lesson. Berlin had taught him that if a man believes in liberty and variety and tolerance and sympathy he cannot breathe the air of the totalitarian State. It all may seem nice upon the surface—but! The tyrant may be charming and intelligent—but! The machinery may work perfectly—but! Something is missing: the human spirit is missing. Voltaire kept faith with the human spirit. He fought its battle against German dictatorship two hundred years before our time.

[1941]

George Crabbe and
Peter Grimes

A lecture given at the
Aldeburgh Festival of 1948

Before I come to George Crabbe or to "Peter Grimes" the poem, or to *Peter Grimes* the opera, I must speak of Aldeburgh.

The situation of this place is curious. A slight rise of the ground —I'll call it a hill, though the word is too emphatic—projects from the fenlands of Suffolk towards the North Sea. On this hill stands the church, a spacious Gothic building with very broad aisles, so that it has inside rather the effect of a hall. At the foot of the hill lies the town—a couple of long streets against which the sea is making an implacable advance. There used to be as many as five streets—three of them have disappeared beneath the shallow but violent waters, the house where Crabbe was born is gone, the street that has been named after him is menaced, the Elizabethan Moot Hall, which used to be in the centre of the place, now stands on a desolate beach. During the past twelve months the attack has been frightening. I can remember a little shelter erected for visitors on the shingle. Last autumn it was at the edge of a cliff, so that fishermen at the high tide actually sat in it to fish. This spring it has vanished, and the waters actually broke into the High Street—huge glassy waves coming in regularly and quietly, and each exploding when it hit the shore with the sound of a gun. This sort of attack went on a hundred and fifty years ago, when Crabbe was alive, but the zone of operation lay further out. Today only the hill is safe. Only at the church, where he preached, and where his parents lie buried, is there security and peace.

North and south of the hill lie marshes. The marshland to the north requires no comment, but that to the south is peculiar, and I had it in mind when I called the situation of Aldeburgh "curious". It is intersected by the river Alde, which flows due east—but when it is within fifty yards of the sea it turns due south, and does not reach the sea for twelve miles, being divided from it by a narrow ridge of shingle. Here again the waves are

166

attacking, and are trying to break through the barrier that keeps them from the river. If they succeed—and they have had some success—Aldeburgh will be menaced on its flank, and the valuable town grazing-lands will disappear into the slime of the estuary.

It is with this estuary of the Alde that we are mainly concerned today. It is here, and not on the open sea or the sea-front, that the action of the poem of "Peter Grimes" takes place. There used to be a little port on the estuary, Slaughden Quay. It was important in Crabbe's day, and was well defined even in my own earlier visits to the district. It is now battered and derelict, and the sea may wash across into it at the next great storm. Here Crabbe worked as a boy, rolling casks of butter about, and much he hated it. Hence Peter Grimes set out to fish. The prospect from Slaughden, despite desolation and menace, is romantic. At low tide the great mud flats stretch. At high tide the whole area is a swirl of many-coloured waters. At all times there are birds and low woodlands on the further bank, and, to the north, Aldeburgh sheltering among a few trees, and still just managing to dominate her fate.

I wanted to evoke these sombre and touching scenes as best I could, in order to give a local habitation and a name to what follows. Crabbe without Aldeburgh, Peter Grimes without the estuary of the Alde, would lose their savour and tang. Now for my story, and the first point I have to make is that Crabbe disliked his native town. Born here in 1754, he grew to manhood in straitened circumstances. He was afraid of his odd rough father who made him roll the casks about; then he was apprenticed to an apothecary; he hated that too, he couldn't even handle a boat properly, he was no use at all. One grim day in the winter of 1779, he walked to the bleak and cheerless Marsh Hill, gazed at a muddy stretch of water called the Leech Pond, and decided to clear out. Leaving "these shores where guilt and famine reign", he set out to seek his fortune in London as a poet. He nearly died of starvation first, and he was rescued not by his fellow townsmen, but by the generosity and insight of Edmund Burke. Burke recognized his genius and had faith in his integrity. From that moment his fortunes were assured; he abandoned medicine and turned to the Church for his profession, took orders, and returned to Aldeburgh three years later in the unexpected role of a triumphant curate.

Again he was unhappy, and no wonder. For he had not concealed his opinions on his home-town, and had indeed described it to Lord Shelburne as a venal little borough in Suffolk. He knew what he thought of his parishioners, and they, for their part, regarded him as an ill-tempered intellectual who, having failed to heal men's bodies, proposed to interfere with their souls. The emotions are recorded with which he mounted the pulpit of Aldeburgh church for the first time. "I had been unkindly received in the place—I saw unfriendly countenances about me, and, I am sorry to say, I had too much indignation—though mingled, I hope, with better feelings—to care what they thought of me or my sermon." The tension only lasted a few months. He got transferred. He was appointed domestic chaplain to the Duke of Rutland, and moved away inland into Leicestershire, where he was happy or anyhow cosy. But his distaste for his native town had been confirmed. Everything seemed to incommode him there. Even his hopes of discovering a new species of trefoil on the beach were dashed. "If I can once more shake off my complaints," he writes, "and gain a little life and spirit, I verily believe that I shall publish an account of my plant." But Sir Joseph Banks reported that the trefoil had been catalogued already. And when, towards the end of his life, he indulged in a visit of sentimentality what were the results?

> Beccles is the home of past years, and I could not walk through the streets as a stranger. It is not so at Aldborough: there a sadness mixes with all I see or hear; not a man is living whom I knew in my early portion of life; my contemporaries are gone, and their successors are unknown to me and I to them.

Beccles, Leicestershire, Wiltshire—anywhere else. It is rare to discover in his writings a reference to his native town that is neither melancholy nor satirical.

Crabbe's antipathy to his birthplace was to play an essential part in the creation of "Peter Grimes". It was not a straightforward antipathy. It was connected with a profound attraction. He might leave Aldeburgh with his body, but he never emigrated spiritually; here on the plane of creation was his home, and he could not have found a better one. This Borough made him a poet, through it he understood Suffolk, and through East Anglia he approached England. He remains here, however far he seems to travel, whatever he says to the contrary. His best work describes the place directly—*The Village, The Parish Register, The Borough*—and its atmosphere follows him when he attempts other themes.

The few dull flowers that o'er the place are spread
Partake the nature of their fenny bed;
Here on its wiry stem, in rigid bloom,
Grows the salt lavender that lacks perfume;
Here the dwarf sallows creep, the septfoil harsh,
And the soft slimy mallow of the marsh;
Low on the ear the distant billows sound,
And just in view appears their stony bound;
No hedge nor tree conceals the glowing sun. . . .

Dull, harsh, stony, wiry, soft, slimy—what disobliging epithets, and yet he is in love with the scene. And the love becomes explicit in a prose footnote which he appends to the passage.

Such is the vegetation of the fen when it is at a small distance from the ocean; and in this case there arise from it effluvia strong and peculiar, half-saline, half-putrid, which would be considered by most people as offensive, and by some as dangerous; but there are others to whom singularity of taste or association of ideas has rendered it agreeable and pleasant.

The sights and the sounds are not beautiful, the smells are putrid, yet through the singularity of his taste and the associations they bring to him he loves them and cannot help loving them. For he had the great good luck to belong to a particular part of England, and to belong to it all his life.

This attraction for the Aldeburgh district, combined with that strong repulsion from it, is characteristic of Crabbe's uncomfortable mind. Outwardly he did well for himself, married money and ended up as a west-country pluralist. Inwardly he remained uneasy, and out of that uneasiness came his most powerful poems. It is natural to remember Wordsworth in connection with him. They were contemporaries, and they had this in common, that they were regional and that their earliest impressions were the most durable. But there the resemblance between them ends. Wordsworth—his superior genius apart—had a power of harmonizing his experiences which was denied to Crabbe. He could encircle them with the sky, he could overawe them with tremendous mountains. Crabbe remains down amongst them on the flat, amongst pebbles and weeds and mud and driftwood, and within earshot of a sea which is no divine ocean. Thus based, he is capable of considerable achievements, and the contradictory impulses possessing him generated "Peter Grimes".

We know how this sombre masterpiece originated. When Crabbe was trying to be a doctor he came across an old fisherman who had had a succession of apprentices from London and a sum of money with each. The apprentices tended to disappear, and the fisherman was warned he would be charged with murder next time. That is the meagre material upon which a poet's imagination worked. According to Edward Fitzgerald—who was a persistent student of Crabbe—the fisherman's name was Tom Brown. Anyhow, he is transformed into Peter Grimes.

The poem occurs in the series of *The Borough*, which was written for the most part away from Aldeburgh, and finished there in 1809. As a narrative, it is one of the best of the series, and it is prefaced by quotations from *Macbeth* and *Richard III* which fix the emotional atmosphere and warn us that the murdered apprentices will live again. It opens with a father-motive; like Crabbe himself, Peter Grimes hates his own father —a pious old fisherman who makes him go to church—and breaks away from him abusively, on one occasion striking him on the head and felling him. Murder is not done, but the wish to murder has been born.

> The father groan'd—"If thou art old" said he,
> "And hast a son—thou wilt remember me."

Peter was indeed to beget sons, though not in the flesh. For the present he gets drunk, and when his father passes away indulges in maudlin grief. It is a prelude to the main tragedy.

Freed from control, the young fisherman proposes to enjoy life—"the life itself" he has called it exultantly—and gambles and drinks. But money is required for such joys, so he develops into a poacher and trespasser, a rustic Ishmael. Then come the sadistic lines:

> But no success could please his cruel soul,
> He wish'd for one to trouble and control;
> He wanted some obedient boy to stand
> And bear the blow of his outrageous hand;
> And hoped to find in some propitious hour
> A feeling creature subject to his power,

and the first of the apprentices arrives, a product of the eighteenth-century workhouse system. Everyone knows he is being mis-handled and starved, no one protects him,

> and some, on hearing cries,
> Said calmly, "Grimes is at his exercise"—

a phrase which is effectively introduced into *Peter Grimes* the opera.

> Thus lived the lad in hunger, peril, pain,
> His tears despised, his supplications vain:
> Compell'd by fear to lie, by need to steal,
> His bed uneasy and unbless'd his meal,
> For three sad years the boy his tortures bore,
> And then his pains and trials were no more.

The second apprentice follows, also with premium, and he too dies. Peter's explanation is that he was playing on the main mast at night, fell into the well where the catch was kept, and hit his head. The jury exonerate him. The third apprentice is a delicate well-mannered child, who rouses the townsfolk to pity and charity and whom Peter dares not beat too hard. He disappears during a voyage at sea. Peter had his fish and wanted to sell it in the London market. They encountered a storm, the boat leaked, the boy fell ill, and before Peter could make harbour both the fish and the boy had died. Such anyhow was Peter's account. But

> The pitying women raised a clamour round,
> And weeping said, "Thou hast thy 'prentice drown'd."

The mayor forbade him to hire any more apprentices (as in the opening of the opera) and none of his neighbours would help him, so henceforward he carried on his trade alone, and melancholy invaded him.

Now begin the depths and, I would add, the flats of the poem —using "flat" in no derogatory sense, but to indicate the glassy or muddy surface upon which the action now proceeds and through which at any moment something unexpected may emerge. Nothing is more remarkable, in the best work of Crabbe, than the absence of elevation. As a preacher, he may lift up his eyes to the hills. As a poet, he was fascinated by

> The bounding marsh-bank and the blighted tree;
> The water only, when the tides were high,
> When low, the mud half-cover'd and half-dry;
> The sun-burnt tar that blisters on the planks,
> And bank-side stakes in their uneven ranks;
> Heaps of entangled weeds that slowly float
> As the tide rolls by the impeded boat.

That is what attracts him—flatness—and upon it the most tragic of his poems deploys. The idea of regeneration, so congenial to Wordsworth and the Lake District, does not appeal to this son of the estuary. Those who sin on the lines of Peter Grimes must sink and sink—incapable even of remorse, though not of fear, incapable of realizing the sun except as a blistering heat, and incapable of observing the stars.

> When tides were neap, and, in the sultry day,
> Through the tall bounding mud-banks made their way ...
> There anchoring, Peter chose from man to hide,
> There hang his head. ...
> Here dull and hopeless he'd lie down and trace
> How sidelong crabs had scrawl'd their crooked race;
> Or sadly listen to the tuneless cry
> Of fishing gull or clanging golden-eye. ...
> He nursed the feelings these dull scenes produce,
> And loved to stop beside the opening sluice. ...

The hanging of the head, the dullness, the nursing of dullness, the lying down motionless in a motionless boat, the dreary contemplation of nature in her trickling exhaustion, the slow downward-bending paralysis of the once active man—they present what the poet too had experienced and the clergyman had combated or ignored. They spring from the attraction and from the repulsion exercised on Crabbe by the surrounding scenery, from the dual feeling which I analysed earlier.

We must consider Crabbe's sensitiveness to dreams in a moment—we are not quite in the world of dreams yet. Peter is still sane and awake. The only sign of abnormality is that he avoids three particular places in the estuary of the Alde; when near them he rows away whistling until they are out of sight. It would seem that here and there the surface of the water is thinner than elsewhere, more liable to be broken from below. He becomes a solitary, seeks men and curses them, and they curse him and he retires to his boat. For a whole winter no one sees him. Next summer he is afloat as before, but no longer fishing. He is gazing, hypnotized by the three places in the stream. "Dost thou repent?" he is asked. The words have a crystallizing effect and shatter him. Quitting his boat, he goes raving mad, rushes over the countryside, and is caught and carried to the parish infirmary. Here, half nightmare, half vision, the story culminates. Grimes himself takes up the tale in the sedate eighteenth-century couplets and the formal diction which Crabbe could not and perhaps did not desire to forgo.

> "I'll tell you all," he said, "the very day
> When the old man first placed them in my way:

172

My father's spirit—he who always tried
To give me trouble, when he lived and died—
When he was gone, he could not be content
To see my days in painful labour spent,
But would appoint his meetings, and he made
Me watch at these, and so neglect my trade.

    "'Twas one hot noon, all silent, still, serene,
No living being had I lately seen;
I paddled up and down and dipp'd my net,
But (such his pleasure) I could nothing get . . .
And so I sat and look'd upon the stream,
How it ran on, and felt as in a dream:
But dream it was not; no!—I fix'd my eyes
On the mid stream and saw the spirits rise;
I saw my father on the water stand,
And hold a thin pale boy in either hand;
And there they glided ghastly on the top
Of the salt flood, and never touch'd a drop:
I would have struck them, but they knew th' intent,
And smiled upon the oar, and down they went.

    "Now, from that day, whenever I began
To dip my net, there stood the hard old man—
He and those boys: I humbled me and pray'd
They would be gone;—they heeded not, but stay'd:
Nor could I turn, nor would the boat go by,
But gazing on the spirits, there was I:
They bade me leap to death, but I was loth to die:
And every day, as sure as day arose,
Would these three spirits meet me ere the close;
To hear and mark them daily was my doom,
And 'Come,' they said, with weak, sad voices,
     'come.'
To row away with all my strength I try'd,
But there were they, hard by me in the tide,
The three unbodied forms—and 'Come,' still
     'come,' they cried. . . .

    "There were three places, where they ever rose,—
The whole long river has not such as those,—
Places accursed, where, if a man remain,
He'll see the things which strike him to the brain;
And there they made me on my paddle lean,
And look at them for hours;—accursed scene!
When they would glide to that smooth eddy-space,
Then bid me leap and join them in the place;

And at my groans each little villain sprite
Enjoy'd my pains and vanish'd in delight.

"In one fierce summer-day, when my poor brain
Was burning hot and cruel was my pain,
Then came this father-foe, and there he stood
With his two boys again upon the flood;
There was more mischief in their eyes, more glee
In their pale faces when they glared at me:
Still did they force me on the oar to rest,
And when they saw me fainting and oppress'd,
He, with his hand, the old man, scoop'd the flood,
And there came flame about him mix'd with blood;
He bade me stoop and look upon the place,
Then flung the hot-red liquor in my face;
Burning it blazed, and then I roar'd for pain,
I thought the demons would have turn'd my brain.

"Still there they stood, and forced me to behold
A place of horrors—they cannot be told—
Where the flood open'd, there I heard the shriek
Of tortured guilt—no earthly tongue can speak:
'All days alike! for ever!' did they say,
'And unremitted torments every day'—
Yes, so they said:"—But here he ceased and gazed
On all around, affrighten'd and amazed . . .
Then dropp'd exhausted, and appear'd at rest,
Till the strong foe the vital powers possess'd;
Then with an inward, broken voice he cried,
"Again they come," and mutter'd as he died.

Crabbe is explicit on the character of Peter Grimes, and
appends an interesting note. "The mind here exhibited is one
untouched by pity, unstung by remorse, and uncorrected by
shame." And he shrewdly observed that "no feeble vision, no
half-visible ghost, not the momentary glance of an unbodied
being, nor the half-audible voice of an invisible one, would be
created by the continual workings of distress on a mind so
depraved and flinty." Grimes is tough, hard and dull, and the
poet must be tough with him, tougher than Shakespeare had to
be with Macbeth, who possessed imagination. He must smash
him up physically with penury, disease and solitude, and then
place indubitable spectres in his path. Physical sufferings have
their effect on any nature:

and the harder that nature is, and the longer time required

upon it, so much the more strong and indelible is the impression. This is all the reason I am able to give why a man of feeling so dull should yet become insane, and why the visions of his distempered brain should be of so horrible a nature.

The poet sees his literary problem very clearly. A sensitive Grimes would mean a different poem. He must make him a lout, normally impervious to suffering, though once suffering starts it is likely to take a strange form.

Grimes in a normal state would be inarticulate. He can only address us effectively through nightmares, and skilful use is made, at the close, of that dream state with which Crabbe was himself too familiar for his own happiness. He recognized its value for his work. He once told Lady Scott, Sir Walter's wife, "I should have lost many a good hit, had I not set down, at once, things that occurred to me in my dreams," and he kept a lamp and writing-material by his bedside in order to record them before they were forgotten. Many of them were unpleasant. He suffered himself from a recurrent one, induced perhaps by opium. He would dream that he was teased by boys who were made of leather so that when he beat them they felt nothing. "The leather lads have been at me again," he would remark in fatigued tones at the rectory breakfast table. Dreams of all types occur in his work. "The World of Dreams" and "Sir Eustace Grey" are terrifying. There is a poignant one at the close of "The Parting Hour" where a desolate man dreams that his wife and children are with him in an enchanting tropical land. And there is a nightmare, rivalling Grimes's in terror and exceeding it in subtlety, where an imprisoned highwayman, condemned to death for murder, dreams that he is innocent and is walking in exquisite weather down to the sea with the girl he loves, and with his sister. The three young people pass through the lanes and over the sheep-walk, where "the lamb browses by the linnet's bed", cross the brook and behold

> The ocean smiling to the fervid sun—
> The waves that faintly fall and slowly run—
> The ship at distance and the boats at hand;
> And now they walk upon the sea-side sand,
> Counting the number and what kind they be,
> Ships softly sinking in the sleepy sea.

On it flows, with a gentleness and sensuousness unusual with Crabbe, in order that the awakening may be the more terrible. They admire

> those bright red pebbles that the sun
> Through the small waves so softly shines upon;
> And those live lucid jellies which the eye
> Delights to trace as they swim glitt'ring by;
> Pearl-shells and rubied star-fish they admire,
> And will arrange above the parlour-fire,—
> Tokens of bliss!—

Then the nightmare asserts itself, the surface is broken:

> "Oh! horrible! a wave
> Roars as it rises—save me, Edward! save!"
> She cries:—Alas! the watchman on his way
> Calls, and lets in—truth, terror, and the day!

This famous passage is more dramatic and more sensitive than anything in "Grimes". More human values are involved, so there is more to lose, the sudden reversal in fortune is only too typical of sleep, and the wave joins the horrors of imagination to those of fact. We are back in the prison which we had forgotten. Truth re-establishes itself, the more relentless for its withdrawal when the criminal walked with those he had loved and lost.

As for Peter Grimes. He has gone to Hell and there is no doubt about it. No possibility of mercy intervenes. A simple rough fisherman over whom some would have sentimentalized, he is none the less damned, the treacherous flatness of the estuary has opened at last. He will sink into the fire and the blood, the only torments he can appreciate. His father has brought him to disaster—that is his explanation, and the father-motive which preluded the tragedy has re-emerged. To push the motive too hard is to rupture the fabric of the poem and to turn it into a pathological tract, but stressed gently it helps our understanding. The interpretations of Freud miss the values of art as infallibly as do those of Marx. They cannot explain values to us, they cannot show us why a work of art is good or how it became good. But they have their subsidiary use: they can indicate the condition of the artist's mind while he was creating, and it is clear that while he was writing "Peter Grimes" Crabbe was obsessed by the notion of two generations of males being unkind to one another and vicariously punishing unkindness. It is the grandsire-grandson alliance against the tortured adult.

The other motive—also to be stressed cautiously—is the attraction-repulsion one. Peter tries to escape from certain places on the stream, but he cannot, he is always drifting back to them.

Crabbe is always drifting back in the spirit to Aldeburgh. The poet and his creation share the same inner tension, the same desire for what repels them. Such parallels can often be found between the experiences of a writer and the experiences of a character in his books, but the parallels must be drawn lightly by the critic, for the experiences have usually been transformed out of recognition and the moral climate changed. To say that Crabbe is Peter Grimes would make that prosperous clergyman indignant and would be false. To say that Crabbe and Grimes share certain psychological tensions might also make him indignant, but it would be true.

And now let us consider *Peter Grimes* the opera; or rather the libretto, for we shall not be much concerned with its music.

The circumstances of its creation are remarkable. The composer, Benjamin Britten, a Suffolk man, was away in the United States, and read there with feelings of nostalgia the poems of Crabbe. They recalled his own country to him, they inspired him, and commissioned by the American conductor Koussevitzky he wrote the opera. It has been accepted as a great work; it has become a national possession and been performed all over the world, and it is a work for which I myself have deep affection.

Now since it bears the same title as the poem people often assume that it is Crabbe set to music. This is not the case. The opera diverges widely from its original, and it is interesting to examine the changes which the composer and his librettist, Mr Montagu Slater, have thought fit to make. They had every right to make them. A composer is under no obligation to stick to his original; his duty is to be original himself. Sometimes he chooses to stick. Verdi's *Otello*, for instance, follows Shakespeare closely—the only addition being the credo introduced for Iago. Bizet's *Carmen*, on the other hand, diverges from Prosper Mérimée's story of the same name, and Donizetti's *Lucia di Lammermoor* owns only the mildest obligations to Sir Walter Scott.

The plot of *Peter Grimes* and the character of its hero are closely interwoven. The curtain rises on the trial of Peter for murdering an apprentice. The scene is the Moot Hall, and the date is 1830—about fifty years later than the presumable date for the action of the poem. Peter is let off with a warning, and we gather that he was innocent. Ellen Orford, the schoolmistress

—who is introduced, with much alteration, from another poem—believes in him, and he hopes to make good and marry her; he hates being an outcast. Then the scene changes to the beach and to that music of the workaday sea which always brings tears into my eyes, it is so lovely, the townsfolk gather, the pleasant time-serving rector (borrowed from another poem) passes, Auntie and her dubious if desirable nieces appear out of another poem at the entrance of the Boar. Peter cannot get help with his boat, people shun him, but he hears of a possible apprentice in the Ipswich workhouse, and Ellen goes off to fetch the boy. The weather turns to storm and the scene to the interior of the Boar. There, in a terrific moment, Peter bursts in on the riotous company. There is silence and he meditates aloud on the Great Bear, the Pleiades, the impossibility of deciphering fate upon the revolving sky. He is revealed as the exception, the poet. The uproar resumes, Ellen enters with the new apprentice, and Peter takes him "home" amongst cries of derision.

"Home" is an upturned boat on the edge of a cliff. Much has happened by the time we reach it—much gossip about Peter's brutality and some evidence of it. The ill-assorted pair enter—the boy terrified, Peter now irritable, now gentle, trying to make friends, dreaming of marriage with Ellen. The neighbours are heard approaching to look into the rumours of cruelty. Peter, enraged, hurries the boy off to their fishing, pushes him out through the cliff door, he slips, falls, and is killed. The next act is a manhunt; there is evidence of murder, voices shout through the fog. Peter realizes that all is up. He launches his boat, sails out into the darkness in it, and sinks it. The new day begins and with it the music of the workaday sea. Some-one sights a sinking boat, but it is too far off to be rescued or identified, and no one is interested, and all is as if nothing had ever been. The chorus gathers, the curtain falls slowly, the opera is over.

It amuses me to think what an opera on Peter Grimes would have been like if I had written it. I should certainly have starred the murdered apprentices. I should have introduced their ghosts in the last scene, rising out of the estuary, on either side of the vengeful graybeard, blood and fire would have been thrown in the tenor's face, Hell would have opened, and on a mixture of *Don Juan* and the *Freischütz* I should have lowered my final curtain. The applause that follows is for my inward ear only. For what in the actual opera have we? No ghosts, no father,

no murders, no crime on Peter's part except what is caused by
the far greater crimes committed against him by society. He is
the misunderstood Byronic hero. In a properly constituted
community he would be happy, but he is too far ahead of his
surroundings, and his fate is to drift out in his boat, a private
Viking, and to perish unnoticed while workaday life is resumed.
He is an interesting person, he is a bundle of musical possibilities,
but he is not the Peter Grimes of Crabbe.

You remember the words in which Crabbe describes his hero.
He is hard and dull, flinty, impervious to sensations, and it was
a problem to Crabbe to make such a character suffer. "The
mind here exhibited is one untouched by pity, unstung by
remorse, and uncorrected by shame." And he gazes downward.
Whereas Grimes in the opera is sensitive, touched by pity, stung
by remorse, and corrected by shame; he needs no apparitions to
remind him of his errors, and he lifts up his eyes to the stars. We
leave him with the knowledge that it is society who sinned, and
with compassion.

The community is to blame. That is one implication of the
opera, and Mr Montagu Slater in his Introduction suggests that
the implication is to be found in Crabbe himself and that the
poet-clergyman was ahead of his times. And the date of the
action is put forward into 1830, the year of revolution, and
extracted from the placid eighteenth century where it was
originally embedded. There is benefit in this operatically, but
it cannot be justified from Crabbe. Crabbe satirized society.
He did not criticize it. Doctrinally he was a Tory parson,
equally averse to idleness and to enthusiasm, and he ascribed
human miseries to human frailties and to fate. As his biographer
Huchon remarks, "he had nothing of the radical or rebel in him.
To make him a sort of early Cobbett is to take a strangely mistaken idea of his character and his ideas. . . . He remained
essentially bourgeois." The implication of a social problem combines with the changes in the action and the transformation of
Grimes's character to make the opera very different from the
poem. The first time I heard it, this worried me rather. I
knew the poem well, and I missed its horizontality, its mud.
I was puzzled at being asked by Grimes to lift up my eyes to the
stars. At the second hearing my difficulty disappeared, and I
accepted the opera as an independent masterpiece, with a life
of its own.

It is time to leave both the opera and the poem behind. I

would like in conclusion to go beyond them and revert to the obscure person who lived at Aldeburgh about two hundred years ago, and whose name was perhaps Tom Brown. He got apprentices from London, they kept disappearing, and he was warned. That is all we know. But he caught the attention of a young surgeon who afterwards specialized in poetry and turned him into Peter Grimes. Two centuries pass. A young musician out in America reads "Peter Grimes". It catches his attention, and inspires him to create an opera. Is that how works of art are born? Do they all depend on a Tom Brown? No, they depend on the creative imagination which will find a Tom Brown somewhere or other, and will accrete round him until he is transformed. So I do not suggest that Aldeburgh need raise a statue to this obscure and unattractive citizen. Still, the fact remains that he happens to be genesis in the whole affair. He is the first step in a series of creative events which has produced your Festival, and if he could ever see anything and if he can see anything now he is feeling surprised.

[1948]

Bishop Jebb's Book

One hundred and thirty-six years ago, John Jebb, who was afterwards Bishop of Limerick, Ardfert and Aghadoe, bought a folio-size notebook. He paid nine-and-ninepence for it to William Watson and Son, Booksellers, 7 Capel Street, Dublin, which was not dear, for it contains six quires of paper. And what paper! Paper manly yet seductive, paper which persuades the lagging and corrects the errant pen, sustains the heavy ink, retains the light, tempts even the twentieth century into calligraphy. In its depths there are two watermarks: one of Britannia, seated in a shield beneath a crown, the other of the date 1799 beneath intertwined initials. The reference must be to the union of England and Ireland, and when the Bishop bought the book he must have felt that that little problem at all events was solved. The book is bound in boards and strong quarter-calf, but the leather recently cracked, like much else in my time, and one of the covers is now loose. This would distress me, if there was anyone to whom I could hand on the book, as it has been handed down to me. But there is no one, and even if I were a clergyman with grandchildren there would be no one. Bequests are coming to their natural end, traditions are retiring to that insecure fortress, the museum. There is not time for the personal memory-sogged past, and there is not room for it either. If after my death—which interests me less than his interested the Bishop—the book should survive, the important thing in it will be the blank pages. Still delightful to write on, they may profit posterity.

The name of the Bishop of Limerick has resounded greatly in my family, but rather megaphonically, like the name of a station shouted out by too energetic a porter. One was so near it that one could not hear it. The bishop, the bishop, the blessed bishop, the bishop's concern, the bishop's regret, his just displeasure, his condescension, his escape from drowning at Rostrevor, his paralysis alleviated at Leamington, all boomed against each other and echoed internally. And when one got outside the family vault there was an even greater obstacle: universal silence.

No one had heard of the Blessed Bishop. Scholars would verify him, ecclesiastics recall him after anxious thought, but he seemed quite lost to general fame. Like a train which has been dispatched in a particular direction, he could be located in that direction and that only. That direction now seems to be me. I have inherited his book. Opening it, I read the initial entry. "Began this common-place-book at Cashel, Wednesday Novem^{er} 11, 1804" —in red ink. Signed "John Jebb" in black ink. And pencilled "Afterwards Bishop of Limerick" by my grandfather.

That was just about the time those two got to know one another. They were both young, strange as it seems—Jebb not thirty. Never averse to the great, he was hanging around the Archbishop of Cashel, and, never idle, he was composing a sermon for the Dublin Magdalen Asylum. But he put all aside when my grandfather, who was a student at Trinity, Dublin, called, and he spoke to him of the superiority of Euripides over Sophocles, of Spenser, Shakespeare, Milton, Dryden, Pope, all through the night. A friendship began, which only ended with his death, thirty years later. When he became bishop my grandfather became his chaplain, courier and trumpeter. When my grandfather wanted to marry, it was the bishop who conducted negotiations for him, just as it was the bride's sisters who conducted them for her. Notes flew between the ponderous parties and have been preserved; the milieu by this time is Clapham and the Clapham Sect. After enormous fuss and copious admonition, the marriage was approved. It was a happy one, and the bride had the additional joy of living under the bishop's roof and nursing him when he ailed. In his will he left them his silver shoe-buckles. So it is alleged. As a matter of fact, they got a little more, this book and others, for instance, but not much more. That made no difference to their devotion. My grandmother, who was the daughter of a banker, may have had her private thoughts, but she did not voice them, and my grandfather, who was absolutely unworldly and who became increasingly provincial, went on from height to height. He wrote his hero's life, he edited his sermons, he published his letters, he called his own first-born after him, and so strong was the force of his will that when he died in his turn the echoing name persisted for a while, and the bishop, the bishop, the blessed bishop could be heard even in the present century by those who held their ear to the ground.

The first two pages of the commonplace book are ruled for an index: a beautiful piece of work. Each letter of the alphabet has a section, and each section is subdivided into five, one for each vowel. When the bishop entered a thought, he underlined the first word in it, and referred appropriately in the index to its page. Thus Pa in the index has references to pages 6 and 12, where "Pastoral Care" and "Parnel's beautiful Hymn to Contentment" are discussed. Po 14 directs us to the Poor in Spirit. The index is beautiful rather than effective, and in continuing the book I have disdained it. He did not write in the book much, and has only filled up eighteen of its pages. His unworthy successor (as I must tediously term myself) has filled over a hundred pages, so perhaps it is my book. But two hundred pages remain virgin, so it is still nobody's. I know what my grandfather would think of my sacrilegious temerity. The sacred volume has passed unsullied from Cashel to Limerick, to Clapham, to quiet rectories in Kent and Essex, and here I am scribbling notes about Marx in it, or copying extracts from Madame de Sévigné. I don't know what the bishop himself would think: he is too far away; indeed I cannot imagine him taking any notice. The spiders' threads one throws backwards into the past seldom stick. As a rule, they encounter complete non-recognition, and return to one.

What do I think of him? Well, he had a beautiful handwriting, anyhow, when he took trouble, small and crystalline; some of his notes at the time of his chaplain's marriage are marvellous—one can scarcely see the piety for the penmanship. And when he hurt his right hand he learned to write almost as beautifully with his left. Also there is a portrait of him which I find sympathetic. It is a sketch by George Richmond, and shows his head sagging forward over a desk upon some papers: the forehead is large, the mouth and chin are planed away by foreshortening. But this is not much to go on, and eulogies add nothing. He was of good family and clever, a scholar and a gentleman, he was efficient at church business, he kept in touch with influential patrons in Dublin and London. If there is anything Irish in him, or of Ireland, it does not appear. Attended by his faithful satellite, he moves complacently through tragic skies.

But it is amusing to see how the book progresses. While not keeping up the index, I have followed the bishop in underlining the first word of every entry, and in ruling a line, clumsily of course, to the left of every page. His spirit also saves me from scandal: we both tend to be non-intimate on the subjects of letters and life, and to saddle Seneca or Ibsen with anything which we do not quite want to say. It would do his reputation

183

no harm if the whole collection was published, and mine no good. His last five entries are: Human Life, Platonists and Stoicks, Miracles, Philosophy, Miracles. My first five entries are: Commonplaces, Isolation, Resentment, Change of Plan, Moll Flanders. I will conclude by transcribing his entry "Journal or Diary":

The utility of keeping one has [been] dwelt upon by many persons remarkable for great attainments and piety. Dr Johnson said that a full and unreserved one would be a very good exercise, and would yield great satisfaction when the particulars were faded from remembrance. He began one himself twelve or fourteen times but never could persevere. The great thing to be recorded, he said, is the state of your own mind; and you should write down everything that you remember; for you cannot judge at first what is bad or good; and write immediately while the impression is fresh for it will not be the same a week afterwards. Pleasant for a man to review his own mind.

I should wish at no very distant day to begin a Journal. The great danger will be that I may be insensibly tempted to deal disingenuously with myself in it. If I could write an *honest* report of my own mind it would under God's blessing do me good. I date this that if I feel indisposed to put my present resolution in hand [?] I may be shamed into it.

Jany 25, 1806. J. J.

A Journal was duly started, but it has perished.

[1940]

Henry Thornton

On March the 31st and April the 1st an exhibition will be held at Clapham, where lived my great-grandfather, and in the school that has been named after him: the Henry Thornton School. The exhibition will be partly commercial and technical, but it will have an historical side, including a collection of prints of Old Clapham; Battersea Rise, my ancestor's home, will be included, and he and the life he stood for will be offered again to the public, it may be for the last time.

What sort of life was it? Let his friend and executor, Sir Robert Inglis, testify: "His piety was fervent, and yet sober; his liberality was magnificent and yet discriminating; his charity was large and yet not latitudinarian; his self-denial was rigorous yet unobtrusive." This is a very fair estimate. Like the man himself, it does not go too far. There is also extant a charming portrait of him by Hoppner, but this does not go too far either; calmness, moderation and restraint dominate in its well-ordered scheme. Mr Thornton's chin is firm without ferocity, his mouth ascetic without fanaticism, his forehead intelligent without fire, in his right hand is a parliamentary bill. The restless modern mind, skimming over all these solidities, finds nothing to laugh at, nothing to condemn, and nothing to die for, and becomes unsympathetic, partly through envy. Here is neither a sinner, a mystic nor an artist—types which the modern mind can comprehend, and in whose presence it does not feel rebuked. Here is only a successful banker, an extensive philanthropist, a devout Christian, an affectionate husband and a judicious father, a loyal friend, an upright citizen, an incorruptible M.P.:

> Nor place or pension e'er got he
> For self or for connection;
> We shall not tax the Treasury
> By Thornton's re-election.

Sound: but not exciting; not even inspiring.

He has two claims on the notice of posterity: a volume of *Family Prayers*, and an essay on Paper Credit.

The prayers were composed from time to time, to be read aloud to his own household at Battersea Rise. In the end, there were over sixty of them, one for each morning and evening in the month. With characteristic modesty, he never thought of publishing them, but they were copied by friends and circulated among other members of the Clapham Sect, and twenty years after his death Sir Robert Inglis gathered them into a volume. This had an enormous success. Between 1834 and 1854 it ran into thirty-one editions, and within living memory our family were still receiving royalties from its sales. The prayers are of the usual evangelical type. They consist of vague contrition, vague thankfulness, and somewhat precise instructions to God on the subject of His own attributes. They borrow their cadences from the Book of Common Prayer and from unimaginative recollections of the Bible, all the splendours and the strangenesses of sacred literature are absent, and it is difficult to understand why their smooth rhetoric was preferred when so much better was to hand, and why the use of them became in the mid-nineteenth century the distinctive sign of true Evangelism:

> O God, who hast commanded us in Thy word to call upon Thy name, and hast declared that Thou hearest and answerest the prayers of those who make their supplications unto Thee, we desire now to offer up our petitions, under a deep sense of our unworthiness, and of Thy manifold and great mercies.

This level is consistently maintained through all sixty prayers; the prose never rises, never falls. "Manifold and great mercies" indeed! What can the words have conveyed to the reader or to the family and the servants who listened to them from opposite ends of the great library at Battersea Rise? To us they mean nothing at all. We get something quite different out of them: no meaning, but an aroma, the aroma of a vanished society, the sense of well-to-do people on their knees, the solid chairs into which the elbows dig, the antimacassared backs against which the foreheads rest, the voice of the master of the house, confronting his Maker in a monotone, and, if the hour be morning, the great virgin breakfast table, clothed all in white like a bride. For three generations it was a problem to religious Englishmen whether the breakfast dishes should come in before prayers and so get cold, or should come in after, which meant a wait, and an

unpleasant sense of hanging in a void between two worlds. I do
not know which decision my great-grandfather took, but there is
a story that in later years his daughter Marianne read the same
passage out of the Bible again and again, because she was
paralysed by the sight of the cat eating the ham, and felt unable
to stop either the cat or herself.

Family prayers went out with the family. When the children
were limited and the servants went into factories and the death-
duties cut property to pieces, these daily gatherings of piety and
plenty came to a natural end. Little houses have been built today
upon the noble lawns of Battersea Rise, and upon the site of its
great library which William Pitt designed, and those little houses
listen to the religious service on the wireless, if they listen at all.
Distracted by earthly chores, they hear from Broadcasting House
the voice of an enlightened clergyman who tries to make religion
realistic and definite and to give spiritual tips; he vibrates like
a weathercock to international troubles, he grapples with daily
trivialities, he enhaloes the ticket-collectors, bus-conductors,
waitresses and L.C.C. ambulances whom we encounter during the
drab suburban day; he even glances at pet animals. A modern
St Francis, he believes in detail. The Henry Thornton prayers
avoid detail, they generalize, they are a discipline and an institution, their well-worn phrases, "manifold mercies" and the rest of
it, would interfere with the general effect if they bore too clear-
cut a meaning. The Clapham Sect listened, rose from its knees,
ate, and then made money—made as much as ever it could, and
then gave as much as it could away. The activity in either direction was immense. Thanks to the economic conditions of the
times, wealth rushed down these worthy people's throats from
morn to eve, and not being psychologists they thought it would
have no effect upon their souls if they purged themselves promptly.
The Devil is subtler than that. He, like Christ, understands the
deceitfulness of riches: the deceitfulness which many a bitter
example now brings to the light. Wealth always fattens the person who swallows it, no matter how promptly he purges, and it is
significant that in spite of his fabulous charities Henry Thornton
left all his nine children extremely well off, and that some of his
money has even descended to myself. Very little; the last trickle
of the golden stream before it expires in the sands of taxation.
Still, enough to remind me that there was an age when to get
rich and to be good were harmonious.

A similar hope is held by the Quakers, to whom the Clapham

Sect has sometimes been compared. They hold it with better reason, because they have what the Claphamites lacked: a touch of mysticism, a sense of the unseen, and a capacity for martyrdom. These impulses, whatever their objective value, do purge the soul, in a way which alms-giving and self-examination cannot; they do lift the participant into a region outside money, whereas charity only keeps man running to and fro, from his business to his deserving cause, and then back to his business. He relieves distress, which the miser doesn't, but he, too, is bound on the wheel. This indifference to the unseen seems to me the great defect in my great-grandfather's set, and the reason why they have not made a bigger name in history. It came out in everything— in the books they collected, in the letters my great-aunts wrote to one another, and in the comments which they made upon life, which are surprisingly dry for people so pious. Poetry, mystery, passion, ecstasy, music, don't count.

Henry Thornton's second claim on the notice of posterity is his treatise on Paper Credit. It has lately been re-edited, with an introduction by an eminent economist, Professor Hayek. Both his father and his brother were directors of the Bank of England, and he married the daughter of a wealthy Yorkshire merchant. Thanks to his training and to his ability, he became one of the leading bankers of his age, in close touch with the provincial banking system which was then springing up, and also in touch with developments in London and with questions of foreign exchange and foreign trade. His treatise, which he published in 1802, had a great effect at the time, and was to be praised by John Stuart Mill, but it was eclipsed by the work of Ricardo, and was almost forgotten by the end of the century. At the time of the War it was rediscovered by economists in America, and according to Professor Hayek it is important for students of the present situation; he speaks of Thornton's acumen, great intellectual power, and width of outlook, and states that the treatise extends far beyond the occasion which evoked it, and is a major contribution to the science of banking.

To the general public the theory of Paper Credit is as remote as Family Prayers, and I wonder with what emotion, if with any, they will see the name of my ancestor when they visit the Clapham exhibition. They will remember him, perhaps, as the man who helped Wilberforce to free the slaves—a great work, to be sure, and a work which now needs all doing over again. For the world has not progressed as Henry Thornton hoped. The evils in human nature, which he realized, and the evils in commercialism, which he could not realize, have combined to pull it down, and the religious remedies he proposed seem today formal and trifling. But they worked well enough in his own circle and on himself. His manuscript diary is in my possession, and I will transcribe from it the final sentence, which was written only a few months before his death in 1815, at the age of fifty-five:

I think if it should please God to gild the evening of the life of my most beloved wife with a few more rays of comfort, sustaining her delicate body and making our children more and more evidently pious, which would be one great joy to her soul, if He should also afford to me that measure of success in business which shall enable me to prepare a good and safe station for my successor in the Banking house in which I am concerned, and if He shall also keep me from falling into any new temptations and dangers, I may consider myself as highly favoured by Providence, for how few can I discover round me who have half my prosperity, or who can look with so little reason for apprehension on a numerous family of children.

[1939]

William Arnold

Oakfield, or Fellowship in the East is not a masterpiece, yet I read it with intense interest, for the reason that its author was Matthew Arnold's brother. Matthew Arnold is of all the Victorians most to my taste: a great poet, a civilized citizen, and a prophet who has managed to project himself into our present troubles, so that when we read him now he seems to be in the room. I took up this novel by his brother with a curiosity that has not been disappointed. It is a strange, quixotic, disillusioned work and it hands out no bouquets, either to Indians or to Englishmen working in India.

Their father, the famous headmaster, helped to start the present public-school system, and laid stress on character and on individual morality. He represented the middle-class conscience, and his children grew up convinced that life meant duty, and hopeful that Christianity meant truth. William Arnold was born in 1828; he was educated at Rugby and Oxford, spending his holidays in the Lakes where the Arnolds had a much-loved house, and he decided to serve humanity in India. Desire for adventure may have contributed, for he went to India as a soldier, as an ensign in the 58th Native Infantry. Then he changed over to the Civil Service. He became Assistant Commissioner to the Punjab, and finally Director of Education there in 1853. While still Assistant Commissioner, he published *Oakfield* under the pseudonym of "Punjabi". The novel was criticized as an anonymous attack on an honourable body of men (how well one knows the phrase!), so he issued a second edition under his own name. His hero is, like himself, educated at Oxford, has also a home in the Lakes, also joins the Indian Army in his twenties, and also switches over to the administration. William Arnold and Oakfield are indeed the same person.

The story makes depressing reading. Oakfield lands at Calcutta full of enthusiasm and the desire to serve, but he gets no pleasure out of India, except from the initial thrill of tropical scenery. He works hard at languages and "passes" in Hindustani and Persian, but gains no understanding of native life, which he regards with a sort of respectful despair. All the talk as to the magnificent work of civilizing Asia through British influence in India is humbug, he concludes; and it has grieved many generous hearts before now to find it so. Until the point of divergence between eastern and western mentality has been discovered, cooperation is impossible. And, though Christianity may be true, to preach it to India is to begin at the wrong end: physical improvement first, then intellectual, then spiritual; that seems the natural order of things. Oakfield is honourable, intelligent and critical—a typical Arnold combination—and he does not shrink from remarking, "The Manchester folks want cotton; and when cotton is wanted, England is ready to begin and consider its duty to India."

His immediate problem, however, is military life and social intercourse with his fellow officers. He is first stationed up the river at Hajeepoor in a bad regiment. The drinking and gambling, the rudeness to the natives, the general lack of propriety and decency keep him in his bungalow as much as possible, and when he does dine in the mess a brother officer sings an improper song and he walks out as a protest. This episode moved me to irreverent laughter, and I am not surprised that the young man was unpopular in his regiment. Nor is he surprised. He is perfectly willing to suffer for his priggishness, since it is part of the high and consistent standard maintained by him in consequence of his education and home life. He is then transferred to Meerut, to a regiment with better traditions, and he gives us a long description of his voyage with congenial companions up the river. The description ignores the river, Allahabad at the moment of the Magh Mela being dismissed with the briefest reference. What interests Oakfield and his fellow passengers is the state of the English Church, the Tractarian Movement at Oxford, the possibilities and the dangers of reform, the positions of Roman Catholicism and of Dissent. India is passed with a puzzled sigh, with a sense of ignorance and impotence. The new regiment is reached, and the most exciting part of the novel begins. For though the officers are gentlemanly and smart they too are affected by the general laxity of European morals in the East; they are shallow and worldly, they get into debt, and, for all their talk of honour, they are unchivalrous to women. Oakfield makes the acquaintance of a Civil Servant, Middleton, and of his sister, and the moment comes when Miss Middleton's name is mentioned too familiarly in the mess. He protests to the senior officer present, and obtains no satisfaction. He is then insulted by Miss Middleton's traducer, and he ought by the unwritten code of honour to challenge him to a duel. He refuses to do so, and when he is challenged he refuses to fight. He is brave enough to endure the charge of cowardice. All this part of the novel is elevated and fine; the writing remains flat, for William Arnold was not an artist. Finally Oakfield loses his temper, turns on his tormentors in an unconventional way and castigates one of them with a horse-whip. There is an appalling row, followed by a ponderous court-martial. Oakfield is acquitted, in view of the provocation he has received and of the illegality of duelling, but his position is no pleasanter in his new regiment than it had been in his old one after the improper song. He carries on with a high hand.

Then comes the Second Sikh War, and at the battle of Chillian-walla he rescues the regimental standard, which has been cap-tured, and rehabilitates himself. He carries on as before. The approval of people whom he does not approve means nothing to this stiff-necked young man. He resigns his commission and be-comes a magistrate, and he works on and on, longing to get home. We are occasionally given glimpses of his home, and the English Lakes gleam in the pages of the book with a radiance denied to the Ganges. Finally he is invalided to England, and there is a poignant passage where as he leaves Calcutta he passes a boatful of young men arriving, enthusiastic about their careers as he had once been about his. He returns to his family, dying—although he does not know it—and with long-drawn Victorian pathos the story closes. One day he inveighs against his official drudgery and cries:

> "Shall I again seek a more busy life, and going on patiently, taking a bushel of falsehood for a grain of truth, casting my bread upon the waters, resume my work in India? Oh!" he exclaimed suddenly. "I cannot do it."

He is told that he will not have to do it. His upright arid career is at an end. He will never have to see India again.

Even today, when conditions both in India and in England are so different, *Oakfield* is a disquieting book. It is so sincere, and it states so fearlessly truths which are unwelcome to the governors and to the governed. If it is priggish, it sticks to its guns; and if it is ineffective it is well aware of its limitations. The characters are longwinded and the action cumbrous. But it has the Arnold in-tegrity. It is the work of a man whose brother was a genius, and who was akin to that brother morally.

By a final touch of irony, the novel is even more autobiographical than its author supposed. It is prophetic as well as retrospective, for William Arnold was destined to fizzle out in much the same way as his hero. He wearied of his work in India; his wife died there; and, like Oakfield, he was invalided home; he too longed to see Westmorland and the Lakes, but, less fortunate here, he died as he was being carried off the boat at Gibraltar. He was only thirty-one. He passes out of history. But at the moment of his disappearance he is transfigured. Matthew Arnold takes him up and glorifies him. Two of his poems, the "Stanzas from Carnac" and "A Southern Night", are an elegy on his dead young brother, and should be read as an epilogue to *Oakfield*. "A Southern Night" is more than an elegy, for it faces up to the tragedy of the inhibited career. There had been no splendour for poor William Arnold. He and his wife—they are "spent ones of a work-day age", they are all too typical of our time, and it is strange, thinks the poet, that they should have been buried so romantically—she by the Himalayan heights, he by these Mediterranean waters.

> Strange irony of fate, alas,
>   Which, for two jaded English, saves,
> When from their dusty life they pass,
>   Such peaceful graves!
>
> In cities should we English lie,
>   Where cries are rising ever new,
> And men's incessant stream goes by—
>   We who pursue
>
> Our business with unslackening stride,
>   Traverse in troops, with care-fill'd breast,
> The soft Mediterranean side,
>   The Nile, the East,
>
> And see all sights from pole to pole,
>   And glance, and nod, and bustle by,
> And never once possess our soul
>   Before we die.
>
> Not by those hoary Indian hills,
>   Not by this gracious Midland sea
> Whose floor tonight sweet moonshine fills,
>   Should our graves be.

Thus is William Arnold glorified—he and Oakfield, whom he had made in his image—and the eternal freshness of poetry descends upon his punkah-swept life. There is certainly some beauty in the world—the poet knows it and connects the dead brother with that beauty:

> And what but gentleness untired,
>   And what but noble feeling warm,
> Wherever shown, howe'er inspired,
>   Is grace, is charm?
>
> What else is all these waters are,
>   What else is steep'd in lucid sheen,
> What else is bright, what else is fair,
>   What else serene?
>
> Mild o'er her grave, ye mountains, shine!
>   Gently by his, ye waters, glide!
> To that in you which is divine
>   They were allied.

[1944]

"Snow" Wedgwood

The interesting correspondence between Robert Browning and Julia Wedgwood features a broken friendship and provides yet another example of the leisurely misunderstandings in which the nineteenth century indulged. Our ancestors were well equipped for the game of epistolary cross-purposes. They had plenty of time, plenty of servants, and they nourished grievances, cherished remarks and entertained regrets with a lavishness which is impossible for their hustled descendants. They had ample opportunities for refining, expanding, correcting, and impairing personal relationships. We may feel, in our slapdash way, that they might have been happier if they had written less, but we must admit that they gave full marks to an important subject. "Love, to most of us, is quite as much the discipline, as the refreshment, of life," writes Miss Wedgwood, and Browning, though proner to paganism, is obliged to agree.

He and she got to know one another in 1864, shortly after Elizabeth Barrett's death. Browning was already famous; Julia ("Snow") Wedgwood was still young. She had an assured position as a member of a respectable, cautious, high-minded middle-class family which managed, somehow or other, to include unconventionality in its make-up; the unconventionality of the Wedgwood clan is notable and very English, and saved it from being stuffy. As the great-granddaughter of Josiah Wedgwood the potter, as the granddaughter of Sir James Mackintosh and the niece of Charles Darwin, she represented a sound intellectual tradition. Though diffuse, earnest and exacting, she was not a prig, and she and the great poet could correspond comfortably. Some of his letters to her are very good; in one of them he re-writes *Enoch Arden*, in another he re-creates the sufferings of Keats. There was mutual sympathy, they were happy, they were becoming intimate. Too intimate? Anyhow, she suddenly broke off the connection, and declined to see Mr Browning any more. She gives her reasons, with circumspection and delicacy, in a letter of which three versions exist, and she takes all the blame (if blame there is to be) upon herself. Browning is frightfully nice, as men often are immediately after a snub, but he feels a fool, and their correspondence dies.

Two years later (they thought it was three years, but it was actually two) they began to write to one another again, chiefly on the high topic of *The Ring and the Book*. Julia has hardened in the interval, she is no longer ecstatic, and, as a critic who will presently produce a work called *The Moral Ideal*, she deplores Mr Browning's preoccupation with Evil and chides him for it carefully. "You know," she writes, "you owe us an adequate translation of what your wife was to you." He replies rather irritably that he owes no such translation to anyone; she insists that he does, and that ends it. Mixed up with their literary and philosophic bout is their personal muddle—they rake up the past and try to understand it better. Just why had they broken? Had Miss Wedgwood heard a report of something which Browning had said or had not said about her, and what in either case was it? Why did Browning suppose she had written to him as she did write? They reached no conclusion except a respectful peevishness.

Mr Richard Curle, who edits this correspondence, provides an introduction which makes "Snow" much too portentous and bleak a female. She was not like that—at least she was not like that when I knew her in her later days. Her deafness made her formidable for strangers, but she was polite and cordial, extremely modest about her work, and decidedly gay. Her support of the Woman's Movement, like her contributions to the *Spectator* under Hutton, has of course been forgotten: the world hasn't the time. But she had fine qualities, of the heart as well as of the head, and they ought to be recorded; she could, for instance, make a close friendship outside her own class, and though it is easy enough to do this today, owing to the social break-up, it was not easy to do it in the nineteenth century, when the Victorian fabric was still intact, and drawing-rooms seemed drawing-rooms and housemaids housemaids for ever.

[1937]

William Barnes

It is surprising that William Barnes has not been more widely worshipped. Perhaps there was a touch of pride in his gentleness, which led him to conceal himself from notoriety beneath the veil of the Dorset dialect. The veil is slight: anyone can lift it after half an hour's reading. Yet it seems to have served his purpose, and to have confined him to the audience whom he loved. He should have been a popular poet, for he writes of matters which move everyone and in a way which everyone can understand. There is no mysticism in him beyond the trust that we shall, through the goodness of God, be reunited to the dead whom we have loved. There is no difficult or disturbing view of society, no crankiness, no harshness of diction or thought. He is truly, sweetly, affectionately, a yes-man, and considering how many worthless yes-men are being boosted today as national assets it is surprising that he should have been left alone, he a clergyman, he a school-master, he of the soil. Propaganda has passed him by. He has been left where he wished, to his own people, and to the few outsiders who have cared to lift the veil and win an easy and a rich reward. To read him is to enter a friendly cottage where a family party is in full swing. One misses many of the allusions, one is not connected with the party by blood, yet one has no sense of intrusion. The party, like all unsophisticated gatherings, welcomes the entire human race. And when, to the jokes and the chatter, there is added the scent of the roses at the casement, and the sighing of the wind down the lane, and the memory of the past loveliness and kindness that are gone—and faith in the future loveliness and kindness that will return with the next generation—the effect is overwhelming. It is impossible to read a poem like "Woak Hill" without tears in one's eyes. Or rather, if one has not tears in one's eyes at the end of "Woak Hill" one has not read it. It is impossible to praise the author of "Uncle an' Aunt" in the balanced language of the study. "I shook hands with you in my heart," wrote an old Dorsetshire servant from her London basement-kitchen. Those are the words in which he has to be praised.

If, suspicious of so much amiability, we start pulling him to pieces, we discover that contrary to expectation he is a scholar. Like A. E. Housman, he knew exactly what he was doing in verse, and he knew what others had done. He sang Dorset because he had to, but not without premeditation; he was not the gifted rustic who smudged some of the effects in Burns. "Woak Hill" itself is composed in an elaborate Persian metre, the Pearl, and even those who discount its pathos are obliged to admire its dexterity. Other poems are written as Ghazels, others imitate or adapt recondite bardic metres, and all of them have their words in the right places. Light words—rose-petals of words, withered leaves, red dowst o' the ridges; but they fall into their places with the assurance of marble.

> Sweet Be'mi'ster, that bist a-bound
> By green an' woody hills all round,
> Wi' hedges, reachèn up between
> A thousan' vields o' zummer green,
> Where elems' lofty heads do drow
> Their sheädes vor haÿ-meäkers below,
> An' wild hedge-flow'rs do charm the souls
> O' maïdens in their evenèn strolls.

The technical skill of "wild hedge-flow'rs" is notable; the verse is heavily pulled up by the lightest element in its subject-matter. We pause, we put on the brake for flowers, and the scenes through which we have been sliding coalesce and are saved from too much smoothness. In the last line the natural speed of the verse is released. Forward we go again, after having been clamped by beauty. It is amazing that a writer who always puts the heart first can so keep his head. His genius worked not by a series of happy hits but by using the poetic intelligence, and it is the more amazing since his prose intelligence was provincial. He believed, for instance, that only Anglo-Saxon words should be employed in English, and he wrote a philological grammar in which vowels become "breath-sounds", and consonants "clippings". To believe this and yet to create touching poetry in which Anglo-Saxon words are mainly employed is a unique achievement.

His life—except for the loss of his beloved wife and for an occasional trouble over his school—was a very happy one. His temperament, though profound, was equable. He was rooted where he could grow, and was never assailed by lusts or nerve-storms. He could live through the Labourers' Revolt of 1830 without its shadows falling across his verse, and he could help his neighbour, Colonel Shrapnel, with some mathematical formulae. Good Colonel Shrapnel was working out a new type of explosive. When the railway was extended to Dorchester it vexed some people, but he and his pupils found some fine geological specimens in the chalk cuttings. Even the new stove so unwisely installed at St Peter's did not function fatally.

> The carbonic acid gas [writes his daughter] which rose from beneath the floor of the aisles had first the effect of making the little children drop down insensible, and one by one they were carried out. Next the more delicate young people succumbed, among whom were two or three of William Barnes's household. At length even the strong ones began to suffer, and went out in groups, leaving the rector preaching to empty benches, very much bewildered to know what was happening, for the heavy fumes had not yet reached him in the pulpit. The streets were full of groups of suffering people, helping to support others more suffering than themselves. One young woman fell into a swoon which lasted three hours....

All this he survived. The little trials of life, like its deeper sorrows, were accepted by him bravely, and with the belief that joy must prevail. For the joy beyond death he had the authority of his Church; for joy upon earth he could point to the recurring generations of village life:

> Vor daughters ha' mornèn when mothers ha' night,
> An' there's beauty alive when the feäirest is dead;
> As when woone sparklèn weäve do zink down vrom the
>   light,
> Another do come up an' catch it instead.

Yet the heart retains its preferences, and joy is compatible with personal loss:

> Zoo smile on, happy maïdens! but I shall noo mwore
> Zee the maïd I do miss under evenèn's dim sky;
> An' my heart is a-touch'd to see you out avore
> The doors, vor to chatty an' zee vo'k goo by.

Out of the goodness of his heart, his muse commends sweetness, modesty, innocent mirth, piety, domesticated manliness. He never destroys and seldom criticizes, and those who believe that no poetry can be great unless it is rebellious will condemn him as too Sunday-schoolish. But a muse can attend a Sunday school. She disobeys all rules. "There is no art without love," he wrote. That too is a rule, and therefore not universally true, but it is true of his own art. He gathered up all the happiness and beauty he could see around him, he invented more, he poured it out as a continuous offering upon the countryside, and when he was told that the offering would from its nature perish he replied: "To write in what some may deem a fast out-wearing speech-form, may seem as idle as the writing of one's name in snow of a spring day. I cannot help it. It is my mother tongue, and is to my mind the only true speech of the life that I draw."

In his old age, as he sat by the fire in the comfortable rectory at Came, he heard the garden gate clanging behind some friends who had just left him, perhaps for ever. The sound moved him to poetry, and he called his daughter and began to dictate "The Geäte a-vallèn to".

> In the zunsheen ov our zummers
>   Wi' the haÿ time now a-come
> How busy wer we out a-vield
>   Wi' vew a-left at hwome,
> When waggons rumbled out ov yard,
>   Red wheeled, wi' body blue,
> And back behind 'em loudly slamm'd
>   The geäte a-vallèn to.

When he had finished dictating he paused, and listened to the sounds clanging back through the centuries. "Observe that word 'geäte'," he said. "That is how King Alfred would have pronounced it, and how it was called in the *Saxon Chronicle*, which tells us of King Edward, who was slain at Corfe's geäte." He paused again and continued: "Ah! if the Court had not been moved to London, then the speech of King Alfred of which our Dorset is the remnant—would have been—the Court language of today."

William Barnes had not many regrets, but this was one of them.

[1939]

Three Stories by Tolstoy

Three short stories by Tolstoy—namely *The Cossacks*, *The Death of Ivan Ilyitch* and *The Three Hermits*—may help us towards an understanding of him.

They are very different, these stories. *The Cossacks* is an early work, full of adventure, it swings ahead, it's about war and love and mountains and ambushes, and it takes place at the foot of the Caucasus. *The Death of Ivan Ilyitch*, written later, is a story of illness and suffering indoors, where we never breathe the fresh air. *The Three Hermits* (also a late work) is a folk-tale about some Holy Men who were so stupid that they could not even learn the Lord's Prayer.

The three stories, although so different, have one thing in common. They all teach that simple people are best. That was Tolstoy's faith. It took various forms at various times of his life and led him into all sorts of contradictions—sometimes he believed in fighting, sometimes in non-violence and passive resistance, sometimes he was a Christian, sometimes he wasn't, was sometimes an ascetic, sometimes a voluptuary, but the idea that simple people are best underlies all his opinions from start to finish. He was himself far from simple—one of the most complex and difficult characters with whom the historian of literature has to deal, he was an aristocrat, an intellectual, a landowner who thought property wrong, he was ravaged with introspection and remorse. But that's his faith, simplicity.

In one of his earlier revolts against society he had retired to the Caucasus and joined the Russian Army there. At that time conditions were primitive, and savage tribes would descend from the mountains to raid the lowlands to the north. To check them the Russian Government subsidized the Cossacks, who were almost equally wild. The Cossacks lived in their own villages, but were a military organization who manned outposts and cooperated with the regular army. They were independent and charming, they loved violence and pleasure, and the women as well as the men went free. The life warmed Tolstoy's imagination, and is responsible for his first masterpiece. *The Cossacks* is loosely written and the plot is simple. A young Russian officer is stationed in a village and falls in love with a Cossack girl, Marianka. She is betrothed to a wild local youngster, who has made good by killing a tribesman. There are complications, and, just as the Russian thinks he has won the girl over, the young Cossack is desperately wounded by the tribesman's brother; Marianka turns away from the officer in fury and returns to her own people, whom she had been tempted to desert. Thus epitomized, the plot sounds thin and stagy, but it is vivified by the character-drawing, by the wealth of incident, and by the splendid descriptions of scenery. It's a story of youth, written by a young man.

Yes, this is the kind of man I am [says one of the Cossacks]. I am a hunter and there isn't another hunter in the regiment like me. I can find and show you every kind of animal and bird—what they are and where they are, I know all about them. And I have got dogs and two guns and nets and a mare and a falcon; got everything I want, thank God! You perhaps may become a real hunter but don't boast of it. I will show you everything. That's the kind of man I am! I will find the scent for you. I know the beast. I know where his lair is and where he goes to drink or lie down. I will make a shooting-hut and I will sit there all night and keep watch for you. What is the use of sitting at home? One only gets warm and gets drunk. And then the women come and make a row, and one's angry. Whereas there—you go out and you smooth down the reeds and you sit and watch as a brave young fellow should. You look up at the sky and see the stars: you look at them and guess the time. The wood stirs and you hear a little noise, and a boar comes out to roll in the mud. You hear how the young eagles cry and how the cocks or the geese in the village answer them—geese only till midnight of course. All this I know.

The Cossacks was published in 1863. It made a great sensation in Russia. He followed it with *War and Peace* and *Anna Karenina*, and by the time he wrote *The Death of Ivan Ilyitch* he was famous.

Ivan Ilyitch is a successful public servant who rises to become a judge. He is a decent fellow—he has had to pull strings to get on, of course, but everyone has to do that—if you're in the Civil Service yourself you realize that, don't you? He married, and for love. Romance doesn't last, of course, and by the time he and his wife are middle-aged they quarrel a good deal. That's not unusual—if you yourself are middle-aged you've experienced it perhaps. When he becomes a judge he takes a charming house at

St Petersburg. He is interested in the house, and supervises its decorating, climbs on a ladder to show a workman how to hang a curtain; he slips and in saving himself knocks his side against the corner of a picture frame. The bruised place aches a little, but the discomfort soon passes off, and that's nothing, is it? He went on with his worldly and respectable life, attended the courts, got in with the best people, gave parties. He had a terrible row with his wife over some cakes. She called him a fool because he had ordered too many and he threatened her with divorce. You know the sort of thing. Still, it passed. The only trouble was—he didn't feel quite well. There was a nasty taste in his mouth at times, his temper got worse, and there was an uncomfortable feeling—not exactly a pain—in his side, where he had banged it against the picture frame. He is persuaded to consult the doctor, who diagnoses—either a loose kidney or appendix trouble. He resumes his daily life—but the pain gets worse.

I won't inflict on you further details of this gruesome story— the most powerful Tolstoy ever wrote. The end is—agonizing death, death embittered by Ivan Ilyitch's knowledge that he is in everyone's way, and that they will be thankful when he is gone, and by the polite pretence around him that he is going to recover. In this bitterness there is one compensation. Among his servants is a young peasant called Gerasim, whose job it is to do the rough work in the house. Gerasim is strong, good-tempered and unsophisticated, and spends his time in doing things for other people without making any fuss. "We shall all die, so what's a little trouble?" says Gerasim. And Ivan Ilyitch discovers before the end that something is wrong with his life: unlike Gerasim he has lived only for himself—even when he was in love with his wife it was for the sake of his own pleasure, and that's what has been wrong. The illumination comes, and at the supreme moment he understands. "In the place of death there was light."

In *The Death of Ivan Ilyitch* Tolstoy criticizes modern civilization. In *The Three Hermits* he shows what civilization needs. A bishop, an excellent man, is on a voyage, and hears of an island where three hermits live, saving their souls. He determines to visit them, and finds them indeed holy and sincere, but so ignorant that they do not even know the Lord's Prayer. He teaches them, but they are so stupid that they have the greatest difficulty in learning it; they try again and again, one gets it right, another gets it wrong; however, the bishop is patient, and does not re-embark until the lesson is learned. He has the satisfaction of leaving the hermits in a row on the shore, saying the Lord's Prayer fairly accurately. By now it is night and the full moon has risen. The ship continues her course, and in the middle of the night something is seen following her rapidly over the sea. It is the three hermits. They have forgotten the Lord's Prayer, and they are running over the surface of the waves to ask the bishop to teach them again.

You will see now what I mean by saying Tolstoy believes in simple people. And he believed in a different sort of simplicity at various times in his life. When he was young, and himself a bit of a rip, he believed in the Cossacks, because they were spontaneous and loved animal violence and pleasure. In *The Death of Ivan Ilyitch* he has shifted his affection to the Russian peasant, Gerasim, who is placid and imperturbable and unselfish. And in *The Three Hermits* he recommends a third type—the saint who is an imbecile in the world's judgement, but walks on the water through the powers of the spirit. Tolstoy was inconsistent. Here are some of his inconsistencies, and they laid him open to attack. But he never wavered in his central faith: simplicity.

Do you yourself believe in simplicity as a cure for our present troubles? And, if so, how do you think simplicity can be worked in a world that has become industrialized? Tolstoy's outlook was agricultural: he never realized the implications of the machine.

[1942]

Edward Carpenter

Edward Carpenter was born at Brighton one hundred years ago. Few people recall him today, and those who do probably dismiss him as a crank. But he was a remarkable fellow, lovable, charming, energetic, courageous, possibly great, and he was once an inspiration in the world of labour. He deserves commemoration.

He came of respectable upper-middle-class parentage. He grew up in stodgy comfort, with no conception of the lives of the poor, and he set forth on what promised to be a typically Victorian career. He went to Cambridge, choosing Trinity Hall as his college because it was "so gentlemanly", read mathematics, rowed, became a Fellow and took orders. Here a little hitch occurred. He had had the religious doubts appropriate to his period, and after he was a clergyman they increased and he was physically ill, and felt that something deeper than his consciousness was pushing him out of the Church: "You've got to go, you've got to go," something said, and he went.

His experience, so far, was not unusual. Other thoughtful and decent young men would become curates in the hope of doing good and then have to be unfrocked, to the dismay of their families. Leslie Stephen is another example. What was unusual with Carpenter was that his difficulties were only partly theological. With him it was really a case of social maladjustment. He was not happy in the class into which he had been born. He wanted to live and work with the manual labourers. As soon as he got clear of the Church he realized this, settled in Sheffield, and that district, then far from gentility, became his home. Here were the people who suited him: artisans, unemployed, toughs, it is to them that his heart went out, and his heart was stronger than his head, although he had a good head. His action does not seem revolutionary today, for he retained his private income of five hundred a year throughout. But it was very revolutionary at the time; it astonished people, and he did not revolt from a sense of duty or in order to make a splash, but because he wanted to. He lived with working-class people, adopted many of their ways, worked hard physically, market-gardened, made and wore sandals, made (but did not wear) a Saxon tunic. He may not have got into another class, but he certainly discarded his own and gained happiness by doing so, and at the end of his life, when I came to know him, he rather mistrusted me because, like himself, I had had the disadvantage of a university education.

His heart made him a socialist. Would he be recognized as one today? It was the socialism of Shelley and Blake. He strove to destroy existing abuses such as landlordism and capitalism, and all he offered in their place was love. He was not interested in efficiency or organization, or party discipline, nor in industrialism, though he tried to be. He believed in Liberty, Fraternity and Equality—words now confined to platforms and perorations. He saw the New Jerusalem from afar, from the ignoble slough of his century, and there is no doubt that it does look more beautiful from a distance. When the armies of the downtrodden enter its gate, as thanks in part to his efforts they are doing today, the New Jerusalem becomes a more ordinary city, where the party leaders book the best rooms. Moreover, he was a mystic, and when he was asked how he combined his socialism with his mysticism he answered, in his gay, quaint way: "I like to hang out my red flag from the ground floor, and then go up above to see how it looks" —a striking answer, but not sound trade unionism. Except by people now elderly, Carpenter must be forgotten today in the labour movements he helped to found. He would not in the least mind. He was absolutely selfless.

This early ardour poured over into a famous volume of poems, *Towards Democracy* (1883). They are in the style and in the spirit of Walt Whitman and have been called Whitman and water—a gibe which amused their author. They expressed his faith, and his love for the individual and for the beauty of nature. These were the only two things he cared about, and he says so repeatedly, sometimes in an economic utterance, like *Civilisation, Its Cause and Cure*, sometimes in philosophic speculation, as in *The Art of Creation*, sometimes in aesthetic criticism (*Angels' Wings*), sometimes in works on sex (*Love's Coming-of-Age* and *The Intermediate Sex*), and best of all in his autobiography, *My Days and Dreams*, written at the end of his life. He demands from society the furtherance of these two things; all else is nonsense. His prose is good, and reveals his sensible and affectionate character. He may have worn sandals, refused to eat meat, supported women's rights before they were fashionable, and disbelieved in vivisection, but he was far, far from being a fool, and the reader who opens him patronizingly will encounter something challenging and tough.

Needless to say, Carpenter had no racial prejudice, and a visit to Ceylon, which he made at the invitation of a Tamil friend, completed his development, and gave him a metaphysical background to the personal emotions and the socialist hopes which he had developed in England. He sat at the feet of an Adept, and he described the elusive experience in "A Visit to a Gnani". As he had looked outside his own class for companionship, so he was obliged to look outside his own race for wisdom. This done, he reached equilibrium. He always gave me the feeling that he had dominated his material and knew where he was in the world and what he wanted. Whether one agreed with him, whether one thought him practical, became a minor question.

He died at Guildford, in 1929. He had worked for a socialism which should be non-industrial, unorganized and rooted in the soil. Society was far from such a socialism when he wrote, and it is further than ever from it today. But that is not the whole of his work.

[1944]

Webb and Webb

Beatrice Webb, who has just died, was one of the great English women of our age. But any homage to her must begin with a summary of her work, for that is what she herself would have wished. Personal gossip, personal relationships, successes, failures —all these she held to be irrelevant: what mattered in her view was work; have you worked? What is your work?

Her work was the investigation of society. She began in the eighties and nineties of the last century, by contributing to an "inquest" into the social conditions of London. This inquest was conducted by her cousin Charles Booth, took seventeen years to publish and ran into many volumes of letterpress and maps; its main aim was the analysis of poverty, particularly in the East End. She followed it by an independent study of the Cooperative Movement in Great Britain, from the seventeenth century until her own day. Then—after her marriage with Sidney Webb—she collaborated with him, and the first outcome of this was their Minority Report on the Poor Law. Both of them had sat on a Royal Commission to examine the problem of poverty; it had issued a report from which they dissented, and in their Minority Report they set in motion the socialist and labour campaign for the break-up of the existing Poor Law system. They then produced, amongst other books, the *History of Trade Unionism*, its sequel *Industrial Democracy*, a treatise in seven volumes on *English Local Government*, and finally, turning from England to Russia, they investigated conditions there and produced yet another monumental survey: *Soviet Communism*.

Such was her work. Who was she?

She was the daughter of a successful railway director, Richard Potter, and she grew up in the heart of Victorianism, amongst the amenities which the nineteenth century lavished upon a happy few. There were nine Miss Potters, and between the country houses and the town houses of their parents they had a very pleasant time. Not a frivolous time, for there was in this wealthy family a strong vein of puritanism and of intellectual seriousness. Herbert Spencer was a close friend, and through him the girl got to know George Eliot, Professor Huxley, G. H. Lewes, etc. It was a full, interesting life, based economically upon capitalism, politically on Liberalism, and philosophically upon individualism, and for the nine Miss Potters it was all very well. But what was going on outside this comfortable existence, these lofty and satisfactory thoughts? Beatrice began to wonder. She knew that "the poor" existed, and she read in the reports of company directors such phrases as "water plentiful and labour docile". But she wanted to know more.

Although her family was prosperous, it had the advantage of humble connections, who had not risen in the world and were still cotton-operators in Lancashire. She got into touch with them, through her old nurse, and made their acquaintance, at first under an assumed name. She liked them, they her, and it is worth noting that she, who was by temperament institutional and bureaucratic, first contacted her subject-matter on the human side. Critics have complained that she was unsympathetic to the individual, and she herself avows that a million sick have always seemed to her more worthy of self-sacrificing devotion than a solitary sick child. She did not believe in a local and sentimental pity. Nor did she believe that poverty could be cured by charity. It could only be cured by altering the conditions in which the poor lived, conditions can't be altered until they are ascertained, and hence her belief in Commissions of Enquiry and note-taking, and questionnaires, and her ultimate conversion to socialism and state-control, and all that her parents detested. Later on when I met her—she was an elderly lady then and a very grand one—I was equally struck by the rigidity of her opinions and by the human charm with which those opinions were expressed. And, reading her early experiences in *My Apprenticeship*, I have come to understand how such a combination occurred.

Her conversion to socialism and to marriage occurred at the same time. About 1890 the firm of Webb and Webb, as they called it, was founded, and few unions have been so productive of private happiness and of public good. They worked as one person: to both of them, the great object in life was work, and the same type of work. When either of them voiced an opinion, they invariably used the word "we". "We think that . . .", "We cannot support the present tendency towards . . ." and so on. It was not a royal "we", or a conceited one. It was rather the well-considered pronouncement of the firm of Webb and Webb. I remember thinking when I visited them in their country home that if I could have confuted the pronouncement it would have been instantly withdrawn. All I could do was to babble, "Well I don't somehow feel like that myself." My remark was listened to, was dismissed, and the next pronouncement followed. I leant back in my deep armchair without any feeling that I had been snubbed. The atmosphere was authentic and noble. They were too serious to score. She sat on one side of the great hygienic fireplace, he on the other—she tall and graceful, he short and compact, and in front of the fire lay a third personage, the dog. The dog formed no part of any social survey and consequently had the Webbs in his power; whatever they instructed him to do he did the reverse. But the human problem lay completely under their control. Alternately they would rise, stand in front of the fire, and begin a sentence beginning "We". William Nicholson's portrait of them shows them thus; a splendid conversation-piece; there are the Webbs, and the fireplace and the dog, and strewn papers, and augustness radiating, and singleness of purpose and unity of faith.[1]

For lunch we had mutton, greens, potatoes, rice pudding—simplest of menus, but supreme in quality and superbly cooked; never have I eaten such mutton, greens, potatoes, rice. Then Sidney Webb took me for a walk. The dog decided to come too, and instantly vanished into a wood. "I cannot think why he always does this," said his master thoughtfully. We continued alone to the open country, through a tract appropriately devoid of birds, and here in the silence he uttered a sentence about himself and his wife: "Our age this year is 157," he said, adding: "our combined ages." When I recall that charming sentence to-day I think too of the closing words of her autobiography, *My Apprenticeship*. There she speaks of "Our Partnership: a working comradeship founded in a common faith and made perfect by marriage; perhaps the most exquisite, certainly the most enduring, of all the varieties of happiness". Soon after we returned from the walk the hired car came round to remove me. They escorted me to it, attentive and courteous to the last, and as soon as it started they started to go back to their work. That was the only time I saw the Webbs, and I could never have been intimate with them: only those who worked with them could be that, and my own schemes for improving society run upon different lines. But

[1] This picture is now in the London School of Economics.

it is a great honour to have met them, and a great enlargement of experience, and I want in particular to pay homage to her who passed away this month in her sleep at the individual age of eighty-five.

[1943]

A Book that Influenced Me

It was rather a little book, and that introduces my first point. One's impulse, on tackling the question of influence, is to search for a great book, and to assume that here is the force which has moulded one's outlook and character. Looking back upon my own half-century of reading, I have no doubt which my three great books have been: Dante's *Divine Comedy*, Gibbon's *Decline and Fall* and Tolstoy's *War and Peace*. All three are great both in quality and in bulk. Bulk is not to be despised. Combined with quality, it gives a long book a pull over a short one, and permits us to call it monumental. Here are three monuments. But they have not influenced me in the least, though I came across them all at an impressionable age. They impressed me by their massiveness and design, and made me feel small in the right way, and to make us feel small in the right way is a function of art; men can only make us feel small in the wrong way. But to realize the vastness of the universe, the limits of human knowledge, the even narrower limits of human power, to catch a passing glimpse of the medieval universe, or of the Roman Empire on its millennial way, or of Napoleon collapsing against the panorama of Russian daily life—that is not to be influenced. It is to be extended. Perhaps those three books were too monumental, and human beings are not much influenced by monuments. They gaze, say "Oh!" and pass on unchanged. They are more likely to be influenced by objects nearer their own size. Anyhow, that has been my own case.

The book in question is Samuel Butler's *Erewhon*, a work of genius, but with Dante, Gibbon and Tolstoy setting our standards not to be called great. It has been better described as "a serious book not written too seriously".

Published as far back as 1872, it is difficult to classify—partly a yarn, partly an account of Utopia, partly a satire on Victorian civilization. It opens with some superb descriptions of mountain scenery; this part is taken from Butler's New Zealand experiences. The hero is a bit of a scamp, and not so much a living character as a vehicle for the author's likes and dislikes, and for his mischievousness. He has left England under a cloud for a distant colony, with the intention of converting some lost tribe to Christianity at a handsome profit. He hears that beyond the mountain range there are terrible figures, and still more terrible sounds. He sets out, and presently discovers enormous and frightful statues, through whose hollow heads the wind moans. They are the guardians of Erewhon. Struggling past them, he enters the unknown country, and the fantasy proper begins. The descent on the further side beyond the statues is exquisitely related, and the scenery now suggests the Italian slopes of the Alps. He is politely imprisoned by the mountaineers until instructions as to his disposal can come up from the capital. But there are two hitches. One of them occurs when his watch is discovered on him. The other is with his jailer's daughter, Yram (Erewhonian for Mary). He and she get on well, and when he catches a cold he makes the most of it, in the hope of being cosseted by her. She flies into a fury.

By now he has learned the language, and is summoned to the capital. He is to be the guest of a Mr Nosnibor, and the account of Mr Nosnibor puzzles him. "He is," says his informant, "a delightful man . . . and has but lately recovered from embezzling a large sum of money under singularly distressing circumstances . . . you are sure to like him." What can this all mean? It's wrong to have a watch, wrong to catch a cold, but embezzlement is only a subject for sympathy. The reader is equally puzzled, and skilfully does Butler lead us into the heart of this topsy-turvy country, without explaining its fantasies too soon. Take the Musical Banks. Erewhon, it seems, has two banking systems, one of them like ours, the other is Musical Banking. Mr Nosnibor, as befits a dubious financier, goes constantly to the first sort of bank, but never attends the offices of the second, though he is ostensibly its ardent supporter. Mrs Nosnibor and her daughters go once a week. Each bank has its own coinage, the coins of the musical banks being highly esteemed, but of no commercial value, as the hero soon discovers when he tries to tip one of its officials with them. Just as in Swift we read for a bit about the Yahoos without realizing that he intends them for ourselves, so we read about the Musical Banks, and only gradually realize that they caricature the Church of England and its connections with capitalism. There was a great row over this chapter as soon as it was understood; the "*enfant terrible*", as he called himself, had indeed heaved a brick.

He also shocked people by reversing the positions of crime and illness. In Erewhon it is wicked to be ill—that is why Yram was angry when the hero had a cold. Embezzlement, on the other hand, is a disease. Mr Nosnibor is treated for it professionally and very severely. "Poor papa," says his charming daughter, "I really do not think he will steal any more." And as for possessing a watch—all machinery invented after a certain date has been destroyed by the Erewhonians, lest it breeds new machines, who may enslave men. And there are further brilliant inventions—for instance, the Colleges of Unreason, who teach a Hypothetical Language, never used outside their walls, and in whom we must reluctantly recognize the ancient universities of Oxford and Cambridge, and their schools of Latin and Greek. And there is the worship of the goddess Ydgrun (Mrs Grundy); the worship is mostly bad, yet it produces a few fine people, the high Ydgrunites. These people were conventional in the right way: they hadn't too many ideals, and they were always willing to drop a couple to oblige a friend. In the high Ydgrunites we come to what Butler thought desirable. Although a rebel, he was not a reformer. He believed in the conventions, provided they are observed humanely. Grace and graciousness, good temper, good looks, good health and good sense; tolerance, intelligence, and willingness to abandon any moral standard at a pinch. That is what he admired.

The book ends, as it began, in the atmosphere of adventure. The hero elopes with Miss Nosnibor in a balloon. The splendid descriptions of natural scenery are resumed, they fall into the sea and are rescued, and we leave him as Secretary of the Erewhon Evangelization Company in London, asking for subscriptions for the purpose of converting the country to Christianity with the aid of a small expeditionary force. "An uncalled-for joke?" If you think so, you have fallen into one of Butler's little traps. He wanted to make uncalled-for jokes. He wanted to write a serious book not too seriously.

Why did this book influence me? For one thing, I have the sort of mind which likes to be taken unawares. The frontal full-dress presentation of an opinion often repels me, but if it be insidiously slipped in sidewise I may receive it, and Butler is a master of the oblique. Then, what he had to say was congenial, and I lapped it up. It was the food for which I was waiting. And this brings me to my next point. I suggest that the only books that influence us are those for which we are ready, and which have gone a little further down our particular path than we have yet got ourselves. I suggest, furthermore, that when you feel that you could almost have written the book yourself—that's the moment when it's influencing you. You are not influenced when you say, "How marvellous! What a revelation! How monumental! Oh!" You are being extended. You are being influenced when you say, "I might have written that myself if I hadn't been so busy." I don't suppose that I could have written the *Divine Comedy* or the *Decline and Fall*. I don't even think I could have written the *Antigone* of Sophocles, though of all the great tragic utterances that comes closest to my heart, that is my central faith. But I do think (quite erroneously) that I could have turned out this little skit of *Erewhon* if the idea of it had occurred to me. Which is strong evidence that it has influenced me.

Erewhon also influenced me in its technique. I like that idea of fantasy, of muddling up the actual and the impossible until the reader isn't sure which is which, and I have sometimes tried to do it when writing myself. However, I mustn't start on technique. Let me rather get in an observation which was put to me the other day by a friend. What about the books which influence us negatively, which give us the food we don't want, or, maybe, are unfit for, and so help us to realize what we do want? I have amused myself by putting down four books which have influenced me negatively. They are books by great writers, and I have appreciated them. But they are not my sort of book. They are: the *Confessions* of St Augustine, Macchiavelli's *Prince*, Swift's *Gulliver*, and Carlyle on *Heroes and Hero Worship*. All these books have influenced me negatively, and impelled me away from them towards my natural food. I know that St Augustine's *Confessions* is a "good" book, and I want to be good. But not in St Augustine's way. I don't want the goodness which entails an asceticism close to cruelty. I prefer the goodness of William Blake. And Macchiavelli—he is clever—and unlike some of my compatriots I want to be clever. But not with Macchiavelli's cold, inhuman cleverness. I prefer the cleverness of Voltaire. And indignation—Swift's indignation in *Gulliver* is too savage for me; I prefer Butler's in *Erewhon*. And strength—yes, I want to be strong, but not with the strength of Carlyle's dictator heroes, who foreshadow Hitler. I prefer the strength of Antigone.

[1944]

Our Second Greatest Novel?

Most people agree that Tolstoy's *War and Peace* is the greatest novel that western civilization has produced. Which novel is the second greatest? I suggest Marcel Proust's *A la Recherche du Temps Perdu.*

Proust was the son of a doctor. He had some Jewish blood in him, and provides another example of the gifts which that wonderful race has given to the world. He was born in 1871, in a French country town which he has immortalized and imparadised as Combray. He went to Paris and entered literary society and smart society, and Paris also has he immortalized—as Dante immortalized the Inferno. He had bad health, and he has immortalized illness. Retiring more and more from the world, sleeping by day, shutting himself up in a room which was lined with cork, he worked and worked, and strove with the aid of memory to throw his sensations and experiences into a work of art. He succeeded. The enormous novel which resulted is not as warm-hearted or as heroic or as great as *War and Peace.* But it is superior as an artistic achievement; it is full of echoes, exquisite reminders, intelligent parallels, which delight the attentive reader, and at the end, and not until the end, he realizes that those echoes and parallels occur, as it were, inside a gigantic cathedral; that the book, which seemed as we read it so rambling, has an architectural unity and pre-ordained form.

The first volume came out in 1913. There are seven volumes in all—seven sub-novels, with the same characters occurring in them, and endless cross-references between them. Proust died before the entire work had been published. To the last moment he was dictating, struggling against a high fever, and refusing to take any nourishment except iced beer. What mattered to him was not life, which he had found unsatisfactory, but art, which alone makes any meaning out of life. On his last day, in November 1922, at three in the morning, he summoned his secretary and dictated a noble passage about the duty of a novelist to do his work as it ought to be done, basing it on laws of goodness, scrupulousness and sacrifice which seem to be derived from some other world. As a result of the effort of dictation, an abscess burst in his lung and he died. Proust was not a very attractive man, or a healthy one. But he possibly produced the second greatest European novel, and he raised that rather tiresome word "art" to an importance and a sublimity which we cannot neglect.

The story is told through a narrator or hero who more or less resembles Proust himself; who grows up with his mother and grandmother—the only characters displaying human integrity; who moves from Combray to the meretricious charm of Paris; who goes into aristocratic society and is disillusioned by it; who goes in for love and is still more disillusioned; who falls ill, and, prematurely aged, finds that his world has aged too yet is none the less fascinating as an object for observation. That is my first point. The second is this: what really matters in the book is not events but the remembering of events. Many tragic events occur and many funny ones, but they take their final shape in the meditations of the narrator. The novel is called not "Things Past", but the "Remembrance of Things Past". For all its realism, it has about it something of a daydream. It plays about with time. It reconsiders the same episode, the same characters, and reaches new results. It keeps turning the stuff of life about and looking through it from this direction and that.

The famous "little phrase" (*la petite phrase*) in the music of Vinteuil serves as an example. This "little phrase" becomes almost an actor, and an actor constantly appearing in a new part. We first hear the name of Vinteuil in hideous circumstances. The composer is dead—an obscure little country organist unknown to fame—and his daughter is defiling his memory. The horrible scene is to radiate in several directions—everything radiates in Proust. Much later, a violin sonata is being performed in Paris, and a little phrase from its slow movement catches the ear of Swann, and steals into his life. Swann is in love with a worthless creature, Odette, and it attends his love. The love affair goes wrong, like most affairs in Proust, the phrase is forgotten. Then it breaks out again when he is ravaged with jealousy, and now it attends his misery and past happiness at once, without losing its own divine character. Who wrote the violin sonata? On hearing it is by Vinteuil, Swann says: "H'm, I once knew a wretched little organist of that name. It couldn't be by him." But it is, and Vinteuil's daughter, who seemed so infamous, has piously transcribed her father's work and published it. Her nature is many-sided, like most natures in Proust.

That seems all. The "little phrase" crosses the book again, but as an echo. Then hundreds, indeed thousands of pages on, when Vinteuil has become a national glory and there is talk of raising a statue to him in the town where he has been so wretched and so obscure, another work of his is performed—a posthumous string sextet. The hero listens—he is in an unknown, rather terrible universe while a sinister dawn reddens the sea. Suddenly, for him and for the reader too, the "little phrase" of the sonata recurs—half-heard, changed, but giving complete orientation, so that he is back in the country of his childhood with the knowledge that it belongs to the unknown. It gives memory a shock, and these shocks and their emotional consequences are Proust's main concern.

So my first point was that the narrator or hero is more or less Proust himself, and my second point—a difficult one, for it takes us into his central problem—is that he is concerned not with events and people as Tolstoy is, but with memories of events and people, and that consequently his novel often has the quality of a daydream, in which the ordinary sequence of time gets interrupted and mixed up. My third point—a straightforward one—is the social scene. He gives a brilliant and malicious picture of the French aristocracy forty or fifty years ago. It was an aristocracy which had wealth and style, but no sense of responsibility, no connection with the land, and no faith in anything except its own superiority to the rest of mankind. Proust saw through it and bowed down to it. He was both a satirist and a snob. He gives, too, a picture, and a disagreeable one, of the bourgeoisie, who force themselves up through the social fabric as the story proceeds, and who are typified by the detestable Monsieur and Madame Verdurin. The working classes come in, as servants and parasites, and are not handled amiably either. The only people who are treated with respect are the hero's mother and grandmother, women incapable of worldliness and meanness, and the artists who, like Proust himself, strive to *understand* the disappointing scene and to give it afterwards a coherence and a beauty it never possesses at the time.

Point number four: Proust as a drawer of character. He is masterly. We live with his people, we see them develop, they behave incredibly, and later on we see why. When they contradict themselves they only become more real. It is an immense gallery of portraits, in which predominate the superb Duchess of Guermantes and the sinister yet touching Baron de Charlus. Even if people only appear for a few minutes, we know them, and hundreds of pages on we shall recognize them if they reappear. The characters are often falling in love with one another, and—here is point number five perhaps—I must allude to Proust's theory of love. It is a gloomy theory and I do not agree with it. He thought, to be brief, that the more deeply people fall in love, the more they distort one another, so that passion is a certain prelude to misunderstanding. He thought, too, that jealousy is inevitable, and that its arrival means the renewal of a love which might otherwise have mercifully died. Long tracts in the latter part of the work are devoted to the "hero's" affair with Albertine. They make depressing reading, and most people skip them.

It is important when tackling Proust to be patient and to be intelligent. He makes no concessions to stupidity. Some writers— and they are great writers—do make concessions. Dickens does, and even Tolstoy does. Proust does not. He expects a constant awareness, both from the mind and from the senses. He was an individualist, he was an invalid, he was a bit of a snob, he belonged to a society which was decadent, and he had no interest in social reform. How dare I suggest that such a creature produced the second best European novel? I dare, because I do not believe that this art business can be swept aside. No violence can destroy it, no sneering can belittle it. Based on an integrity in man's nature which lies deeper than moral integrity, it rises to heights of triumph which give us cause to hope. Proust was an artist and a tremendous one; he found in memory the means of interpreting and humanizing this chaotic world, and he has given the results in *Remembrance of Things Past*.

[1943]

Gide and George

Two modern writers of European reputation, the Frenchman André Gide and the German Stefan George, offer contrasted reactions to the present chaos. I will begin with Gide.

Gide is an old man now.[1] He has written a number of novels including *The Immoralist*, his most disquieting work, *The Caves of the Vatican*, expressing his pagan side, and *The Narrow Gate*, which expresses his Protestant pietistic side. He has also written criticisms and plays, and a fascinating and frank autobiography of his early life, he has kept journals, been active at conferences, helped to run the chief French literary magazine. And now he is an old man. And when his country collapsed three years ago he might naturally have done what some French writers actually did—that is to say, collaborated with Hitler or at all events with Vichy. He refused. Retiring to unoccupied France, he continued to express truths which he alone, owing to his prestige, was able to get into print. Instead of playing for safety, he used his high position to uphold still higher the torch of freedom. Then Hitler advanced again and occupied the south. Gide got away to Tunis, and when the Allied armies captured it this spring they found him there. He has honoured us as well as his own country by his conduct, and he has advanced the republic of letters.

Yet I do not want to present Gide as a hero. He would not wish it and he isn't the type. He is not a hero. He is a humanist. The humanist has four leading characteristics—curiosity, a free mind, belief in good taste, and belief in the human race—and all four are present in Gide. His curiosity—he is always inquiring, he's interested in society and its break-up, in his own character and other people's, in virtues and in vices too: in forgery as much as in the ecstasies of the saints: in self-denial and in self-indulgence. And secondly, he has a free mind. He is indifferent to authority, and he is willing to pay the penalty for independence. For example, he once went to the Congo, and he was so disgusted by economic imperialism and its exploitation of the

[1] He died in February 1951.

African Negro that he became a Communist, at some personal inconvenience. Later on he went to Russia, and what he saw of Communism there compelled him at even greater inconvenience to renounce it. I'm not saying either of these decisions is correct. I only want to point out that here's a man with a free mind, indifferent to authority, indifferent sometimes to logic, indifferent to everything except what he believes to be true. He has remained an individualist in an age which imposes discipline. His third characteristic is that he believes in good taste. Gide is a literary man, not a scientist, not a prophet, and his judgements tend to be aesthetic. He's subtle and elusive—sometimes annoyingly so—he sets great store by charm, he's more interested in harmony than in doctrine.

Fourth, he believes in humanity. He is not cynical about the human race. And consequently—for it is a consequence—he has no class prejudice and no colour prejudice. I remember so well the last time I met him: it was in an international congress of writers at Paris in the thirties, and he had to make a speech. A tall, willowy figure, he undulated on the platform above the vast audience, rather full of airs and graces and inclined to watch his own effects. Then he forgot himself and remembered the human race and made a magnificent oration. His thesis was that the individual will never develop his individuality until he forms part of a world society. As his thought soared, his style became fluid, and sentimentality passed into affection. He denied that humanity would cease to be interesting if it ceased to be miserable, and imagined a social state where happiness will be accessible to all, and where men, because they are happy, will be great. At that time the menace of Fascism was already darkening our doorways, and it seemed to us, as we listened to Gide, that here was a light which the darkness could not put out. It is not easy, in a few words, to give a picture of a very complicated individual; let me anyhow make it clear that he reacts to the European tragedy as a humanist, that the four characteristics of humanism are curiosity, a free mind, belief in good taste, and belief in the human race, and that he has been prepared to suffer for his belief; they have not been just for the study and the cloister; and consequently men honour him.

Now there are other reactions to the European tragedy besides humanism. Let us turn to Stefan George and see what he did in the face of the approaching darkness—George, a fine lyric poet, a sincere man of high ideals and of an iron will. He died exactly ten years ago, in 1933, after the establishment of Hitler's power. He was born in a very different Germany, in 1868. Well educated, and versed in European culture, he thought of his country as one among many, and owed a special debt, in his early poems, to France. By nature he was a recluse. He wrote for a small circle of friends and was accepted by them as their chief. Then he had an intense personal experience which exalted his poetry but did not improve his judgement, and as a result of that experience the circle of friends hardened into a cult, and George almost assumed the airs of a priest. Domineering and humourless, he trained his young disciples and began to send them out into the world. He taught them to despise the common man and to despise women, to prefer instinct to brains, and to believe in good birth, and in state organization. A friend of mine who attended the University of Heidelberg used to see these disciples of George in the streets, "almost dancing, tall, graceful and athletic, with their heads thrown back, as if they were trying to avoid the sight of common humanity". It seemed like the coming of a new aristocracy, and George himself was a natural aristocrat, just as Gide is a natural democrat. He was an exceptional person, highly gifted as a poet, a lofty idealist with something of a prophet's grandeur. He knew it, and he made the mistake of thinking that when a person is exceptional he ought to be a leader. The idea of leadership, so seductive and so pernicious both for the leaders and the led, invaded this fine artist. The swastika was stamped on the covers of his latest books, his poems spoke of a Führer and a New Reich, and he found a cure for the evils of his age not in humanism, like Gide, but in authority. That was his reaction to the approaching European tragedy: authoritarianism.

The Nazis were not slow to take him up. From their point of view he was one of them. The National Socialists, it has been well said, have a peculiar gift for adopting and defiling ideas that have been of real value in their time, and they did not spare Stefan George. They patronized him, and he had the misery of seeing his work exploited by cads—the greatest misery which a fastidious writer can undergo. He saw his ideals put into practice by Hitler, and it was more than he could stand. Doctor Goebbels wrote to him—no doubt with Hitler's approval—and offered him high honours as a poet in the gangster state. To his glory, he never answered the letter. Germany had become intolerable, and in 1933 he went away to Switzerland to die. That is his end— a sad end but a dignified one. The poet whom the Nazis claim as their own could not stand their foulness and preferred to die in exile.

Creative writers are always greater than the causes that they represent, and I have not interpreted either Gide or George in this brief summary of their respective attitudes. I have, for instance, conveyed nothing of the quality of their emotion or their style, nor is it possible to do so except by quotations. But they neatly illustrate two contrasted reactions in this age of misery: the humanist's reaction, and the authoritarian's.

[1943]

Gide's Death

I never knew Gide well, but we exchanged letters now and then, and I saw something of him in Paris at an international writers' conference in 1935. Like many others at that date, he was then hopeful of the Russian experiment, he was not scared by its economic and social heresies, and he had not foreseen its contempt for individual freedom or its regimentation of the intellect and of taste. He made a moving speech at the conference about the greatness of Man, who will become greater still when no men suffer from misery or want. He was the humanist unafraid.

He was also as slippery as a trout. He entertained myself and a friend at a restaurant, stood us a delightful dinner with promise of a still more delightful talk after it, and then—*il se sauva* when the coffee arrived, he saved himself, he was gone. André Malraux went with him. I still remember the disappearance of those two distinguished backs, and our mild disappointment. In what diverse directions were they finally to vanish! That, too, none of us then foresaw.

I saw Gide once more, after Paris. He did not see me. It was in a remote valley in the Crau, in Provence. He was leaning over a bridge with a friend, looking at a rushing turbid stream, silent, and looking upstream. It is thus that I most clearly see him. Distinguished as ever, he was also content. I realized more clearly how much he had got out of life, and had managed to transmit through his writings. Not life's greatness—greatness is a nineteenth-century perquisite, a Goethean job. But life's complexity, and the delight, the difficulty, the duty of registering that complexity and of conveying it. Unlike some others who have apprehended complexity, he was a hard worker. He wrote and wrote and travelled and wrote, and oh how he has helped us in consequence! He has taught thousands of people to mistrust façades, to call the bluff, to be brave without bounce and inconsistent without frivolity. He is the humanist of our age—not of other ages, but of this one.

His equipment contained much that was unusual and bewildering. He was what *The Times* obituary notice of him sagely termed "heterodox" (i.e. homosexual), he had in many ways a pagan outlook, yet he had also a puritanical and religious outlook, which was inherent in his upbringing and sometimes dominated him. He had also, and above all, a belief in discovering the truth and following it. This comes out in the fascinating exchange of letters between him and Paul Claudel. Claudel, an authoritative authoritarian, had much that Gide believed himself to lack—more genius, more influence, more money, more will-power, more everything—and he tried to impose his formidable personality upon his correspondent, and to convert him to his own strongly held views. He was a fisher of men. He cast his net. But the fish escaped. Wavering, yielding, tempted, flustered, Gide nevertheless slipped through the meshes and continued his undulating course upstream. *Il se sauva.* He saved himself instead of being saved, and left Paul Claudel planted on the bank.

Gide had not a great mind. But he had a free mind, and free minds are as rare as great, and even more valuable at the present moment. He has died at the age of eighty-one. No one could wish old people to live on in days like these, yet I wish he had found time to write me a promised letter on the subject of *Howards End.* Year after year I have heard through mutual friends that he was contemplating one. It would have been a precious and a provocative possession.

[1951]

Romain Rolland and the Hero

There died a couple of months ago a French writer who is of international importance. Whether he was a great writer is debatable, but he did address all humanity, not merely his own nation. Romain Rolland is not as celebrated today as he was a quarter of a century back, when he seemed to be of the first rank, and to have almost the stature of Tolstoy. There are two reasons for this decline in reputation. He did not fulfil his early promise as a novelist, the world did not fulfil his hopes; and he started out with passionate hopes. He became isolated, he was partly forgotten.

He was born in 1866. Although he came from the heart of France, and became a professor at Paris, he had strong Teutonic sympathies, which we must bear in mind if we are to understand him. He had an enormous admiration for German music, and for much German literature, and he cherished a rather Teutonic cult for the great man. With him, the cult was beneficent, for greatness, in his vision, meant not power over others, not dictatorship, but creation, exploration. All the same, his lifelong insistence on the Hero is not very French, and it has its distant parallel in the sinister cult which has produced Hitler. He combined hero-worship with belief in the people, and by "the people" he meant not the stodgy "common man" who is being so boosted by our administrators today, but the people as a fiery instinctive emotional force, the people who made the French Revolution. The "hero" and the "people" were his twin stars, and whenever they shine he sees his way through the uncongenial tangle of his century.

His most important work is the enormous novel *John Christopher*. The theme of it is the hero as musician. There are ten volumes, and I can remember our excitement at the beginning of the century when they were coming out. We were full of hopes then, easily held hopes, we did not know the severity of the problems which Fate was reserving for us, and the volumes were both civilized and inspiring, and how few books are both! They were intensely human, they had integrity, they possessed the culture of the past, yet they proclaimed that culture is not time-bound or class-bound, it is a living spirit to be carried on. "Have you read the latest *John Christopher?*" we were saying. "Has he got to Paris yet?" As the series proceeded, our excitement slackened. However, the author pushed his great achievement through, and was awarded the Nobel Prize for literature in 1916. Romain Rolland had entered the First World War.

He was shattered by it to an extent which we can scarcely comprehend. Today we are all of us tougher, and though we still cherish hopes they are protected by a very necessary crust of cynicism. We are no longer surprised. He—who had known what was best in Germany, and there was much good in that Germany—he, who was an inheritor of France, saw the two precious civilizations destroying each other, and the imperialism of Russia slinking up behind. While loyal to France, he became an internationalist, and a precursor of the League of Nations, and addressed to the youth of his country a pamphlet entitled *Above the Battlefield.*

> For the finer spirits of Europe there are two dwelling-places; our earthly fatherland, and that other City of God. Of the one we are the guests, of the other the builders. To the one let us give our lives and our faithful hearts; but neither family, friend nor fatherland nor aught that we love has power over the spirit, which is the light. It is our duty to rise above tempests, and thrust aside the clouds which threaten to obscure it; to build higher and stronger, dominating the injustice and hatred of nations, the walls of that city wherein the souls of the whole world may assemble.

The title *Above the Battlefield* was unfortunate. It suggested that the writer felt himself superior to his fellows, and it annoyed people who were brave or vulgar-minded or both—and it is possible to be both. He became unpopular in his own country, and stayed for the rest of the war in Switzerland working on prisoners' relief. When peace came he had some further success as a dramatist. He had always been interested in a People's Theatre, where the people could be given what they understood and could participate in, and not what the upper classes thought nice for them. He had longed for the popular stage of ancient Greece to be reborn in the modern world. And he had himself written plays, dealing with mass-revolution and freedom (a play on Danton, for instance), and some of these were performed, under the direction of Reinhardt. But it is as the author of *John Christopher* and *Above the Battlefield* that he is best remembered.

Romain Rolland knew and understood a great deal about music, and whatever he says is worth reading. He wrote a long and important work on Beethoven, also on Handel; he could appreciate composers as diverse from one another as Berlioz and Hugo Wolf. He did not like Brahms—most Frenchmen and many Germans do not—and he had only a contemptuous tolerance for Debussy. What he demanded was vitality, robustness, from which alone the mysterious filaments of the spirit can sprout. He felt music as a breath from the vanished centuries, to be transformed by our lungs into the song of the moment and the prophecy of the future; music is the god which each generation must make into flesh. It was the deepest thing for him, and anyone who has felt its depth is bound to join in homage to him. I am not qualified to say whether he is a sound musical interpreter. He is certainly a thrilling one, and here is the heart of him, without doubt. There is a scene in the opening volume of *John Christopher* where the hero, still a baby, touches the piano for the first time, and experiments in the marriage of sounds. I have never come across a scene like it in literature, for it is not merely poetic, not merely good child-psychology: it seems to take us inside a special chamber of the human spirit, and make us co-creators.

The opening volumes of *John Christopher* are the best. They take place in a little princely city of the old Germany, on the banks of the Rhine. The child's forebears have been musicians here for generations in a quiet way, but he himself is anything but submissive and he does not fit in. The young Beethoven is in the writer's mind, and he has supplied other details from his own youth. Explosive, moody, inconsiderate, uncouth, John Christopher is all the same good: affectionate, generous, trustful. He suffers atrociously from poverty, and the cruelty of his drunken father, and from a fear of death which is only tempered by his disgust at life. Violent longings, powers outside him shake him. His genius is recognized, but not fully recognized; he is too large for the little town, and when he is actually rude to its Grand Duke he is expelled and escapes to France. In these early volumes we get, besides the impression of genius and character, a brilliant and sympathetic account of the old Germany which will never return; we sit in little shops and go for Sunday walks or to a performance at the local opera; we make love, with discretion, to this girl or that; we are narrow-minded and serious, and past us all the time flows the Rhine. *Dawn* and *Morning* (volumes one and two) are delightful. In volume five we get to Paris, and the interest rather flags. John Christopher's comments and escapades are less exciting, and his surroundings have lost their vividness. He discovers, after a good deal of grumpiness, that Paris is not France, gets into touch with the people, and makes close friends with a fine-natured Frenchman, Olivier. By now he is famous, and there is a touching episode when he visits a provincial admirer—a humble and sincere old man whom he has never seen. The visit is a success—just a success; we are on tenterhooks all the time lest it be a failure, for the great musician is extremely irritable, and the humble old man is an admirer of Brahms, and a bit of a bore.

The final volume, *The New Day*, passes into mysticism. The hero, mortally sick, finds himself fording a river which is partly the Rhine of his youth, partly the river of death. The crossing is hard, and on his shoulder is seated a child. Heavier grows the burden, and from the bank he has left come cries of "You'll never succeed". He stumbles, he is drowning—and then the water becomes shallow. The sun rises. Bells burst into music, and he reaches the further shore. John Christopher is saved. And he has not merely saved himself. He is not just the artist. He is Christopher the saint. He has carried on his shoulders, through the troubles of our century, the divine spirit of man, so that it may live and grow. "Child, who are you?" he asks. And the child answers, "I am the day which is going to be born."

I don't think the work will live like another French panorama-novel of the period—the novel of Proust. It is too episodic and diffuse, the conception sags, the satire is often journalistic and the style flat. But Romain Rolland was a far bigger person than Proust from the social and moral point of view; he cared about other people and tried to help them, he fought for a better world constantly and passionately, and he moved across frontiers to-wards internationalism as surely as the Rhine moves through Germany to the universal sea. He may be forgotten today, but insight and sincerity such as his will return to a world which needs them badly, and through other lips he will inspire youth once more and clarify its hopes.

[1945]

A Whiff of D'Annunzio

Poet, hero and cad, D'Annunzio presents a test problem to the Englishman. Byron, to whom he has been compared, was difficult enough, and was sent by us on a continental pilgrimage from which he has never returned. D'Annunzio is even more troublesome, since his poetry is more poetical than Byron's, his heroism more histrionic and his caddishness not an aristocratic freak but innate in his bones and bowels. And he has no sense of humour—the "saving grace" as we are pleased to call it. Faced by such a problem, the Englishman becomes uncritical and unjust, thinks himself profound when he castigates and acute when he is merely being nasty, refuses to admit that an ill-bred egoist can be a genius and a leader of men, and suspects shoddiness because there is no underlying moral worth. D'Annunzio, a very great southerner, is not thus to be judged. His standards are not ours, and if we ask him to sign a suburban gentlemen's agreement he will impale us contemptuously upon the point of his pen as he did President Wilson. How are we to approach him? His secretary and sometime publisher, Signor Tom Antongini, has written a book which may help us. It is not much of a book, but it breathes his atmosphere and accepts his ideals.

His leading passion was the Renaissance passion for earthly immortality. And he knew that immortality cannot be won by talking. Effort must accompany advertisement, and as a writer, a patriot and a lover he worked very hard. By the time he died he had a number of books to his credit, a still larger number of mistresses, and the city of Fiume. It is no small haul. It is a substantial hostage against oblivion. So long as Italy is Italy, he will not be forgotten. He, Paderewski and T. E. Lawrence stand out as the three artists who achieved fame as men of action during the 1914–1918 war, and of the three he is the most spectacular. He will win the prize which he wanted and which he certainly deserves.

There is another prize—the silence that does not even say it is silent; D'Annunzio knew nothing about that. In some words which were engraved in his retreat, the Vittoriale—words which his biographer accepts as mysterious but which we find muddled—he claims to approach the gods *Princeps et Praeco,* as a Prince and a Herald. He was always heralding, always heading some sumptuous embassy of his own creation, always clothing his actions in a gorgeous rhetoric which concealed them. Here again he belongs to the garrulous, restless, processional Italian Renaissance. "I go to awake the Dead," cried the fifteenth-century scholar Cyriac of Ancona, meaning that he was getting on with his Greek studies. "I go towards the Light," cries D'Annunzio, meaning that he has ratted in the Chamber of Deputies from the Conservatives to the Socialists. The actions are not unimportant, the phrases are striking. But the Light, the Dead, remain as they were, in silence.

Signor Antongini, who was with him while he was writing *The Martyrdom of St Sebastian,* is interesting in this connection. He suggests that that particular play was inspired not by religious mysticism but by a pair of female legs. D'Annunzio was full of spiritual ideas, but he could not use them until he had had the good fortune to see Ida Rubinstein dancing in a ballet. Then he exclaimed, "Here are the legs of St Sebastian for which I have been searching in vain all these years," and poetry poured from his pen. No doubt the anecdote exaggerates, still it emphasizes the point that his contacts with life were sensuous and local in their character: certain gestures, certain limbs, certain spots of soil in the Abruzzi and elsewhere, served as jumping-off grounds for his art, and impelled him into orations about human destiny. Nothing he writes is profound. Yet he is never superficial, because he is excited by what he touches and sees, or hopes to touch. "We ate oranges as if they were bread." Why has this phrase, in its half-remembered Italian, lingered in my mind for nearly thirty years? It is a phrase from his drama *The Dead City,* and, placed where he placed it, it brought out the taste of the newly picked fruit and the feeling of it between the lips and the teeth: not pulp, not juice, but a unity, bread-like, divine. The characters—poor mortals, they had fallen in love as they should not—discussed such an orange amidst the aridities of Greece, and it passed as a tangible presence behind the veil of their prose, it lent importance to their fate, like the peaches and pears surrounding a Crivelli Madonna. There are several lists in Signor Antongini's tribute, which will repel the reader by their triviality and expensiveness, yet he had better study them, because they indicate D'Annunzio's aesthetic sources—lists of fruits, mottoes, scents, horses, villas, women, dogs. Most of these, including the women, had to be renamed after the poet handled them, so that he might have an additional sense of power. They are defiled by his possessiveness, but they are evidently necessary to his art.

The women deserve particular attention, from Duse the Divine down to poor Madame de B——, whose confessions fill an entire chapter. She describes her first and last visit to the poet's villa at Florence. "On the pillar on the left I read 'Beware of the dog!' and on the right 'Beware of the master'." Her knees trembled, she rang the bell. "The first shock in store was for my nostrils, the air was heavy with incense," and before many minutes she had been seduced. A few minutes more, and she was bowling away in a carriage lined like a coffin with roses. She told Signor Antongini of her fall many years later. It had become her great, her tender memory. He mentioned her name with due discretion to his employer, who only said: "Madame de B——? I think I remember her vaguely. She was at the time of *La Figlia di Jorio*."

By now we are well into the waters of the Mediterranean. Our trouble is that, to the northerner, such an inscription as "Beware of the dog—Beware of the master" is essentially comic. Yet neither Signor Antongini nor D'Annunzio nor Madame de B—— finds anything funny in it or anything vulgar; it is to them a cynical proclamation of virility, which she who ignores ignores at her peril. This makes them antipathetic, so we must remind ourselves in conclusion that the Mediterranean is also the sea of courage and of splendour. D'Annunzio's courage is unquestionable. He possessed both grit and dash; he could urge Italy into the War, fight in the trenches, fly over Vienna, occupy and administer Fiume against the approval of the Allies and of his own government, and he could watch his own appendix be cut out under a local anaesthetic. And his splendour—that too is incontestable, although by our standards it is often encumbered by *bric-à-brac*. He could write like music, like scents, like religion, like blood, like anything, he could sweep into the folds of his magnificent prose whatever took his fancy, and then assert it was sacred. There has been nobody like him. Fascism wisely accepted him after a little demur, and we had better do the same. We can anyhow hail him by two of the titles which he claims: poet and hero.

[1938]

The Complete Poems of
C. P. Cavafy

The first English translation of Cavafy was made by Cavafy.

The occasion is over thirty years ago now, in his flat, 10 rue Lepsius, Alexandria; his dusky family-furnished flat. He is back from his work in a government office; the Third Circle of the Irrigation employs him as it might have employed many of his heroes. I am back from my work, costumed in khaki; the British Red Cross employs me. We have been introduced by an English friend, our meetings are rather dim, and Cavafy is now saying with his usual gentleness, "You could never understand my poetry, my dear Forster, never." A poem is produced—"The God Abandons Antony"—and I detect some coincidences between its Greek and public-school Greek. Cavafy is amazed. "Oh, but this is good, my dear Forster, this is very good indeed," and he raises his hand, takes over, and leads me through. It was not my knowledge that touched him but my desire to know and to receive. He had no idea then that he could be widely desired, even in the stumbling North. To be understood in Alexandria and tolerated in Athens was the extent of his ambition.

Since that distant day, many other translators have had a shot. The shooter most to my taste is George Valassopoulo. He had the advantage of working with the poet and he has brought much magic across; Cavafy is largely magic. But Valassopoulo only translated, and only wished to translate, some of the poems. What was needed, and has been happily found, is a translator for them all, for all the 154 of them: Professor John Mavrogordato. This eminent scholar has done a most valuable piece of work, lucid, faithful, intelligent; he has enabled us to read what Cavafy wanted to say, and to read it in its proper perspective. For Cavafy as a historical poet, or as an erotic poet, or an introspective one, would fail to convey that Mediterranean complexity. We need all of him if we are to understand anything.

All the poems are short. They are learned, sensuous, ironic, civilized, sensitive, witty. Where's their centre? Courage enters,

233

though not in an ordinary nor a reputable form. Cavafy appreciates cowardice also, and likes the little men who can't be consistent or maintain their ideals, and can't know what is happening and have to dodge.

> Be afraid of grandeurs, O my soul;
> And if you cannot conquer your ambitions
> With hesitation always and precautions
> Follow them up.

Be afraid, if you are Caesar, of that obscure person in the crowd; he may be Artemidorus trying to warn you against death. Be afraid lest, into your comfortable flat, Pompey's head is carried on a trencher. Be afraid if, like Nero, you lie asleep, of the obscure tumblings in the cupboard; your little household gods are falling over each other in terror, because they, not you, can hear the approaching footsteps of the Erinyes. And if you are brave your courage is only genuine when, like those who fought at Thermopylae, you know you are certain to perish.

Courage and cowardice are equally interesting to his amoral mind, because he sees in both of them opportunities for sensation. What he envies is the power to snatch sensation, to triumph over the moment even if remorse ensues. Perhaps that physical snatching is courage; it is certainly the seed of exquisite memories and it is possibly the foundations of art. The amours of youth, even when disreputable, are delightful, thinks Cavafy, but the point of them is not that: the point is that they create the future, and may give to an ageing man in a rue Lepsius perceptions he would never have known.

> The years of my youth, my life of pleasure—
> How clearly I see the meaning of them now.
>
> What unnecessary, what vain repentances . . .
>
> But I did not see the meaning then.
>
> Under the dissolute living of my youth
> Were being formed the intentions of my poetry,
> The province of my art was being planned.
>
> And that is why my repentances were never lasting.
> My resolutions to control myself, to change,
> Used to endure for two weeks at most.

The attitude recalls Proust's, but the temperament differs.

Cavafy is never embittered, never the invalid. He is thankful to
have lived, and

> Young men even now are repeating his verses.
> His visions pass before their lively eyes.
> Their healthy brains enjoying,
> Their welldrawn, tightskinned flesh,
> Even now are moved by his revelations of beauty.

He has something of the antique faith in fame. He is not a
super-sensitive Frenchman. He is not English. He is not even
British. Alexandria's his home.

> Environment, of house, of city centres, city quarters
> Which I look upon and where I walk; years and years.

> I have created you in the midst of joy and in the midst of
>   sorrows;
> With so many circumstances, with so many things.

> And you have been made sensation, the whole of you, for me.

Alexandria is the city which he creates and over which he leans,
meditative, when sorrows and triumphs recur; the city over
which Antony, nearly two thousand years before him, may have
leant when the music sounded and the God abandoned him.
It is in Alexandria that he died in 1933 at the age of seventy;
the Greek Hospital lay close by to receive him.

His material as a poet, then, begins with his own experiences
and sensations: his interest in courage and cowardice and bodily
pleasure, and so on. He begins from within. But he never
makes a cult of himself or of what he feels. All the time he is
being beckoned to and being called to by history, particularly
by the history of his own race. History, too, is full of courage,
cowardice, lust, and is to that extent domestic. But it is something
more. It is an external inspiration. And he found in the expanses
and recesses of the past, in the clash of great names and the
tinkle of small ones, in the certified victories and slurred defeats,
in the jewels and the wounds and the vast movements beginning
out of nothing and sometimes ending nowhere: he found in
them something that transcended his local life and freshened and
strengthened his art. Demurely, ironically, he looks into the
past, for he knew the answers. Cleopatra did not win Actium.
Julian did not reinstate paganism. Anna Comnena took the
wrong side. The Senate sit in state to receive the barbarians;

news comes that there are no more barbarians, so the Senate have nothing to do. Sometimes there is a double irony; the Prince from western Libya impresses the Alexandrians by his reticence and dignity; he is actually a most ordinary youth, who dare not speak because of his awful Greek accent,

> and he suffered no little discomfort
> Having whole conversations stacked inside him.

"Exactly what I feel in England," a Greek friend remarked to me. The irony became triple as he spoke, and Cavafy would have appreciated this further turn of the screw.

There is, however, nothing patronizing in his attitude to the past, nor have his cameos the aloofness of Heredia. The warmth of the past enthralls him even more than its blunders, and he can give the sense of human flesh and blood continuing through centuries that are supposed to be unsatisfactory. A tomb here, an inscription there; coloured glass worn by an emperor and empress at their coronation because they have no jewels. Sometimes the supernatural appears, and not always ominously: as in "One of their Gods", it may enrich voluptuousness:

> When one of them was passing through the market
> Of Seleukeia, about the hour of evenfall,
> Like a tall, a beautiful, a perfect youth,
> With the joy of incorruptibility in his eyes,
> With his black and perfumed hair,
> The passers-by would look at him,
> And one would ask another if he knew him,
> And if he was a Greek of Syria, or a stranger. But a few
> Who observed with greater attention
> Would understand and draw aside;
> And while he disappeared under the arcades,
> In the shadows and in the lights of evening,
> Going towards the quarter which at night only
> Lives, with orgies and debauchery,
> And every kind of drunkenness and lust,
> They would wonder which it could be of Them,
> And for what disreputable sensuality
> He had come down to the streets of Seleukeia
> From those Majestical, All-holy Mansions.

The idea that the Divine should descend to misbehave, so shocking to the Christian, comes naturally enough to a paganizing Greek, and the poem (which I first knew in a Valassopoulo translation) sums up for me much that is characteristic. And how admirable is its construction! Only two sentences, and the second one descending and descending until the final abrupt ascent.

His attitude to the past did not commend him to some of his contemporaries, nor is it popular today. He was a loyal Greek, but Greece for him was not territorial. It was rather the influence that has flowed from his race this way and that through the ages, and that (since Alexander the Great) has never disdained to mix with barbarism, has indeed desired to mix; the influence that made Byzantium a secular achievement. Racial purity bored him, so did political idealism. And he could be caustic about the claims of the tight-lipped little peninsula overseas. "Aristocracy in modern Greece?" he once exclaimed. "To be an aristocrat there is to have made a corner in coffee in the Peiraeus in 1849." The civilization he respected was a bastardy in which the Greek strain prevailed, and into which, age after age, outsiders would push, to modify and be modified. If the strain died out—never mind: it had done its work, and it would have left, far away upon some Asian upland, a coin of silver, stamped with the exquisite head of a Hellenizing king. Pericles, Aristides, Themistocles, schoolroom tyrants: what did they know of this extension which is still extending, and which sometimes seemed (while he spoke) to connote the human race?

Half humorously, half seriously, he once compared the Greeks and the English. The two peoples are almost exactly alike, he argued: quick-witted, resourceful, adventurous. "But there is one unfortunate difference between us, one little difference. We Greeks have lost our capital—and the results are what you see. Pray, my dear Forster, oh pray, that you never lose your capital."

That was in 1918. British insolvency seemed impossible then. In 1951, when all things are possible, his words make one think—words of a very wise, very civilized man, words of a poet who has caught hold of something that cannot be taken away from him by bankruptcy, or even by death.

[1951]

Virginia Woolf

The Rede Lecture, delivered in the
Senate House, Cambridge

When I was appointed to this lectureship the work of Virginia
Woolf was much in my mind, and I asked to be allowed to speak
on it. To speak on it, rather than to sum it up. There are two
obstacles to a summing-up. The first is the work's richness and
complexity. As soon as we dismiss the legend of the Invalid
Lady of Bloomsbury, so guilelessly accepted by Arnold Bennett,
we find ourselves in a bewildering world where there are few
headlines. We think of *The Waves* and say, "Yes—that is
Virginia Woolf"; then we think of *The Common Reader*, where she
is different, of *A Room of One's Own* or of the preface to *Life As We
Have Known It*: different again. She is like a plant which is supposed to grow in a well-prepared garden bed—the bed of
esoteric literature—and then pushes up suckers all over the place,
through the gravel of the front drive, and even through the flagstones of the kitchen yard. She was full of interests, and their
number increased as she grew older, she was curious about life,
and she was tough, sensitive but tough. How can her achievement be summed up in an hour? A headline sometimes serves a
lecturer as a lifeline on these occasions, and brings him
safely into the haven where he would be. Shall I find one
today?

The second obstacle is that 1941 is not a good year in which to
sum up anything. Our judgements, to put it mildly, are not at
their prime. We are all of us upon the Leaning Tower, as she
called it, even those of us who date from the nineteenth century,
when the earth was still horizontal and the buildings perpendicular. We cannot judge the landscape properly as we look down,
for everything is tilted. Isolated objects are not so puzzling; a
tree, a wave, a hat, a jewel, an old gentleman's bald head look
much as they always did. But the relation between objects—
that we cannot estimate, and that is why the verdict must be left
to another generation. I have not the least faith that anything
which we now value will survive historically (something which
we should have valued may evolve, but that is a different proposi-

tion); and maybe another generation will dismiss Virginia Woolf as worthless and tiresome. However, this is not my opinion, nor I think yours; we still have the word, and I wonder whether I cannot transmit some honour to her from the university she so admired, and from the central building of that university. She would receive the homage a little mockingly, for she was somewhat astringent over the academic position of women. "What? I in the Senate House?" she might say. "Are you sure that is quite proper? And why, if you want to discuss my books, need you first disguise yourselves in caps and gowns?" But I think she would be pleased. She loved Cambridge. Indeed, I cherish a private fancy that she once took her degree here. She, who could disguise herself as a member of the suite of the Sultan of Zanzibar, or black her face to go aboard a Dreadnought as an Ethiopian[1]— she could surely have hoaxed our innocent praelectors and, kneeling in this very spot, have presented to the Vice-Chancellor the exquisite but dubious head of Orlando.

There is, after all, one little lifeline to catch hold of: she liked writing.

These words, which usually mean so little, must be applied to her with all possible intensity. She liked receiving sensations— sights, sounds, tastes—passing them through her mind, where they encountered theories and memories, and then bringing them out again, through a pen, onto a bit of paper. Now began the higher delights of authorship. For these pen-marks on paper were only the prelude to writing, little more than marks on a wall. They had to be combined, arranged, emphasized here, eliminated there, new relationships had to be generated, new pen-marks born, until out of the interactions something, one thing, one, arose. This one thing, whether it was a novel or an essay or a short story or a biography or a private paper to be read to her friends, was, if it was successful, itself analogous to a sensation. Although it was so complex and intellectual, although it might be large and heavy with facts, it was akin to the very simple things which had started it off, to the sights, sounds, tastes. It could best be described as we describe them. For it was not about something. It was something. This is obvious in "aesthetic" works, like *Kew Gardens* and *Mrs Dalloway*; it is less obvious in a work of learning, like the *Roger Fry*, yet here too the analogy holds.

[1] See Adrian Stephen, *The Dreadnought Hoax*. See, still more, an unpublished paper which she herself once wrote for a Women's Institute, leaving it helpless with laughter.

We know, from an article by R. C. Trevelyan, that she had, when writing it, a notion corresponding to the notion of a musical composition. In the first chapter she stated the themes, in the subsequent chapters she developed them separately, and she tried to bring them all in again at the end. The biography is duly about Fry. But it is something else too; it is one thing, one.

She liked writing with an intensity which few writers have attained, or even desired. Most of them write with half an eye on their royalties, half an eye on their critics, and a third half-eye on improving the world, which leaves them with only half an eye for the task on which she concentrated her entire vision. She would not look elsewhere, and her circumstances combined with her temperament to focus her. Money she had not to consider, because she possessed a private income, and though financial independence is not always a safeguard against commercialism it was in her case. Critics she never considered while she was writing, although she could be attentive to them and even humble afterwards. Improving the world she would not consider, on the ground that the world is man-made, and that she, a woman, had no responsibility for the mess. This last opinion is a curious one, and I shall be returning to it; still, she held it, it completed the circle of her defences, and neither the desire for money nor the desire for reputation nor philanthropy could influence her. She had a singleness of purpose which will not recur in this country for many years, and writers who have liked writing as she liked it have not indeed been common in any age.

Now the pitfall for such an author is obvious. It is the Palace of Art, it is that bottomless chasm of dullness which pretends to be a palace, all glorious with corridors and domes, but which is really a dreadful hole into which the unwary aesthete may tumble, to be seen no more. She has all the aesthete's characteristics: selects and manipulates her impressions; is not a great creator of character; enforces patterns on her books; has no great cause at heart. So how did she avoid her appropriate pitfall and remain up in the fresh air, where we can hear the sound of the stable-boy's boots, or boats bumping, or Big Ben; where we can taste really new bread, and touch real dahlias?

She had a sense of humour, no doubt, but our answer must go a little deeper than that hoary nostrum. She escaped, I think, because she liked writing for fun. Her pen amused her, and in the midst of writing seriously this other delight would spurt through. A little essay called *On Being Ill* exemplifies this. It starts with the thesis that illness in literature is seldom handled properly (De Quincey and Proust were exceptional), that the body is treated by novelists as if it were a sheet of glass through which the soul gazes, and that this is contrary to experience. There are possibilities in the thesis, but she soon wearies of exploring them. Off she goes amusing herself, and after half a dozen pages she is writing entirely for fun, caricaturing the type of people who visit sick-rooms, insisting that Augustus Hare's *Two Noble Lives* is the book an invalid most demands, and so on. She could describe illness if she chose—for instance, in *The Voyage Out*—but she gaily forgets it in *On Being Ill*. The essay is slight, still it does neatly illustrate the habit of her mind. Literature was her merry-go-round as well as her study. This makes her amusing to read, and it also saves her from the Palace of Art. For you cannot enter the Palace of Art, therein to dwell, if you are tempted from time to time to play the fool. Lord Tennyson did not consider that. His remedy, you remember, was that the Palace would be purified when it was inhabited by all mankind, all behaving seriously at once. Virginia Woolf found a simpler and a sounder solution.

No doubt there is a danger here—there is danger everywhere. She might have become a glorified *diseuse*, who frittered away her broader effects by mischievousness, and she did give that impression to some who met her in the flesh; there were moments when she could scarcely see the busts for the moustaches she pencilled on them, and when the bust was a modern one, whether of a gentleman in a top-hat or of a youth on a pylon, it had no chance of remaining sublime. But in her writing, even in her light writing, central control entered. She was master of her complicated equipment, and, though most of us like to write sometimes seriously and sometimes in fun, few of us can so manage the two impulses that they speed each other up, as hers did.

The above remarks are more or less introductory. It seems convenient now to recall what she did write, and to say a little about her development. She began back in 1915 with *The Voyage Out*—a strange, tragic, inspired novel about English tourists in an impossible South American hotel; her passion for truth is here already, mainly in the form of atheism, and her passion for wisdom is here in the form of music. The book made a deep impression upon the few people who read it. Its successor, *Night and Day*, disappointed them. This is an exercise in classical realism, and contains all that has characterized English fiction, for good and evil, during the last two hundred years: faith in personal relations, recourse to humorous side-shows, geographical exactitude, insistence on petty social differences: indeed most of the devices she so gaily derides in *Mr Bennett and Mrs Brown*. The style has been normalized and dulled. But at the same time she published two short stories, *Kew Gardens* and *The Mark on the Wall*. These are neither dull nor normal; lovely little things; her style trails after her as she walks and talks, catching up dust and grass in its folds, and instead of the precision of the earlier writing we have something more elusive than had yet been achieved in English. Lovely little things, but they seemed to lead nowhere, they were all tiny dots and coloured blobs, they were an inspired breathlessness, they were a beautiful droning or gasping which trusted to luck. They were perfect as far as they went, but that was not far, and none of us guessed that out of the pollen of those flowers would come the trees of the future. Consequently when *Jacob's Room* appeared in 1922 we were tremendously surprised. The style and sensitiveness of *Kew Gardens* remained, but they were applied to human relationships, and to the structure of society. The blobs of colour continue to drift past, but in their midst, interrupting their course like a closely sealed jar, stands the solid figure of a young man. The improbable has occurred: a method essentially poetic and apparently trifling has been applied to fiction. She was still uncertain of the possibilities of the new technique, and *Jacob's Room* is an uneven little book, but it represents her great departure, and her abandonment of the false start of *Night and Day*. It leads on to her genius in its fullness: to *Mrs Dalloway* (1925), *To the Lighthouse* (1927) and *The Waves* (1931). These successful works are all suffused with poetry and enclosed in it. *Mrs Dalloway* has the framework of a London summer's day, down which go spiralling two fates: the fate of the sensitive worldly hostess, and the fate of the sensitive obscure maniac; though they never touch they are closely connected, and at the same moment we lose sight of them both. It is a civilized book, and it was written from personal experience. In her work, as in her private problems, she was always civilized and sane on the subject of madness. She pared the edges off this particular malady, she tied it down to being a malady, and robbed it of the evil magic it has acquired through timid or careless thinking; here is one of the gifts we have to thank her for. *To the Lighthouse* is, however, a much greater achievement, partly because the chief characters in it, Mr and

Mrs Ramsay, are so interesting. They hold us, we think of them away from their surroundings, and yet they are in accord with those surroundings, with the poetic scheme. *To the Lighthouse* is in three movements. It has been called a novel in sonata form, and certainly the slow central section, conveying the passing of time, does demand a musical analogy. We have, when reading it, the rare pleasure of inhabiting two worlds at once, a pleasure only art can give: the world where a little boy wants to go to a lighthouse but never manages it until, with changed emotions, he goes there as a young man; and the world where there is pattern, and this world is emphasized by passing much of the observation through the mind of Lily Briscoe, who is a painter. Then comes *The Waves*. Pattern here is supreme—indeed it is italicized. And between the motions of the sun and the waters, which preface each section, stretch, without interruption, conversation, words in inverted commas. It is a strange conversation, for the six characters, Bernard, Neville, Louis, Susan, Jinny, Rhoda, seldom address one another, and it is even possible to regard them (like Mrs Dalloway and Septimus) as different facets of one single person. Yet they do not conduct internal monologues, they are in touch amongst themselves, and they all touch the character who never speaks, Percival. At the end, most perfectly balancing their scheme, Bernard, the would-be novelist, sums up, and the pattern fades out. *The Waves* is an extraordinary achievement, an immense extension of the possibilities of *Kew Gardens* and *Jacob's Room*. It is trembling on the edge. A little less—and it would lose its poetry. A little more—and it would be over into the abyss, and be dull and arty. It is her greatest book, though *To the Lighthouse* is my favourite.

It was followed by *The Years*. This is another experiment in the realistic tradition. It chronicles the fortunes of a family through a documented period. As in *Night and Day*, she deserts poetry, and again she fails. But in her posthumous novel *Between the Acts* she returns to the method she understood. Its theme is a village pageant, which presents the entire history of England, and into which, at the close, the audience is itself drawn, to continue that history; "The curtain rose" is its concluding phrase. The conception is poetic, and the text of the pageant is mostly written in verse. She loved her country—the country that is the countryside, and emerges from the unfathomable past. She takes us back in this exquisite final tribute, and she points us on, and she shows us through her poetic vagueness something more solid than patriotic history, and something better worth dying for.

Amongst all this fiction, nourishing it and nourished by it, grow other works. Two volumes of *The Common Reader* show the breadth of her knowledge and the depth of her literary sympathy; let anyone who thinks her an exquisite recluse read what she says on Jack Mytton the foxhunter. As a critic she could enter into anything—anything lodged in the past, that is to say; with her contemporaries she sometimes had difficulties. Then there are the biographies, fanciful and actual. *Orlando* is, I need hardly say, an original book, and the first part of it is splendidly written: the description of the Great Frost is already received as a "passage" in English literature, whatever a passage may be. After the transformation of sex things do not go so well; the authoress seems unconvinced by her own magic and somewhat fatigued by it, and the biography finishes competently rather than brilliantly; it has been a fancy on too large a scale, and we can see her getting bored. But *Flush* is a complete success, and exactly what it sets out to be; the material, the method, the length, accord perfectly, it is doggy without being silly, and it does give us, from the altitude of the carpet or the sofa-foot, a peep at high poetic personages, and a new angle on their ways. The biography of Roger Fry—one should not proceed direct from a spaniel to a Slade Professor, but Fry would not have minded and spaniels mind nothing—reveals a new aspect of her powers, the power to suppress herself. She indulges in a pattern, but she never intrudes her personality or over-handles her English; respect for her subject dominates her, and only occasionally—as in her description of the divinely ordered chaos of Fry's studio with its still-life of apples and eggs labelled "please do not touch"—does she allow her fancy to play. Biographies are too often described as "labours of love", but the *Roger Fry* really is in this class; one artist is writing with affection of another, so that he may be remembered and may be justified.

Finally, there are the feminist books—*A Room of One's Own* and *Three Guineas*—and several short essays, etc., some of them significant. It is as a novelist that she will be judged. But the rest of her work must be remembered, partly on its merits, partly because (as William Plomer has pointed out) she is sometimes more of a novelist in it than in her novels.

After this survey, we can state her problem. Like most novelists worth reading, she strays from the fictional norm. She dreams, designs, jokes, invokes, observes details, but she does not tell a story or weave a plot, and—can she create character? That is her problem's centre. That is the point where she felt herself open to criticism—to the criticisms, for instance, of her friend Hugh Walpole. Plot and story could be set aside in favour of some other unity, but if one is writing about human beings one does want them to seem alive. Did she get her people to live?

Now there seem to be two sorts of life in fiction: life on the page, and life eternal. Life on the page she could give; her characters never seem unreal, however slight or fantastic their lineaments, and they can be trusted to behave appropriately. Life eternal she could seldom give; she could seldom so portray a character that it was remembered afterwards on its own account, as Emma is remembered, for instance, or Dorothea Casaubon, or Sophia and Constance in *The Old Wives' Tale*. What wraiths, apart from their context, are the wind sextet from *The Waves*, or Jacob away from *Jacob's Room*! They speak no more to us or to one another as soon as the page is turned. And this is her great difficulty. Holding on with one hand to poetry, she stretches and stretches to grasp things which are best gained by letting go of poetry. She would not let go, and I think she was quite right, though critics who like a novel to be a novel will disagree. She was quite right to cling to her specific gift, even if this entailed sacrificing something else vital to her art. And she did not always have to sacrifice; Mr and Mrs Ramsay do remain with the reader afterwards, and so perhaps do Rachel from *The Voyage Out* and Clarissa Dalloway. For the rest—it is impossible to maintain that here is an immortal portrait gallery. Socially she is limited to the upper-middle professional classes, and she does not even employ many types. There is the bleakly honest intellectual (St John Hirst, Charles Tansley, Louis, William Dodge), the monumental majestic hero (Jacob, Percival), the pompous amorous pillar of society (Richard Dalloway as he appears in *The Voyage Out*, Hugh Whitbread), the scholar who cares only for young men (Bonamy, Neville), the pernickety independent (Mr Pepper, Mr Bankes); even the Ramsays are tried out first as the Ambroses. As soon as we understand the nature of her equipment, we shall see that as regards human beings she did as well as she could. Belonging to the world of poetry, but fascinated by another world, she is always stretching out from her enchanted tree and snatching bits from the flux of daily life as they float past, and out of these bits she builds novels. She would not plunge. And she should not have plunged. She might have stayed folded up in her tree singing little songs like "Blue and Green" in the *Monday or Tuesday* volume, but fortunately for English literature she did not do this either.

So that is her problem. She is a poet, who wants to write something as near to a novel as possible.

I must pass on to say a little—it ought to be much—about her interests. I have emphasized her fondness for writing both seriously and in fun, and have tried to indicate how she wrote: how she gathered up her material and digested it without damaging its freshness, how she rearranged it to form unities, how she was a poet who wanted to write novels, how these novels bear upon them the marks of their strange gestation— some might say the scars. What concerns me now is the material itself, her interests, her opinions. And, not to be too vague, I will begin with food.

It is always helpful, when reading her, to look out for the passages which describe eating. They are invariably good. They are a sharp reminder that here is a woman who is alert sensuously. She had an enlightened greediness which gentlemen themselves might envy, and which few masculine writers have expressed. There is a little too much lamp-oil in George Mere-dith's wine, a little too much paper crackling on Charles Lamb's pork, and no savour whatever in any dish of Henry James's, but when Virginia Woolf mentions nice things they get right into our mouths, so far as the edibility of print permits. We taste their deliciousness. And when they are not nice we taste them equally, our mouths awry now with laughter. I will not torture this great university of Oxbridge by reminding it of the exquisite lunch which she ate in a don's room here in the year 1929; such memories are now too painful. Nor will I insult the noble college of women in this same university—Fernham is its name—by reminding it of the deplorable dinner which she ate that same evening in its Hall—a dinner so lowering that she had to go to a cupboard afterwards and drink something out of a bottle; such memories may still be all too true to fact. But I may without offence refer to the great dish of Bœuf en Daube which forms the centre of the dinner of union in *To the Lighthouse*, the dinner round which all that section of the book coheres, the dinner which exhales affection and poetry and loveliness, so that all the characters see the best in one another at last and for a moment, and one of them, Lily Briscoe, carries away a recollection of reality. Such a dinner cannot be built on a statement beneath a dish-cover which the novelist is too indifferent or incompetent to remove. Real food is necessary, and this, in fiction as in her home, she knew how to provide. The Bœuf en Daube, which had taken the cook three days to make and had worried Mrs Ramsay as she did her hair, stands before us with "its confusion of savoury brown and yellow meats, and its bay leaves and its wine"; we peer down the shiny walls of the great casserole and get one of the best bits, and, like William Bankes, generally so hard to please, we are satisfied. Food with her was not a literary device put in to make the book seem real. She put it in because she tasted it, because she saw pictures, because she smelt flowers, because she heard Bach, because her senses were both exquisite and catholic, and were always bringing her first-hand news of the outside world. Our debt to her is in part this: she reminds us of the importance of sensation in an age which practises brutality and recommends ideals. I could have illustrated sensation more reputably by quoting the charming passage about the florist's shop in *Mrs Dalloway*, or the passage where Rachel plays upon the cabin piano. Flowers and music are conventional literary adjuncts. A good feed isn't, and that is why I preferred it and chose it to represent her reactions. Let me add that she smokes, and now let the Bœuf en Daube be carried away. It will never come back in our lifetime. It is not for us. But the power to appreciate it remains, and the power to appreciate all distinction.

After the senses, the intellect. She respected knowledge, she believed in wisdom. Though she could not be called an optimist, she had, very profoundly, the conviction that mind is in action against matter, and is winning new footholds in the void. That anything would be accomplished by her or in her generation, she did not suppose, but the noble blood from which she sprang encouraged her to hope. Mr Ramsay, standing by the geraniums and trying to think, is not a figure of fun. Nor is this university, despite its customs and costumes: she speaks of "the light shining there—the light of Cambridge".

No light shines now from Cambridge visibly, and this prompts the comment that her books were conditioned by her period. She could not assimilate this latest threat to our civilization. The submarine perhaps. But not the flying fortress or the landmine. The idea that all stone is like grass, and like all flesh may vanish in a twinkling, did not enter into her consciousness, and indeed it will be some time before it can be assimilated by literature. She belonged to an age which distinguished sharply between the impermanency of man and the durability of his monuments, and for whom the dome of the British Museum Reading Room was almost eternal. Decay she admitted: the delicate gray churches in the Strand would not stand for ever; but she supposed, as we all did, that decay would be gradual. The younger generation—the Auden-Isherwood generation as it is convenient to call it—saw more clearly here than could she, and she did not quite do justice to its vision, any more than she did justice to its experiments in technique—she who had been in her time such an experimenter. Still, to belong to one's period is a common failing, and she made the most of hers. She respected and acquired knowledge, she believed in wisdom. Intellectually, no one can do more; and since she was a poet, not a philosopher or a historian or a prophetess, she had not to consider whether wisdom will prevail and whether the square upon the oblong, which Rhoda built out of the music of Mozart, will ever stand firm upon this distracted earth. The square upon the oblong. Order. Justice. Truth. She cared for these abstractions, and tried to express them through symbols, as an artist must, though she realized the inadequacy of symbols.

"... Then the beetle-shaped men come with their violins [said Rhoda]; wait; count; nod; down come their bows. And there is ripple and laughter like the dance of olive trees. . . .

"'Like' and 'like' and 'like'—but what is the thing that lies beneath the semblance of the thing? Now that lightning has gashed the tree and the flowering branch has fallen . . . let me see the thing. There is a square; there is an oblong. The players take the square and place it upon the oblong. They place it very accurately; they make a perfect dwelling-place. Very little is left outside. The structure is now visible; what is inchoate is here stated; we are not so various or so mean; we have made oblongs and stood them upon squares. This is our triumph; this is our consolation. . . ."

The consolation, that is to say, of catching sight of abstractions. They have to be symbolized, and the square upon the oblong is as much a symbol as the dancing olive trees, but because of its starkness it comes nearer to conveying what she seeks. Seeking it, "we are not so various or so mean"; we have added to the human heritage and reaffirmed wisdom.

The next of her interests which has to be considered is society.

She was not confined to sensations and intellectualism. She was a social creature, with an outlook both warm and shrewd. But it was a peculiar outlook, and we can best get at it by looking at a very peculiar side of her: her feminism.

Feminism inspired one of the most brilliant of her books— the charming and persuasive *A Room of One's Own*; it contains the Oxbridge lunch and the Fernham dinner, also the immortal encounter with the beadle when she tried to walk on the college grass, and the touching reconstruction of Shakespeare's sister— Shakespeare's equal in genius, but she perished because she had no position or money, and that has been the fate of women through the ages. But feminism is also responsible for the worst of her books—the cantankerous *Three Guineas*—and for the less successful streaks in *Orlando*. There are spots of it all over her work, and it was constantly in her mind. She was convinced that society is man-made, that the chief occupations of men are the shedding of blood, the making of money, the giving of orders and the wearing of uniforms, and that none of these occupations is admirable. Women dress up for fun or prettiness, men for pomposity, and she had no mercy on the judge in his wig, the general in his bits and bobs of ribbon, the bishop in his robes, or even on the harmless don in his gown. She felt that all these mummers were putting something across over which women had never been consulted, and which she at any rate disliked. She declined to cooperate, in theory, and sometimes in fact. She refused to sit on committees or to sign appeals, on the ground that women must not condone this tragic male-made mess, or accept the crumbs of power which men throw them occasionally from their hideous feast. Like Lysistrata, she withdrew.

In my judgement there is something old-fashioned about this extreme feminism; it dates back to her suffragette youth of the 1910s, when men kissed girls to distract them from wanting the vote, and very properly provoked her wrath. By the 1930s she had much less to complain of, and seems to keep on grumbling from habit. She complained, and rightly, that though women today have won admission into the professions and trades they usually encounter a male conspiracy when they try to get to the top. But she did not appreciate that the conspiracy is weakening yearly, and that before long women will be quite as powerful for good or evil as men. She was sensible about the past; about the present she was sometimes unreasonable. However, I speak as a man here, and as an elderly one. The best judges of her feminism are neither elderly men nor even elderly women, but young women. If they, if the students of Fernham, think that it expresses an existent grievance, they are right.

She felt herself to be not only a woman but a lady, and this gives a further twist to her social outlook. She made no bones about it. She was a lady, by birth and upbringing, and it was no use being cowardly about it, and pretending that her mother had turned a mangle, or that her father Sir Leslie had been a plasterer's mate. Working-class writers often mentioned their origins, and were respected for doing so. Very well; she would mention hers. And her snobbery—for she was a snob—has more courage in it than arrogance. It is connected with her insatiable honesty, and is not, like the snobbery of Clarissa Dalloway, bland and frilled and unconsciously sinking into the best armchair. It is more like the snobbery of Kitty when she goes to tea with the Robsons; it stands up like a target for anyone to aim at who wants to. In her introduction to *Life As We Have Known It* (a collection of biographies of working-class women edited by Margaret Llewellyn Davies) she faces the fire. "One could not be Mrs Giles of Durham, because one's body had never stood at the wash-tub; one's hands had never wrung and scrubbed and chopped up whatever the meat may be that makes a miner's supper." This is not disarming, and it is not intended to disarm. And, if one said to her that she could after all find out what meat a miner does have for his supper if she took a little trouble, she would retort that this wouldn't help her to chop it up, and that it is not by knowing things but by doing things that one enters into the lives of people who do things. And she was not going to chop up meat. She would chop it badly, and waste her time. She was not going to wring and scrub when what she liked doing and could do was write. To murmurs of "Lucky lady you!" she replied, "I am a lady," and went on writing. "There aren't going to be no more ladies. 'Ear that?" She heard. Without rancour or surprise or alarm, she heard, and drove her pen the faster. For if, as seems probable, these particular creatures are to be extinguished, how important that the last of them should get down her impressions of the world and unify them into a book! If she didn't, no one else would. Mrs Giles of Durham wouldn't. Mrs Giles would write differently, and might write better, but she could not produce *The Waves*, or a life of Roger Fry.

There is an admirable hardness here, so far as hardness can be admirable. There is not much sympathy, and I do not think she was sympathetic. She could be charming to individuals, working-class and otherwise, but it was her curiosity and her honesty that motivated her. And we must remember that sympathy, for her, entailed a tremendous and exhausting process, not lightly to be entered on. It was not a half-crown or a kind word or a good deed or a philanthropic sermon or a godlike gesture; it was adding the sorrows of another to one's own. Half fancifully, but wholly seriously, she writes:

> But sympathy we cannot have. Wisest Fate says no. If her children, weighted as they already are with sorrow, were to take on them that burden too, adding in imagination other pains to their own, buildings would cease to rise; roads would peter out into grassy tracks; there would be an end of music and of painting; one great sigh alone would rise to Heaven, and the only attitudes for men and women would be those of horror and despair.

Here perhaps is the reason why she cannot be warmer and more human about Mrs Giles of Durham.

This detachment from the working classes and labour reinforces the detachment caused by her feminism, and her attitude to society was in consequence aloof and angular. She was fascinated, she was unafraid, but she detested mateyness, and she would make no concessions to popular journalism, and the "let's all be friendly together" stunt. To the crowd—so far as such an entity exists—she was very jolly, but she handed out no bouquets to the middlemen who have arrogated to themselves the right of interpreting the crowd, and get paid for doing so in the daily press and on the wireless. These middlemen form after all a very small clique—larger than the Bloomsbury they so tirelessly denounce, but a mere drop in the ocean of humanity. And since it was a drop whose distinction was proportionate to its size she saw no reason to conciliate it.

"Now to sum up," says Bernard in the last section of *The Waves*. That I cannot do, for reasons already given: the material is so rich and contradictory, and ours is not a good vintage year for judgements. I have gone from point to point as best I could, from her method of writing to her books, from her problems as a poet-novelist to her problems as a woman and as a lady. And I have tried to speak of her with the directness which she would wish, and which could alone honour her. But how are all the points to be combined? What is the pattern resultant? The

best I can do is to quote Bernard again. "The illusion is upon
me," he says, "that something adheres for a moment, has round-
ness, weight, depth, is completed. This, for the moment, seems
to be [her] life." Bernard puts it well. But, as Rhoda indicated
in that earlier quotation, these words are only similes, compari-
sons with physical substances, and what one wants is the thing
that lies beneath the semblance of the thing; that alone satisfies,
that alone makes the full statement.

Whatever the final pattern, I am sure it will not be a depressing
one. Like all her friends, I miss her greatly—I knew her ever
since she started writing. But this is a personal matter, and I
am sure that there is no case for lamentation here, or for the
obituary note. Virginia Woolf got through an immense amount
of work, she gave acute pleasure in new ways, she pushed the
light of the English language a little further against darkness.
Those are facts. The epitaph of such an artist cannot be written
by the vulgar-minded or by the lugubrious. They will try,
indeed they have already tried, but their words make no sense.
It is wiser, it is safer, to regard her career as a triumphant one.
She triumphed over what are primly called "difficulties", and she
also triumphed in the positive sense: she brought in the spoils.
And sometimes it is as a row of little silver cups that I see her
work gleaming. "These trophies," the inscription runs, "were
won by the mind from matter, its enemy and its friend."

[1941]

Two Books by T. S. Eliot

1 Notes towards the Definition of Culture

There is T. S. Eliot who is a poet, and there are also two Mr Eliots who write criticism. The poet does not enter into this particular volume; his great achievement lies elsewhere, and it has been awarded the highest possible honours, both in this country and abroad.

The two critics do enter. They dominate the scene, and although they never contradict one another there is a difference between them which must be noted. They differ according to the audiences they address. Most of the book is addressed to sophisticated and highly educated people, and it is, on the whole, not satisfactory. At the end of it, three broadcasts are printed; these were intended for popular audiences and they are a success. It would seem that, when Mr Eliot is wishing to instruct, his prose remains lucid, considerate and assured; his excellent handbook on Dante is an example of this. When on the other hand he is writing for people who may answer him back, he becomes wary and loads his sentences with qualifications and precautions which make them heavy. The very title of the book is ominous. It is not about culture nor about a definition of culture, nor does it even offer notes on a definition. It offers "notes towards the definition". By its caution and astuteness the title forestalls many possible objections. But what cumbersome English!

The broadcasts were intended for a German-speaking audience, and were translated into German for that purpose. In the first of them, Mr Eliot speaks of the unity of European culture, and ascribes the richness of English to our continental connection. In the second, he describes the break-up of European culture during the last twenty years, and refers to the *Criterion*, the admirable review which he once edited. The third broadcast is the least satisfactory, because he advances in it towards a definition of culture, and then retires without making it clear how far he has been. Culture is connected with the family, if we interpret the family rightly. It is also connected—in certain circumstances—with much else. It is assuredly connected with

Christianity. Here we reach firmer ground. We feel—and he would wish us to feel—that his religious faith is more important to him than anything else, and that art and literature are only valid in their relation to it. The relation may be negative: "only a Christian culture could have produced a Voltaire or a Nietzsche." But as far as Europe is concerned the relation must exist. Where there is not Christianity there is nothing. And it has to be Christianity of an approved type: Mr Eliot grows increasingly theological. Smartly over the knuckles does he rap a certain book called *The Churches Survey Their Task*. They surveyed it wrongly. The rap occurs in the main body of the work. Here we may pursue, in greater detail and with superior caution, the ideas exposed in the broadcasts. There is much that is subtle and profound, much that is provocative, and we are bound to admit at the end that culture is even more important than we guessed. Unfortunately she has not become more accessible. Through the criss-cross of reservations and postulates we can scarcely catch sight of her outline, or see where she is going.

The book is prefaced by a quotation from Lord Acton: "I think our studies ought to be all but purposeless." The quotation does not seem appropriate in view of Mr Eliot's purposeful interest in polemical Christianity. Acton, too, was a deeply religious man. But he was also a convinced liberal, and Mr Eliot, for all his many-sidedness, cannot be described as that.

[1949]

2 *The Cocktail Party: A Comedy*

A comedy where one of the characters is crucified on an ant-hill is not comic in the usual sense of the word, and readers of *The Cocktail Party* will do well to arm themselves against difficulties. On the stage, those difficulties may diminish; the play was well received when it was produced at the Edinburgh Festival last year, and it is having a tremendous success in New York. The faces and voices and clothes of the characters may help to establish a perspective which is unobtainable through words.

Where does the mere reader find himself?

In an operating-theatre—a spiritual one. He has realized in the first act that something is wrong with some of the characters, perhaps with all of them; they chatter miserably and endlessly, and drink unprofitably, and Lavinia, the wife who should be helping Edward her husband to throw the party, has just deserted him. In the second act the reader gets a dramatic surprise—his big laugh, if the phrase be permissible. He discovers that three of the worthless guests were really doctors, who were mingling with their unsuspecting patients in order to gather information about them. Surgeon-in-chief is Sir Henry Harcourt-Reilly, previously an anonymous buffoon and now enthroned in his consulting-room. With him work Julia, previously mistaken for an ill-natured feckless old woman, and Alex, mistaken for a globe-trotter with pseudo-connections which turn out to be genuine. The patients arrive. Edward and Lavinia are confronted with one another, to their mutual indignation, and the similarity of their cases emphasized. They are refused any spectacular cure. They are followed by Celia, the girl with whom Edward has intrigued. Celia's position is different, is unique. She has a sense of sin—not for anything specific, but a general sense, and she desires to "atone". A way is pointed out to her, and accepted by her, no fee is charged her, and she is assigned to a "sanatorium" the outcome of which no one can foresee, not even the experts. A fourth patient is expected, but he is too much immersed in worldliness, and does not come. The act ends in a solemn and touching libation to the safety of Celia. It has become clear to the reader that he is actually in the presence of the Church, which is directing its children, through its priesthood, on their appropriate paths.

In the third act he learns what has happened. Edward and Lavinia are reconciled, are living together happily and civilly in their old flat, and are about to throw yet another cocktail party. It is the best they can achieve. Their quarrel was not important, nor is their reconciliation. The worldly young man has become still more worldly. As for Celia, we hear that she has chosen the path of Devotion and Dedication, has become a nurse and a nun, and has perished agonizingly amongst savages. Her sufferings are dwelt on, are indeed gloated over, and no doubt this is consonant with the author's religious outlook and with his "comedy". But aesthetically the sufferings disturb the reader and distract him. The Christian ethic of atonement, which has been impending over his head since the end of the second act, comes down with too sudden a bump. He hears the doctor-priests analysing the successful martyrdom as they sip their drinks, and he wonders.

The difficulties of *The Cocktail Party* do not extend to its diction. It is most beautifully and lucidly written. T. S. Eliot can do whatever he likes with the English language. This time he has selected a demure chatty verse form which seems to be like prose, but it is full of turns and subtle echoes, and always open for the emotional intensity he occasionally needs. On the stage, such diction may well carry all before it, and, reinforced by sound stagecraft, may place affairs in a less puzzling perspective.

[1950]

The Ascent of F6

This play is not easy to focus. It is short and straightforward, yet at least four pairs of spectacles are necessary before we can examine it properly. Let us start by looking at it through a heroic pair.

Behold Michael Ransom, known to his friends as M.F.! He is a gifted, sensitive, ascetic, altruistic mountaineer, who crowns a noble life with a glorious death. Aeroplanes locate his body on the summit of the virgin peak known as F6, which he alone has scaled. His body perishes, his name liveth for evermore. A national hero, akin to Colonel Lawrence in temperament and to Captain Scott in fate—that is what we see through this pair of spectacles, but the play is by Messrs Auden and Isherwood, and the spectacles soon slip off the nose and smash into nasty splinters. Try another pair.

Try the politico-economic outlook. F6 now appears to be situated on the boundary of two colonies, British Sudoland and Ostnian Sudoland, and the expedition to scale it is really a political ramp. The British and the Ostnians are racing one another to the top, for reasons of prestige, and if the British lose they will have trouble with the natives down in the coffee plantations, and no dividends. Thus viewed, the play becomes a satire of familiar type, the type instituted over thirty years ago by Hilaire Belloc in his brilliant novel *Mr Burden*. The situation is old, the machinery up-to-date, for Auden and Isherwood can show us the working-up of public opinion through broadcasting. Little Mr and Mrs Everyman in their poky flat—they are caught by the F6 propaganda, they listen spellbound to the important personages who come to the microphone; as they hear about the terrible mountain and the glorious young man, their own lives become less drab and boring, and they actually dash off and have a weekend at Hove, though they can ill afford it, as they realize on their return. "He belongs to *us* now," they cry, as they gaze at the obelisk erected to Ransom, after his death, by Big Business. Sudoland is safe. The natives work. The coffee comes. The curtain falls.

But focus again; this time upon Ransom himself. F6 now appears as a test for his character, which he fails to surmount. He suffers from the last infirmity of noble minds: thinking he pursues virtue and knowledge, he really pursues power. And at the crisis, in the nightmare-cloud on the summit, he sees that his motive has been impure, and, as evidence of this, the ghosts of the friends whom he has killed. He has sacrificed them in devoting himself. He had tried to turn back, but as soon as he set foot on the mountain all were doomed.

Why is F6 so fatal? Chormopuloda the natives call it, and it is haunted by a demon, they say. There is a monastery by the upper glacier, and the monks there spend their time less idly than might be supposed, restraining the demon by their meditations from irrupting onto the plains. The abbot explains to Ransom that the demon takes different forms for its temptations; he does not reveal that to Ransom himself it will take the form of his own mother. Mrs Ransom has appeared earlier in the play. It is she who made her son go, when he shrank from the temptation of power. She wants him to be brave, for her sake, and to be happy, provided she supervises his happiness. Cornelia, the mother of the Gracchi! For her other son, James, is the politician who organizes the ramp. Cornelia-Jocasta! For our final pair of spectacles is provided by Freud. When the cloud lifts from the summit of the mountain, Ransom finds his mother waiting for him, reabsorbing that which she has sent forth, frustrating that which she has created. He has never escaped her. He re-enters the womb. The lyric finale suggests *Peer Gynt*, but there is a bitterness in it which neither Åse nor Solveig conveys. She sings to her little boy:

> Reindeer are coming to drive you away
> Over the snow on an ebony sleigh,
> Over the mountain and over the sea
> You shall go happy and handsome and free.

But the chorus retorts:

> True, Love finally is great,
> Greater than all; but large the hate,
> Far larger than Man can ever estimate.

Mother-love, usually sacrosanct, becomes a nasty customer in this exciting play.

The Ascent of F6 is a tragedy in a modern mode, full of funniness and wisecracks. It is not an entertainment, for all its lightheartedness, because its details fit into its grave general plan. Unlike its predecessor, *The Dog beneath the Skin*, it moves onward instead of after its own tail; the changes from poetry to prose, from monastery to mike, advance the action, the amusing subordinate characters never blur the genius and the pathos of Ransom.

[1936]

The Enchafèd Flood

T. E. Lawrence, that desert hero, once told me that he did not think highly of the sea. He considered it overrated. He enjoyed teasing sailormen and found them easy game, and when on board would make such remarks to them as, "I've been sitting upstairs on the veranda. I think I'll go now and rest in my room." Their infuriated reactions amused him. He never crossed the line, I think, but he would have regarded that ordeal as an opportunity for experiencing vulgarity. He was the aggressive landlubber—a refreshing type and a modern one. The landlubber gets covered with tar and chucked overboard, he turns green and is sick, but he has had his laugh and his say. He has made fun of the sea.

Sacrilege!

Yet the sea today certainly is in retreat. Occasionally it reasserts itself, as in the Kon-Tiki expedition, and occasionally, through the fringe of oil and dead birds and the chonking and bobbing of metal objects, we catch a glimpse of it from the shore. But it is in retreat poetically. A poet is needed to arrest it, to restore Neptune his majesty, to wet Canute his feet, to float the Old Man in the Boat. Auden is such a poet. He has the necessary power, and a contemporary vision that can include the past. He takes us back to the romantics, including Lear, he lends us their ears and their fears, and with their help revivifies the mass of water from whose shallows we came, and contrasts that mass with the desert, into which we try to retreat, and with the City, which we are trying to build and have never built. The nineteenth century helps him—Wordsworth, Shelley, Blake, Tennyson, Melville, Baudelaire, Rimbaud, Ibsen, Kierkegaard. They understand the expedition, the setting-out, the heroic leap, and sometimes they understand how expeditions end. The age of reason cannot help. Voltaire, Rousseau understand nothing. They cannot with their common sense interpret this trinity of Sea, Desert, City. They mock on, mock on. And, their salutary mirth in my ears, I turn me to *The Enchafèd Flood*.

It reprints lectures. Critics who have decided that lectures must not be reprinted will doubtless complain of it on this account; anyhow it is a good old game, complaining of Auden, and a safe one. The admonitory note, the professional quote, are certainly present in him, but underlying them is imaginative passion, and the words "We must love one another or die". The effort to grasp the universe, and where it threatens us, persists here as in his poems. The threat alters because we alter, and neither seas nor deserts now menace directly. They are symbols. And he plunges us into that world of symbols which is so chancy in its effects, and from which we emerge illuminated, or dazed. For myself, I am not too dazed. That is what happens to me when reading this writer. He elicits a response which I cannot always explain. Because he once wrote "We must love one another or die", he can command me to follow him.

The first section, "The Sea and the Desert", contrasts and compares these protagonists. They are alike in that they are wildernesses, which beckon to the outlaw and the hero, and they both contain earthly paradises—the Happy Island and the Oasis respectively. They differ in that the sea breeds life. The blessed creatures and the slimy things seen by the Ancient Mariner dwell there, so does Moby Dick; it is wild and lonely but vital. To the city of today—the squalid unbuilt or ruined city—the sea still calls, though its waters choke and destroy us as soon as they are tasted. Its romance is more powerful than the desert's— and T. E. Lawrence knew this really.

The second section, "The Stone and the Shell", interprets a dream of Wordsworth's with which the book started. Wordsworth dreamt that he encountered a knight, half Ishmael and half Don Quixote, who held in the one hand a stone, which belongs to the desert and symbolizes precise knowledge, and in the other hand a shell, symbolic of poetry and prophecy, and murmurous of the sea. Both the stone and the shell are needed for the perfect city, but the knight must know how to control their opposing magics. He cannot, the waters gain on him, and Wordsworth awakes. Auden has at this point much symbolism on his hands—an extensive bag of tricks. He too fails to control it, I think; anyhow this is the section of the book where I found myself getting dazed. I felt I had strayed into a conjuror's parlour, and that the objects hurtling around me were not real. It is a feeling one often experiences when reading the romantics, and it comes and it goes.

It has gone in the final section. This is called "Ishmael—Don Quixote". The two types of heroes are analysed, Ishmael more particularly, and there is a discussion of Moby Dick. Melville is very profoundly explored today, especially in the United States, and like all ploughed-up authors his surface has got rather bumpy. Fortunately Auden is a poet, who understands what poems feel like as well as what they mean, and who does not rely too much upon incest and castration. The sea guides him—perhaps through his Icelandic blood. Real and symbolic voyages coincide and by the end of the discussion we have a clearer vision of Ahab's tragedy.

The Enchafèd Flood, it should now appear, is itself a poem. Though its tone is critical, it is not constructed like a lecture course or a thesis. Brooding in it is the ruined or unbuilt city, and we must either build it or die. We cannot escape any more to the sands or the waves and pretend they are our destiny. We have annihilated time and space, we have furrowed the desert and spanned the sea, only to find at the end of every vista our own unattractive features. What remains for us, whither shall we turn? To the city which we have not yet built, to the unborn polity, to the new heroism.

> The heroic image [today] is not the nomad wanderer through the desert or over the ocean, but the less exciting figure of the builder, who renews the ruined walls of the city. Our temptations are not theirs. We are less likely to be tempted by solitude into Promethean pride: we are far more likely to become cowards in the face of the tyrant who would compel us to lie in the service of the False City. It is not madness we need to flee but prostitution. Let us, reading the logs of their fatal but heroic voyages, remember their courage.

Auden's hope—reinforced in his case by Christian dogma—is the world's hope and its only hope. For some of us who are non-Christian there still remains the comfort of the non-human, the relief, when we look up at the stars, of realizing that they are uninhabitable. But not there for any of us lies our work or our home.

[1951]

Forrest Reid

When one has been friends with a writer for thirty-five years, and he dies, and one is asked to write about him—well, one wishes to write about him, but the books recede, and little details, of doubtful interest to the public, take their place. No doubt Forrest Reid's trilogy of *Young Tom*, *The Retreat* and *Uncle Stephen* is a unique chronicle of boyhood. No doubt, again, *Apostate* is a memorable spiritual biography. Nor will *Illustrators of the Sixties* be superseded. But smaller things intrude. Moreover, to those who knew and loved him, he was more than a creator of books. He existed in his own right, and by the right of being unlike anyone else. His integrity, his affection, his patience and humorous irritability, his prejudices and occasional ruefulness about them—how can it all be conveyed without overdoing the tang or missing it out? Good temper, bad temper—which was it? One didn't know, didn't care, only knew that there was a great deal of it and that its charm was irresistible. He was the most important person in Belfast, and, though it would be too much to say that Belfast knew him not, I have sometimes smiled to think how little that great city, engaged in its own ponderous purposes, dreamed of him or indeed of anything. He who dreamed and was partly a dream. A dream compounded not only of visions, Mediterranean and Celtic, but of the "moral fragrance" which he prized and pursued and diffused.

Into which falls his voice. "Och, it'll do you no harm"—of whisky. Or "Tea or coffee? Tea, I think. It's apt to be the more successful." Or "What did he want to use that foul language for? Remus only gave him a wee nip." For Remus and all dogs he had unbounded love. For cats he entertained a proportionate regard, and his visits to Bloomsbury were rendered tolerable by a cemetery, where cats confabulated upon some railed-in tombs. Except for its animals, which included moles, he did not appreciate England. He came over to the place mainly to play croquet, in which he was expert, and, whirled from one championship ground to another in a car, acquired a special view of its geography. Each time it was nicer to him than he expected, which showed what he had been thinking in the intervals.

For his own country, for Northern Ireland, his feeling was passionate—a regional feeling, not political, and not hardening into theories. Happy the man who has such feelings, happy the district for which they are felt! He has given to the Lagan, and Newcastle, Co. Down, and Ballycastle, something which they can keep for ever, if they are worthy.

He entered no cultural swim, and for this his independence of character was responsible. He could not fit into any clique, he was never the right shape, and, though not truculent or aggressive, he never softened his opinions. For a long time he maintained that all women novelists, with the exception of Jane Austen, are bad, which did not commend him to the sisterhood. When his loyalty was once given it was irremovable. Year in, year out, whatever the metropolitan fashions, he reverenced Henry James. He had indeed hoped for closer literary contact with James, but the Master was scared of *The Garden God*, a Platonic but Hellenic romance, and somewhat withdrew. Reid was hurt and surprised, but not affronted. His high estimate of James's character and art did not waver. Another loyalty went out to Walter de la Mare, to whom he has devoted a detailed and affectionate study.

His critical attitude, especially about poetry, was childish and firm. Poems are people. They either evoke a sympathetic response from us or they do not, and if they do not we had better move away. In his last book, *The Milk of Paradise*, he writes: "After all, the personal appeal in poetry is everything, because without it, for the particular reader concerned, there *is* no poetry." What a contrast to the highly equipped modern critic who, until he has applied his tests and noted how the poem reacts to them, cannot know whether the poem is good, and, if good, good in what way and how good in that way! Reid kept to what he liked. This might have made his outlook arbitrary and whimsical, but he was saved here by the inner gravity of his spirit, and his natural good taste. In *The Milk of Paradise* he quotes, and discusses on an even note, hackneyed poems like "Lucy Gray", recondite poems like Dobell's "Orphan's Song", and controversial excerpts from Poe. There was his heart, thus it happened to respond. He left others to their own responses, nor was he curious to discover what these were.

Believing as he did (and as I do) in the past, he would approve a reference to our first meeting. It was in 1911, the year *The*

Bracknels was published. I had written to thank him for that delicate and disturbing novel, without knowing who he was or where he lived. I received an answer from round the corner. We were both of us in Belfast, and from this happy coincidence much depended. He and his friends invited me to lunch, the first of their endless hospitalities. There was pheasant—a delicious meal and an attentive dog. In the afternoon we rowed through sunlight and shadow up the Lagan, then a lovely stream haunted by his sort of ghosts. In the next year, when *Following Darkness* appeared, it was dedicated to me. Perhaps that is why I have a special feeling for it. Some critics sensed satanism in its title, and became excited. Idiots, they had forgotten Puck's "Following darkness like a dream". Towards the end of his life, he rewrote *Following Darkness* as *Peter Waring*, but I have never cared to read this later version. The earlier is so connected with happy visits to Ireland, with the Mourne Mountains, with cats and dogs muddling round a fire, with the glint from his spectacles and the turns in his voice.

[1947]

English Prose
between 1918 and 1939
The W. P. Ker Lecture, delivered in the
University of Glasgow

This is a period between two wars—the Long Weekend it has
been called—and some of the books published in it look backward—like Siegfried Sassoon's *Memoirs of an Infantry Officer*—
and try to record the tragedy of the past; others look forward and
try to avert or explain the disaster which overtook Europe in the
thirties. And even when they are not directly about a war—
like the works of Lytton Strachey or Joyce or Virginia Woolf—
they still display unrest or disillusionment or anxiety, they are still
the products of a civilization which feels itself insecure. The
French lady, Madame de Sévigné, writing letters during the wars
of the late seventeenth century, can feel tranquil. The English
lady, Jane Austen, writing novels in the Napoleonic wars, can
feel tranquil. Those wars were not total. But no one can write
during or between our wars and escape their influence. There,
then, is one obvious characteristic of our prose. It is the product
of people who have war on their mind. They need not be gloomy
or hysterical—often they are gay and sane and brave—but if they
have any sensitiveness they must realize what a mess the world
is in, and if they have no sensitiveness they will not be worth
reading.

We can conveniently divide the long weekend into two
periods—the 1920s and the 1930s. The division is not hard-and-
fast, still it is helpful. The twenties react after a war and recede
from it, the thirties are apprehensive of a war and are carried
towards it. The twenties want to enjoy life and to understand
it; the thirties also want to understand but for a special purpose:
to preserve civilization. They are less detached. In *Life among
the English* Rose Macaulay contrast the two periods neatly:

> The twenties were, as decades go, a good decade; gay, decora-
> tive, intelligent, extravagant, cultured. There were booms in
> photography, Sunday film and theatre clubs, surrealism, steel

furniture, faintly obscure poetry, Proust, James Joyce, dancing, rink-skating, large paintings on walls of rooms.

The next decade was more serious, less cultured, less aesthetic, more political. The slump blew like a cold draught at its birth, war stormed like forest fire at its close; between these two catastrophes Communists and Fascists battled and preached, and eyes turned apprehensively across the North Sea towards the alarming menace which had leaped up like a strident jack-in-the-box from a beer-cellar to more than a throne.

Rose Macaulay is a wise guide, tolerant, generous-minded, liberal, courageous, cheerful, and her judgements of society and social values are always sound. She sums up the two decades very well.

But of course there is more to say. There are influences in this world more powerful than either peace or war. And we cannot get a true idea of our period and the books it produces until we look deeper than fashions or politics or the achievements and failures of generals. For one thing, there is a huge economic movement which has been taking the whole world, Great Britain included, from agriculture towards industrialism. That began about a hundred and fifty years ago, but since 1918 it has accelerated to an enormous speed, bringing all sorts of changes into national and personal life. It has meant organization and plans and the boosting of the community. It has meant the destruction of feudalism and relationships based on the land, it has meant the transference of power from the aristocrat to the bureaucrat and the manager and the technician. Perhaps it will mean democracy, but it has not meant it yet, and personally I hate it. So I imagine do most writers, however loyally they try to sing its praises and to hymn the machine. But however much we detest this economic shift we have to recognize it as an important influence, more important than any local peace or war, which is going on all the time and transforming our outlooks. It rests on applied science, and as long as science is applied it will continue. Even when a writer seems to escape it, like T. E. Lawrence, he is conditioned by it. T. E. Lawrence hated the progress of industrialism, he hated what your city of Glasgow and my city of London stand for. He fled from it into the deserts of Arabia and the last of the romantic wars, in the search of old-time adventure, and later on into the deserts of his own heart. I think he was right to fly, because I believe that a writer's duty often exceeds any duty he owes to society, and that he often ought to lead a forlorn retreat. But of course the flight failed. Industrialism did T. E. Lawrence in in the long run, and it was not by the spear of an Arab but by a high-power motor-bike that he came to his death.[1] We must face the unpleasant truths that normal life today is a life in factories and offices, that even war has evolved from an adventure into a business, that even farming has become scientific, that insurance has taken the place of charity, that status has given way to contract. You will see how disquieting all this is to writers, who love, and ought to love, beauty and charm and the passage of the seasons, and generous impulses, and the tradition of their craft. And you will appreciate how lost some of them have been feeling during the last quarter of a century, and how they have been tempted to nostalgia like Siegfried Sassoon, or to disgust like Evelyn Waugh and Graham Greene.

But this economic movement, from the land to the factory, is not the only great movement which has gathered strength during our period. There has been a psychological movement, about which I am more enthusiastic. Man is beginning to understand himself better and to explore his own contradictions. This exploration is conveniently connected with the awful name of Freud, but it is not so much in Freud as in the air. It has brought a great enrichment to the art of fiction. It has given subtleties and depths to the portrayal of human nature. The presence in all of us of the subconscious, the occasional existence of the split personality, the persistence of the irrational, especially in people who pride themselves on their reasonableness, the importance of dreams and the prevalence of day-dreaming—here are some of the points which novelists have seized on and which have not been ignored by historians. This psychology is not new, but it has newly risen to the surface. Shakespeare was subconsciously aware of the subconscious, so were Emily Brontë, Herman Melville and others. But conscious knowledge of it only comes at the beginning of the century, with Samuel Butler's *The Way of All Flesh,* and only becomes general after 1918—partly owing to Freud. It gathers strength now, like the economic movement, and, like it, is independent of war or peace. Of course, writers can be stupid about it, as about anything else, they can apply it as a formula instead of feeling it as a possibility; the stupid psychologist who applies his (or her) formula in season or out

[1] See Christopher Caudwell, *Studies in a Dying Culture*; a brilliant criticism of the period from a Communist standpoint.

and is always saying "You think you don't but you do" or "You think you do but you don't" can be absolutely maddening. But the better minds of our age—what a rich harvest they have reaped! Proust in France to begin with; Gertrude Stein and her experiments in uninhibited talk—not too successful in her own case but influential; Dorothy Richardson's novels, another pioneer in this country; the later work of D. H. Lawrence, the novels of Virginia Woolf, Joyce, de la Mare, Elizabeth Bowen. History too has profited. This new method of examining the human individual has helped to reinterpret the past. Aldous Huxley's *Grey Eminence* is one example—it gives a fresh view of Cardinal Richelieu and his adviser Father Joseph—a fresh view of their insides. Livingston Lowes's *The Road to Xanadu* is another example: a fresh view of the genius and make-up of Coleridge. And then there is the great work of a Christian historian, Arnold Toynbee, *A Study of History*, which regards history as a record of what men think and feel as well as of what they assert and achieve, and tries, with this extra material, to account for the rise and fall of civilizations. Professor Toynbee comes to the conclusion that they rise and fall in accord with a religious law, and that except the Lord build the house their labour is but lost that build it; or, if you prefer the language of Freud to that of the Old Testament, that the conscious must be satisfactorily based on the subconscious.

So, though we are justified in thinking of our period as an interval between two wars, we must remember that it forms part of larger movements where wars become insignificant: part of an economic movement from agriculture to industrialism, and of a psychological movement which is reinterpreting human nature. Both these movements have been speeded up, and writers have in my judgement been worried by the economic shift but stimulated by the psychological. Remember too, in passing, another factor, and that is the shift in physics exemplified by the work of Einstein. Can literary men understand Einstein? Of course they cannot—even less than they can understand Freud. But the idea of relativity has got into the air and has favoured certain tendencies in novels. Absolute good and evil, as in Dickens, are seldom presented. A character becomes good or evil in relation to some other character or to a situation which may itself change. You can't measure people up, because the yard-measure itself keeps altering its length. The best exponent of relativity in literature known to me is Proust, though there are instances in English too. Most of Proust's people are odious, yet you cannot have the comfort of writing any of them off as bad. Given the circumstances, even the most odious of them all, Madame Verdurin, can behave nobly. Proust and others have this attitude—not because they know anything about science, but because the idea of relativity, like the idea of the subconscious self, has got about and tinged their outlook.

A word must now be said on the special character of prose. Prose, unlike poetry, does two things. It serves us in daily life and it creates works of art. For instance, I travelled from Euston to Glasgow on prose, I am talking prose now, and, like Monsieur Jourdain, I am astonished at finding myself doing so. For prose, besides serving our practical ends, also makes great literature.

Now, one of the problems which a critic has to tackle is that these two uses of prose are not watertight, and one of them is as it were constantly slopping over into the other. The practical popular prose is always getting into the deliberate artistic prose which makes books. Indeed, if it didn't, the artistic prose couldn't live very long, as it would get stale and stuffy. It has to be replenished by contemporary speech. And in this period of ours there has been a great deal of this replenishment. New words and phrases—and, what is more important, the new habits of thought expressed by them—are rapidly absorbed by authors and put into books. That is one tendency of our period, and it may be called, for want of a better word, the popular tendency. The writer feels himself part of his people. He enters or wants to enter into their ways. And he wants to be understood by them, and so he tries to be informal and clear. I'll give several examples of it. Here is a little example, taken from letter-writing. In 1918, if I had had a letter from a stranger it would certainly have begun "Dear Sir". Today, if I have a letter from a stranger, it will probably begin "Dear Mr Forster". One form of address doesn't mean more than another, but the convention is a more friendly one. I expect it came in, like other speak-easies, from America. It shows which way the wind of words is blowing. Another sign is the speeches of public men. Public men are becoming less formal—some of them because of the influence of the radio, for they know if they broadcast too pompously listeners will switch off. Others are informal by instinct, like Winston Churchilll, whose speeches sound and read more democratic than those of the Prime Ministers of the last war. Novelists too—

they practise the friendly unpatronizing tone; Christopher Isherwood's *Mr Norris Changes Trains* is an example of this. Isherwood—who is extremely intelligent—always writes as if the reader were equally intelligent. He is an example of democratic good manners. He trusts his public. Another novelist—Ernest Hemingway—introduces a new technique of conversation. Another straw which shows which way this wind is blowing is the tendency of official notices and proclamations to become more intelligible. They do so reluctantly, for the bureaucrat who gives his meaning clearly is afraid he may be giving something else away too. Still, they do it. They tend to issue orders which we understand. And since we live under orders this is a good thing.

I could continue this list of the popular tendencies in prose. We have had an example in the demand from high quarters for Basic English—and I expect it is a useful commercial idea, though I cannot see what it has to do with literature, or what it can do to literature, except impoverish it. I'll conclude with an example of another kind, a reference to the English of the Authorized Version of the Bible. This, the great monument of our seventeenth-century speech, has constantly influenced our talk and writing for the last three hundred years. Its rhythm, its atmosphere, its turns of phrase, belonged to our people and overflowed into our books. Bunyan, Johnson, Blake, George Eliot, all echo it. About ten years ago an edition of the Bible came out called *The Bible Designed to be Read as Literature.* Its publication gave some of us a shock and caused us to realize that the English of the Authorized Version had at last become remote from popular English. This was well put in a review by Somerset Maugham. The English of the Bible, he agreed, is part of our national heritage, but it is so alien to our present idiom that no writer can study it profitably. I shall soon be quoting from a writer who has studied it, still Somerset Maugham is right on the whole, and there is now an unbridgeable gulf between ourselves and the Authorized Version as regards style, and the gulf widened about 1920, when those other influences we have discussed became strong. Quotations from the Bible still occur, but they support my contention: they are usually conventional and insensitive, introduced because the author or speaker wants to be impressive without taking trouble. Listen to the following advertisement of Cable and Wireless in *The Times* of 28 July 1943. The advertisement is reporting a speech made by a cabinet minister, Colonel Oliver Stanley, at a Cable and Wireless staff lunch:

When the end comes, when victory is won, then history will begin to assess merit. We shall all of us be searching our conscience. . . . We shall be discussing who succeeded and who failed. . . . I have no doubt at all, when we come to discuss the part that Cable and Wireless has played, what the verdict of the nation will be—"Well done thou good and faithful servant!"

No doubt Cable and Wireless has done and deserved well, but I do not feel it can be suitably congratulated in the words of St Matthew's Gospel, and if the English of the Bible had been in Colonel Stanley's blood instead of in his cliché-box I do not think he would have used such words. It is an example of insensitiveness to the Authorized Version and of the complete divorce between Biblical and popular English. (A similar example, this time of insensitiveness to Milton, was the slogan "They also serve" on a war-workers' poster.)

So much for this popular tendency in prose. I have suggested that it takes various forms, bringing freshness and informality and new usages and democratic good manners into literature, but also bringing vulgarity and flatness. Now for the other tendency to which I will attach the name esoteric: the desire on the part of writers—generally the more distinguished writers— to create something better than the bloodshed and dullness which have been creeping together over the world. Such writers are often censured. You may complain that Lytton Strachey, Virginia Woolf, James Joyce, D. H. Lawrence and T. E. Lawrence have done little to hearten us up. But you must admit they were the leading writers of our age. It is an age that could not produce a Shakespeare or even a Madame de Sévigné or a Jane Austen: an age in which sensitive people could not feel comfortable, and were driven to seek inner compensation: an age similar in some ways to that which caused St Augustine to write *The City of God*. St Augustine, though he looked outside him, worked within. He too was esoteric. These writers look outside them and find their material lying about in the world. But they arrange it and re-create it within, temporarily sheltered from the pitiless blasts and the fog.

A further word on T. E. Lawrence. The *Seven Pillars of Wisdom* is a most enigmatic book. Lawrence made good in the world of action and was what most of us regard as a hero—brave, selfless, modest and kind by nature yet ruthless at need, loyal and the inspirer of loyalty, magnetic, a born leader of men, and victorious at Damascus in the last of the picturesque wars. Such a man, even if not happy, will surely be true to type. He will remain the man of action, the extrovert. But when we read the *Seven Pillars* we find beneath the gallant fighting and the brilliant description of scenery—sensitiveness, introspection, doubt, disgust at the material world. It is the book of a man who cannot fit in with twentieth-century civilization, and loves the half-savage Arabs because they challenge it. This comes out in the following quotation; note in the final sentence the hit at "vested things": at the innate commercialism of the West which ruined the peace of Versailles.

> Their mind [the Arabs'] was strange and dark, full of depressions and exaltations, lacking in rule, but with more of ardour and more fertile in belief than any other in the world. They were a people of starts, for whom the abstract was the strongest motive, the process of infinite courage and variety, and the end nothing. They were as unstable as water, and like water would perhaps finally prevail. Since the dawn of life, in successive waves they had been dashing themselves against the coasts of flesh. Each wave was broken, but, like the sea, wore away ever so little of the granite on which it failed, and some day, ages yet, might roll unchecked over the place where the material world had been, and God would move upon the face of those waters. One such wave (and not the least) I raised and rolled before the breath of an idea, till it reached its crest, and toppled over and fell at Damascus. The wash of that wave, thrown back by the resistance of vested things, will provide the matter of the following wave, when in fullness of time the sea shall be raised once more.

The *Seven Pillars* for all its greatness is too strange a book to be typical of the period, and the same applies to another curious masterpiece, James Joyce's *Ulysses*. For a typical example I'd take Lytton Strachey's *Queen Victoria*. This is important for several reasons. It came out at the beginning of our period, it is an achievement of genius, and it has revolutionized the art of biography. Strachey did debunk of course: he hated pomposity, hypocrisy and muddle-headedness, he mistrusted inflated reputations, and was clever at puncturing them, and he found in the Victorian age, which had taken itself very, very seriously, a tempting target for his barbed arrows. But he was much more than a debunker. He did what no biographer had done before: he managed to get inside his subject. Earlier biographers, like

Macaulay and Carlyle, had produced fine and convincing pictures of people; Lytton Strachey makes his people move; they are alive, like characters in a novel: he constructs or rather reconstructs them from within. Sometimes he got them wrong: his presentation of General Gordon has been questioned, so has his brilliant later work on Elizabeth and Essex. But even when they are wrong they seem alive, and in the *Queen Victoria* his facts have not been seriously challenged; and, based on dry documents, a whole society and its inhabitants rise from the grave, and walk about. That was his great contribution. He was a historian who worked from within, and constructed out of the bones of the past something more real and more satisfactory than the chaos surrounding him. He is typical of our period, and particularly of the twenties—throughout them his influence is enormous; today it has declined, partly because people are again taking themselves very, very seriously, and don't like the human race to be laughed at, partly because Strachey had some tiresome imitators, who have brought his method into discredit. However, that doesn't matter. Reputations always will go up and down. What matters is good work, and *Queen Victoria* is a masterpiece. It is a pageant of the historical type, but as the grand procession passes we—you and I, we little readers—are somehow inside the procession, we mingle unobserved with royalty and statesmen and courtiers and underlings, and hear their unspoken thoughts.

Even a frivolous passage, like the one about the boy Jones, has its historical function. Lytton Strachey was a gay person who loved fun and nonsense, and he knew how to make use of them in his work. Through the episode of the enigmatic boy Jones, an undersized youth who repeatedly entered Buckingham Palace and hid there in the year 1840, was discovered under sofas, and confessed "that he had 'helped himself to soup and other eatables ... sat upon the throne, seen the Queen, and heard the Princess Royal squall'", Strachey re-creates the domestic confusion existing there, and makes the period come alive. Then he passes on to more serious topics.

What was he serious about? Not about political ideals or social reform. Like T. E. Lawrence, he was disillusioned, though in another way. He believed, however, in wit and aristocratic good manners, and he was implacable in his pursuit of truth. He believed, furthermore, in fidelity between human beings. There, and there only, the warmth of his heart comes out. He is always moved by constant affection, and the Queen's love for the Prince Consort, and for his memory, makes the book glow and preserves it from frigidity. Strachey's belief in affection, like his fondness for fun, is too often forgotten. Here is the famous passage describing the Queen's death, with which the book closes. He begins by being the dignified historian; then he dismisses his subject tenderly, and launches the Queen as it were on an ebbing tide, carrying her backwards through the manifold joys of life till she vanishes in the mists of her birth.

By the end of the year the last remains of her ebbing strength had almost deserted her; and through the early days of the opening century it was clear that her dwindling forces were kept together only by an effort of will. On January 14, she had at Osborne an hour's interview with Lord Roberts, who had returned victorious from South Africa a few days before. She inquired with acute anxiety into all the details of the war; she appeared to sustain the exertion successfully; but, when the audience was over, there was a collapse. On the following day her medical attendants recognized that her state was hopeless; and yet, for two days more, the indomitable spirit fought on; for two days more she discharged the duties of a Queen of England. But after that there was an end of working; and then, and not till then, did the last optimism of those about her break down. The brain was failing, and life was gently slipping away. Her family gathered round her; for a little more she lingered, speechless and apparently insensible; and, on January 22, 1901, she died.

When, two days previously, the news of the approaching end had been made public, astonished grief had swept over the country. It appeared as if some monstrous reversal of the course of nature was about to take place. The vast majority of her subjects had never known a time when Queen Victoria had not been reigning over them. She had become an indissoluble part of their whole scheme of things, and that they were about to lose her appeared a scarcely possible thought. She herself, as she lay blind and silent, seemed to those who watched her to be divested of all thinking—to have glided already, unawares, into oblivion. Yet, perhaps, in the secret chambers of consciousness, she had her thoughts, too. Perhaps her fading mind called up once more the shadows of the past to float before it, and retraced, for the last time, the vanished visions of that long history—passing back and back, through the cloud of years, to older and ever older memories—to the spring woods at Osborne, so full of primroses for Lord Beaconsfield—to Lord Palmerston's queer clothes and high demeanour, and Albert's face under the green lamp, and Albert's first stag at Balmoral, and Albert in his blue and silver uniform, and the Baron coming in through a doorway, and Lord M. dreaming at Windsor with the rooks cawing in the elm-trees, and the Archbishop of Canterbury on his knees in the dawn, and the old King's turkey-cock ejaculations, and Uncle Leopold's soft voice at Claremont, and Lehzen with the globes, and her mother's feathers sweeping down towards her, and a great old repeater-watch of her father's in its tortoiseshell case, and a yellow rug, and some friendly flounces of sprigged muslin, and the trees and the grass at Kensington.

You'll remember what I said before about the new psychology being in the air, and this last long lovely drifting sentence, with its imaginings of the subconscious, could not have been created at an earlier date.

A word on the authors whom I have mentioned. I have kept to those who may be said to belong to our period, who were formed by it, and received its peculiar stamp. Authors like Arnold Bennett, Galsworthy, Wells, Belloc, Chesterton, Frank Swinnerton, Norman Douglas, Bertrand Russell, Lowes Dickinson, George Moore, Max Beerbohm, did good work after 1920, and some of them are still active. But they got their impressions and formed their attitudes in an earlier period, before the first of the two world wars. D. H. Lawrence presents a special difficulty. Does he come in or not? His finest novels, *The White Peacock* and *Sons and Lovers*, were published round about 1912, and he displays all his life a blend of vision and vituperation which seem to date him further back still—right back to Carlyle. On the other hand, he was alive to the new economics and the new psychology, and well aware, when he died in 1930, that the war to end war had ended nothing but the Victorian peace. My own feeling is that he does come into our survey.

To sum up my remarks. Our period: a long weekend between two wars. Economic and psychological changes already in existence intensify. Writers are intimidated by the economic changes but stimulated by the psychological. Prose, because it is a medium for daily life as well as for literature, is particularly sensitive to what is going on, and two tendencies can be noted: the popular, which absorbs what is passing, and the esoteric, which rejects it, and tries to create through art something more valuable than monotony and bloodshed. The best work of the period has this esoteric tendency. T. E. Lawrence, though heroic in action, retreats into the desert to act. Lytton Strachey is disillusioned, except about truth and human affection.

As for assessing the value of our period, I am disposed to place it high, and I do not agree with those numerous critics who condemn it as a failure, and scold mankind for enjoying itself too much in the twenties and for theorizing too much in the thirties. We are plunged in a terrific war, and our literary judgements are not at their best. All our criticism is or ought to be tentative. And tentatively I suggest that the long weekend did valuable work, and I ask you to pause before you yield to the prevalent tendency to censure it.

[1944]

An Outsider on Poetry

I have written very little poetry in my life, and only two lines of modern poetry. Here they are:

> I will pull down Hastings, you shall see
> Companion to India as a boat gnawed.

I wrote them last year in a dream, and managed on waking to transcribe them before the censor stopped me—that censor who from Porlock or elsewhere always attends on our sleep and prevents us from communicating what we have learned in it. On their merits I need not pronounce. They seem to me poetry because they scan, and modern because they are obscure and minatory. Most feebly credentialled by them, I approach the thirty-six poets of *Poetry of the Present*, Mr Geoffrey Grigson's anthology of the thirties and forties.

One has need of some sort of credential. The outsider, the proser, even if he is modest and sensitive, goes wrong in the poetry world very quickly. He can hear music, he can recognize ideas, but the marriage between music and ideas, out of which the poem is born, often eludes him, with the result that his judgement is unreliable, he praises where he ought to blame, and vice versa. He is constantly entering a world for which he is not prepared. He is prepared for the poetry of the past. Critics have laid down the lines within which he may wander. But the present demands an unaided opinion, which he hesitates to give. The safer course is not to read the stuff, and to hold the comfortable hope that what is worthy in it will survive. Meanwhile the poets are far from comfortable, for if they are not read they will not get published. Their fate is symbolic: the present indifference to contemporary poetry—contrasting so lamentably with the curiosity of the twenties and thirties—is part of the general menace to literature.

I read it from time to time myself. I cannot pretend to be as curious about it as I am about contemporary music, but now and then, perhaps through some personal experience, perhaps through my profound belief that poets know best, I venture, I venture into the present's whirlpool, and find something hitting my hand. It is uncommonly like a stone, and since it may not be a precious stone practical people ignore it. There, however, the stone is. Through some slight affinity in myself, I hold it, I remove it from the waters with respect, I listen and look.

There's been discomfort here. That is my first impression. The person who has created this little object does not find the universe a soft or sunny spot. Through his imagination, he has heard danger coming, he has seen war-clouds, he has felt the social tremble underfoot, and maybe he has detected disunion in his own heart. He is minatory like my own doggerel. How should he not be? It began with Auden, and the various people who have complained of Auden have never managed to avoid his note,

> never will be perfect like the fountains;
> We live in freedom by necessity,
> A mountain people dwelling among mountains.

The threat may be lifted to the heroic, it may be subdued into an anxiety, it may be masked by compassion or sharpened by satire, but in some form or other it is the heritage of most of the contributors to this volume.

> The blackbirds sing and I see no end of agony,
>   The pink and the white blossom
>
> Spangles the chestnuts, the theatres pour into the
>   streets
> The unimaginative. And the earth renews
> In Europe its solar gaiety, and the earth moves on
>   To no destination.
>   (Kenneth Allott)

What's to become of the world if Money should suddenly die?

Should suddenly take a toss and go down crack on his head?
If the dance suddenly finished, if they stopped the runaway bus,
if the trees stopped racing away?
If our hopes come true and he dies, what's to become of us?
                                        (Bernard Spencer)

> When I was born on Amman hill
> A dark bird crossed the sun.
> Sharp on the floor the shadow fell;
> I was the youngest son.

And when I went to the County School
I worked in a shaft of light.
In the wood of the desk I cut my name:
Dai for Dynamite.

The tall black hills my brothers stood;
Their lessons all were done.
From the door of the school when I ran out
They frowned to watch me run.

(Vernon Watkins)

The seven-branched cactus
Will never sweat wine:
My own bleeding feet
Shall furnish the sign.

The rock says "Endure".
The wind says "Pursue".
The sun says "I will suck your bones
And afterwards bury you."

(Sidney Keyes)

That seems the generalization to which the outsider can cling
as the little objects dash against his hand: minatory: the anxiety
of those who, through their temperament, apprehend more than
the rest of us, and have special powers for communicating their
dreams. It is only a generalization, and the poem I most admired
stands right beyond it on the calm lake of oriental philosophy:

But now beyond question, the swans sail on together,
Wing answering wing, as parting of a breath
Is close to its indrawing.
And the god in one sees himself in the other,
For his self-knowledge is the sailing of two swans.

But the swans do not know themselves possessed.
They go on their own way in their distant world.

(E. J. Scovell)

And there are other poems which express no view, but rest
content with the immediate sensation, the present image:

The scent of the conifers, sound of the bath,
The view from my bedroom of moss-dappled path,
As I struggle with double-end evening tie,
For we dance at the Golf Club, my victor and I.

(John Betjeman)

Wild Wilbur paces by the caves
His limbs are long his smile is wide
his hands are dangling side to side
his eyes are fixed upon the waves.

The birds sing in his healthy ears
the waves spill round his anklesocks
sometimes he spits upon the rocks
sometimes he picks his nose with tears.

(James Kirkup)

That contemporary poetry should often be obscure and odd never surprises me; the poet, however traditional his equipment, is always an innovator and likely to puzzle his elders. He has seen something old in a new way, and he may even have seen something new. When reading him it is desirable to be good-tempered; so many readers get cross out of a sense of duty; they are proud of being irritated by modern verse, and of detecting any affectations in it. They enjoy sneering at it, and one small thing that we can do for it and for literature generally is to call their bluff and ask them to explain why they are sneering.

[1949]

Mohammed Iqbal

I met Iqbal once, thirty years ago, and only in passing. He is
dead now and lies in honour outside the great mosque in Lahore,
his own city. I visited his grave last winter. He is constantly
mentioned in India—quite as often as Tagore, with whom he is
contrasted. Over here he is little known; so I shall venture to
allude to him, although I can only read him in translation.

Iqbal was an orthodox Moslem, though not a conventional
one. He was highly educated, and partly in Europe; he was
not cosmopolitan, and the basis of his culture remained oriental.
By profession he was a lawyer. He wrote both prose and poetry.
The poems are mostly in Urdu, some are in Persian, and a few
in Punjabi. As for his politics, he was once in sympathy with
a united India, but in later life he changed, and adherents of
Pakistan now claim him as a prophet. Whatever his opinions,
he was no fanatic, and he refers to Hindus and to Christians with
courtesy and respect.

All the same he was a fighter. He believed in the Self—the
Self as a fighting unit—and his philosophy is not an enquiry into
truth but a recommendation as to how the fight should be carried
on. Fight we must, for man is the vice-regent of God upon
earth. We must fortify our personalities. We must be hard.
We must always be in a state of tension and try to be supermen.
In one poem, Satan complains to God that men are not worth
tempting because they are weak and have never discovered their
Selves:

> O master of all . . .
> Association with mankind has debased me. . . .
> Take back from me this doll of water and clay.[1]

So might the button-moulder in Ibsen's play complain of Per
Gynt. Iqbal reminds us of Nietzsche too. Renunciation of the
Self is a form of cowardice, and therefore a crime. We cannot

[1] The translations are from an interesting monograph by Mr S. A. Vahid,
published in Lahore [as revised by the author for the edition published in
London by John Murray, 1959—Ed.].

bear one another's burdens, and we must not expect to be redeemed.

Now he combines this doctrine of hardness and of the Self with a capacity for mysticism. The combination makes him remarkable as a poet. Even in a translation, one can see the sudden opening-up of vistas between the precepts. It is not the mysticism that seeks union with God. On this point the poet is emphatic. We shall see God perhaps. We shall never be God. For God, like ourselves, has a Self, and he created us not out of himself but out of nothing. Iqbal dislikes the pantheism which he saw all around him in India—for instance, in Tagore—and he castigates those Moslem teachers who have infected Islam with it. It is weakening and wrong to seek unity with the divine. Vision—perhaps. Union—no.

Such—if an outsider may summarize—is his philosophy. It is not a philosophy I like, but that is another matter. There is anyhow nothing vague about it, nothing muzzy. It gives us a shock and helps us to see where we are. It is non-Christian. It is, in a sense, anti-humanitarian. It inspires him to write poems. They follow the orthodox forms, but they contain matter which is excitingly modern. Take, for instance, this poem in which Man defiantly addresses God on the ground that Man has proved the better artist of the two:

> Thou didst create night and I made the lamp,
> Thou didst create clay and I made the cup.
> Thou didst create the deserts, mountains and forests,
> I produced the orchards, gardens and groves;
> It is I who turn stone into a mirror,
> And it is I who turn poison into an antidote!

Or consider this strange poem on the subject of Lenin. Lenin has died, and finds himself in the presence of the Deity whom he had supposed to be an invention of the priests. He is not intimidated, but speaks his mind. God exists, to be sure. But whose God is he? The starving peasant's? The God of the East, who worships the white man? Or of the West, who worships the Almighty Dollar?

> Thou art All Powerful and Just, but in Thy world
> The lot of the hapless labourer is very hard!
> When will this boat of Capitalism be wrecked?
> Thy world is waiting for the Day of Reckoning!

The angels are moved by the dead Bolshevik's bluntness, and

they sing to their Lord like the angels at the opening of Goethe's *Faust*, but not in the same strain:

> Intellect is still unbridled, Love is not localized;
> O Painter Divine, Thy painting is still lacking in something.
> Lying in ambush for mankind are the libertine, the theo-
>   logian, the leader and the monk.
> In Thy Universe the old order still continueth!

The Almighty is moved in his turn. He bows to the criticism of Lenin, and he orders the angels to burn every cornstalk in the field which does not nourish the cultivator, to give the sparrow strength to fight the falcon, and to smash up the glasshouse of modern civilization. Iqbal never identifies hardness with oppression, or the Self with selfishness. The superman he seeks may come from any class of society.

Here is an uncontroversial lyric, "Loneliness". The poet is speaking, and his words gain pathos when we remember his creed of hardness:

> To the seashore I went and said to a restless wave,
> "Thou art always in quest of something. What ails thee?
> There are a thousand bright pearls in thy bosom,
> But hast thou a heart like mine in thy breast?"
> It merely trembled, sped away from the shore, and said
>   nothing!
> I betook myself to the presence of God, passing beyond the
>   sun and the moon, and said:
> "In Thy world not a single particle knows me,
> The world has no heart and this earthly being of mine is
>   all heart.
> The garden is charming, but is not worthy of my song."
> A smile came to His lips but He said nothing!

Mohammed Iqbal is a genius and a commanding one, and, though I often disagree with him and usually agree with Tagore, it is Iqbal I would rather read. I know where I am with him. He is one of the two great cultural figures of modern India, and our ignorance about him is extraordinary.

[1946]

Syed Ross Masood

Contributed to the
Memorial Number of an Urdu journal

Masood had many English friends, but I may claim to be the oldest and most intimate of them. I have known him since 1907, and we kept in touch the whole time. I have been with him in England and in Switzerland and have twice visited him in India[1] and have also been his guest in France and in Germany. I cannot speak of our affection here—it is not the time or the place—but I am thankful to pay this tribute to it and to his memory. There never was anyone like him and there never will be anyone like him. He cannot be judged as ordinary men are judged. My own debt to him is incalculable. He woke me up out of my suburban and academic life, showed me new horizons and a new civilization, and helped me towards the understanding of a continent. Until I met him, India was a vague jumble of rajahs, sahibs, babus and elephants, and I was not interested in such a jumble; who could be? He made everything real and exciting as soon as he began to talk, and seventeen years later when I wrote *A Passage to India* I dedicated it to him out of gratitude as well as out of love, for it would never have been written without him.

Masood was essentially an artist. Those who knew him as an official may be surprised at this statement, but though his career was of a practical character his temperament was aesthetic. He lived by his emotions and instincts, and his standards were those of good taste. "Don't be so damned inartistic," he would say if he wanted to criticize my conduct. For logic, and for ethical consistency, he had very little use. He had an artist's recklessness over money; he was fantastically generous, incredibly hospitable, and always happiest when he was giving something away. He was a patron of the arts and a connoisseur; he loved good books, coins and engravings: when he went to Japan, he made a collection of coloured prints there, and gave them to me afterwards. His aesthetic judgements were not always sound, but they were always vehement and came from the very depths of his being. As a

[1] First at his home in Aligarh, and then in Hyderabad, Deccan, where he was Director of Education.

young man he had an unbounded admiration for the poetry of Alfred de Musset, and in later life when a play of Tolstoy's was put on in London and took his fancy he went to see it eight times. A professional critic may smile at his enthusiasms, but men of wider outlook will understand them, and recognize their sincerity and their stimulating effect on others. One might disagree with him but he never left one cold. With his temperament, he naturally felt most at home in the country that has honoured art most, and that country is neither India nor England but France. He loved Paris, and he spoke French well.

What did he think of the English? He handled them splendidly. If they patronized him, he let them have it back, very politely, and I have often been amused at the way in which Englishmen and Englishwomen who had begun by giving themselves airs were obliged to drop them, and to yield to his masterful personality and his charm. There is a story that he was once involved in a "railway-carriage" incident. He was stretched full-length in an empty compartment when a British officer bounced in and said, "Come on! Get out of this." Masood looked up quietly and said, "D'you want your head knocked off?", whereupon the officer exclaimed, "I say, I'm awfully sorry, I didn't know you were that sort of person," and they became excellent friends. Whether this story be true or not, it is certainly true that on another occasion when returning on a P. & O. he contracted to shave an Australian miner all the way from Bombay to Marseilles for the sum of one guinea, and that he kept the contract. That was how he handled the Anglo-Saxons. He overwhelmed them by his energy and his unconventionality of address.

That was how he handled them, but what did he think of them? Leaving aside his English friends, whom he placed in a class apart, what did he feel about the Ruling Race as a whole? Perhaps his private thoughts are best expressed in a remark which has always amused me: "As for your damned countrymen, I pity the poor fellows from the bottom of my heart, and give them all the help I can." He was irritated by the English, he was sometimes bitter about them, but he realized that they were awkwardly placed in India, and he extended, half humorously, his sympathy towards them in their plight. He did not really dislike them, and I attribute his tolerance to his early upbringing: when he was a little boy at Aligarh, he lived with Sir Theodore and Lady Morison, and his lifelong friendship with both of them coloured his outlook and made him less exacting.

Masood's real work, of course, lay with his own community in his own country, and those who shared it will write about him best. But I knew him very well, from a particular angle, and I have tried to keep to that angle in this inadequate contribution to his memory. When his official career is described, it must not be forgotten that he was essentially an artist, and I have tried to emphasize this. And, when his services to Islam, to India and to the Urdu language are commemorated, it must not be forgotten that he was loved and indeed adored by men and women who differed from him in creed, race and speech, but were able nevertheless to recognize his genius and the greatness of his heart.

[1937]

A Duke Remembers

Men, Women and Things, the Duke of Portland's reminiscences, is more of a bag than a book. The reader who opens it will assist at a tremendously aristocratic shoot, where many birds fall dead but none are wantonly wounded. In the foreground move the guns, always titled and often royal, then come the highly paid keepers, and further off, also doing their duty and drawing their screw, slink the beaters. It is a very good-tempered book. Great names hurtle through the air, to fall at our feet with scarcely a feather disarranged. It is also a self-assured book, hence its strength. If the writer stopped to think what he was aiming at, he would be lost, the pen would drop from his hand. But he never stops, he just writes, just as he just shoots, dresses or rides. He has worn the best clothes all his life, killed the best animals, and he had the best friends, and with the same flair he uses the best words. Hit or miss! There's no getting away from that truth, is there? And it's a hit all the time with the Duke of Portland. Duke, Duke, you're cute, as those lively if backward people the Americans would say. Oh Duke, give us more! And this is indeed the third volume of his reminiscences. They make the pleasantest reading, that is to say, he is so loyal to his peers, so considerate to his dependants, and so resourceful and jolly when confronted with the plebs, that we do not notice the triviality of their subject-matter or their narrowness of outlook.

> In her younger days, "Skittles" often hunted with the Quorn Hounds, riding horses lent her by an admirer of Hebrew origin, who hunted from Melton. One day he and his horse fell into a brook. "Skittles" jumped over them both, turned round, kissed her hand and said, "Moses in the bulrushes, I see!" This is only one of the many good stories I have heard about "Skittles".

There is something faintly wrong in this good story about Skittles, but we dash past it, the racy anecdote carries us. We join too in the baiting of various provincial mayors. Mayors are absurd, they show the wrong sort of awe at the approach of royalty, with the result that a drop of sweat falls from the nose of one of them onto Queen Alexandra's glove. "Fortunately the Lady in Waiting had a handkerchief at hand", so no real harm was done. (The mentality of the Duke here is precisely that of the Mayor, but he doesn't notice that, nor do we.) We relish, too, the wit of Sir Frederick Milner. Interrupted at a political meeting by a radical grocer, Sir Frederick dubbed him "Treacle Tommy". The grocer was furious and retorted with "Frothy Fred", but this was not nearly as clever, and when the election results came out it was the "froth" that rose to the top, while the "treacle" sank to the bottom, its natural home.

Yes, the general effect of the book is pleasant. The writer is a man of energy, good humour and natural sense, who has inherited and enhanced a great name, held a high post in the royal household, and found the world agreeable. He does not like the present day. Women are plainer, driving deteriorates, of the thirteen great London houses of his youth only four remain as private residences, and as for the country, the estates around Welbeck are let, or empty, and their staffs of servants are seeking employment elsewhere. Such are the results of Treacle Tommy and time. But the Duke is too good a sportsman to grumble: "For all this, I believe human nature is, and will always be, the same; it may therefore be only the outward and visible form of things which has so much altered. I hope that the new world, though I do not always agree with its ways, holds just as many possibilities of happiness, good-fellowship and enjoyment of life as that which I knew, and shall try to some extent to describe."

In a sentence such as this the landed aristocrat seems the only democrat, and our hearts go out to him. But he is far away from us really. His touches of arrogance and patronage, his childish interest in uniforms, and the clouds of retainers behind which he can retire, combine to make him a very queer bird. No doubt the arrogance is unconscious, but the aristocrat does practise, more than most men, the art of switching off when a person or a situation incommodes him. Graciousness and bleakness alternate. Hence the mixed impression he makes upon the general public, and the reprisals he occasionally provokes. A regrettable incident once happened at Nottingham. Lord Roberts, attended by the Duke himself, was decorating veterans there, and one of the men, just as the ribbon was going to be pinned on him, opened his coat, and out popped the head of a kitten. A kitten was the last thing which the Commander-in-

Chief had expected, and he so hated cats that he stepped back and trod on the Duke's toe. All must deplore the veteran's conduct, yet the public is bound to pop out a kitten occasionally, or it would burst. It has, every now and then, to remind the governing classes that they must not take themselves and their awards too seriously, and if it is ever afraid to do this England will cease to be England.

[1937]

Mrs Miniver[1]

A working-class man I know—he grew up in a Gloucestershire village—has told me of the reactions of the villagers there to the parson thirty years back. The parson was not disliked, he was a kindly, friendly fellow, who had the right word for every occasion. But when the right word was spoken and he passed out of earshot, swinging his stick and looking right and left at the sky, the villagers came into their own for a moment, and used foul language about him. They had to, to clear their chests and to get rid of their feeling of incompetence. To preserve their manhood and their self-respect, they had to splutter a little smut.

Mrs Miniver, the gifted heroine of Miss Jan Struther's sketches, invites a similar reaction. She, too, has the right word for every occasion. What answer can the villagers make to a lady who is so amusing, clever, observant, broad-minded, shrewd, demure, bohemian, happily-married, triply-childrened, public-spirited and at all times such a lady? No answer, no answer at all. They listen to her saying the right things, and are dumb. They watch her doing the right things in the right way, and are paralysed. Even if they disgrace themselves by spluttering smut in her hearing, she is not put out, for the class to which she and the parson belong has grown an extra thickness of skin in the last thirty years. "Touchée!" she would exclaim, with her little ringing laugh, and pass on untouched. She is too wonderful with the villagers, she has them completely taped. Taxi-men, too. One day she overhears two ridiculous fat bottle-nosed taxi-men talking about the subconscious self. She takes the absurdity back to her husband, whose sense of humour coincides with her own, and if the taxi-men had turned the tables and ridiculed *her* she would have taken that back, too. She has learned the defensive value of honesty, which was unknown to her immediate forebears, and consequently nothing short of physical violence can ever do her in. Even when the Highlanders take off their trousers at the Games she is not disconcerted; it is the governess who looks the other

[1] The book, not the film.

291

way. And she writes so well, knowing just where to place each word. And she has delighted thousands upon thousands of readers of *The Times* and been the subject of two *Times* leaders and of innumerable letters to *The Times* calling her charming, and she has been a clue in *Times* crossword puzzles. Why do a few of us stand glum by the roadside as the gallant little pageant passes? Is it not just our own silly jealousy that prevents us from following in her train?

Perhaps. But there is another possibility, which is more interesting to examine. It concerns the odd social fabric of these islands. Mrs Miniver is beyond doubt a lady. But she is equally certainly not an aristocrat. Although her name is vaguely heraldic and her son at Eton and her brother-in-law the McQuern of Quern, she comes out of the top drawer but one. She thinks she is in the top drawer of all, and that her good behaviour is the best kind of behaviour. It may be morally the best. But socially— no, and her quiet assurance that she is socially "it" becomes rather trying. There is something the little lady has not got—some grace or grandeur, some fierce eccentricity, some sense of ancient lineage or broad acres lost through dissipation, something which makes patronage acceptable, even if it hurries the patron to the guillotine. She may be able to give chapter and verse for a distinguished ancestry, but distinction does not course in her blood. She has her own style, but she has not Style. Look at her treatment of poverty. She and her husband are poorish and not ashamed of it, which is very nice of them, but a fatal error for those who wish to seem always in the right. Her shabby old car, her unsnobbishness in living only in Kent, are deftly exploited, and serve to snub another lady who has smarter cars and lives in Gloucestershire. But dinginess is a dangerous weapon. It may break in the hand if used carelessly. She assumes that it will work in the social sphere as effectively as it does in the humorous and the moral, and that she can create the atmosphere of Madame de Sévigné by behaving like Mrs Carlyle.

That—so far as one can put one's finger upon an elusive spot —is the trouble with Mrs Miniver and with the class to which she and most of us belong, the class which strangled the aristocracy in the nineteenth century, and has been haunted ever since by the ghost of its victim. It is a class of tradesmen and professional men and little government officials, and it has come into power consequent on the Industrial Revolution and Reform Bills and the Death Duties. But it has never been able to build itself an appropriate home, and when it asserts that an Englishman's home is his castle it reveals the precise nature of its failure. We who belong to it still copy the past. The castles and the great mansions are gone, we have to live in semi-detached villas instead, they are all we can afford, but let us at all events retain a Tradesmen's Entrance. The Servants' Hall has gone; let the area-basement take its place. The servants themselves are going; Mrs Miniver had four, to be sure, but many a suburban mistress batters the registry offices in vain. The servants are unobtainable, yet we still say, "How like a servant!" when we want to feel superior and safe. Our minds still hanker after the feudal stronghold which we condemned as uninhabitable.

This is not a great tragedy, according to present standards of sadness. Something much worse than middle-class complacency and facetiousness has got loose in the world today. But it is worth noting, and the working classes sometimes note it for themselves, and let out a hoot. They have something which the middle classes have not and the aristocracy once had: spontaneity, natural gaiety, recklessness. They are losing it, for their betters have insisted upon their being insured, and insurance always has a soddening effect upon the spirits. But they retain enough of it to miss the point of the jokes in *Punch*, and to make rude noises when moral worth dons a plumed hat and masquerades as social distinction. There is a natural sympathy between the top drawer and the bottom. The "castle" and the "hovel" have understood one another, and have even approximated in type. Those who had everything have felt easy in the presence of those who had nothing; and vice versa. A society constituted thus was not just and could not be permanent, but in the intervals of persecution and rebellion there was a harmony in the fabric of England which has been lost. The top drawer has now gone. The bottom drawer is being reorganized and dusted out. The top drawer but one makes its little jokes and imposes its whimsies and ideals as if nothing else was obtainable. And certainly there are worse things. But there are other things.

People still go on studying the English National Character. And Mrs Miniver furnishes useful material. But the world moves so fast under the relentless lash of science that national characteristics are not likely to be of much importance in the future. They have a factitious value, especially in wartime, because they are exploited by rival governmental gangs, but the forces that form human nature have moved elsewhere. Just as Gloucestershire and Kent have become alike, so will England, Germany, Russia and Japan become alike. Internationalism, unavowed or avowed, is a cert. Bloodstained or peaceful, it is coming. As it looms on the eastern horizon, the little differences of the past lose their colour, and the carefully explored English temperament seems in particular scarcely worth the bother that has been taken over interpreting it.

[1939]

In My Library

You are soon in my library and soon out of it, for most of the books are contained in a single room. I keep some more of them in a bedroom and in a little sitting-room and in a bathroom cupboard, but most of them are in what we will politely term the library. This is a commodious apartment—twenty-four feet by eighteen—and a very pleasant one. The ceiling is high, the paint white, the wallpaper ribboned-white, and the sun, when it shines, does so through lofty windows of early Victorian Gothic. Even when it does not shine, the apartment remains warm and bright, for it faces south. Round the walls are a dozen wooden bookcases of various heights and shapes, a couple of them well designed, the others cheap. In the middle of the room stands a curious object: a bookcase which once belonged to my grandfather. It has in its front a little projecting shelf supported on two turned pillars of wood, and it has a highly polished back. Some say it is a converted bedstead. It stood in a similar position in the middle of his study over a hundred years ago—he was a country clergyman. Bedstead or not, it is agreeable and original, and I have tried to fill it with volumes of gravity, appropriate to its past. Here are the theological works of Isaac Barrow, thirteen volumes, full morocco, stamped with college arms. Here are the works of John Milton, five volumes, similarly garbed. Here is Evelyn's Diary in full calf, and Arnold's Thucydides, and Tacitus and Homer. Here are my grandfather's own works, bearing titles such as *One Primeval Language*, *The Apocalypse Its Own Interpreter* and *Mohammedanism Unveiled*. Have you read my grandfather's works? No? Have I read them? No.

My grandfather, then, is one of the influences that I can trace in my little collection. I never knew him in the flesh. He must have been rather alarming. His character was dogmatic and severe, and he would not approve of some of the company which I oblige him to keep today. For close by, in a bookcase between the two windows, lurk works of another sort—Anatole France, Marcel Proust, Heredia, André Gide—the type of Frenchman whose forerunners he denounced in a sermon preached to his village in 1871 on the occasion of the fall of Paris. It is ironical that the book belonging to him which I most cherish should be a French book. This is a great encyclopaedia in fifty-two volumes— the *Biographie Universelle* of 1825. Each volume bears his dignified bookplate with our family arms and also the bookplate of Sir James Mackintosh, its previous owner. It is in bad condition— all the backs off—but it is a useful work of reference of the leisurely type, and makes excellent reading. There is nothing slick about it. It dates from the days before the world broke up, and it is a good thing occasionally to go back to these days. They steady us.

The next influence I have to note is that of his daughter, my aunt. I inherited her possessions, and had to sell or give away most of her books before I could fit into my present quarters. But I kept what I liked best, and enough to remind me of her cultivated and attractive personality. She was a maiden lady of strong character, and a great reader, particularly of good prose. Trollope, Jane Austen, Charlotte Yonge, Malory, sound biographies of sound Victorians—these have come down from her. Books on birds also—Bewick and Morris. The birds remind me of her bookplate. She had a charming personal one of a foliated arabesque round a shield, and from the arabesque peep out birds, dogs and a squirrel—some of the living creatures who surrounded her country home where she led a quiet, happy and extremely useful life. She was interested in crafts—she started classes for leatherwork in the village. She was herself a designer and worker, she designed and executed book-covers which were made up at the binder's, and my shelves (to which we now return) are enriched by several examples of her skill. Here are the Letters of Charles Darwin (whom she had known), and Ruskin's *Praeterita*, and Ruskin's *Giotto*—a fine example in pigskin, introducing the legendary O of Giotto and her own initials. The most ambitious of all her bindings—*The Rubáiyát of Omar Khayyám*—I gave away after her death to an oriental friend. I still miss that lovely book and wish I possessed it. I still see the charming design with which she decorated its cover—polo-players adapted from an ancient Persian miniature—a design for which the contemporary dust-jacket is a poor substitute.

However, I am contemporary myself and I must get on to myself and not linger amongst ancestral influences any longer. What did I bring to my library? Not much deliberately. I have never been a collector, and as for the first-edition craze, I place it next door to stamp-collecting—I can say no less. It is non-adult and exposes the book-lover to all sorts of nonsense at the hands of the book-dealer. One should never tempt book-dealers. I am myself a lover of the interiors of books, of the words in them—an uncut book is about as inspiriting as a corked-up bottle of wine— and much as I enjoy good print and good binding and old volumes they remain subsidiary to the words: words, the wine of life. This view of mine is, I am convinced, the correct one. But even correctness has had its disadvantages, and I am bound to admit that my library, so far as I have created it, is rather a muddle. Here's one sort of book, there's another, and there is not enough of any sort of book to strike a dominant note. Books about India and by Indians, modern poetry, ancient history, American novels, travel books, books on the state of the world, and on the world-state, books on individual liberty, art-albums, Dante and books about him—they tend to swamp each other, not to mention the usual pond of pamphlets which has to be drained off periodically. The absence of the collector's instinct in me, the absence of deliberate choice, have combined with a commendable variety of interests to evolve a library which will not make any definite impression upon visitors.

I have not a bookplate—too diffident or too much bother. I cannot arrange books well either; shall it be by subjects or by heights? Shall a tall old Froissart stand beside *The Times Atlas*, or beside a tiny Philippe de Commines? I do not bang or blow them as much as I should, or oil their leather backs, or align those backs properly. They are unregimented. Only at night, when the curtains are drawn and the fire flickers, and the lights are turned off, do they come into their own, and attain a collective dignity. It is very pleasant to sit with them in the firelight for a couple of minutes, not reading, not even thinking, but aware that they, with their accumulated wisdom and charm, are waiting to be used, and that my library, in its tiny imperfect way, is a successor to the great private libraries of the past. "Do you ever lend books?" someone may say in a public-spirited tone of voice at this point. Yes, I do, and they are not returned, and still I lend books. Do I ever borrow books? I do, and I can see some of them unreturned around me. I favour reciprocal dishonesty. But the ownership of the things does give me peculiar pleasure, which in-creases as I get older. It is of the same kind, though not so strong, as the desire to possess land. And, like all possessiveness, it does not go down to the roots of our humanity. Those roots are spiritual. The deepest desire in us is the desire to understand, and that is what I meant just now when I said that the really important thing in books is the words in them—words, the wine of life—not their binding or their print, not their edition value or their bibliomaniac value, or their uncuttability.

One's favourite book is as elusive as one's favourite pudding, but there certainly are three writers whom I would like to have in every room, so that I can stretch out my hand for them at any moment. They are Shakespeare, Gibbon and Jane Austen. There are two Shakespeares in this library of mine and also two outside it, one Gibbon and one outside it, one Jane Austen and two outside it. So I am happily furnished. And, of course, I have some Tolstoy, but one scarcely wants Tolstoy in every room. Shakespeare, Gibbon and Jane Austen are my choice, and in a library one thinks of Gibbon most. Gibbon loved books but was not dominated by them. He knew how to use them. His bust might well stand on my grandfather's bookcase, to my grandfather's indignation.

[1949]

The London Library

In May 1841 the London Library was launched on the swelling tides of Victorian prosperity. It celebrates its centenary among the rocks. It is unharmed at the moment of writing—not a volume out of action—but the area in which it stands is cloven by the impacts of the imbecile storm. All around it are the signs of the progress of science and the retrogression of man. Buildings are in heaps, the earth is in holes. Safe still among the reefs of rubbish, it seems to be something more than a collection of books. It is a symbol of civilization. It is a reminder of sanity and a promise of sanity to come. Perhaps the Nazis will hit it, and it is an obvious target, for it represents the tolerance and the disinterested erudition which they so detest. But they have missed it so far.[1]

Why should a private subscription library, which appeals to only a small section of the community, arouse exalted thoughts?

The answer to this question is to be found in the Library's history, and in its present policy. Speakers at its annual meetings are fond of saying that it is unique, which is more or less true, and that it is typically English, which greatly understates its claims. It is not typically English. It is typically civilized. It pays a homage to seriousness and to good sense which is rare in these islands and anywhere. It has cherished the things of the mind, it has insisted on including all points of view, and yet it has been selective. Ephemeral books, popular successes, most novels, many travelogues and biographies have been excluded from its shelves. And technical treatises, such as have helped to make the mess outside, have not been encouraged either. Of course it has had its lapses; one can find trash in it, and specialization-lumber also. But its policy has always been to send those who want trash to the chain-libraries, and those who want lumber to their appropriate lumber-room. It caters neither for the goose nor for the rat, but for creatures who are trying to be human. The desire to know more, the desire to feel more,

---

[1] They hit it in 1944.

and, accompanying these but not strangling them, the desire to help others: here, briefly, is the human aim, and the Library exists to further it.

So much for its seriousness. Its good sense is equally remarkable. For it would be possible to have these admirable ideals, but to render them unacceptable through red tape. That is the great snag in institutionalism. There may be fine intention and noble provision, but they often get spoiled by the belief that the public cannot be trusted, that it is careless, dishonest, grubby, clumsy, that it must on no account be "allowed access" to the shelves, and is best served from behind a wire netting. The London Library, though an institution, will have nothing to do with this fallacy. It takes the risks. Its members can go all over its book-stores. There is a price to be paid; books do get stolen, or taken out without being entered, or taken out in unauthorized quantities, or kept out too long, or dog's-eared, or annotated in the margin by cultivated scribes who should know better; but it is worth it, it is worth treating the creatures as if they were grown-up, the gain to the humanities outweighs the financial loss. Moreover, it is the tradition of the library to help the student rather than to snub, and this promotes a decent reaction at once. And "help" is indeed too feeble a word; the officials there possess not only goodwill, but wide and accurate knowledge, which is instantly placed at the inquirer's disposal.

The library owes its origin to the spleen and to the nobility of Thomas Carlyle. The spleen came first: Carlyle needed books of reference while he was writing his *Cromwell*, he could not afford to buy them all, and the journey from Chelsea to the British Museum Library was a vexatious one. Besides, when he got to the British Museum he found other people reading there too, which gave him the feeling of a crowd, and it is impossible to work in a crowd: "add discomfort, perturbation, headache, waste of health." Grumbling and growling at his miserable fate, be betook himself to the drawing-room of Lady Stanley of Alderley in Dover Street, and burst forth there; even in Iceland, he said, the peasants could borrow books, and take them away to read in their huts during the Arctic night; only in London was there this "shameful anomaly". The company tried to soothe him or to change the subject, but his growls continued; books, books, one ought to be able to borrow books. And before long he effected one of his junctions between private peevishness and public welfare, and persuaded other men of distinction to combine with him in launching a library. Gladstone, Hallam, Grote, Monckton Milnes joined him. A meeting was held at the Freeman's Tavern to promote a scheme for "a supply of good books in all departments of knowledge". Lord Eliot was in the chair, and Carlyle made a fine speech. It is said to be his only speech. Here are some sentences from it:

> A book is a kind of thing that requires a man to be self-collected. He must be alone with it. A good book is the purest essence of the human soul. . . . The good of a book is not the facts that can be got out of it, but the kind of resonance that it awakens in our own minds. A book may strike out of us a thousand things, may make us know a thousand things which it does not know itself. . . . The founding of a Library is one of the greatest things we can do with regard to results. It is one of the quietest of things; but there is nothing that I know of at bottom more important. Everyone able to read a good book becomes a wiser man. He becomes a similar centre of light and order, and just insight into the things around him. A collection of good books contains all the nobleness and wisdom of the world before us. Every heroic and victorious soul has left his stamp upon it. A collection of books is the best of all Universities; for the University only teaches us to read the book: you must go to the book itself for what it is. I call it a Church also—which every devout soul may enter—a Church but with no quarrelling, no Church-rates. . . .

At this point, Carlyle was interrupted by laughter and cheers, and sat down good-temperedly. His speech is too optimistic, in view of our present information; also too subjective in its emphasis on the "resonance" from books; also too little aware of the power of concentration possessed by many readers, which enables them today to continue through an air-raid. But it is a noble utterance. It recalls us to the importance of seriousness, and to the preciousness and the destructibility of knowledge. Knowledge will perish if we do not stand up for it and testify. It is never safe, never harvested. It has to be protected not only against the gangster but against a much more charming and seductive foe: the crowd. "I know what I like and I know what I want," says the crowd, "and I don't want all these shelves and shelves of books. Scrap them."

The Library started in two rooms at 49 Pall Mall, with five hundred members, and three thousand books. Conditions were Spartan; no ink or paper was provided, and for a time there was no clock. In 1845 it moved into St James's Square, and now it has a a membership of four thousand, and about four hundred and seventy thousand books, together with various luxuries, including a comfortable reading-room. Its rise is largely due to a great librarian, Sir Charles Hagberg Wright, who died last year. Hagberg Wright had a European connection, and a European outlook. He was free from the insularity which has such a numbing effect on the collecting of books, and it is largely thanks to him that one feels the library to be not English but civilized. For the moment it has one overwhelming problem before it: that of not getting smashed and not getting burnt. But if normality returns it will have the task of getting into touch with the thought and literature of the Continent, however repellent the mental state of the Continent may be. And—a more congenial task—it will have to get up to date on America. It has never admitted, and it must never admit, the idea of exclusion; in Hagberg Wright's wise little pamphlet, *The Soul's Dispensary*, there are some pertinent remarks on this, and a curious account of the war which he had to wage after the last war with various government departments before he could regain liberty for the reimportation of foreign literature.

[1941]

Places

A Letter to Madan Blanchard[1]

The London Library
St James's Square
London

April 1931

My dear Madan,

Captain Wilson keeps telling me about you, and I feel I should like to write you a line. I shall send it by airmail to Paris, but from Paris to Genoa in a pre-war express. At Genoa the confusion will begin. Owing to the infancy of Mussolini the steampacket will not start on time, and will frequently put in for repairs. So slow is the progress that the Suez Canal may close before it can be opened, and my letter be constrained to cross Egypt by the overland route. Suez is full of white sails. One of them, tacking southward, will make India at last, another bring tidings of Napoleonic wars on a following breeze. Smaller boats, duskier crews. Brighter dawns? Quieter nights anyhow. The world is unwinding. What of Macao, where no news follows at all? What of the final transhipment? The last little vessel scarcely moves as she touches the Pelews, the waves scarcely break, just one tiny ripple survives to float my envelope into your hand. As the tide turns, I reach you. You open my letter a hundred and fifty years before it is written, and you read the words "My dear Madan".

Before I forget, there are messages. Don't lose the compass

---

[1] My correspondent is not imaginary. See *An Account of the Pelew Islands, situated in the western part of the Pacific Ocean. Composed from the journals and communications of Captain Henry Wilson, and some of his officers, who, in August 1783, were there shipwrecked in the Antelope, a packet belonging to the Honourable East India Company,* by George Keate, Esq., F.R.S. and S.A. (Dublin, Luke White, 1788.)

See also India Office, *Marine Records,* 570a and 570c, where his name is spelt Blanshard.

See furthermore Rupack Street, Rotherhithe, London, S.E.

you asked for. Maintain the pinnace and her tackle in proper repair. Help the natives to work any iron they recover from the wreck, and look after the arms and ammunition for them. £23 8s. 3d. wages are still due to you—do you want them? Above all Captain Wilson asks me to "request Blanchard he will never go naked, like the natives, as, by preserving the form of dress his countrymen have appeared in, he will always support a superiority of character; that he may be better enabled to follow this advice, he was furnished with all the clothes we could spare, and directed, when these were worn out, to make himself trowsers with a mat." He hopes that all this has been done, and that you have not forgotten your Sundays. You may follow Pelew customs in other ways. He sees no objection to two wives, since Abba Thulle offered them, indeed a refusal might well cause offence, but Sunday stands apart. Knot a string to remind yourself of it, or count coral insects, or something. Prince Lee Boo saw the importance of Sunday as soon as he landed in England, and has indeed gone so far as to be buried in Rotherhithe Church. How about baptizing your Cockilla and Cockathey?—though this is my suggestion, not the Captain's. He says that I am not to plague you with niceties, especially as you can't read, and indeed wants me to draw a picture of a church and a pair of trousers, and leave it at that. But I'm writing, because there's just a chance that, on the turn of the tide, the answer to my question may float back to me.

I want to know why you stopped behind when the others went.

At the present moment I'm stuffed in between books, and old ladies with worried faces are making notes in long armchairs, so I feel it natural enough you should stop. The ends of the earth, the depths of the sea, the darkness of time, you have chosen all three. But when you chose them you were stuffed in somewhere or other yourself, latitude 6° 25′ N., longitude 136° E., date 12 November 1783, so what were your grounds for deciding? Did it start as a joke? Your mates never took you seriously, and Wilson talks of your dry sense of humour. You helped them to the very last to build the sloop, you even came aboard as she was moving to show where a sail had been stowed, then you took leave without the least regret, "as if they were only sailing from London to Gravesend, and were to return with the next tide". They couldn't believe their eyes when you went and sat down with the savages and the canoes, it seemed like a dream. Even Prince

Lee Boo was amazed. He pointed to you as the canoes fell
astern, and then he pointed to himself and said: "I go with his
people, he stop with mine. But I go with wise English, he stop
with the savage Pelew. I go to visit King George and God, he
only visit King Abba Thulle my father. Oh mystery! How
curious!" Captain Wilson then invited him to dine, after which
he started being sick.

That ramshackle craft got safely to China, looking more like
a packing-case than a sloop, with every sort of rag flapping, and
the black and white magic stuff still showing round the stern.
The John Company officials at Canton were not too pleased
with the vision. They had sent out the *Antelope*, you see, one
of their best vessels, and this was what came back, and they
questioned Wilson pretty straightly over what had happened.
I suspect—owing to my knowledge of history—that the *Antelope*
had been despatched to annex the Pelew Islands for Great Britain,
instead of which the Pelews have annexed the *Antelope*, and she
now forms part of the coral reef at Oroora. Wilson had to
explain this away as well as he could, also the disappearance of
the stores, the death of Quarter-Master Godfrey Minks (drowned
through swimming ashore with two suits of clothes on), the
mortality among the Chinese crew (occurring no one remembered when) and the absence of two dogs and yourself. On
the other hand, he could point to Prince Lee Boo, and this
certainly calmed the officials. Lee Boo was a hostage, though
the word was never used, he ensured the good behaviour of his
father. The Company's plan was to educate him in England,
and send him back to rule the islands for us; he was to take
with him horses, dogs, cows, pigs, goats, seeds, clothes, rum, and
all that makes life bearable; he was to oust Qui Bill from the
succession, conquer the Artingalls with musket fire, and reign
over corpses and coconuts in a gold-laced suit. The small-pox
had something to say to all that, and there will be no more talk
of annexation yet awhile. You may rest in peace, my dear
Madan, if rest is what you want, and your king Abba Thulle
has saved his kingdom at the moment he lost his son. Such an
amiable youth, and so intelligent. First he was puzzled by
houses, then he called everything a house; at Portsmouth he
was "put into a little house which was run away with by horses,
most agreeable, the trees and fields went the other way", and so
reached London, which was "all fine country, fine house upon
house up to sky", and skipped about half the night in a four-

poster bed, peeping between the curtains, and crying, "In England a house for everything. How wise!" He must have been charming. But I am more intrigued by you, about whom I know nothing except that you preferred the ends of the earth, the depths of the sea. Answer this letter if you can—there are various methods—and let me know why you went native, and how you are.

I meant to break the Prince's death to you gradually, but the news is already out, besides, I don't see why you should mind. I enclose his picture—it will amuse you, and you will hardly recognize who it is. You saw him going on board man-naked, with masses of wild fruit in his arms. Well, in a week they taught him to wear clothes like these, in a fortnight he wouldn't take even a waistcoat off except in the dark, and a year later you might have seen him in Mrs Wilson's dining-room at Rotherhithe, offering her, with exquisite grace, three small cherries in a spoon. He had offered them in his hand at first, whereat the old lady had smiled slightly—you too may not know, but cherries are never handed in the hand. Observing her smile, he resorted to a spoon, and "a blush actually forced itself through his dusky complexion". Nothing was too refined for him, or too moral; he embraced civilization with the grace of a courtier and the integrity of a curate. He admired all Englishmen. He adored all Englishwomen; he called the old ones "mother"—the young ones—we shall never know. I wish he hadn't died—he must have been a dear. He seems to have loved his country. He was always talking about it, and collecting rubbish to sow there when he got back. His chief treasure was two little barrels of blue glass on stands, which an official gave him in Canton. His chief pleasure: driving in St James's Park, close to where I am writing to you now. The Wilsons would not take him about much, for fear of infection. He went to see Lunardi go up in a balloon, but failed to mistake the balloon for a house, so was bored. Most days he was at school—an Academy for young gentlemen close by, and many a merry tale did he bring back, but never an unkind prank. The Wilsons were devoted to him—he and young Harry used to practise javelin-throwing for hours in the attic—and there is no doubt that he came to his end among friends. You can tell this or not tell it to Abba Thulle as you like. Probably you had better not tell it, for the noblest of savages is apt to be deranged by the death of a son, and whatever else this letter does I do not want it to do you harm.

Though the good CAPTAIN and his household strove
Each other to excel in deeds of love . . .
Will this, when told thy father, noble Chief!
Stop the strong current of resistless grief?
Has not imagination, in alarms,
Pourtray'd his son return'd with arts and arms,
To bless his kingdom with a lasting race
Of warriors all, and all in love with peace?
Shall he, regardless of each social tie,
Calmly resign LEE BOO, without a sigh?
And will unmoved thy gen'rous uncles stand
To hear thou died'st regretted in our land?
Ah no! . . .

This is from an anonymous poem which someone sent Wilson
after the funeral. I, too, feel, "Ah no!" If the generous uncles
realize that we have, with the best intentions, committed murder,
they will not be unmoved, and when they see you alone among
them, and you're just his age—well, perhaps they'll make you
their king instead, but I wouldn't risk it. I would watch Abba
Thulle tying a knot in a string at every full moon until his son
comes back with the wise English, and I would say nothing.

What about your own relatives? I don't even know whether
you're English or French. I find you signed on to the *Antelope*
at Falmouth, but that means anything, and the books in the
library here make their usual imbecile noises when I mention
your name. Here are *Métamorphoses, mœurs et instincts des insectes*,
by Emile Blanchard. Would this attract you as a connection?
Or Samuel Laman Blanchard's *Collected Poems*. May I send
them you? Or a letter from Pierre Blanchard, *Sur les questions
qui divisent l'Eglise gallicane*. Or Edward Blanchard's *Descriptive
Guide to the Great Western Railway*. Or Frank Nelson Blanchard's
A Revision of the King Snakes: Genus Lampropeltis. This is what is
termed research. The Madans offer even wider scope to the
earnest student, but I shall not pursue it beyond *Thelyphthora, a
Treatise on Female Ruin*. This helpful work was composed by
one Martin Madan, only three years before the *Antelope* struck,
and him, if anyone, I assign to you as uncle. I haven't any news
about your mates either—they scattered and got other jobs—
Nick Tyacke, little Will Cobbledick and all. Young Mr Devis
stopped in India, to paint portraits there, the rest of the party
proceeding to England as aforesaid, via St Helena. The two
arrow wounds he got on your expedition still hurt him in the

309

jaw. Do you remember when Mr Devis drew Abba Thulle's wives, and they were so frightened—Ludee in particular, that very pretty one? Are your Cockilla and Cockathey very pretty too? I suggested to Wilson that they might be, which would explain your vagaries, and he answered yes, they very well might be, but no one knew, since they had not arrived from the interior by the time the sloop sailed. He also said that you were known to have formed "no special attachments on the island"—it seems rather to have been a general feeling, something connected with the Artingall wars. It was in a canoe among savages and Englishmen mixed, coming back from the second war, that you said, "I mean to live here for ever." Wilson was irritated, for he had noticed nothing remarkable about you; you were like any other seaman at £2 a month, good-tempered, inoffensive, quiet, enjoyed fighting—the usual thing; he took it for insolence when you stuck to it, and perhaps still isn't quite sure. "Did you ever want to stop on there yourself, sir?" I asked him. He sighed, "Ah well, ah well," and looked at his wrist. The bone with which Abba Thulle invested him still encircles his wrist, he won't have it removed, and polishes it every evening to keep his luck, as he was told. "This denotes that I am a Rupack, or noble, of the first rank," he continued, smiling, "and it was conferred on me by the natives in front of one of their public assembly halls or 'Pyes'." Dr Keate says the bone belongs to a whale, but in my judgement it is a merman's, for they are not uncommon in the China seas." I questioned him more on the Pyes, and he said, "Ah well, the Pyes, most remarkable, most." I like to hear him sigh "Ah well". It runs under so much of his talk. He will never forget the three months he spent on the island, or the Apples of Paradise they brought him the morning he sailed, or the canoes escorting him over the reef while they cried, "Come again to us, good Englishman, come!" The English will not come again—at least I hope not. Your island has swung away from ours into what we choose to call darkness, and into what I can't help calling life.

Look at Lee Boo! Think how it ended, in spite of all the care they took. Mr Sharp (your late surgeon) never let him out of his sight, and as soon as the first trace of infection appeared they sent for Doctor Carmichael Smith too. Doctor Smith examined him, and told the Wilsons at once that he must die. A few days later he knew it himself. He was walking across the room, saw himself in the glass, and was disgusted—shook his head, and said that his father and mother, thousands of miles away, were grieving. To Mr Sharp he said: "Good friend, when you go back to Pelew, tell Abba Thulle that Lee Boo take much drink to make small-pox go away, but he die; Captain Wilson, Mother Wilson, very kind—all English very good men—much sorry he could not speak to the King the number of fine things the English had got—he do all they tell him, but he die." The little barrels of blue glass were to be given to the king. As long as Doctor Smith was with him, he complained of his symptoms in case he could be cured, but at other times he thought only of his friends. To add to their misery, old Mrs Wilson lay ill in the next room, and he kept calling out to her "Lee Boo do well, mother," to comfort her, or tried to visit her, and had to be stopped. Hot baths, blistered back and legs—the boy endured it all, sensible, unselfish, ultra-civilized to the last. What he really thought, no one knew or has dared to guess. He managed to pass away without distressing the Christians or disappointing the philosophers, and he has a tablet in Rotherhithe churchyard consequently. John Company paid for it, and for the funeral, too, though the Wilsons would gladly have settled it all themselves. All Rother-hithe attended—the two little painted figures up on the alms-houses couldn't ever have looked down on so vast a concourse—officials from London, all the young people from the Academy, although it was their Christmas holiday. The stone was put up after a year, which gives enough time for all flesh to decay.

To the Memory
of Prince LEE BOO,
A native of the PELEW, or PALOS Islands;
and Son to ABBA THULLE, Rupack or King
of the Island COOROORAA;
who departed this Life on the 27th of December 1784,
aged 20 years;
This Stone is inscribed,
by the Honourable United EAST INDIA COMPANY,
as a Testimony of Esteem for the humane and kind Treatment
afforded by HIS FATHER to the Crew of their Ship
the ANTELOPE, Captain WILSON,
which was wrecked off that Island
in the Night of the 9th of August 1783.

Stop, Reader, stop!—let NATURE claim a Tear—
A prince of *Mine*, LEE BOO, lies bury'd here.

I almost shed a tear, but not quite; he was rather too harmless a blackamoor—such a puppet, he always did as he was bid, and people like that don't seem quite real. The people who touch my imagination are obstinate suddenly—they do break step, and I always hope they'll get by without the sergeant punishing them. It was so like poor Lee Boo that he loved above all things to see the Guards drilling in the Park. They are drilling there still, so are the ladies in the long chairs in this library, so are the books in the shelves. If it isn't one set of rules it's another, even for heroism. I ought to feel free myself, as I've health, strength, and am middle-aged, yet I can't keep my hat on in a church, for instance, even if no one's looking, and if I'm fighting never manage to hit below the belt. While not getting fussed over this, I can't but remember the people who managed better, and it's in order to meet them in the flesh that I study history. Here and there, as I rake between the importancies, I come across them —the people who carried whimsicality into action, the salt of my earth. Not the professional whimsies—their drill's dearer than anyone's—but the solid fellows who suddenly jib. The queer thing is, we all admire them—even when we're hard-bitten disciplinarians like old Wilson. They've got hold of something which we know is there, but have never dared to grasp in our hands. A sort of stinging nettle. I went down to the tomb the other day, and thought, "No, he isn't quite good enough, he was stung when he wasn't looking, which happens to anyone." I took down a lot of notes about Rotherhithe church, the neighbourhood, Shad Thames, etc., thinking they would interest you, but if they interested you you'd have come back to them, so I tore the notes up and wandered about feeling rather tired and out of place, then I got across the river to Stepney, and through the City, in at Aldgate and out at Newgate, back to this part, where I live now.

Well, that concludes my news, and now it's your turn. I will enclose you one more poem, and then I'm done:

O'er the mighty Pacific whose soft swelling wave
A thousand bright regions eternally lave,
'Mid rocks red with coral and shellfish abounding,
The note of the parrot and pigeon resounding:
Crowned with groves of banana and taper bamboo
Rise the gay sunny shores of the Isles of *Pelew*.

This is how a Miss Heisch, before she married a Mr Hookey, imagined your present home. I laughed the first time I read her poem, but the second time I found myself sighing "Ah well!" Write to me if you possibly can—I suppose on the bark of some tree. Lower it one evening as the tide turns, and watch it drift out through the coral reefs. The monsoons will hurry it west-ward, and the spray begin whispering "Progress" against it. Swifter boats, paler crews, and an intelligent interest among savants as it is raised aboard in a dredge off, let us say, Réunion. "C'est bien une lettre?" Pourquoi pas? It is addressed? Apparently! Then forward it onward to England. The waves are rising, the world's winding up, but King George is still on his throne, so's God. Boom! Before the last echo of 1815 dies away, 1914 strikes, and here we are. Your letter now takes to the air. Heavily surcharged, liable to customs duty, enterable under income tax, subject to quarantine, notifiable, censorable, confiscatable, it crashes through the library window, and explodes in my hand. None of the old ladies notice it—they are still researching. I wait until the envelope of smoke has vanished, I find my right spectacles, and I decipher, a hundred and fifty years after it was written, the single word "aaa".

What can "aaa" mean? Perhaps you have forgotten your English. I will send for a Pelew dictionary. While it is coming I have one more thing to say to you.

Once I used to come across an Irish clergyman—an unusual fellow, I never liked him much, he died before your time. He invented a group of islands to relieve his feelings on, and oddly enough placed some of them south-east of Formosa—that's to say, more or less where you actually are. One of these islands contained very small men, another very large ones, a third was inhabited by horses, and the fourth flew. The clergyman was too bad-tempered to take much notice of what he was doing: I mean, whether the men were big or little they were intended to make men of his own size look small, and so with his horses: he didn't care for horses but he hated people, and used horses for saying so. Well, in one of the islands he imagined men living for ever. It sounded like Paradise, but of course there was a catch—I will not tell you what, but it is a terrifying one, and nothing he has ever said to me has upset me more. If he is right on the subject of eternal youth in the southern seas, don't answer this letter, in fact you won't want to. But if I am right, send the answer that tells everything, the answer I have imagined, "aaa" (Pelew for Yes).[1]

Yours ever,
E. M. Forster.

[1] My letter was never delivered. An explanation for this can be found in *A Supplement to the Account of the Pelew Islands; compiled from the journals of the Panther and Endeavour, two vessels sent by the Honourable East India Company to those Islands in the year* 1790, by the Reverend John Pearce Hockin, of Exeter College, Oxford, M.A. (London, printed for Captain Henry Wilson by W. Bulmer and Co., Cleveland Row, 1803.)

[1931]

India Again

It was a dull, cold Friday morning in October 1945 when I left England. Two days later, on the Sunday afternoon, I was in India. Below me lay the desert of Rajputana, baked by the sun and blotched with the shadows of clouds. The plane came down for half an hour near the dragon-shaped fort of Jodhpur, then took off again, and it was Delhi. I felt dazed. And we had travelled so fast that we were ahead of schedule, and had no one to meet us. Suddenly very slow, instead of very quick, we jogged in a tonga through the Delhi bazaars, our luggage in front, our legs hanging down behind, the dust rising, the sun setting, the smoke drifting out of the little shops. It became dark and the sky was covered with stars. Were we lost? No. An unknown host, an Indian, received us, and next day I stood on the high platform of the Great Mosque, one of the noblest buildings in India and the world. Profound thankfulness filled me. The sky was now intensely blue, the kites circled round and round the pearl-gray domes and the red frontispiece of sandstone, sounds drifted up from Delhi city, the pavement struck warm through the soles of my socks; I was back in the country I loved, after an absence of twenty-five years.

I was bound for a conference of Indian writers. The All-India Centre of the P.E.N. Club had invited us. The people I was to meet were nearly all Indians, of the professional classes—doctors, lawyers, public servants, professors at the university, businessmen. Many of them were old friends or the sons of old friends. They were what is termed "intellectuals" and they lived in towns. I did not see much of the countryside nor of the industrial conditions. I met a few Englishmen but not many, and have often looked round a crowded room and observed that I was the only westerner in it. Such are my credentials, or, if you prefer, such are my limitations.

The big change I noticed was the increased interest in politics. You cannot understand the modern Indians unless you realize that politics occupy them passionately and constantly, that artistic problems, and even social problems—yes, and even economic problems—are subsidiary. Their attitude is, "First we must find the correct political solution, and then we can deal with other matters." I think the attitude is unsound, and used to say so; still, there it is, and they hold it much more vehemently than they did a quarter of a century ago. When I spoke about the necessity of form in literature and the importance of the individual vision, their attention wandered, although they listened politely. Literature, in their view, should expound or inspire a political creed.

Externally the place has not changed. It looks much as it did from the train. Outside the carriage windows (the rather dirty windows) it unrolls as before—monotonous, enigmatic, and at moments sinister. And in some long motor drives which I took through the Deccan there were the same combinations of hill, rock, bushes, ruins, dusty people and occasional yellow flowers which I encountered when I walked on the soil in my youth. There is still poverty, and, since I am older today and more thoughtful, it is the poverty, the malnutrition, which persists like a ground-swell beneath the pleasant froth of my immediate experience. I do not know what political solution is correct. But I do know that people ought not to be so poor and to look so ill, and that rats ought not to run about them as I saw them doing in a labour camp at Bombay. Industrialism has increased, though it does not dominate the landscape yet as it does in the West. You can see the chimneys of the cotton mills at Ahmedabad, but you can see its mosques too. You can see little factories near Calcutta, but they are tucked away amongst bananas and palms, and the one I have in mind has an enormous tree overhanging it, in whose branches a witch is said to sit, and from whose branches huge fruit occasionally fall and hit the corrugated iron roofs with a bang, so that the factory-hands jump. No—externally India has not changed. And this changelessness in her is called by some observers "the real India". I don't myself like the phrase "the real India". I suspect it. It always makes me prick up my ears. But you can use it if you want to, either for the changes in her or for the unchanged. "Real" is at the service of all schools of thought.

It is when you leave the country, or the streets of the town, and go into the private houses, that you begin to notice a second great alteration, second only to politics—namely the lifting of purdah, the increasing emancipation of women. It struck me particularly in cities which are largely Moslem, such as Lahore and Hyderabad, where women once kept rigidly behind the veil. I have been in my life three times to Hyderabad, some of my happiest Indian days were spent there, so I have been able to trace this change. My first visit was in 1912 and then I saw scarcely any Indian women. My second visit was in 1921, when I was admitted into some family circles and saw a good deal of what may be called "semi-purdah"—ladies coming out into company, but not coming avowedly, and retiring at any moment behind the veil if they felt disposed to do so. Today, purdah has broken down at Hyderabad, except amongst the most conservative, and at the receptions to which I went the women sometimes outnumbered the men. Since they kept to their lovely Indian saris, the effect was exquisite; it was a delight to look round at so much gracefulness and graciousness, at so many and such well-chosen colours. I don't know how far into society this lifting of the veil has extended. But I imagine that sooner or later the change will extend to the villages and transform the Indian social fabric from top to bottom. Our world does not go back, though whether it progresses God alone knows, and in India, as in the West, women will shortly have the same opportunities as men for good and for evil.

The receptions I have been mentioning usually took the form of buffet dinners—they are an innovation since my time. Long tables are loaded with Indian food, and sometimes one table is labelled "vegetarian" and the other "non-vegetarian". You help yourself, or are helped. I take away pleasant memories of these buffet dinners, memories of Indians moving elegantly through well-filled rooms, with well-filled plates in their hands, and miraculously conveying food to their mouths in the folds of a chapatti. There is rationing, but its workings are mysterious and I did not grasp them or suffer from them. For the well-to-do, life is much easier in India than in England. The shops are full of tinned delicacies for those who can afford them—butter, cheese, even plum puddings. For the poor, life is much harder there than here.

The Indians I met mostly talked English. Some of them spoke very well, and one or two of them write in our language with great distinction. But English, though more widely spoken than on my last visit, is worse spoken, more mistakes are made in it, and the pronunciation is deteriorating. "Perpéndicule" for "perpendicular". "Pip" into my office for "pop". Here are two tiny slips which I noted in a couple of minutes, and both of them made by well-educated men. The explanation, I think, is that Indians at the schools and universities are now learning their English from other Indians, instead of from English teachers as in the past. Furthermore, they have little occasion to meet our people socially and so brush it up; intercourse is official and at a minimum, and even where there are mixed clubs the two communities in them keep apart. So it is not surprising that their English is poor. They have learned it from Indians and practise it on Indians.

Why talk English at all? This question was hotly debated at the P.E.N. conference of All-India writers. Writers from central or upper India were in favour of Urdu or Hindi as a common language for the whole peninsula. Writers from Bengal favoured Bengali, and it has great claims from the literary point of view. Writers from the south, on the other hand, preferred English. The debate, if I may say so, continues, and into it, as into every-thing, come politics. I mention it to indicate the trend of events, the change in emphasis. Meanwhile, in this uneasy interregnum, English does get talked and gets interlarded in the oddest way with the Indian vernacular. I was travelling one day to Baroda in a crowded second-class carriage. Indians, my luggage, their luggage, myself and a number of loose oranges were piled up together in confusion, and the Indians were arguing. Their language was Gujarati, but they used so many English words that I followed what they were saying. They were arguing about religion and free-thought. I intervened and was welcomed into the conversation, which was now carried on entirely in English out of courtesy to me. I did not follow it the better for that, but they peeled me an orange and we parted friends. Indeed, it is difficult to conclude an Indian railway journey on any other note. Their response to ordinary civility is immediate. I don't think they are particularly friendly in the street—if you ask them the way they are suspicious. But squashed in a railway carriage they seem to expand. And my reason for wanting English to be the common language for India is a purely selfish reason: I like these chance encounters, I value far more the relationships of years, and if Indians had not spoken English my own life would have been infinitely poorer.

My visit ended all too soon. On a Friday afternoon in Decem-ber—it was again a Friday—I was walking about in the sunshine of Karachi. And on the Sunday evening I was in London.

Our train was icy cold, it arrived at Waterloo two hours late, midnight, thick fog, refreshment-rooms closed, waiting-rooms closed, local trains gone, no taxi could leave the station. The grumpy railway policeman to whom we appealed was glad we were uncomfortable, and said so, while a poster on the wall exhorted us to practise even greater austerity, since it was peace time. It was not much of a return, it was not like the arrival in Delhi, and as the policeman's sulky bulky back disappeared into the gloom I found it understandable that not everybody should care for England.

2

The conference I had attended was held at Jaipur. A thousand people, nearly all of them Indians, were assembled in the great town hall. It is a magnificent apartment. At one end was a platform, on which sat Mrs Naidu, the president of the conference, the Prime Minister of Jaipur, and other notables. At the lower end five big arches opened onto the outer world. The arches were hung with straw curtains, through which could be seen the tops of trees and the roofs of the Maharajah's palace, sweltering in the October sunshine. Above the arches, high on the wall, ran a lattice, and behind it every now and then shadowy gracious figures passed, just discernible against the brightness. Silent as ghosts, colourless though not formless, they were the figures of ladies going to their purdah galleries to watch our deliberations. Or perhaps they were coming away from their purdah galleries because we had bored them. I don't know. But that sort of cloud movement high up in the thickness of the wall, that ethereal shuttle playing left to right or right to left behind the lattice, went on all the time, and gave a sense of spaciousness and of strangeness. We might be the future, but we were observed by the past.

Down in the hall we plodded away at our agenda. We had come to discuss literature as a unifying force, the future of the Indian languages, the Indian copyright act, a scheme for an encyclopaedia, and so on. Fascinating to me, though I knew nothing of the subjects, was the symposium on the Indian languages. Twenty minutes were allotted to each. There were sixteen languages in all, and so writers from all parts of the peninsula could learn what was being done elsewhere, and could contact their colleagues, perhaps for the first time. A sense of enlargement and of complexity stole over the audience as they discussed whether, despite all these languages and perhaps through them, India could not be one. In fact we slid towards politics. Everything out there does. But we did not go over the edge. It remained a conference of writers, and the organization which convened it is pledged to be non-political.

Out of school we amused ourselves. We rode on elephants— though I myself find such a ride elevating rather than amusing. We looked at the curious pink city of Jaipur—an early example of town-planning—and went to the romantic ancient capital of the state which lies above it in a crack of the hills, and is said to have as its neighbour a fabulous hoard of jewels. We entered a Hindu temple—a rare experience in these days for the non-Hindu; twenty-five years ago, if my memory serves, entry was not so difficult. We attended a political demonstration. We ran over a cobra. But the conference dominated, and I would like to refer, before leaving it, to the moving address made by the Prime Minister of Jaipur, Sir Mirza Ismail. He described the atmosphere in which all modern writers must function, and held it to be their duty to keep in touch with the world, but not as politicians. Not much of the oratory was of his high order or struck his international note. But his concern with moral issues was typical of other speakers, and typical, too, his indifference to art for art's sake. Listening to him and to others, I felt that India had indeed changed. The Jaipur conference would have been impossible twenty-five years back.

When it was over, I travelled about, meeting many writers, and acquiring a good many books. These last are following after me in a boat and have not yet arrived. When I have digested them I shall have a better general notion of the Indian literary scene. Here meanwhile are a few notes. Book production: very active, though the authors are miserably paid. Short stories are popular; I read some excellent ones in Bengal. Poetry often echoes T. S. Eliot or Auden. Drama is not prominent. Criticism weak. Indians have a marked capacity for worship, or for denunciation, but not much critical sense, as criticism is understood in the West. As for great writers, there is no one alive today of the stature of Tagore, or of Iqbal. I have had the honour of meeting each of these great men once. Both are dead now, and their disappearance has impoverished the scene.

The cinema. Since my last visit to India, a film industry has sprung up. I believe it is the second largest in the world. It has its headquarters in Bombay. Its results are evident, and in the cities advertisements brighten the walls or hang from the lamp-posts. They often take the form of a youth and a maiden. The maiden gazes before her at the traffic, the youth gazes down the nape of the maiden's neck; and thousands of passers-by see them and go in the evening for more. I went twice myself, but had no luck. My first film was crude anti-Japanese propaganda. It was shown in a remote Indian state, in an excellent little modern cinema; you could not have wanted a better-designed house—very simple, with a royal box at the back. The hero was a police inspector, who sang a good deal, and the heroine, who also sang, tricked some fifth columnists. No money had been spent on it, and there was no talent in it. The other Indian film I saw was at Delhi: an ambitious historical film on the subject of the Emperor Humayun. This was much better—decent photography and acting—but I could not agree with my ardent young host who declared it was far superior to our *King Henry V*. That remark, though I did not tell him so, was an example of the Indian un-critical spirit. The production of *Humayun* was fussy and the camera was always on the move. But though I was not fortunate with my two pictures I am certain that a great future awaits the Indian film industry. There is the climate, there is the scenery; for subjects there is the dramatic history, and the varied contem-porary life; and Indians have an innate power of acting naturally and of looking graceful. So I wish that youth and maiden on the advertisements well, even when they warble a duet.

Of modern architecture, the chief example I saw was the great new university at Hyderabad. This is an interesting innovation. It is built in the American fashion on a campus, a wide open space several miles from the centre of the city, in beautiful country, among flowering shrubs. And it attempts to blend two styles of architecture which occur in the Hyderabad state—one style being Mohammedan, and the other derived from the famous Buddhist caves of Ajanta. It is an ambitious work and there is nothing comparable with it over here; you could put dear little Cambridge down in the middle of it. And another achievement—this time in engineering—is the titanic steel bridge over the Hugli at Calcutta. It connects the squalid railway station with the tousled city, and the contrast between it and both of them is overwhelming.

Painting and sculpture: are they progressing? A good deal

may be heard about them in the future. For painting, Bengal is the chief centre. I went to several studios in Calcutta, and I also visited Santaneketan—the home and the creation of Tagore. Santaneketan, about eighty miles from Calcutta, is an impressive little place, a sort of cultural and humanistic university. I spent a night there, and understood why it has exercised a mystic influence on many of its sons. You will either know a great deal about Santaneketan or else you will never have heard of it. It is that kind of place. Its name means "The Home of Peace". The painters whom it has nurtured tend to the religious, the gentle, the ethereal. Down in Calcutta, on the other hand, are pictures which are definite, robust, and based on the folk art of Bengal. Folk art there has a genuine existence among the people—I saw, for instance, a delightful collection of dolls which had been made in the villages. Each doll was a joy and sometimes a terror, too— dolls can be both at once. And the art of the best-known Calcutta painter, Jamini Roy, came out of the villages and is based on the earth. I went to Mr Roy's studio. Many small white rooms were filled with his work, for he is prolific. Although a Hindu, he once made an imaginative approach to Christianity, and his "Christian" pictures, particularly of the Last Supper, have great poignancy. I met other excellent painters too—younger men, who call themselves the Calcutta Group, and there has been an exhibition of Bengal art at Government House under the auspices of the Governor's wife, Mrs Casey, and the Calcutta Group has helped her with it.

To the tragic problem of India's political future I can contribute no solution. And perhaps you may think that there was not much justification for allowing a person of my type to go out at a moment of crisis. If you think that, you will agree with a chorus of indignant colonels at Delhi who were overheard exclaiming, "What next! Fancy sending out old gentlemen who fall ill and can do no possible good." As regards myself, the colonels were not accurate. Old I am, gentleman I may or may not be, ill I was not. I have never felt better. And did I do any good? Yes, I did. I wanted to be with Indians, and was, and that is a very little step in the right direction.

And turning from myself to people who are far more important than I am, namely to the young, I do pray that young English people who like Indians and want to be with them will be encouraged to go to their country. Goodwill is not enough. Of that I am too sadly convinced. In fact, at the present moment goodwill out there is no use at all. The reactions to it are instantly cynical. The only thing that cuts a little ice is affection or the possibility of affection. Whatever the political solution, that can surely do no harm. But it must be genuine affection and liking. It must not be exercised with any ulterior motive. It must be an expression of the common humanity which in India and England and all the world over has been so thwarted of late, and so despised.

[1946]

Luncheon at Pretoria

I have only been to Pretoria once, but it was a great success. It happened back in the twenties. I was staying with some acquaintances at Jo'burg—thus we called it—and the idea was that we should go to lunch with some acquaintances of theirs over at Pretoria. We were to drive over and see the sights, and, after lunch, attend an official reception at Union Buildings.

This idea was carried out with good humour. The drive was, to be sure, not a remarkable one. The boundless spaces of South Africa were in a measured mood, they rolled inadequately, and every now and then a label was stuck in them to show that we were passing the entrance of private property. The dust was like any other dust, and there was a good deal of it, and the trees were grayish and lanky. But Pretoria turned out to be a dear little place, with the touch of two civilizations upon it. Down below were the straight streets of quiet modest Dutch houses, and the statue of Oom Paul by the railway station. Up on the hill was a fine Imperial effort: Union Buildings, with its pavilions, its long terraces, its two domes. An agreeable morning was spent, the sights were indicated and viewed with complaisance, and then it was time for lunch.

The Pretoria acquaintances of my Jo'burg acquaintances were bankers. They lived in a very good-class suburb. The husband was away on business, so his wife, a dignified, handsome and civil lady, had to do the honours. She welcomed us to her cool marblified house, which had a commodious drawing-room, a dining-room, a hall, and (as I was to discover later) the usual offices. There were eight or ten guests, all going on to the government reception, like ourselves. They behaved as guests do, or did, behave. We went into the drawing-room and talked a little, and then we went into the dining-room and talked a little more and ate and drank a little. It would be unjust to call us a set of dull dogs. We were not dogs, we were not even dull. We were not amusing or bored or critical or cross or anything. We were just a collection of well-fed people who did not know one another well and did not want to. This sort of entertainment used to go on—and pray why not?—all over the padded portions of the globe. The acquaintances gather and goggle, their mouths fall open, food goes into the mouths and noises come out, neither at the call of necessity, and never simultaneously. (Belching is confined to the Tribes without the Law.) Sometimes the mouths open sideways to express deference, benignity or repletion. Wearing a blue serge suit which had cost, when new, eleven pounds, I performed these antics with my peers, I too simpered pleasantly.

Then came the dish which transformed our lives.

It was a chicken fricassee.

It was a fricassee of the moister persuasion. The birds lay low in the water, and the various vegetable adjuncts scarcely broke its steaming surface. The mixture swished and trembled upon an enormous oval platter, which no doubt was of silver, having regard to the status of the house. The house-boy carried it round, inclining towards each guest with deference but without intimacy, and each guest, without looking at the house-boy, swayed both hands leftward, and removed a moderate portion to the plate. When he came to me, he tilted the platter a little, to convenience me further. A piece of chicken dragged its moorings and slid to the edge, another followed, and then the gravy gathered in a great tidal wave, gathering strength as it moved, and rolling little onions in its depths. I was busy simpering, and had no conception of what was upon me. Something stung my wrist. The platter had overbalanced, and the entire fricassee poured over me and splashed onto the carpet.

"Sah, sorry sah, sorry," said the house-boy, waving his foot which had been scalded. I answered with a shriek of laughter. Why is laughter so difficult to describe? I hooted, I yelled, I shrieked. I saw a merrythought perching on my waistcoat and went all faint. An onion bumped, I thought I should have died. Up jumped our hostess, flung away her napkin, took hold of me where I was dry, and led me to a suitable apartment. She too was weak with laughter. The guests jumped up, waving their arms and spluttering, more Negroes came running to the cries, the children's Scotch Nanny appeared with a bottle of ammonia from the nursery. Not a moment was to be lost if I were to be got right for the government reception. "Sah, sah, sorry," repeated the house-boy. He had lost his head, but without animation. I gave him my trousers—in some ways our gravest problem. He dropped them upon the tessellated pavement of the hall, and they were there, a lamentable concertina, when other guests arrived. Our hostess lent me her husband's sky-blue Japanese dressing-gown. Though not of the best period, it was a sumptuous garment, and clad in it I hopped round the house like a tropical bird, now taking a sip of coffee in the dining-room, now putting in some work at the pantry sink. "He likes to look like that," she wailed, indicating me to the newer arrivals. "He always looks like that. He likes to."

Afterwards, rationalizing the incident, she praised me without stint, she interpreted my hysteria as a deliberate piece of good manners, designed to save her lunch party. It is true that most bankers would not have laughed. Their sense of values is too sound. And King Edward VII is said to have ill-brooked the arrival of a tureen of anchovy sauce upon his shirt-front, at a moment when he was cementing the Entente Cordiale. But it was not true that I had behaved well. I could not help myself; except in the severely scientific sense, I was not behaving at all. "You were wonderful, quite marvellous," she insisted. Pleasant it was to walk by her side into Union Buildings, and in my blue serge suit too. Miracles had been wrought upon it by the Nanny and Negroes, and for a short time I did not look so bad. Towards the end of the reception some ominous clouds appeared, and the drive back to Jo'burg was altogether too searching. I arrived with every grease-spot stencilled in African dust.

So next day it went to the cleaners, and was back in time to be packed for my journey northward. It came out for a mayoral tea in Rhodesia. The noted pattern reappeared, faint at first, then unmistakable. I had it seen to again on the boat, and wore it for a lunch at Mombasa. Three days of the red soil of Uganda finished it off, and by Egypt it was clear that it could not be worn again. So when I got home I claimed from the insurance people and told them the whole story. They forked out four pounds, but not graciously. They said that the under-writers had expressed surprise.

[1940]

The United States

America is rather like life. You can usually find in it what you look for. If you look for skyscrapers or cowboys or cocktail parties or gangsters or business connections or political problems or women's clubs, they will certainly be there. You can be very hot there or very cold. You can explore the America of your choice by plane or train, by hitch-hike or on foot. It will probably be interesting, and it is sure to be large.

I went there for the first time at the age of sixty-eight. By sixty-eight one is, so to speak, a pilgrim grandfather who knows very clearly what to look for when he disembarks. I had no doubt as to what I wanted to discover in America. It was to provide me with scenery and individuals. The scenery was to be of two sorts—gigantic and homely. The individuals were not to be representative—I never could get on with representative individuals—but people who existed on their own account and with whom it might therefore be possible to be friends. That is the America I looked for and was to find. My visit was a complete success from my own point of view.

After a respectful glance at New York, I went a hundred miles north into the Berkshires. It was April. The trees were leafless—thousands and thousands of birch trees, their trunks whiter than the birch trees here, milk-white, ghost-white in the sharp sunshine, covering the sides of the valley and the crests of the hills; and among the birches pushed pine and hemlock—which is like a not very dark green yew. Was I in England? Almost, but not quite. That was again and again to be my sensation, and in the Arizona Desert I was to feel I was almost but not quite in India, and in the Yosemite Valley that it was not quite Switzerland. America is always throwing out these old-world hints, and then withdrawing them in favour of America. To return to the Berkshires: after a few days' quiet the snow descended and silence became absolute. The country became primeval and polar—endless purity, under spreading motionless trees. I can never be grateful enough for those opening days of silence and snow. They imposed proportion. They made me realize that America is not all town; such a generalization would be truer of England. It is country—controlled no doubt by mechanized gadgets, still it is country. I was glad I had not gaped too long at the New York skyscrapers. Exciting as they are, they mislead. They do not epitomize what lies behind them. Presently the snow melted. Where it had lain appeared dark brown earth and occasional pale lilac hepaticas, and the spring began—in double quick time compared to our spring.

The Berkshires are homely scenery. Gigantic scenery is more difficult to describe, but I will make an attempt. Suppose yourself walking on a Surrey common near Bagshot. There are a good many fir trees about, the soil is sandy, and the prospect rather dull. Suddenly the common stops, and you are standing without any warning on the brink of a precipice which is one mile deep. One mile into the tortured earth it goes, the other side of the chasm is miles away, and the chasm is filled with unbelievable deposits of rock which resemble sphinxes draped in crimson shawls. That, as far as I can get it into a single sentence, gives you my first impression of the Grand Canyon of the Colorado River, but the Grand Canyon would need many sentences to describe and many books. It is the most astounding natural object I have ever seen. It frightens. There are many colours in it besides crimson—strata of black and of white, and rocks of ochre and pale lilac. And the Colorado River itself is, when one gets down to it, still more sinister, for it is muddy-white and very swift, and it rages like an infuriated maggot between precipices of granite, gnawing at them and cutting the Canyon deeper. It was strange after two days amongst these marvels, and terrors, to return to the surface of the earth, and go bowling away in a bus between little fir trees.

The second item I sought in America was the human, the individual. My work lay mainly in universities, and there and elsewhere I found the individuals I sought. I had expected generosity and hospitality. I had not expected so much tact, charm and sensitiveness; here was the delightful surprise. Wherever I went I found delicate understanding of our troubles in Britain over food and clothing, and a desire to help that was never patronizing. This was not confined to the highly educated classes. I recall a cheap eating-house in Nevada where some strangers came up and asked what they could send. I remember the chambermaid in the hotel at Salt Lake City who when I offered her a tip replied, "I don't like to take your money, brother, you need it more than I do." That is the sort of remark which comes from the heart and goes to the heart, and in the light of it and the warmth of it I found difficulty in examining the defects of the American character. The defects are, I suspect, lack of discrimination, emotionalism, and a tendency to narrow the idea of freedom into freedom to make money. "What else have we fought the war for?" a business acquaintance inquired. But I cannot feel these defects are basic. My friends reassure me against this, and not only my friends: the faces of strangers lighting up everywhere, compassionate, respectful, anxious to help. The individuals I met were mostly of Anglo-Saxon stock; I also knew some Swedish and some Italian farming people, made some oriental contacts, and had one or two Mexican friends. I did not have the good fortune to get to know any Negroes. On the whole I saw as much of the human landscape as an elderly traveller may reasonably expect, and I liked it.

But now comes a qualification. Although the Americans I encountered were full of charitable feelings towards Great Britain, I cannot say that they showed much interest in us otherwise. I have often been asked since my return home: "What do they think about us over there?" Indeed, it is often the only thing English people want to know. The answer, not very flattering to our pride, is that the Americans scarcely think about us at all. They are curious about our Royal Family, they are grateful and appreciative towards Mr Churchill, they are—or were—enthusiastic over British films. That is all. They do not discuss our Empire. India, over which they have been so critical in the past, is now scarcely in the news and seems to bore them. Even Palestine was seldom mentioned. An explanation of this indifference is that they concentrate, as we all do, on home affairs, and that when they do think of foreign affairs they think of Russia. China to some extent, but mostly Russia. Russia is always weighing on their minds. They are afraid of war, or that their standard of life may be lowered. I shall never forget a dinner party, supposedly given in my honour, at which one of the guests, a journalist, urged that atomic bombs should be dropped upon the Soviet Union without notice, and quoted with approval a remark which he inaccurately ascribed to Oliver Cromwell: "Stone-dead hath no fellow." "That's good, isn't it, Tom?" he called to another journalist. "Stone-dead hath no fellow". Tom agreed that it was very good, and they shouted, "Stone-

329

dead hath no fellow" in unison or antiphonically for the rest of the evening. They were cultivated men, but as soon as the idea of Russia occurred to them their faces became blood-red; they ceased to be human. No one seemed appalled by the display but myself, no one was surprised, and our hostess congratulated herself afterwards on the success of her party. This obsession over Russia should be realized by all who would understand America, and it explains in part her lack of interest in us.

I did not encounter such hysteria elsewhere, and maybe did not frequent the circles where it is likeliest to occur. Most of the people I was with were not influential or highly placed: many of them were teachers, and some of them were young—students, or they practised music or painting or acting or the ballet, or they were doing small commercial jobs or working on the land. My general impression was of good temper and goodwill and hope-fulness. I could darken the picture, no doubt. I do not take the Statue of Liberty in New York harbour as seriously as she takes herself. And I did encounter hints of oppression and of violence, and of snobbery. But the main verdict is favourable, and I do beg anyone who happens to have fallen into the habit of nagging at America to drop it. Nagging is so insidious. It often resides not in what is said but in the tone of voice. It proceeds not from considered criticism but from envy and from discontent—and, of course, life out there is far more comfortable for the average man than it is here. The food is nicer, if dearer, the clothes are nicer and cheaper, the cold drinks are not lukewarm, and the railway carriages are not dirty. But these advantages over ourselves should not embitter us against the people who enjoy them. Nor should we charge it against all Americans that their politicians do what our politicians tell them, and tell us, they ought not to do.

I chanced to end my three months' visit in the same district of the Berkshires where it had begun. Now it was high summer. The little spring from which I fetched water every day had al-ready begun to flag. The meadows were full of flowers—ox-eye daisies, black-eyed susans, orchids, and an under-carpet of creeping jenny; the meadows sloped down to a brook where the farm-hands bathed. There were swallow-tail butterflies and fritillaries, and the bobolink, a very agreeable bird, skipped from post to post carolling, and another bird, the phoebe, repeated "phoebe, phoebe, phoebe", whence its name. At night there were fireflies to remind us that this was in the latitude of Madrid.

Thunderstorms did not disconcert them, and I would watch their flash vanish in the superior brilliancy of lightning, and reappear. Some of them flew at the level of the grass, others across the curtain of birch trees. They were extraordinarily bright; it was a good year for fireflies, and the memory of them sparking in the warm rain and the thunder is the latest of my American impressions, and the loveliest.

[1947]

Mount Lebanon

Two hundred years ago, Ann Lee, a Quaker of Manchester, England, went to New England and became a Shaker. She founded a sect. The early records of the Shakers are curious and show fantastic elements which have disappeared. There was an attempt to rectify Christianity in the interests of the female—an attempt also made by Mariolatry in the Middle Ages. Mother Ann made a half-hearted bid for equality with Christ, and there are hymns—not sung today—in which homage is paid to them both as the co-regents of the universe, and Adam celebrated as bisexual. This had to be dropped. The sect did not take the intransigent route of Mormonism, it dug up no plates of gold, and commended itself to its neighbours by hard work, good if dull craftsmanship, satisfactory bank-balances, honesty, and celibacy—recruiting its ranks from orphanages. It became a quiet community of men and women—simple folk who liked to feel a little different; even the simplest have this weakness. Meetings were held where sometimes they were seized by the Spirit and shook; otherwise nothing remarkable occurred.

The sect today has almost died out, for its industry has been superseded by industrialism, and orphans have something better to do. But a few settlements of aged people survive, or recently survived, and the friends with whom I was stopping in Massachusetts in 1947 were in touch with the most considerable of these settlements: Mount Lebanon, where Mother Ann herself had once dwelt. It was arranged that we should call at Mount Lebanon. We had with us a pleasant journalist from the *New Yorker* who had been commissioned to write the Shakers up, though I never saw his article—only what he wrote up on me. It was a twelve hours' expedition. The month was April but the weather wintry, and myriads of birch trees were bare and sharp against the sky. We ascended to a broad pass with a view over sub-Alpine scenery, half-covered with snow. The settlement was downhill, below the high-raised modern road. Life had shrunk into one enormous house, a huge wooden box measuring a hundred and eighty feet long and fifty feet thick, and it was five or six storeys high. We knocked at the door, and an old lady peeped out and greeted us in a dazed fashion. This was Elderess Theresa. Further down the box another door opened and another old lady peeped out. This was Sister Susan, and she was bidden to retire. They seemed a bit dishevelled, and it was agreed we should go away for lunch and come back again; they wished they could have entertained us. My friends were in great excitement. The experience was more romantic for them than it was for me, and the idea of home-made chairs hanging from pegs on a wall filled them with nostalgia. It was part of the "dream that got bogged", the dream of an America which should be in direct touch with the elemental and the simple. America has chosen the power that comes through machinery, but she never forgets her dream. I have seen several instances of it. The most grotesque was the handicraft fair in Greenwich Village, where pieces of copper, wood and wool, which had been bothered into ugly shapes at home, were offered for sale at high prices. Another instance is the yearning for Mexico, whose peasants were drunk and dirty, but they did sing. And another instance was these Shakers, to whom, having had our lunch at a drug store, we returned.

They had smartened themselves up no end. Elderess Theresa wore a dove-coloured cape, and Sister Susan's hair had been combed. Sisters Ellen, Ada, Mamie and Ruth also appeared— the first-named sensible and companionable and evidently running the place. Each had plenty of room in the vast building, since the community had shrunk: it was like an almshouse where the inmates are not crowded and need not quarrel, and they seemed happy. I had a touching talk with the Elderess, now ninety-one, who had come from England, and dimly remembered a baker's shop in the Waterloo Road, and the voyage in a sailing ship away from it. She did not regret the days when Mount Lebanon had eighty inmates. "It is much better like this," she said. Her room was full of mess and mementoes, all of which she misdescribed as Shaker-made. It was nothing to the mess in the apartment of Sisters Ada and Mamie, who kept kneeling without obvious reason on the carpet and crackling toilet-paper at the parrot to make him dance. On their wall ticked a clock which had the face of a cat, and a cat's tail for pendulum. Up and down the enormous passages Sister Susan stalked, her raven locks flying, and gesticulating with approval on the presence of so many men. We saw the dining-room, where a place was laid, a little

333

humourously, for Christ. We saw the communal meeting-room. Did they—er—shake ever? No—nobody shook now. Did they—er—meet here for prayer? No, said the Elderess complacently. We used to meet once a month. Now we never meet. They were in fact bone idle and did not even know it. I found myself wishing that other groups, the Oxford for instance, would imitate them.

While the *New Yorker* questioned them, I went out and looked at the five or six other houses which completed the original Mount Lebanon colony (Shaker houses are always in little colonies). They were empty except for ponderous wooden machinery. The ground still sloped into a view, and bright streams and pools of water twinkled at every corner. The sun shone, the snow melted, the planks steamed. The simplicity of the buildings was impressive but not interesting. I went back into the main building to meet Brother Curtis. For the sisters above described only occupied half the huge house. On each floor, in the longitudinal central passage, was a door, which was locked or supposed to be locked, and beyond the doors, all alone in the other half, dwelt the enigmatical Brother Curtis. He could also be reached by walking along outside. He was a healthy elderly man in overalls, very stupid from the *New Yorker* point of view, though probably not from his own. Much time was spent in trying to make him say something characteristic; he was understood to have different ideas on carrying in logs from the sisters' ideas, but since he carried in the logs his ideas prevailed. Perhaps he had been interviewed before. He had a roguish twinkle. Then we took our leave. One of our party found a tin dust-pan in the attic, and was allowed to purchase it; and I myself became an object of envy because the Elderess presented me with a ruler. It is an ordinary wooden ruler, it is eighteen inches long, it rules, but little more can be said of it. We waved goodbye—Sister Susan again bursting out of her special door—and that is the last I saw of these gentle harmless people, though the *New Yorker* returned on the following day to consolidate his investigations. To me, the Shakers were interesting because they interested. My companions were moved by them to a degree which I could not share; they were a symbol of something which America supposes herself to have missed, they were the dream that got bogged. Mount Lebanon has, I believe, now been closed down.

[1951]

334

Ferney

Cultivated monkeys, Charles and I clung to the iron palings of the park. Froggy as well as monkey, he appreciated better than I did what we saw, but even to me the sight was an exciting one. For this was Ferney. So this was Ferney! This was the house that Voltaire built, those were the trees he planted, here his niece, Madame Denis, and others whom I read about afterwards in *La Vie Intime de Voltaire*, by Perey and Maugras, a very entertaining book—here Madame Denis, anyhow, lived, as shapeless as my sentence, but generally liked. With a heart like a warming-pan and a figure like a dumpling, Madame Denis queened it here and reigned it, acted it and reacted it, danced it, reasoned it, unreasoned it, she drove in from Geneva to take possession covered with diamonds, she flounced away to Paris in a pet, she sneaked back. Voltaire was pleased when she arrived, thankful when she left, delighted when she returned. However, that is enough about Madame Denis for the moment. She is all in the book. We are clinging to the park railings.

Our feet slithered upon the uncomfortable parapet. We wished they were more prehensile. Craning our noses to the left, we could see the chapel. It was a small and simple structure, and it looked a trifle *moisi*. I cannot think of the right English equivalent of "moisi". "Mouldy" will not do. "Moisi" must stand. After all, we are in France. That always was the advantage of Ferney—it was just in France, and Voltaire, who preferred a pop-hole to a moat, could be over the border into Switzerland if he felt nervous, and back again if his nerves relaxed or reversed. The chapel ranked with the *loca senta situ* of which Virgil speaks, it had acquired the art of neglect with dignity, and had no wish to look trim. On its frontal was the famous inscription, "Deo erexit VOLTAIRE", and we saw with delight that the lettering of the Voltaire was twice the size of the Deity's. Proportion had been observed. Listen, while you look at this, to what they sang to him in the October of 1767, on the occasion of the feast of St Francis of Assisi. They had begun the day by going to Mass, at two o'clock they had dined in state, a vast concourse of people, at six o'clock they attended a performance of two plays at his private theatre, and when this was over the actors and actresses, including Madame Denis, came forward in their brilliant dresses and grouped themselves around him and sang:

> L'Eglise, dans ce jour, fait à tous ses dévots
> Célébrer les vertus d'un pénitent austère.
> Si l'Eglise a ses saints, le Pinde a ses héros,
> Et nous fêtons ici le grand nom de Voltaire.

Then came fireworks, then an enormous supper, and then a ball at which Voltaire, who was over seventy, danced until midnight. Yes: the chapel has done well to observe proportion.

Straight ahead of us lay the chateau. It was quiet enough now, no singing, no guests, no work, the shutters were closed, the doors locked, and a man in an apron was sweeping up the leaves of 1939—not many of them, for our year was still at its June. Tourists were not admitted, and we were, we knew, almost the last of our sinewy tribe. Soon we should have to skedaddle for our tram. Lucky, happy we, to get this last peep at one of the symbols of European civilization. Civilization. Humanity. Enjoyment. That was what the agreeable white building said to us, that was what we carried away. It was not a large building and that has been part of the disaster. It was too small to cope with the modern world. A Ferney today would have to be enormous, with rolling staircases and microphones, if it was to function proportionately, and if it was enormous could it be Ferney? Even Voltaire felt that he saw too many people, and that the universe, though fortunately bounded by Russia, was upon too cumbrous a scale. He could just illuminate it, but only just, and he died without knowing that he was the last man who would ever perform such a feat, and that Goethe would die asking for more light. On the crest of a wave Ferney sparkled. The boundaries of the universe were to extend bewilderingly, the common people were to neglect the pursuit of agriculture, and, worst of all, the human make-up was to reveal deadnesses and depths which no acuteness could penetrate and no benignity heal.

His end was actually at Paris, and technically not happy. "Count no man happy until he is dead," saith the spirit of dullness. Happiness up to one's final collapse is the better criterion, and this Voltaire achieved. The pains and fears of his last moments (which most of us are doomed to share) altered the sum of his life but inappreciably. The death-bed or death-tumble or death-jumble, death-battle, death-rattle, death-splinter, death-squirt, appalling as it will be to each deserted and dying individual, is a transition, not an epitome. It has no retrospective force. It does not taint (except in a gleam of diseased memory) any of the triumphs that have gone before. Against that over-emphasis, that priestly organization of the death-moment, Voltaire had himself protested, it was part of the infamous thing he had tried to crush. His real end was Ferney, and there we saw him that afternoon, as a house and trees.

Suppose he had come out as a person, and seen our snouts, what would he have done? He would probably have gone in again. But he would possibly have been very kind, and with a twentieth-century kindness, for he had an up-to-date heart. When his secretary's children pestered him with questions which the eighteenth century deemed foolish, he would answer the questions seriously, and put aside his work to do so. When a waiter was nice to him at Mainz, he insisted on stopping at the hotel kept by the waiter's father at Strasbourg. It turned out to be a dreadful doss-house, but he would not leave it, although he was at the height of his fame, for the reason that he had made a friendly compact with the Mainz waiter. Humanity to him was not a platform gesture. He got down to brass tacks over it. Humanity meant saving the Calas family, or being respectful to his secretary's children, or to an unimportant little domestic. "Oh, but that is not the whole story," saith the spirit of dullness, looking up from its ledger; "he was also a capricious, shifty, cruel, litigious, indecent, panicky capitalist; I have it all down." And that exercise of a summing-up goes on, summing up an achievement which is a pattern, not a sum, and a pattern so intricate that the eye rests with the most conviction upon the spots of gold. Whether he would have greeted us is doubtful. Madame Denis, ever too sensitive to externals, would have recoiled with a *moue*, I fear. But they would certainly have caught sight of us. I want to make that plain, for it brings out the restricted character of the site. It was more of a packet than a park. We and the chateau and the man sweeping leaves and the chapel and the porter's lodge were all bunched up together among residential greenery. There was nothing august or wide-sweeping in the demesne, though two hundred years ago, before the trees grew up, there must have been views of the lake. Oddly enough, I catch a parallel with Max Gate as I try to reconstruct. A nest made by a celebrated literary man, going a little untidy. But, whereas Hardy belonged to the soil, the soil belonged to Voltaire, and one has not, when visiting Ferney, any poignant sense of locality. Here is merely a place which he happened to buy and make his own, after Cirey and Potsdam and Les Délices had failed, and it is appropriate that he should have failed to die in it, and that his corpse should have been bandied about in revolutions, and perhaps got mixed up with Rousseau's.

But one cannot cling for ever to an alien pale, or peep for ever at a scene with which curiosity and hope are one's only links. Monkeys must let go. "I am content to have seen Ferney," remarked Charles, as he dusted his paws. I popped the object into my pouch for future use. One never knows, and I had no idea how precious it would become to me in a year's time, nor how I should take it out, and discover that it had turned faintly radioactive. We caught the tram back to Geneva all right, crossed the almost unguarded frontier, and then we departed to our respective cages, which were closed and locked not long after we entered them.

[1940]

Clouds Hill

I used to stop at Clouds Hill in the old days with T. E.—I can't ever think of him as Colonel Lawrence. It's not exactly a show-place, there's not much to see, only a tiny four-roomed cottage hidden away in a four-acre dell of rhododendrons in the Dorset-shire heathland. But it's charming and it's unusual, indeed there's something magical about it.

I first went there back in 1924. T. E. was then a private in the Tank Corps at Bovington Camp. We met down in a pub to talk over the *Seven Pillars*, the early version of which he had allowed me to see. We scarcely knew one another, and the talk was de-cidedly sticky. Then he said, in a casual, diffident way, that there was an old cottage where he and his fellow soldiers sometimes went when they were off duty, to get a little peace and quiet or to play the gramophone: would I care to come up and see it? He took me up through the bleak, ungracious desert of Bovington Camp by a straight road which mounts slightly, and then falls over into a little dip into peacefulness and wildness. There was Clouds Hill. I liked the place at once. His friends were friendly, I felt easy, and to feel easy was, in T. E.'s eyes, a great recommendation. Two Greek words are over the door. He carved them himself. *Ou phrontis*—meaning roughly: "I don't care." They came, he told us, out of a story in Herodotus, a story about a young man who was going to marry a king's daughter, but unfortunately during the dinner party he got drunk, stood on his head on the table and began dancing with his legs in the air. The king was shocked at such conduct in a prospective son-in-law, and said to him severely: "You have danced away your bride." But the young man didn't care. He replied: *Ou phrontis*, "I don't care," and continued to wave his legs in the air. That is the motto T. E. chose for Clouds Hill. We weren't to care, as soon as we were in-side; we were to feel easy, and not worry about the world and its standards.

In those days the two bottom rooms were full of firewood and lumber. We lived upstairs, and the sitting-room there looks now much as it did then, though the gramophone and the books have gone, and the fender with its bent ironwork has been remodelled. It was, and it is, a brownish room—wooden beams and ceiling, leather-covered settee. Here we talked, played Beethoven's symphonies, ate and drank. We drank water only, or tea—no alcohol ever entered Clouds Hill, in spite of the story from Herodotus. We drank out of pretty cups of black pottery. And we ate out of tins. T. E. always laid in a stock of tinned dainties for his guests. There were no fixed hours for meals and no one sat down. If you felt hungry you opened a tin and drifted about with it. It's a grand way to feed; the drawback is that you may lose count of how much you are eating. That didn't matter to T. E., who scarcely ate at all, but the rest of us sometimes went too far. You always know a place better when you've been ill in it, and I've been quite ill at Clouds Hill, from overeating out of those treacherous tins.

When I stopped there, I used to sleep in the little room opposite—it is nattily fitted up today with a bunk and drawers, it has a porthole and looks like a ship's cabin, but then it was all anyhow. T. E. slept in camp, coming out when he could during the day, as did the rest of the troops. It was fine being alone in Clouds Hill at night: so silent—and those were the times when there still was silence. Silence scarcely exists now—it is a lost luxury. One night the silence was disturbed by a nightjar, which perched on the roof above my head and churred and churred—the sort of fantastic thing that would happen at Clouds Hill. It's annoying to be kept awake by a bird even when it's a nightjar, so I went into the garden and shouted at the thing. It kept on churring. Finally I threw a stone. This missed the nightjar, as I had intended, but smashed a tile, which I hadn't intended. T. E. was delighted when he heard of the mishap. He liked his visitors to leave these little evidences of their presence behind them. He declared that the whole affair was an extremely good omen, he refused to have the tile replaced, and it is still broken today.

I don't know whether these trivial remarks convey the atmosphere of the place—the happy casualness of it, and the feeling that no one particularly owned it. T. E. had the power of distributing the sense of possession among all the friends who came there. When Thomas Hardy turned up, for instance, as he did one sunny afternoon, he seemed to come on a visit to us all, and not specially to see his host. Thomas Hardy and Mrs Hardy came up the narrow stairway into the little brown room and there they were—the guests of us all. To think of Clouds Hill as T. E.'s home is to get the wrong idea of it. It was rather his *pied-à-terre*, the place where his feet touched the earth for a moment, and found rest. I was to have stopped there yet again in May 1935, the date of his tragedy. I have been down there since, with thoughts which were necessarily sad, and there came into my mind an inscription which I once saw on a gateway in India: "Jesus—on whom be peace—said: The world is a bridge: pass over it, but build no house on it." Clouds Hill is not so much a house as a point where T. E.'s feet tarried for a little on their all too swift passage through this world.

The ground floor has no memories for me—except that there are a couple of twisted candlesticks, which used to be upstairs. The big lower room was fitted up by him in later years to sleep in, and for his books. He had a good collection, of modern stuff specially. For instance there was Bernard Shaw's *St Joan*, inscribed "To Private Shaw from Public Shaw". And there was a copy of Hardy's *Dynasts* with two inscriptions: the first "Colonel Lawrence from Thomas Hardy", and the second "To T. E. Shaw for his comfort in camp from Lawrence". He, as it were, passed the book on from one of his personalities to another! All these treasures have gone, and in the empty shelves has been arranged an exhibit of photographs. Some of these are from negatives which he himself took when he was out East, others are photographs of him; there are illustrations to the *Seven Pillars* and to *Crusaders' Castles*, and a couple of photographs of the rooms as they used to be, and so on. The little room opposite—that's now a bathroom containing a snowy and hygienic bath. Nothing of the sort in my time. I remember one of our party retiring into a corner with a coin, tossing it, and muttering to himself: "Heads I wash, tails I don't. Tails. I've won." And that represented our general attitude to washing. We did not allow it to win too easily. But—if I may mention so unheroic an article—a hot bottle did figure. T. E.'s kindness and consideration over trifles were endless, and after he had returned to camp one would find a hot bottle in the bed, which he put there in case his precious visitor's feet should be cold. That was so like him. The harder he lived himself, the more anxious he was that others should fall soft. He would take any amount of trouble to save them.

There's a little piece of grass outside the house, also "The Nook", a pleasant semicircle of rising terraces which he contrived. And a visit should end in a climb through the rhododendrons

341

behind to the upper lip of the dell. There you get a surprising and a noble view, right away down to the sea, and incidentally a new idea of rhododendrons. They don't seem like ornamental bushes any more, they become part of the landscape. We used to pull the dead wood out of them for fires, and it burned splendidly. Clouds Hill, viewed from above its rhododendrons, shrinks into a tiny box. You get instead the vast expanses of the purple heath surrounding it, where gentians can be found, and sundew. T. E. cared intensely for the English countryside; he was hoping to explore it quietly upon a push-bike when the end came.

[1938]

Cambridge

It is difficult to meditate on one's dear old university without falling either into snobbery or priggishness. I am a prig, and Mr Steegman sometimes disconcerts me. For instance, when he says in his book:

> The poor man from the elementary school really does not get very much out of Cambridge. He is not likely to make many friends, and will almost certainly remain a fish out of water. He would be much wiser to go to one of the newer universities where he would feel less discontented with his lot. Discouraging though it may be for social reformers, the man from the elementary school is unquestionably excluded from everything that makes Cambridge worth while.

Oh dear. As we push off in our punt, Mr Steegman doing all the work and doing it with efficiency and grace, as we glide under Clare Bridge and through the Gate of Honour and down the Combination Room of John's, this little quotation worries me, like a pea under the cushions, and I ask myself what is wrong with it, or, if nothing, what is wrong with me. The prig tries to get down to brass tacks, in fact. What am I prepared to bequeath the place which I have loved for forty years, and where I have made my best friends? Do I really want the whole of its architecture to be remodelled into bed-sitting-rooms? Do I want its courts to be asphalted, and its lavatories to plunge and roar with municipal self-righteousness? Lavatories were few and far once. They belonged to the Silent Service, and were called Fourths because one of them was rumoured to lurk in the fourth court of Trinity. Ivy peeped. To go to one was an expedition only rivalled by the taking of a bath. Those hardships are vanishing. Hardship is vanishing, but so is style, and the two are more closely connected than the present generation supposes. The food that arrived on heads from the kitchens—lukewarm but from the kitchens—will soon arrive no more.

The punt drifts on, floating away from the cafeteria and cash register down the broadening stream. Here is the Pitt Press, charming, the freshman's first chapel. If we rise up a certain staircase in Caius, we can see the far-away tower of the Pitt Press through the whole breadth of the Senate House, shimmering and bending behind two thicknesses of glass. This is my private discovery. I announce it half asleep. And now the Campanile of the University Library is mercifully concealed behind the Chestnuts of Jesus, and now we bob in the Market Piazza, where a fine new building, the Guildhall, has arisen in the nick of time. How happy am I that Mr Steegman should praise the new Guildhall! The centre of the town will never go smartiboots now, and never become a civic centre. What a lot my guide knows! How deftly he steers! I drowse. A cushion falls into the Pem. And then again that disquieting pea.

This time the pea is feminine in gender.

> While the various parliamentary reforms can be defended as well as attacked, it is unusual to find anyone defending Girton and Newnham. . . . Cambridge owes a great deal to the munificence of such women as the Lady Clare, the Countess of Pembroke, Queen Margaret, the Lady Margaret, and the Countess of Sussex. But these pious Foundresses founded their colleges for men and the argument is pointless. . . . The most serious indictment of the women students, apart from the fearsomeness of the women which those students almost always become unless they marry quickly and forget it all, is the complete pointlessness of their being there.

So women, like elementary-school men, must be banned from our precinct, because they cannot enter properly into its social life. Does not the rest of the educational world lie open, hood upon hood, gown upon skirt, mortar-board upon corduroy, until the appointments board creaks? O spare Cambridge! Is not the city a little one? Is she not unparalleled? Oxford, her swollen sister, is so distended by endowments as to be unrecognizable, and her old Gothic ornaments hang around her neck like a broken locket which she may at any moment swop. Cambridge still keeps her antique shape. No idealistic millionaire has yet raped her. The dons at her High Tables still rise into civilized conversation out of tired grunts. O leave her where she is and as she is, leave her to her peculiar destiny. She, Edinburgh and Bath are the only towns in Great Britain to retain any style, and she is unique, because to style she adds intellect and the power to mould a certain type of male. So keep off, you women, elementary and otherwise; you shall gain nothing from the Cam, not even a degree—that was the little trick it played you, ha ha! Horny-handed miners, meagre-faced technicians, high-collared clerks—go where you will feel less discontented, and where your fellow students will not decline to be your friends. Indians, be so good as to remain at Patna. Americans, have you not Carolina for your portion?

> In North Carolina the poets are fewer,
> We never were much at literature.

The phantoms fly as I sing. So varied, but all so unsuitable, they fly and educate themselves where and how they will, and our punt drifts on, and Mr Steegman and myself are soon engaged in a passionate dispute on the subject of the Chimney at Jesus. What! He would destroy the Chimney? What! He calls it a "depressing flagged path between high walls"? I cannot contain my rage, and utter a series of little Cambridge shrieks. For the Chimney, to me, is part of a delicate dramatic effect; at the end of its calculated dullness rises Alcock's rich Gate Tower, promising a different world—a promise faithfully fulfilled. I like, too, to think that Coleridge stole down it when he ran away to enlist in the Dragoons, and that Malthus paced up it as he planned how to decrease the human race and, incidentally, our troubles. I do not know its date—perhaps it did not exist in their day. All the same, hands off!

This is my major architectural quarrel with Mr Steegman, so it may be gathered how fully, in this department, I accept him. He might perhaps have mentioned the court of Emmanuel which lies across Emmanuel Street—I always like it, although it did destroy a group of picturesque cottages. And he might have mentioned—nobody does—the carving on the wooden west door of the chapel of King's. Still, unlike the Chimney, these are no matters for a blood feud. On we drift, and as each noted building appears and reappears I am delighted by the comments of a learned and courageous mind. The work of the young Wren, of Gibbs, Wilkins and Cockerell, is focused with that of the anonymous medieval builders, until we see our Alma Mater advancing physically down the centuries, not always logically or gracefully, but to the measure that fascinated her sons,

> So that if at night, far out at sea over the tumbling waves, one saw a haze on the waters, a city illuminated, a whiteness even in the sky, such as that now over the Hall of Trinity

where they're still dining, or washing up plates, that would be the light burning there—the light of Cambridge.

How splendidly these words express our faith! How unlucky that they should have been written by a woman!

The book is a guide to Cambridge, in the fuller sense of the word guide. Three parts. Cambridge as it was—historical; as it is—architectural; and modern Cambridge—mainly soci with surmises on what is to come.

> The Fellows went into Chapel on Monday before noon. . . . After prayers and sacrament they began to vote. . . . Thus they continued, scrutinizing, and walking about, eating, and sleeping; some of them smoaking. . . . At the hour of two in the morning . . . never was a more curious, or a more divert- ing spectacle. Some wrapped in blankets, erect in their stalls like mummies; others, asleep on cushions, like so many Gothic tombs. Here a red cap over a wig; there a face lost in a rug. One blowing a chafing dish with a surplice sleeve; another warming a little negus. . . .

This is from the historical section. We have backed into the eighteenth century, and are assisting at the election of a Provost of King's. The eighteenth century is an appropriate landing- stage, our punt moors, and I get out on the steps of the Whig- Conservative Club. Prig's feelings are mixed. He has enjoyed his conducted tour, and found himself more of a snob than he intended. The selective Cambridge he loved cannot possibly sur- vive, except as a museum piece. But the Cambridge-open-to-all, the in-accordance-with-national-needs-Cambridge will only be a technical finishing-school, an educational crammery, a degree- monger, not a university at all. I dislike Mr Steegman's hopes, but I share his fears, and in this dilemma I proffer a third solu- tion—that of razing the whole sacred area to the ground. The dons and other portable valuables could first be transplanted to a safer spot, and Hitler would do the rest free of charge. She would survive as a memory then. And a memory can do more than either a mummy or a travesty towards civilizing the world.

But if it came to a vote I am against my guide. I know so many elementary-school men who ought to have gone up twenty or thirty years ago, and who would have given as well as gained. And I know so many women who have retained their learning in spite of marriage, and their charm in spite of spinsterhood. He will say that these are exceptions, and will also point out that he holds no brief for rank or wealth. This is true, but his conception of Cambridge lacks generosity, he is always scrutinizing the entrance lists, he will risk nothing which is not familiar to him socially; and if generosity is excluded the idea of a university becomes meaningless.

> I have been drawn to think rather of the tens who have failed than of the units who have succeeded, and of the ore which lies buried in our social strata than of the bright coins which circulate from hand to hand. If a field of coal, or of some other mineral, lies unworked and unused, yet it is always there. It may be kept for some future age when its wealth will be more needed, and posterity will bless the prescience and parsimony of their ancestors who refrained from using it. But the human mind is born and lives and perishes. If it is unenlightened it passes away into its native darkness.

This is generosity, this is the warmth without which all education is senseless, and it is not to be laughed away by dubbing it Social Reform.

(Writing as I am on an academic theme, I had better give authority for my quotations throughout. The first two are from Mr Steegman's *Cambridge*, the third was imported from America by Lowes Dickinson, the fourth is from Virginia Woolf's *Jacob's Room*, the fifth is quoted by Mr Steegman from Cooper's *Annals of Cambridge*, and the final one is from Oscar Browning.)

[1941]

347

London Is a Muddle

London is a muddle, and not always an unpleasant one. At the present time the muddle is being hidden away, as far as possible, for this is Coronation Year, but it remains, and it will re-emerge. If you want an example, look out of your bedroom window, even if the bedroom is in a hotel. Your view is sure to be "spoiled" by something vulgar or shabby, but it may be redeemed by something charming, entertaining, antiquated. Anyhow, it will not be all of a piece.

Or go for a walk. You need not even leave the main thoroughfares, you need only look sideways from them with a little attentiveness, and you will see to right or to left the casualness and the confusion which are the Spirit of London. Stand, for example, at the City end of London Bridge. What do you see at the first glance? An enormous building called Adelaide House. Built in an Egyptian style, it towers into the sky, it plunges into the depths; in its vast cube are accommodated hundreds of businessmen with their clerks, typewriters and anxieties all complete, all making money as hard as they can for the sake of the Empire, and upon its roof, which is flat, are a garden, an orchard and a putting-green, where the anxieties of the businessmen can take another form. Adelaide House attempts to set the pace. It is pompous and practical; it suggests that London is a mart, a hub, a focus, a last word on something or other; it bullies the visitor as he approaches from the Surrey side. Wait a minute, though. What is that narrow chasm beneath, and what is that building down in the chasm, nestling against Adelaide's flank? Descending by a ponderous and grimy stairway, you reach Lower Thames Street. Here quite another pace is set and quite another language spoken. Fish and their retainers from Billingsgate throng it in the early morning, lorries and drays rumble at all times. London Bridge is high above, and higher still—nearly two hundred feet in the air—the businessmen are phoning or putting. And the building crouched in the chasm? What is that? Oh, that is only a third London—

348

that is only one of Sir Christopher Wren's best churches, St Magnus the Martyr. It is crouched between the grubbiness and the hygienic tiles, indifferent to both, still leading its own life, and letting the waves of traffic and business roar over its head. Notice the passage going through its tower and leading to a blank wall. A hundred and fifty years ago that passage was the footway of old London Bridge; people went by it to go over the river. The city has piled itself up, like a geological series, and, perhaps, the process will continue until a skin of unsmashable glass is stretched over her, as in H. G. Wells's dream.

This Adelaide-Billingsgate-Magnus combination is typical of London, which is an untidy city, and ought not to be tidied up.

Though attempts have been made to tidy her. Wren himself made one of them, and drew up a town-planning scheme after the Great Fire. The present Bishop of London, on the other hand, thinks that it is Wren who needs tidying, and he pulls down a City church whenever he can. St Magnus the Martyr has eluded him hitherto, but he has recently scored a success in the demolition of All Hallows, Lombard Street. Another attempt at tidying up was made over a hundred years ago by Nash, in the West End. It was a good attempt. Nash planned to connect Carlton House, where the Prince Regent lived, with Regent's Park. His plan today is unrecognizable, but it made some progress, and I am old enough to remember what his Regent Street looked like while it was still untouched. I wish it was there today, for a bad muddle, instead of a good one, has superseded it. It was not great architecture, but it knew what it was doing, and where it was going; it was reasonable and refined. Of course, it had to be scrapped. Greed moulds the landscape of London, as of other great cities, and the Regent Street frontages were too valuable to be occupied by such lowly piles. Besides, they belong to the Crown, and the Crown seems even greedier and more unaesthetic than most landlords. So Nash went, and the present insipid mixture took his place.

If you want a muddle, look around you as you walk from Piccadilly Circus to Oxford Circus. Here are ornaments that do not adorn, features that feature nothing, flatness, meanness, uniformity without harmony, bigness without size. Even when the shops are built at the same moment and by architects of equal fatuity, they manage to contradict one another. Here is the heart of the Empire, and the best it can do. Regent Street exhibits, in its most depressing aspect, the Spirit of London.

349

However, you can easily escape. Go, for a change, up the Caledonian Road, and lean over the bridge which crosses the canal. A much pleasanter muddle awaits you. A queer smell hangs about, sweetish and not disagreeable, and seems to rise from the water. The surroundings are grubby and cheerful, the colouring quiet, as is usual with London colouring, the district poor. The smell comes from the locust beans which are used for making cattle-food in an adjoining factory, and the little boys of the district go bathing at suitable times and steal the locusts. Yes, they pinch them. Almost like John the Baptist, though not quite, they tie them up in handkerchiefs, and push them before them through the savoury waters of Jordan, devouring them as soon as they reach shore. This, too, is London—a London undreamt of in Regent Street—nor is it the only vision to be gained from this particular bridge. Turn the other way and you will have a little surprise. For the canal disappears into the side of a hill. Pitch darkness, no lamps, no towpath. It has vanished under the heights of Pentonville. It keeps its course for over half a mile, absolutely straight, so that when the tunnel is empty the swimmers can see a tiny spot of daylight at its further end. Occasionally a string of barges passes through behind a tug, on its way to the docks.

They are typical, these surprises, these oddnesses. No doubt, all cities which are large and old contain them—they are certainly to be found in Paris. But London has a deceptive air of dullness. One does not expect her to indulge in irregularities and pranks. The businessmen inside Adelaide House, the shops of Regent Street—these seem, at the first sight, to set the pace. Only when one prowls about and loiters and wastes time do the competitors become visible: the church of St Magnus hiding in Lower Thames Street, the canal hiding in the depths of Pentonville, the little boys pushing their cargoes across the canal. There is something more in the City than the getting of money and the spending of it; there is even something which escapes the denunciations of Blake.

> I wander thro' each charter'd street,
> Near where the charter'd Thames does flow,
> And mark in every face I meet
> Marks of weakness, marks of woe.

Blake is on the right lines, but he goes too far on them. London is full of injustice, joylessness and smugness, but there is good temper and rebelliousness in her, too.

Dickens realized this, and so did another great novelist, whose name is not quoted in this connection as often as it should be: Daniel Defoe. Defoe's Moll Flanders is the apotheosis of the Cockney: not criminal, not law-abiding, not respectable, warm-hearted. Next time you go down the little passage which leads to St Bartholomew's, Smithfield, give a thought to Moll Flanders, for it was here that she robbed of a gold necklace a little girl who was coming back from a dancing-class. She thought of killing the little girl, too, but desisted, and, conscious of the risk the child had run, she became indignant with the parents for "leaving the poor little lamb to come home by itself, and it would teach them to take more care of it another time". Give a thought to her when you are stifled with cant, for she is the goods. I used to loathe London when I was young. Living an immense distance away (to be precise, in Hertfordshire), I used to denounce her for her pomp and vanity, and her inhabitants for their unmanliness and for their unhealthy skins. Like Blake, I went too far. Time has tamed me, and, though it is not practicable to love such a place (one could as easily embrace both volumes of the Telephone Directory at once), one can love bits of it and become interested in the rest. She does not pay for being smartened up, and these Coronation arrangements, with their false splendour and false orderliness, do her wrong. She can be casual and gentle. Leave Regent Street for ever. Walk instead through the unsmart squares which lie east of the King's Cross Road—the group which begins with Percy Circus and ends in Arnold Bennett's Riceyman Steps. Or walk as close as you dare to the south bank of the river from Blackfriars Bridge to Tower Bridge—an excellent expedition, including possibilities of trespass and the best available view of St Paul's. Or go up the river to Battersea church, where Blake was married, or down it to Rotherhithe church, where Prince Lee Boo lies buried— he who once was prince of the Pelew Islands. And then return to where you first started from—that is to say, to the City end of London Bridge. Lean over the chasm by Adelaide House again, and allow a few words of one of our living poets to slide through your mind:

> O city city, I can sometimes hear
> Beside a public bar in Lower Thames Street,
> The pleasant whining of a mandoline
> And a clatter and a chatter from within
> Where fishmen lounge at noon: where the walls

Of Magnus Martyr hold
Inexplicable splendour of Ionian white and gold.

T. S. Eliot has felt and has well expressed the muddle of London—the muddle which need not be unpleasant.

[1937]

The Last of Abinger

Written in a Surrey not free from worry, these notes are unlikely to please the nature-lover. Nor are they documentary enough to interest the historian. Most of them come from a commonplace book. The date of the final entry (which is partly a dream) is Monday, 27 July 1946.

EVENING WALK round by the yew-wood on the Pilgrims' Way that I have kidded myself into thinking terrifying. It isn't. The junipers looked like men, the yew-roots were silvery in the last light, and resembled skeletons or snakes, a ghostly little plant or two waved at the entrance of the great warm cave. . . . Yet it isn't, it isn't. And a rabbit moving suddenly in the dark as I came down—it isn't either. The really terrifying things are bacteria or the small trefoil that spoils my rockery. I have not time to see or feel this. I waddle on under a rucksack of traditional nature-emotions, and try to find something important in the English countryside—man-made, easily alterable by man. George Meredith, my predecessor on these downs, could upset himself with a better conscience.

HONEYSUCKLE BOTTOM. The path is blocked by trees that have fallen in the snow. Wild, wild, wilder than the genuine forests that survive in the south of Sweden. I excite myself by learning the names of the woods on the Ordnance Map, by hearing a wryneck, and by seeing a swallow and a bat—all three phenomena early. Think I will learn the names of all the fields in the parish. Wish I had talked to old men.

BLIND OAK GATE. The soil of our parish consists of greensand and of chalk, and is unpropitious to earthquakes. Since the days of King John, who once behaved very badly indeed near Paddington Farm, tragedy has averted her face. The Tillingbourne is too shallow to get drowned in, the banks of the Smugglers' Lane too sloping to be leapt off fatally, and, though there are wells, millponds, quarries, a tower upon Leith Hill and several high wellingtonias, these may not rank as natural dangers; they are artificial death-traps which have been constructed by man for his own destruction, often unsuccessfully. Similarly with the mechanically propelled vehicles which certainly do rush along at lethal speeds; they have always gathered impetus outside the parish boundaries, and similarly with the aeroplanes. Left to itself, there is not a safer place in England than Abinger.

Yet, if not a bang, there is a whimper. Here and there, in this ten-mile ribbon of fluffy Surrey, comes a rumble of occurrences below. One of these rumbles is at Holmbury Camp, where the brow of the heathland is furrowed by neolithic frowns. The other, better known to me, is at Blind Oak Gate.

Blind Oak Gate lies at the extreme north. The tracks leading up to it from the south climb up the clean chalk of the downs, and the sun shines into their ruts. Then begins a brash of bushes —hawthorn, sloe, bramble, heightening into holly and ash, and the sunlight gets frittered away. The ridge of the downs is crossed inadvertently, and after a hundred yards the traveller— for he has become a traveller—reaches this queer clearing. It slopes and slides, descending to the quarter of the north. It has no special shape. Eight or ten paths converge on it—some so unobtrusive that they fail to get counted. It is surrounded by trees, some of which are big, and many of which are undamaged. Tucked away at the top of it is a pond. The pond is small and shallow, and pretty ranunculus covers it in June. But what is it doing up a hill? Like the paths, it is trying to hide itself. It is the centre of the whole affair, if affair there be. When the traveller has passed, the pond rises on its elbow and looks around it. When he returns, it lies back, and only a dribble through silver-weed reveals its dubious bed.

Many years ago, at Cairo, I encountered as a traveller the ruinous Mosque of Amr. The neighbourhood was deserted, the sunlight violent. I stood outside the enclosure and peeped. There was nothing particular to look at—only old stones—but peace and happiness seemed to flow out and fill me. Islam means peace. Whatever the creed may have done, the name means peace, and its buildings can give a sense of arrival, which is unattainable in any Christian church. The tombs at Bidar give it, the Gol Gumbaz at Bijapur, the Shalimar Gardens at Lahore, the garden-houses at Aurangabad. But it came strongest from the Mosque of Amr, and I learned afterwards, with superstitious joy, that others besides myself had noticed this; that the Mosque had been in early days the resort of the Companions of the Prophet; that the sanctity of their lives had perfumed it; that the perfume had never faded away. Anyhow, I remember the feeling and am grateful for it, and it is the exact opposite of the feeling I get at Blind Oak Gate. No peace here. Only a sense of something vaguely sinister, which would do harm if it could, but which cannot, this being Surrey; of something muffled up and recalcitrant; of something which rises upon its elbow when no one is present and looks down the converging paths. Anyone who knows the novels of Forrest Reid will realize what I am trying to say. He, better than any living author, can convey this atmosphere of baffled malevolence, this sense of trees which are not quite healthy and of water which is not quite clear. Yes—something is amiss. Our parish ingredients have been wrongly combined for once, and I can't honestly say I am sorry.

The Blind Oak and the Gate, which lent their names to the clearing, are both gone. The oak goodness knows when. The gate was pulled up for a lark by a boy who is now a middle-aged butcher. He and some other boys set to work and dragged it over the crest of the downs to the great chalk-pit on the southern slope, where they crashed it. The place, deserted by its sponsors, has been left to its very own self, and who knows what it is up to during autumn nights? Not I. But I have sometimes stood there of a late afternoon, and flirted with the shadow of the shadow of evil. When I can go there no longer, I shall still remember it: it will remain as a faint blur opposite the calm cleansing sunlight of the Mosque of Amr. And when its trees are cut down, and its pond emptied and its levels altered, it will not exist anywhere except in my memory. Cursing feebly, Blind Oak Gate will have been cleaned up for ever, and I can't honestly say I shall be glad.

THE OLD CRAB TREE near the second chalk-pit on the downs has been blown down this spring, but is flowering as in other years. Neither sad nor glad that this should be, yet my heart beats to its importance. My head and deepest being said: "We approve of your heart—*it* is important—but why exercise it over nonsense? Only those who want, and work for, a civilization of grass-grown lanes and fallen crab trees have the right to feel them so deeply." Most people who feel as I do take refuge in the "Nature Reserve" argument, so tastelessly championed by H. G. Wells. The moment nature is "reserved" her spirit has departed for me, she is an open-air annex of the school, and only the semi-educated will be deceived by her. The sort of poetry *I* seek resides in objects Man *can't* touch—like England's grass network of lanes a hundred years ago, but today he can destroy them. The sea is more intractable, but it too passes under human sway. Peace has been lost on the earth, and only lives outside it, where my imagination has not been trained to follow, and I am inclined to agree with Gerald Heard that those who do follow will abandon literature, which has committed itself too deeply to the worship of vegetation. To substitute the worship of motor-pumps is unsatisfactory, because it is mere assertiveness, and can never rise out of the advertisement-catalogue atmosphere. The man who says, "Look what I'm doing!" is merely reassuring himself that he has done it. Hence the quantity of empty noises in Walt Whitman.

FALLEN ELMS. Have seen so many of them in the past week that I ought to be able to describe them in a few vivid words. All the black outer twigs are crashed and stamped into the earth and stain it like the ghost of a tree. The wood, where it splits, suggests commonness; where it is sawn and shows ruddy—chocolate surrounded by white—distinction. Reggie B. showed me the sawn top of a great one used as a table; the old fellow what walks on two sticks says they were put to many uses when he was young, only coffins now. Three fell across the garden, seventeen in Hackhurst Lane, one a double elm or cuckold, which broke the steps, one of the pair by the drive gate has shown a surround of cracks as if it will heel over into the field, one leans across the public path into the wood and rests on three ashes. The flesh of fallen ashes is beautifully pink here and there where sawn, and smells different to the elm's, though here again I can't describe or even remember the difference.

CAT IN WOOD washing its face on the grand new oak stump with amphitheatre of hollies behind it. After a time turned and saw me—cat I knew slightly but not in that place. We stared, motionless, but it gradually lowered its head after a bit. I guessed what was up—it wouldn't take its eyes off mine, yet wanted to get them down to a place where they couldn't be on them. A frond of fern was enough, and cat bolted.

356

SANDY FIELD, between Deer Leap and the Railway. Here, a few years ago, three black cinerary urns of the first century A.D. were found, the most perfect of which was given to the B.M. by Mrs E., now herself dead. I saw it there, proffered by a polite colonel, and today went to the field. There is a pond, large but difficult to find, and no doubt of the Silent Pool type, for it lies under the down. This was crammed with carp, and when it was cleared out some of them stocked Paddington. Ernest R. told me all this. Up in Deer Leap is a tumulus, spiky with trees, and the field called Great Slaughter Field is on the other side. (Great Sloe Tree Field really.) Peaceful feeling after turning out this tiny pocket of history. Pond lies on watershed and drains towards Mole.

BUNCH OF SENSATIONS. Listening in the late dusk to gramophone records I did not know; smoking; the quarter-moon shone as the light faded, and brought out sections of my books; motors coming down the Felday road shone through the window and flung the tulip-tree—and pane—shadows on the wallpaper near the fireplace. When the music stopped I felt something had arrived in the room; the sense of a world that asks to be noticed rather than explained was again upon me.

PADDINGTON. Gently and happily relate the evening. In some sort of poetry if it is was mine after the vexatious little prosaic day. I go down to Paddington, old Empson fishing there, and chub, dace, bream, pike, perch, gudgeon are all mentioned as being in the pond. Seldom caught because they find so much in the mud, and their fins break the surface like tiny sea-serpents or float like sticks. There was a woman once nearly drowned bathing—she had been making a film of the Clock House, and bathed. The ropes flayed her arms. The fish moved, the trees regrouped, the lovely summer night came on. I did not want fun or wit or lust, sat on a rail by a young couple and heard old Empson talk. Did not want anything else, or think of my approaching expulsion from unexplored paradises. One gentle fact after another hit me—as that a pigeon's nest is close. Teeth of the pike, dorsal fin of the perch, they hurt, the fin is poison. Old Empson and I are old and moderate friends, he regrets I am going but did not say, he wanted to talk about fish. The loveliness of indifference! The restfulness! The happiness not mystic or intense! Nothing hanging on it.—Now it is 1.0 a.m. I lie down on

357

my pond, but first will read what I have written.—Have done
so.—My hour at Paddington has not come through. I have not
the vocabulary, my mind is not sufficiently equable. Yet I still
see the fishes' tails breaking the water and the small white float
which they never approached.—I am sleepy, I should like the
kindly meaninglessness in my dreams. I must go to my pond, to
its depths which are not deep, only a couple of feet, but out of
sight.

[1927?–1946]

Source and Textual Notes

A: *Two Cheers for Democracy* (London, Edward Arnold, 1951).

B: *Two Cheers for Democracy* (New York, Harcourt, Brace, 1951).

C: For every item but three, at least one earlier published version, as listed by Miss B. J. Kirkpatrick in *A Bibliography of E. M. Forster* (London, Hart-Davis; second, revised impression, 1968) and specified below under individual titles.

D: For thirteen items as specified below, at least one typescript (TS) or complete or partial manuscript (MS); at King's College, Cambridge, unless otherwise stated.

E: *Nordic Twilight* (London, Macmillan, 1940; see below under "Three Anti-Nazi Broadcasts").

The text of this volume is, with the exceptions noted below, that of *A*. It has been collated word by word with *B*, *C* and *D*, and also with the 1970 reprint of the Penguin Books edition of 1965. The absence from this last, however, of any variants other than obvious compositors' errors merely confirms the strong probability, in the absence of evidence to the contrary, that Forster (who died in June 1970) neither made nor authorized any alterations to *Two Cheers for Democracy* after its simultaneous publication in London and New York on 1 November 1951.

There are a number of substantive differences between *A* and *B*, all of them noted below. In a few places *B* corrects a manifest error in *A*; such corrections apart, it is *A* which represents Forster's latest wishes. This is because, at some stage after Edward Arnold had sent Harcourt, Brace the "corrected" galley-proofs from which *B* was set, Forster made further corrections and additions to *A* (including the insertion of the essay on Cavafy) which were either not transmitted to New York— possibly on the mistaken assumption that Forster would be seeing American proofs also—or received there too late for incorporation in *B*.

In the Introduction I have mentioned and illustrated some of the ways in which, to a varying extent, Forster revised these essays, talks and reviews for publication in volume form. It would be tedious, in a volume intended for general use, to list the many minor changes made by Forster at successive stages, and a handful only of the more interesting ones are noted below (italic being used for variant words). In a number of cases, however, a variant reading in *C*, or occasionally *D*, confirmed my suspicions (or convinced me where I had entertained

359

none) that the reading given by *A* (*B*, etc.) is incorrect. This need surprise no one who is familiar with the phenomenon known as "proofreader's illusion", or with the tendency of texts to deteriorate progressively with resetting. More worthy of remark is the pre-eminent authority which, for the reasons given below, I attach to one *C* item (the *Horizon* version of "The *Raison d'Être* of Criticism") *as a whole*.

All substantive departures from *A*, then, including one or two emendations where even the earliest extant version is, I believe, corrupt, are duly noted below. The word "substantive" excludes matters of spelling, word division, the use of italic (other than for emphasis), capitalization and punctuation. In 1951 some attempt was made—certainly by the publisher of *A* rather than the author—to impose such uniformity in these matters as is desirable; in the Abinger Edition the attempt has merely been more persistent. Also, double quotation marks have been adopted for non-fiction as well as fiction, and the terminations "-ize" and "-ization", which are acceptable either side of the Atlantic, substituted for the exclusively British forms. Punctuation, of course, is much less a matter of obeying rules or of choosing consistently between equally valid alternatives, much more an integral part of the writer's craft. Nevertheless, I have ventured here and there—without, I believe, encroaching on the author's prerogatives of meaning, emphasis and tone—to change the punctuation in the interests of consistency or clarity. An example occurs in the essay on Gibbon: "He could be affectionate and grateful—to Lord Sheffield, to the rather tiresome old aunt who had been good to him when he was a boy at Putney—but he never developed his emotions." The structure of that sentence is clear; it is obscured, surely, by Forster's—or a compositor's—careless use of a comma instead of the second dash. Much the same applies to initial capitals. Their use in the sentence "Enter the Science of Psychology" is clearly deliberate and ironical; but when we find, for example, "communist" in one essay and "Communist" in another there are at least three simple explanations of the discrepancy which are far more plausible than any hypothetical nuance or change of attitude.

A problem arises when Forster misquotes from other writers, or quotes from a faulty text, or mis-spells their fictional characters (William Banks for Bankes) or pseudonyms (Comberback—in this volume; in *Abinger Harvest* Comberbacke—for Comberbache).[1] Misquotation may, of course, be significant, for Freudian reasons such as Forster mistrusted, or because its correction would invalidate an argument or destroy a rhetorical effect; examples of the latter occur on page 231, line 10 (D'Annunzio, as reported by Antongini, claimed to be going towards *Life*), and on page 247, lines 36–7, where the echo "shining . . . shines" would be lost if "shining" was corrected to Virginia Woolf's "burn-

---

[1] See *Collected Letters of Samuel Taylor Coleridge*, ed. E. L. Griggs, vol. 1 (Oxford, Clarendon Press, 1956), p. 66.

ing". Elsewhere, it seemed more pedantic to preserve such lapses than silently to correct them—as Forster would surely have done if, say, it had been suggested to him in 1925 ('see "Anonymity"') that Blake's poem begins "Whether on Ida's *shady* brow" (not "snowy").

Here and there, however, what purports to be quotation is actually Forsterian paraphrase or even invention; examples are duly noted.

In the Dedication, B names Roerick (so spelled) first. In the Prefatory Note, B has, for "may be regarded as a key", "is, in its way, the key", and, in the fourth paragraph, after the first and last sentences respectively, "Each item in it is dated." and "Lectures reprint comparatively well." B's Acknowledgements name the American publishers of Lawrence and Strachey, omit "Harvard", and refer to "an Urdu periodical [or rather, an organization] whose title I have mislaid". Minor corrections to A have here been made.

THE LAST PARADE

C: New Writing (editor: John Lehmann), Autumn 1937. An intriguing statement, in the first paragraph, that "the body of Mr Justice Avory continues to decay" is found only in *C*; Avory, who died in 1935, was perhaps remembered by Forster for his performance while representing the Crown against Oscar Wilde in 1896.

THE MENACE TO FREEDOM

C: Spectator, 22 November 1935 (one of a series of nine articles on "Aspects of Freedom" by various contributors).

JEW-CONSCIOUSNESS

C: New Statesman and Nation, 7 January 1939 ("Comment and Dream: Jew-Consciousness").

OUR DEPUTATION

C: New Statesman and Nation, 14 January 1939 ("Comment and Dream: On a Deputation").

RACIAL EXERCISE

C: Time and Tide, 18 March 1939, in "Notes on the Way" series. Instead of "at least eight to one against" (beginning of seventh paragraph) B has C's "eight to one that you cannot".

POST-MUNICH

C: New Statesman and Nation, 10 June 1939 ("The 1939 State").

GERALD HEARD

C: Listener, 14 September 1939 (review of *Pain, Sex and Time,* headed "The Trigger").

THEY HOLD THEIR TONGUES

C: New Statesman and Nation, 30 September 1939. At the end of the third paragraph the quotation from Matthew 18:20 (in Forster's version, "*When* two or three . . .") has here been corrected each time it occurs (as in the preceding essay): although the phrase has no quotation marks when repeated, the repetition needs to be exact.

THREE ANTI-NAZI BROADCASTS

C1: Listener, 26 September ("Two Cultures: The Quick and the Dead"), 3 and 10 October 1940. *C2: London Calling,* 26 September ("The Nazis and Culture"), 3 and 10 ("What Would Germany Do to Britain If She Won?") October 1940. *E:* Forster's pamphlet *Nordic Twilight* (London, Macmillan, [10 September] 1940); a copy at King's College, Cambridge, is inscribed, in Forster's hand, "Alternative, and perhaps preferable, to this are three Broadcasts enclosed"—from which it appears that he allowed Edward Arnold, when publishing *Two Cheers for Democracy,* to choose between *C1* and the longer *E.* The latter has several readings of which those in *A, B* and *C* appear to be corruptions, and the following variants from *E* have been preferred: on page 32, last line, "sends, it" to "sends it, it"; on page 37, "Condemning . . . Condemning" to "Concerning . . . Concerning"; on page 38, line 32, "banned" to "barred"; on page 39, line 8, "had" to "have had" (*C:* "have, or rather had,"); and, on page 40, line 10, "act" to "art". "Condemning" is confirmed by the source quoted (and cited in *E*): Eva Lips, *What Hitler Did to Us* (London, Michael Joseph, 1938), page 82. The "quotations" from Hitler are paraphrases.

TOLERANCE

C1: Listener, 31 July 1941, and *C2: Vital Speeches of the Day,* 15 October 1941, both as "The Unsung Virtue of Tolerance" (Kirkpatrick C369; C437, "Toward a Definition of Tolerance", is a different work, as is an item not listed in Kirkpatrick, "Tolerance", *Picture Post,* 8 July 1939). In the first sentence of the fourth paragraph, the second dash is from *C; A* and *B* have a comma.

RONALD KIDD

C: New Statesman and Nation, 23 May 1942.

THE TERCENTENARY OF THE "AEROPAGITICA"

C: Listener, 7 December 1944 ("A Tercentenary of Freedom"). Forster's quotations are here particularly erratic (*B* being worse than *A*), with, in addition, a seemingly random scatter of archaic spellings in a largely modernized text. For this edition the text is that of *Milton's Prose,* edited by Malcolm W. Wallace (World's Classics, Oxford University Press, reprinted, 1947). On page 51, line 31, *B* has "The answer" instead of *A*'s "He answers" (and *C*'s "Milton answers").

THE CHALLENGE OF OUR TIME

C1: Listener, 11 April 1946 ("The Challenge of our Time: The View of the Creative Artist"; fourth in a series of eleven talks). *C2: The Challenge of our Time*, by Arthur Koestler . . . E. M. Forster [and others] (London, Percival Marshall, 1948). At the very end of the second paragraph, *B* omits ", that, ". In the fifth paragraph, "personal relationships" is *C*; *A* and *B* have the singular.

GEORGE ORWELL

C: Listener, 2 November 1950 (review of *Shooting an Elephant*).

WHAT I BELIEVE

C1: Nation (New York), 16 July 1938 ("Two Cheers for Democracy"; first in a series entitled "Living Philosophies"). *C2: London Mercury*, September 1938 ("Credo"). *C3: What I Believe* (London, Hogarth Press, 1939). *C4: I Believe*, by W. H. Auden . . . E. M. Forster [and others] (London, Allen & Unwin, 1940). *D:* autograph MS fragment in an otherwise blank notebook, probably representing a first attempt at this essay: "Well, I believe in having different sorts of people, and in letting them think and speak & act as they like, so far as that is possible. The modern state tends to produce only two sorts, the bosses and the bossed, both of them pretty nasty, and n [. . .]"

In the second sentence, "Age of Faith" is here capitalized for consistency with the first sentence of the next paragraph; the tone is equally ironic. On page 71, the Keatsian "holiness of the Heart's *affections*" corrects the ". . . Affection" of *A* and *B*—which in turn "corrects" the ". . . Imagination" of *C1–4*. *C1* and *C4* have this final sentence: "Until psychologists and biologists have done much more tinkering than seems likely, the individual remains firm and each of us must consent to be one, and to make the best of the difficult job."

ANONYMITY: AN ENQUIRY

C1: Atlantic Monthly, November 1925. *C2: Calendar of Modern Letters* (editor: Edgell Rickword), November 1925. *C3: Anonymity* (London, Hogarth Press, [1 December] 1925); a copy at King's College, Cambridge, served as press copy for *A*. *D:* page 2 only of an autograph MS, possibly a paper read at the Working Men's College, 28 February 1924, on which the essay was based.

C2 and *C3* differ little from each other, but significantly from *C1*. Many of the variants can only have resulted from authorial revision, and *C1* (hence its designation as such) is clearly the unrevised version: it is scarcely possible, for example, on page 83, line 37, to imagine Forster *inserting* the superfluous "during our reading" before "we are always exclaiming"—and producing an ugly jingle in the process. Two of the *C1* variants, however—in the fourth paragraph, "an old gentleman" for "old gentlemen"; in the sixth, "how they illuminate passion!" for "they illuminate passion."—are at first sight extremely tempting. I have not adopted them, for the following reasons: (a) if the C2/3 readings are compositors' errors, they are of a kind (especially the second) which it would be hard for even a careless author to overlook in proof; (b) we can hardly suppose that *two* compositors made the same two mistakes, and the alternative explanation—that C2 was set from C3 or vice versa—seems on balance less likely than that they were set from different copies of the same TS; (c) since only an editor (or possibly printer) with some rigid ideas on grammar can have been responsible for C1's "whom" in the first sentence, it seems not unlikely that the same mind boggled at what, on this hypothesis, are two calculated irregularities: the elliptical shift from plural to singular, and the avoidance of an expected rhetorical parallelism.

On page 78, line 41, "pure information" is C1–3; A and B—but not the corrected copy of C3—have "the pure information". On page 82, A (alone) has the comic "Priestley" for "Priestly".

ART FOR ART'S SAKE

C: *Harper's Magazine*, August 1949, described as a "slightly emended version of an address delivered before a combined meeting" of the two bodies named on page 87 (incorrectly in A and B). Closely related is "The New Disorder" (*Horizon*, December 1941, and elsewhere; Kirkpatrick A27, B14, C373). In the third and fourth sentences B follows C in reading "Fifty years ago . . . fifty" where A has "Sixty . . . sixty".

THE DUTY OF SOCIETY TO THE ARTIST

C: *Listener*, 30 April 1942.

DOES CULTURE MATTER?

C: *Time and Tide*, 16 November 1935, in "Notes on the Way" series; and (second half) *Spectator*, 4 October 1940. The *Spectator* article ends with a paragraph which mentions that Forster has been "greatly helped this year by reading Locke's little work on the Understanding, and greatly pleased by *The Portrait of a Lady*".

THE RAISON D'ÊTRE OF CRITICISM

C1: *Harper's Magazine*, July 1947 ("On Criticism in the Arts, Especially Music"). C2: *Horizon*, December 1948. C1 states: "This essay was delivered as an address at the Harvard Symposium on Music, under the title 'The Raison d'Etre of Criticism in the Arts'. It has been slightly revised for magazine publication." The revision was probably done by Forster himself, or at least approved by him; and there is no evidence to suggest that he reverted to a pre-publication version as a basis for either C2 or A (which uses the lecture title cited by C1).

The crucial points in the relationship between C1, C2 and A are, first, that *A* derives, unmistakably, not from *C2* but from the earlier *C1*; and, second, that this cannot be explained by supposing that the variant readings in *C2* represent the work of the editor of *Horizon* (Cyril Connolly) or a member of his staff which Forster was either unaware of or chose to ignore. One or two of these variants—those of the type represented by the change, in the second paragraph, from "my paper" to "my survey"—could just be explained in this way (though a footnote, "A lecture given in May 1947 at a Symposium of Music at Harvard", seems designed partly to account for such phrases); and one omission of five or six lines might conceivably have been made in proof for copy-fitting purposes. As against these possibilities, however, several changes—including *additions*—could not conceivably have been the work of any-one but Forster himself. It is clear, therefore, that the reason why he used *C1* rather than *C2* as a basis for *A* was simply that he had forgotten about *C2* or, more probably, had no copy available at the time.

Moreover, it is clear that Forster exercised much more care and concentration over *C2* than over *A*—indeed, it would be surprising if in revising some seventy essays for volume publication he never flagged. And at one point in the preparation of *C2* he noticed and corrected, though not quite fully, an error in *C1* which destroys the required argu-ment; whereas in *A*, at this point, he merely tied up a comparatively insignificant loose end. The passage in question (page 122 in *A*) reads, in *C1* (editor's emphasis of crucial words):

> For now our trouble starts. We can readily agree that *criticism* has educational and cultural value; *the artist* helps to civilize the com-munity, builds up standards, forms theories, stimulates, dissects, encourages the individual to enjoy the world into which he has been born; and on *its* destructive side, *it* exposes fraud and pretentiousness and checks conceit. These are substantial achievements. But I would like if I could to establish *its* raison d'être on a higher basis than that of public utility. I would like to discover some spiritual parity between *it* and the objects *it* criticizes. . . .

Clearly something has gone wrong here. Not only is there a shift from "the artist" to an unrelated "its"; but the thing referred to is evidently *criticism*, and the list of "substantial achievements" corresponds not to those of the *artist*, but to those—detailed in the preceding pages, and recapitulated in almost identical terms at the end of both *C1* and *C2*—of the *critic* (or criticism). The combination of these two flaws, and the unlikelihood of the second having resulted from a mere *lapsus calami*, suggests that what Forster actually wrote may have been something like (my emphases):

> . . . We can readily agree that criticism has educational and cultural value; *it draws attention to* the artist, helps to civilize . . . [then as before]

365

and that the italicized words (or similar ones) were accidentally omitted at some stage, and a comma removed to make sense—the wrong sense. In *C2*, however, Forster has restored the correct sense by changing "artist" to "critic", "it exposes" to "he exposes", and "its raison d'être" to "the *raison d'être* of criticism"; this is perfectly adequate, except that he has forgotten to make the further contingent change of "its destructive side" to, say, "the destructive side". In *A*, on the other hand, he has merely changed "it exposes" to "criticism exposes", thereby supplying an antecedent for "its"—but leaving the *artist* responsible for what are actually the "substantial achievements" of *criticism*.

In this passage, clearly, the text of *C2* (with the "contingent change" mentioned above) must be preferred. Of the remaining variant readings peculiar to *C2*, several are indisputably improvements, others more questionably so, one apparently a misprint. Except for this last, I have incorporated all changes to *C1* made in *C2*, as well as—following normal practice, and hence without comment—those made in *A*. The result is in the nature of a conflated text, but the decision—which affects the very title—seems justified by the special circumstances.

The remaining *C2/A* discrepancies, in summary form, are as follows (figures denote page and line):

105: 3 criticism / criticism in the arts
105: 5 it may be remembered in / you will remember in your
105: 18 agree, I think, / agree
106: 39 controversy which not even Professor Saintsbury had read / controversy
106: 41 Except / Except perhaps
107: 28 raising one / raising it
108: 25 the Garden [*capital added*] / his garden
109: 12 taste / taste, nor perhaps to yours
109–10 Op. 97! He has turned to gaiety / Op. 97: turning away
110: 8 our / the
112: 21 act. How / act, and ask you to observe how
112: 28 spoke and then knew / knew
113: 13 valuable. But if / valuable, but what meanwhile has become of Monteverdi's Vespers, or the Great Mosque at Delhi, or the Frogs of Aristophanes, or any other work which you happen to have in mind? I throw these three objects at you because they happen to be in my own mind. I have been hearing the Vespers, seeing the Frogs, and thinking about the Delhi Mosque. If
113: 16 a particular work of art / Vespers, Mosque, and Frogs
113: 17 at once, if we are sensitive, / at once
114: 26 recipient / spectator
114: 37 that key / the key
115: 23 At / You remember how, at
115: 30 great critic / critic
115: 31 she was an archangel: she / she
115: 33 she was Mephistopheles: she / she

116: 1 tentatively / tentatively in the presence of an expert audience
116: 20 It / There must be many artists, musicians and others here, and it
116: 21 musicians in their work today / them in their work
117: 38 needs / wants
118: 36 unfavourable; it does not and cannot go to the heart of things [*tentative editorial emendation of* them] / unfavourable

Finally, the text given here incorporates three editorial emendations of what, in view of the hash made elsewhere by *C1*, are almost certainly printing errors: on page 113, line 14, "obtainable" for "attainable"; on page 114, line 12, "the nature" for "a nature"; and, on page 117, line 27, "what Fate" for "that Fate".

THE C MINOR OF THAT LIFE

C: Abinger Chronicle, June 1941. At the end of the fourth paragraph *B* shares with *C* an additional sentence: "And Wagner chooses its fellow-brilliant, E, for the close of *Tristan*, where the lovers leave this unreality of light for the darkness, and Verdi [*C adds:* , his inspired follower,] chooses E for the end of *Otello*." Forster doubtless deleted this in proof on discovering that *Tristan* ends, not in E, but in B.

NOT LISTENING TO MUSIC

C1: Listener, 19 January 1939 ("How I Listen to Music"; first in a series of talks by various speakers).

NOT LOOKING AT PICTURES

C: New Statesman and Nation, 15 July 1939 ("Not looking at Art").

JOHN SKELTON

C: none. In view of the footnote on page 135, quotations have not been checked. On page 137, bottom, "way" is an emendation of "away".

"JULIUS CAESAR"

C1: Listener, 7 January 1943 ("Why *Julius Caesar* Lives"; first in a series of talks on set books in the B.A. course in English literature at Calcutta University). *C2: Books and Authors* (B.B.C. pamphlet, Oxford University Press, 1946), pp. 1–5 ("Shakespeare's *Julius Caesar*"). In the third and last paragraphs, the italic "*is*" is *C2* each time. In the last sentence, *B* follows *C*'s "our *comprehension and* enjoyment".

THE STRATFORD JUBILEE OF 1769

C: Spectator, 23 April 1932.

GIBBON AND HIS AUTOBIOGRAPHY

C1: London Calling, 30 July 1942 ("Edward Gibbon, the Historian"; "broadcast in the B.B.C.'s North American service"). *C2: Talking to*

India, by E. M. Forster . . . and others, edited with an Introduction by George Orwell (London, Allen & Unwin, 1943), pp. 11–16 ("Edward Gibbon"). In Forster's second sentence, the first "he" is in *C1* and *C2* only. On page 160, line 29, "twenty-three" is *B*'s correction of "twenty-seven" (*A, C1, C2*)—an error arising from a wrong date (1760 for 1764) in the first sentence of *C1*.

VOLTAIRE AND FREDERICK THE GREAT

C1: Listener, 23 January 1941 ("But . . ."). *C2: London Calling,* 30 January 1941 ("When Voltaire Met Frederick the Great"). *D:* TS of talk, B.B.C. Overseas Service, 17 January 1941. The relationship between the various versions is not entirely clear, but it is safe to say that *A* (and therefore *B*) derives from *C1*; that *C1* departs from *D* at a number of points where *C2* does not; and that some of these departures— "hostess" for "host was" in the first paragraph, "still more civilized" for "much more civilized" in the seventh, "studies art books" for "studies and books" in the ninth—produce absurdities that are eliminated in *A*, though only in one case by a return to the reading of *C2* and *D*. It follows that several readings which are common to *A, B* and *C1* but not to *C2* and *D may* represent less obvious errors in *C1*; and at two points I have adopted such readings. In the eighth paragraph, "*care* to keep house" seems more likely to be what Forster wrote than the slightly unidiomatic "come . . ." ("come *and* keep house would be more natural); and in the first sentence of the tenth paragraph "The visit went *wrong shortly*" gives exactly the sense required, which ". . . very slowly" does not.

On page 163, 25 June 1750 is the correct date ; all earlier versions have 13 June 1751.

GEORGE CRABBE AND PETER GRIMES

C, D: none. (Broadcast talks on *Peter Grimes,* 1945, and on Crabbe, 1960, are quite different.) On page 168, line 12, "and" is an editorial interpolation. The following are editorial emendations: page 171, line 23, "invaded" for "invades"; page 172, line 1, "even" for "ever", page 177, line 35, "mildest" for "wildest".

BISHOP JEBB'S BOOK

C: New Statesman and Nation, 7 December 1940 ("The Blessed Bishop's Book"). The transcriptions have here been corrected.

HENRY THORNTON

C: New Statesman and Nation, 1 April 1939. In the second paragraph, "*an* affectionate husband" is *B* and *C; A* has "and . . .".

WILLIAM ARNOLD

C: Listener, 12 October 1944 ("An Arnold in India"). In the third paragraph, three pairs of quotation marks, probably the misguided

368

handiwork of a *C* editor, have here been removed. Two of the "quotations" ("All the talk . . . humbug" and "physical improvement . . . order of things") are in fact paraphrase, while "and it has grieved many generous hearts before now to find it so" is not even a paraphrase of Oakfield's sentiments, but Forster's comment. The quotation with which the paragraph ends is genuine enough—but comes from the Dedication, so that it is not Oakfield but his creator who "does not shrink" etc.

"SNOW" WEDGWOOD

C: Listener, 13 October 1937 ("More Browning Letters"; review of *Robert Browning and Julia Wedgwood*, edited by Richard Curle). In the last sentence, "and housemaids housemaids" occurs only in *A*.

WILLIAM BARNES

C: New Statesman and Nation, 9 December 1939 ("Homage to William Barnes").

THREE STORIES BY TOLSTOY

C: Talking to India, by E. M. Forster . . . and others, edited with an Introduction by George Orwell (London, Allen & Unwin, 1943), pp. 117–21 ("Tolstoy's Birthday"). *D1:* TS (carbon) of talk, B.B.C. Eastern Service, 16 September 1942, in series "We Speak to India: Some Books". *D2:* TS (photocopy) of talk, B.B.C. African Service, 18 March 1943, in series "Books and People". *A* omits some introductory remarks on Tolstoy; also—with some loss of point—the end of the story of the three hermits. In *D1* this reads: "The bishop replies: 'Your own prayer will reach the Lord. It is not for me to teach you. Pray for us sinners.' The three hermits then turn and walk back to the island over the sea."
On page 202, line 10, "vivified" is *D1*; other versions have "alive". The quotation that follows corresponds to no published translation.

EDWARD CARPENTER

C: Tribune, 22 September 1944. *D1:* TS (carbon) of talk, B.B.C. Eastern Service, 29 August 1944, in series "We Speak to India: Some Books". *D2:* TS (photocopy) of "book talk", B.B.C. Home Service, 25 September 1944. The *D* material has been much rearranged in *C*, on which *A* is based. In the fifth paragraph, "*in* his autobiography" is *C*; *A* and *B* have "is . . .".

WEBB AND WEBB

C: none has been traced. *D:* TS (carbon) of talk, B.B.C. Eastern Service, 26 May 1943, in series "We Speak to India: Some Books"; with an additional final paragraph, on *My Apprenticeship*.

A BOOK THAT INFLUENCED ME

C: New Statesman and Nation, 15 July 1944, in series "Books in General".
D1: TS (carbon) of talk, B.B.C. Home Service, 17 April 1944, in series
"Books That Have Influenced Me". *D2:* TS of talk, B.B.C. African
Service, in similar series. *C* and *D1* are longer than *A* and *D2*, the extra
material consisting mainly of a preamble on how the history of literature
tends to be "influences,'influences all the way", and (in *D1* only) a paragraph on Butler's life. The latter includes a quotation from his *Note-
books*—"I am the *enfant terrible* of literature and art. If I cannot . . . get
the literary and scientific bigwigs to give me a shilling, I can . . . heave
bricks into the middle of them "—whose omission leaves in some obscurity
the reference to heaving a brick on page 213, last line.

In the first paragraph, "to make us feel small in the right way"
was, in *C*, *D1* and *D2*, not merely "a function" but "*the chief* function
of art". On page 214, the remark attributed to Mr Nosnibor's daughter
is a figment. On the same page, the plural (and correct) "Colleges of
Unreason" is found only in *D1* and *D2*.

OUR SECOND GREATEST NOVEL?

C: Listener, 15 April 1943 ("The Second Greatest Novel?"; talk,
B.B.C. Indian Service). In the fifth paragraph, the remark attributed to
Swann is Forster's paraphrase. In the penultimate paragraph, "distort"
is an editorial emendation of "distorted".

GIDE AND GEORGE

C: Listener, 26 August 1943 ("Humanist and Authoritarian").
D: TS (carbon), with autograph corrections, of talk, B.B.C. Eastern
Service, 15 August 1943, in series "We Speak to India: Some Books".
The autograph MS (see Kirkpatrick C382) in the Academic Center,
University of Texas, is a different work. Many of the corrections to *D*
were clearly intended for microphone delivery only, and have not been
incorporated in *C* or *A*.

In the third line, "reactions" is an editorial emendation (cf. the final
sentence) of *A*'s and *B*'s "reaction". In the final paragraph, *A* and *B*
read: "I have not interpreted either Gide or George *to you* . . ."; Forster
has removed many other references to his audience, and the survival
of this one was surely inadvertent. (See also the Introduction.)

GIDE'S DEATH

C: Listener, 1 March 1951 (letter, headed "André Gide: a Personal
Tribute").

ROMAIN ROLLAND AND THE HERO

C: Listener, 8 March 1945. *D:* autograph MS headed, in an unidenti-
fied hand, "Commissioned by John Morris for transmission to India".
D omits the penultimate paragraph and more, adding instead three

paragraphs on Rolland's interest in India, and in particular his book
on Gandhi. On page 228, line 34, "*a* fear of death" is *C* and *D*; *A* and
B omit the article.

A WHIFF OF D'ANNUNZIO

C: Spectator, 22 April 1938 ("A Mediterranean Problem"; review of
D'Annunzio by Tom Antongini). In the second paragraph, for "1914–
1918 war" *B* has *C*'s "last war-period". In the penultimate paragraph,
the speech attributed to D'Annunzio is Forster's paraphrase.

THE COMPLETE POEMS OF C. P. CAVAFY

C: Listener, 5 July 1951 ("In the Rue Lepsius"). Omitted from *B*.

VIRGINIA WOOLF

C1: Virginia Woolf (Cambridge University Press, [May] 1942); there
is a dedication to Leonard Woolf and a note: "This, with a few addi-
tions, is the text of the Rede Lecture which was delivered in the Senate
House, Cambridge, on May 29, 1941. The lecture was also given, in a
somewhat different form, at the Royal Institution of Great Britain on
March 5, 1942." *C2: Atlantic Monthly*, September 1942 ("The Art of
Virginia Woolf"). *C3: Virginia Woolf* (New York, Harcourt, Brace,
[September] 1942). *C4: Wine and Food*, Spring 1943 (extract, headed
"Virginia Woolf's 'Enlightened Greediness'"). *D:* autograph MS,
heavily corrected.

In the first paragraph, *D* has "*between* the flagstones", and the
"through . . ." of all published versions perhaps represents a typist's
error—there is another "through" a few words earlier—rather than a
deliberate conceit. On page 240, line 40, before "Her pen . . .", *D*
has: "It was important to be mischievous: it might even be important
to get bored, for the sense of boredom can warn one of the approaching
abyss, and stop one from crashing."

TWO BOOKS BY T. S. ELIOT

C: Listener, 20 January 1949 ("The Three T. S. Eliots") and 23 March
1950 ("Mr Eliot's 'Comedy'").

"THE ASCENT OF F6"

C: Listener, 14 October 1936 ("Chormopuloda"; review of the published play). On page 258, line 27, "finale" is an emendation of "final".

"THE ENCHAFÈD FLOOD"

C: Listener, 26 April 1951 ("The Unbuilt City"; review of Auden's
book).

FORREST REID

C: Listener, 16 January 1947.

ENGLISH PROSE BETWEEN 1918 AND 1939

*C: The Development of English Prose between 1918 and 1939: The fifth
W. P. Ker Memorial Lecture . . . 27th April 1944* (Glasgow, Jackson, 1945).
On page 267, line 26, "relationships" is *C*; *A* and *B* have the singular.
On page 270, line 15, "them" is an editorial emendation of "these",
as, in the same paragraph, is "influence" of "influences". On page
271, line 11, *C* has: "Still they do it. *Under the lash of Mr A. P. Herbert
they do it.*" On page 274, line 41, *B* has "infidelity" for "in fidelity".

AN OUTSIDER ON POETRY

C: Listener, 28 April 1949 (review of *Poetry of the Present*, edited by
Geoffrey Grigson). In the sentence before the Scovell quotation, *B*
has "the poem *which* I most admired" (*C:* "one poem which I much
admired"); in the one after it, *B* follows *C*'s "And *then*, other poems . . .".
In the final sentence *B* omits "to explain" (*C* has "just").

MOHAMMED IQBAL

C: Listener, 23 May 1946 ("A Great Indian Poet-Philosopher").
D: TS (carbon) of "book talk", B.B.C. Home Service, 8 May 1946.
Between the second and third quotations, "the white *man*" is *D*; *A*,
B and *C* all have ". . . men".

SYED ROSS MASOOD

C: Urdu, October 1937, with an accompanying letter to the Editor.

A DUKE REMEMBERS

C: Listener, 8 December 1937 ("Ducal Reminiscences"; review of
Men, Women and Things, by the Duke of Portland). In the final sentence,
where *A* has "if it is ever afraid", *B* follows *C*'s "*when* it is afraid".

"MRS MINIVER"

C: New Statesman and Nation, 4 November 1939 ("The Top Drawer
but One"; review of Jan Struther's book). In the third sentence, *B*
has "stock" for "stick".

IN MY LIBRARY

C1: London Calling, 26 May 1949 ("Bookshelves of a Lover of Words";
third, following Desmond MacCarthy and Harold Nicolson, in a series of
talks entitled "In My Library"). *C2: Listener*, 7 July 1949. *C3: New
York Times Book Review*, 11 September 1949 ("On the Meaning of a
Man's Books").

THE LONDON LIBRARY

C: New Statesman and Nation, 10 May 1941 ("The Centenary of the
London Library").

A LETTER TO MADAN BLANCHARD

C: A letter to Madan Blanchard (London, Hogarth Press, 1931). Some of the passages in quotation marks are from the books by Keate and Hockin which Forster cites; some are an amalgam of Keate and Forster; one (page 307: "I go with his people . . .") seems to be pure Forster.

In the fourth paragraph, *B* follows *C* in locating Pelew at "latitude 16′ 25″ N., latitude 126 E." Evidently Forster became aware at a late stage that this was incorrect; the latitude he had doubtless taken from Keate, page 7 (without noticing that the shipwreck, though only three pages ahead, was still nine days away), while "126" is probably an error for "136" as taken from Keate's map. On page 311, line 21, "up on" is an editorial emendation of "upon". On page 312, lines 30–31, "the City," is an editorial interpolation; without some such interpolation the passage makes little sense.

INDIA AGAIN

C: Listener, 31 January and 7 February 1946 ("India after Twenty-Five Years").

LUNCHEON AT PRETORIA

C: Abinger Chronicle, January 1940. In the penultimate paragraph, "sense of *values*" is *C*; *A* and *B* have the singular.

THE UNITED STATES

C: Listener, 4 September 1947 ("Impressions of the United States"). In the third paragraph, "under spreading" is an editorial emendation of "underspreading".

MOUNT LEBANON

C: Listener, 24 May 1951.

FERNEY

C: New Statesman and Nation, 2 November 1940 ("Happy Ending").

CLOUDS HILL

C: Listener, 1 September 1938. *D:* TS (photocopy) of talk, B.B.C. Regional and Western Programmes, 15 April 1939, in series "The House and the Man". In the fifth paragraph, where *A* has "on a gateway", *B* follows *C*'s "upon a mosque".

CAMBRIDGE

C: New Statesman and Nation, 29 March 1941 (review of John Steegman's book).

LONDON IS A MUDDLE

C: Reynolds News, 9 May 1937 ("City of Odd Surprises"). On page 351, line 13, *C* has "stifled with *Coronation* cant".

THE LAST OF ABINGER

C: Abinger Chronicle, September 1944 ("Abinger Notes") and June 1940 ("Blind Oak Gate"; a longer version). *D:* the commonplace book mentioned in the introductory paragraph and described in "Bishop Jebb's Book"; it has been edited for publication by Forster, with omissions and concealment of names—though at least two changes, noted below, almost certainly represent mere errors of deciphering or transcription. *C* lacks "Paddington", *D* "Blind Oak Gate".

The second half of the introductory paragraph shows successive stages of revision:

C: They come unaltered from a common-place book which I have had by me for the last twenty years, and local readers may perhaps care to re-write them mentally.

B: Most of them come from a common-place book which I have had by me for many years. (Final entry, July 27th, 1946.)

A: Most of them come from a common-place book. The date of the final entry (which is partly a dream) is Monday, July 27th, 1946.

In "Honeysuckle Bottom", "three phenomena" is *D*; Forster appears to have misread his own writing to produce "these pleasures" (*A*, *B* and *C*). In the third paragraph of "Blind Oak Gate", "covers" is an editorial emendation of "cover", as is "up a hill" of "up hill".

In "Fallen Elms", the semi-colon (replacing a comma) after "commonness" represents an editorial attempt to clarify a sentence-structure that has caused trouble: in place of *D*'s pair of dashes, *C* has a hyphen and a dash, *B* a pair of hyphens, *A* a hyphen and a comma. In the last sentence, "elm's" is *D*; *A*, *B* and *C* have "elms".

"Cat in Wood" has two extra final sentences in *D*: "Mem: do not want to stroke cat's genitals. Didn't know anyone did until last week." Similarly, in *D*, "Bunch of Sensations" ends: ". . . upon me, my restless and feeble brain was at peace for a tick or two. Then it started again, with lust and the sense of humour, its faithful companions."

In "Paddington", the words "lie down on my pond, but first" and the two final sentences are missing from *B*; Forster's restoration in proof of the unabridged entry is presumably related to the simultaneous insertion (see above) of "(which is partly a dream)".

Annotated Index

This index—like those in other non-fiction volumes of the Abinger Edition—is intended to serve three purposes:

(1) The tracing of any given passage or *obiter dictum*, however imperfectly remembered; to the extent that many passages and sayings are liable to be remembered by a particular word rather than by the underlying idea, the index partakes also of the nature of a concordance. Thus, the reader who recalls, and wishes to trace, the passage with the striking image of a writer dipping a bucket into his lower personality will find it indexed under both "buckets" and "personality: two levels of". If, on the other hand, what comes to mind is the idea of the part played by the *subconscious* (or *unconscious*) in artistic *creation*, it will be equally possible to identify the passage via any of the italicized words.

(2) The pinpointing of what Forster has said on any given topic, be this a person, a place, an event, or a concept such as culture or freedom or love or science. In the case of writers, quotations from their works (whether acknowledged as such or otherwise) are, where identified, indexed under their names, since the frequency with which one writer quotes another is not without interest. In the case of concepts, Forster's own words have been used wherever possible, without inverted commas, and with cross-references between related headings.

(3) The provision, in an unobtrusive yet accessible form, of brief expository notes. In writing these I have tried to avoid the irrelevant and the obvious—while remembering that some readers are younger, or more curious, or less knowledgeable, than others. To take two examples from the opening essay. Sir Malcolm Campbell, once a household name, may well be an unfamiliar one to many people today (and especially to those who feel about speed as Forster did); in the index they will find an explanation both of who he was and of why, in the autumn of 1937, Forster singled him out for ironic reference. Later in the essay is a paragraph on "Satan". Those who remember, or have read about, the Italo-Abyssinian war of 1935–6 will at once identify this figure as Benito Mussolini. For others the identification may be less easy; if they turn to "Satan" in the index, however, they will be referred to Mussolini, where those who are still puzzled by "He sprays savages with scent" will find an explanation. In much the same way, a number of quotations or near-quotations for which Forster has given no source are indexed under one or more key words (e.g. "stone-dead") as well as under

authors. (This has not, however, been done with the numerous Biblical phrases, which are almost certain to be recognized as such, and are merely listed under Bible.)

This third function is not one commonly performed by an index, but the incorporation, in this one, of all expository notes seems to offer some advantages. While footnotes are unsightly and irritating to those who do not need them (the few in this volume are Forster's own), *occasional* reference to terminal notes, however well-signposted, is likely to be more laborious than such reference to an alphabetical index. In reality, however, readers of books with terminal notes tend to insert a thumb or forefinger in the end-pages, and (whether the notes are flagged in the text or not) to keep flicking the pages anxiously backwards and forwards lest they miss some gem. Forster deserves a better fate than to be read in such a way; and I hope that nobody will turn to this gemless index who is not conscious of a genuine and specific need to do so.

Subheadings are arranged in order of first page reference, unless some other arrangement—alphabetical, chronological or thematic—seemed likely to be more helpful; Shakespeare's plays, for instance, are given in alphabetical order. Famous books, plays etc. are normally entered only under their authors.

Unless otherwise stated, parenthetic dates after names refer to life-spans, not to reigns etc. A distinction is made between, for example, "(*b.* 1800)" (implying failure to discover the date of death) and "(1900–)" (implying that the person in question was believed to be alive at the moment of going to press.

Forster is abbreviated to F. throughout.

OLIVER STALLYBRASS

Abba Thulle, King of Coorooraa, 306–11 *passim*
"Abide with me" (H. F. Lyte), 90
Abinger, Surrey, 353–8
achievement, varieties of, 70
Ackerley, J. R. (1896–1967), viii. *See also* Paris
Acton, Lord (1834–1902), 254
address, forms of, 270
aeroplanes, 10, 25, 69, 72; and two or three gathered together, 29
aesthetic stock exchange, the, 105
affection: Lytton Strachey's belief in, 275; the only thing that cuts ice in India, 323. *See also* friendship; love

"affections, the holiness of the Heart's" (Keats, *q.v.*), 71
Ahmedabad, 316
air-raids, *see* Second World War
Ajanta, 96, 321
albatross: sportsman, naturalist and, 81
Aldeburgh, Suffolk (where the sea's "implacable advance" has been arrested, since the 1953 floods, by the construction of a concrete and steel piled sea wall, complemented by groynes and beach nourishment), 166–170, 180; F.'s lectures at Festival, 133–49, 166–80
Alexandria, Egypt, 233, 235

ANNOTATED INDEX

Aligarh, 285, 286

Allott, Kenneth (1912–): quoted, 279

America, 327–34; is mongrel for ever, 18; source of speakeasies, 270; London Library and, 302. *See also* Middle West

American Academy: F. addresses, 87–93

Americans, 328–30; lively if backward, 288; their dream, 333, 334; have Carolina, 345, 409

anger: correlated with hope, 5

Anglo-Saxon words: William Barnes's use of, 198

Anna Comnena (1083–1148; turned to the writing of history after failure of intrigues against her brother, John II Comnenus), 235

anonymity (F.'s *obiter dicta* on which were described as "delightful" by Robert Bridges in a letter to F., 4 December 1925), 77–86

Antigone (Sophocles), 29, 90, 215

antisemitism, 12–14; German, 36–37, 45; in story about "Skittles", 288. *See also* racial prejudice; racial purity

Antongini, Tom: *D'Annunzio*, 230–232

Antony (Marcus Antonius, *c.* 83–30 B.C.): allusion to Plutarch's story of music and revelry being heard leaving Alexandria during night before his death, 235

Aristides (Athenian leader during Persian Wars), 237

aristocracy: F.'s, 70–2; in modern Greece?, 237; transference of power from, 267; aristocratic good manners, 274; Duke of Portland a representative of, 288–90; strangled in nineteenth century, 292

Aristophanes (*c.* 450–385 B.C.): *Frogs*, 366; *Lysistrata*, 249

Aristotle (384–322 B.C.), 106

Arizona, 327, 326

Arne, Thomas (1710–78): *Judith*, 155

Arnold, family: characterized, 191, 192

Arnold, Matthew (1822–88): "The Progress of Poesy", 106; "Southern Night" quoted, 193

Arnold, Thomas (of Rugby; 1795–1842): edition of Thucydides, 295

Arnold, William (1828–59), 190–4

art: Nazi and Soviet attitudes to, 5–6; advantage of spending on, 24; Hitler on, 36; for art's sake (being a self-contained harmony), 57–8, 87–93, 320; its privilege to exaggerate, 68; merely one of the things that matter, 87, 90; purpose and nature of, 95–8, 212; infectious nature of, 113–114; eternal freshness of, 114; alone makes meaning out of life, 216; Proust's service to, 217; based on an integrity deeper than moral integrity, 219; palace of, a pitfall, 240–1; and the pleasure of inhabiting two worlds at once, 243; most honoured in France, 286. *See also* culture; literature; music; pictures

artist, the: his need for freedom, 36, 57, 96–7; his *fin-de-siècle* trappings, 87, 91; as bohemian, 90–1, 98; his unique value, 91–92; duty of society to, 94–8; ought perhaps to be alone, 117; comprehensible to the modern mind, 185; his recklessness over money, 285. *See also* writer, the; *and individual names*

arts, the: criticism's role in, 105–

377

books: that do and do not influence, 212, 214–15; owned by F., 295–8; uncut, as inspiriting as a corked-up bottle of wine, 297; lent and borrowed by F., 297; Carlyle on, 301
Booth, Charles (1840–1916), 208
Bosch, Hieronymus (c. 1450–1516), 127
Boswell, James (1740–95): at Stratford as "Corsica Boswell" (his *Journal of a Tour to Corsica* having been published in 1768), 155, 156
bottlenecks: a vicious circle of, 61
Bowen, Elizabeth (1899–), 269
Brahms, Johannes (1833–97), 228, 229; Fourth Symphony, 113, 124; Violin Concerto, 123
bravery, *see* courage
breathlessness, inspired, 242
Bridges, Robert (1844–1930): "Poor Poll" quoted, 54
British Broadcasting Corporation: and Sedition Bill, 47; and Will Hay fade-out incident (2 November 1935), 100. *See also* broadcasting
British Empire: Nazis and, 38; London as centre of, 348, 349
British Museum Reading Room, 248, 300
Britten, Benjamin (1913–): *Peter Grimes*, 177–80
broadcasting (radio; wireless), 10, 94, 99; censorship in, 52; big opportunity of, 107; religious, 187; influence of, on prose style, 270. *See also* British Broadcasting Corporation
Brontë, Emily (1818–48), 79, 268
Brown, Tom (fisherman), 170, 180
Browning, Oscar (historian, described in *Goldsworthy Lowes Dickinson* as "friend and enemy to so many generations of

Kingsmen"; 1837–1923): presidential address to Education Section at Birmingham Social Science Congress, 1884 (quoted from H. E. Wortham's biography, as recorded in F.'s commonplace book, *q.v.*, in 1927), 347
Browning, Robert (1812–89): and "Snow" Wedgwood, 195–6
brutality: and ideals, 247
buckets: and the lower personality (or subconscious), 83, 111, 117
Bumble, Mr (state official), 95–8
Bunyan, John (1628–88), 271
bureaucracy: Milk Marketing Board as symbol of, 11
bureaucrat, the: growing power of, 267; his aversion to clarity, 271
Burke, Edmund (1729–97), 167
Burns, Robert (1759–96), 198
business relationships: and personal ones, 66
businessmen: anxieties of, 348
"but": F.'s use of, 118; Voltaire's, 164
Butler, Samuel (1835–1902): views summarized, 214; *Erewhon* (chapter 22), 118; its influence on F., 212–15; *The Way of All Flesh*, 79, 268
Byron, Lord (1788–1824): and D'Annunzio, 230; "So, we'll go no more a roving", 79
Byzantium: a secular achievement, 237

C minor, *see* Beethoven; music
Cable and Wireless: not to be congratulated in the words of St Matthew, 271–2
caddishness: freakish and innate, 230
Caesar, Julius (100–44 B.C.): murder of, 66; Shakespeare's play,

creation (creativeness; creativity; the creative state or impulse): is disinterested, means passionate understanding, 41; its allies, 41; varieties of, 67; under shadow of sword (etc.), 69, 72; an achievement in itself, 70; and Creator, 82; in literature, 83–4, 86; unconnected with mateyness, 90–1; nature of, exemplified by Coleridge, described by Claudel, 111–12; need for imagination in, 180

Creon, King of Thebes, *see* Sophocles

Cretinist ancestry, possible need for, 18

crime: and illness, in *Erewhon*, 214

crisis: behaviour in time of, 21–4

Criterion, The, 253

critic, the modern, 264

criticism: a cooler ally of creation, 41; permitted by democracy, 67; its *raison d'être*, limitations and dangers, 105–18; called a charming parasite, a gadfly, an imp, 110; Virginia Woolf and, 240; should be tentative, 277; Indian weakness in, 320

Crivelli, Carlo (fifteenth century), 127, 231

Cromwell, Oliver (1599–1658): did not say, "Stone-dead hath no fellow" (*q.v.*), 329

crooners: and Sir Richard Terry, 99–100; in a cultureless world, 101

culture: freedom necessary for, 31–5; English, summarized, 31; German, likewise, 34; importance of, 99–104; no longer a social asset, 102; T. S. Eliot on, 253–4. *See also* art; civilization; taste

curiosity: a characteristic of

humanism, 220–1; Virginia Woolf's, 238, 251; about poetry, 278

Curle, Richard (1883–1968), 196

cynicism: necessity for a crust of, 227

Cyriac of Ancona (*c.* 1390–1450), 231

Czechoslovakia: Nazi treatment of, 38

D'Annunzio, Gabriele (1863–1938), 230–2

Dante Alighieri (1265–1321), 84, 99, 114, 216, 253, 297; and the holders of tongues, 28–9; his intolerance, 46; his attitude to Brutus and Cassius, 66; a cultural test-case, 101; *Inferno* (III: 5–6) quoted, 101; *Divine Comedy* one of F.'s three great books, 212, 215

Darwin, Charles (1809–82), 195, 296

Davies, Margaret Llewellyn (*b.* 1861): *Life As We Have Known It,* 250–1

Day Lewis, Cecil (1904–72): *The Poetic Image* quoted, 116

Dead, Book of the, 30

death: expectation of, makes men separate, 73; has no retrospective force, 337

death-duties, 187, 292

Debussy, Claude (1862–1918), 228; and Monet (cf. *Howards End,* chapter 5), 123

decadence: some people's name for civilization, 68

Decontamination, Ministry of, 28

Defoe, Daniel (whom in 1919 F. had not yet read, to Virginia Woolf's amazement; 1661?–1731): *Moll Flanders,* 351; subject of entry in commonplace book, 184

Giles, Mrs, of Durham, 250–1

Giono, Jean (whose pacifism landed him in prison in 1939; 1895–1970), 23

Giorgione (c. 1477–1510): Castelfranco Madonna, 127

girls: kissed by men to distract them from the vote, 249

Glasgow, 267

Gloucestershire: village life in, 291; smarter than Kent?, 292, 293–4

Gluck, C. W. von (1714–87): Orfeo, 123

God: City of, 11; as creator, 82, 83, 84, 86; imagination compared to, by Shelley, 86; instructed on His own attributes, 186; Iqbal and, 282–4; Voltaire and, 335

Goebbels, Paul Josef (1897–1945), 40, 53, 222

Goethe, Johann Wolfgang von (1749–1832): 46, 336; archenemy of Nazis, 37; Faust, 115, 284

Gogh, Vincent van, see van Gogh

golf: a source of anxiety, 348

good temper: not enough, 65

goodness: Blake's preferred to St Augustine's, 215

goodwill: cuts no ice in India, 322–3

Gourmont, Remy de (1858–1915), 23

governing class, see ruling class

Gracchi, see Cornelia

Grand Canyon, 327–8

grandsire–grandson alliance, 176

Gray, Thomas (1716–71), 155

Great Man, the: belittled, 70; Rolland's cult of, 226

Greece, ancient, 103, 237; saw Man's first attempt to become an individual, 9. See also Athens

Greece, modern: Cavafy on, 237

greed: moulds great cities, 349

greediness, enlightened, 246

Greek Anthology, 82

Greeks, the: and the English, 237

"green thought" (Marvell), 129

Greene, Graham (1904–ᅟ), 268

Greenwich Village, 333

Grigson, Geoffrey (1905–ᅟ), ed.: Poetry of the Present, 278–81

Group Movement, see Oxford Group

Grundy, Mrs: mocked in Erewhon (which much influenced F.), 214

Guatemala, death of Emperor of, 85

guests: behaviour of, 324

habit: or faith?, 30

Hall, Henry (1899–ᅟ), 99

Handel, G. F. (1685–1759), 228

happiness: Solon quoted on, 336

hardness: does not even pay, 54–5; Virginia Woolf's admirable, 250; Iqbal's, 282–4

Hardy, Thomas (1840–1928), 337–8; and T. E. Lawrence, 340–1

Hare, Augustus (1834–93): Two Noble Lives, 241

harmony: in art, 57, 88, 90, 91; between man and his surroundings, lack of, 89; mystic, 89; contrasted with doctrine, 221; in the fabric of England, 293

Harrison, Frederic (1831–1923): Carlyle and the London Library quoted, 300–1

Harvard University: F. addresses Symposium on Music at, 105–118

Hay, Will (1888–1949): and B.B.C. fade-out incident, 100

Haydn, Joseph (1732–1809): Shaw on, 109–10

Hayek, F. A. von (1899–   ), 188
head, *see* heart; intellect; intelligence
Heard, Gerald (1889–   ; original of William Propter in Aldous Huxley's *Time Must Have a Stop; see also* G. H. Thomson, "Forster, Gerald Heard and Bloomsbury", in *English Literature in Transition*, vol. 12, 1969), 356; *Pain, Sex and Time*, 25–7
heart and head: in William Barnes, 198; in Edward Carpenter, 205
Heart, Change of, *see* Change
"Heart's affections, the holiness of the" (Keats, *q.v.*), 71
Heidelberg, University of, 222
Heine, Heinrich (1797–1856; his denouncer was Adolf Bartels, *q.v.*), 37
Heisch, Miss, later Mrs Hookey: poem on the Pelew Islands, 312–13
Hemingway, Ernest (1898–1961), 271
Henry VIII (1491–1537), 133, 143–5; the age of, 137–8, 148
Herbert, A. P. (later Sir Alan; 1890–1971), 372
herd, the: fear of, disguised as loyalty, 9
Heredia, José-Maria de (1842–1905), 236, 295
hero, the: Carlyle and, 40, 215; worship of, a dangerous vice, 69–70; Gide not an example of, 220; Romain Rolland and, 226–9; D'Annunzio as, 230, 232; T. E. Lawrence as, 260, 272–3
Herodotus (fifth century B.C.): T. E. Lawrence's inscription from, 339
Hertfordshire: F.'s childhood home in, 55, 56; his denuncia-

tions of London from, 351
highbrow, the: eclipse of?, 91
Hinduism: and non-Hindus, 320
history: effect of knowing, 10; and literature, 84; and psychology, 269; F's motive in studying, 312. *See also* past, she
Hitler, Adolf (1889–1945), 11, 22, 41, 220, 222, 226; arouses pity as well as horror and disgust, 26–7; speech, 18 July 1937, when opening the House of German Art at Munich ("quotations" are from F.'s commonplace book, *q.v.*, where he has paraphrased Hitler's speech; *see* Norman H. Baynes, ed., *The Speeches of Adolf Hitler*, London, O.U.P., 1942, vol. 1, pp. 587–92), 34, 36; compared with Frederick the Great, 163, 164; foreshadowed by Carlyle, 215; would destroy Cambridge free of charge, 346
Hoare, Sir Samuel (later Lord Templewood; 1880–1959; Home Secretary, 1937–9), 15–16
Hockin, J. P.: *Supplement to the Account of the Pelew Islands*, 314; quoted, 309
"holiness of the Heart's affections" (Keats, *q.v.*), 71
Holy Roman Empire: 56
Home Office: 67
Home Secretary: F. on a deputation (*q.v.*) to, 15–16
Homer, 82, 295
honesty: Virginia Woolf's, 250; defensive value of, 291
Hookey, Mrs, *see* Heisch, Miss
hope: correlated with anger, 5
Hoppner, John (1758–1810), 185
Horace (65–8 B.C.), 69
Housman, A. E. (1859–1936), 198; "Far in a western brookland", 79

Huchon, René (1872–1940): *Un Poète Réaliste Anglais (George Crabbe and his Times)* quoted, 168 (second quotation; letter to Edmund Cartwright, 22 July 1794), 175 (on "the leather lads", citing Edward Fitzgerald), 179

Hulbert, Jack (actor and comedian; 1892–), 3

human aim, the: summarized, 299–300

humanism: as reaction to European tragedy, 221; contrasted with authoritarianism, 223

humanist, the: four characteristics of, exemplified by Gide, 220–1, 223, 224

humanity: Voltaire's, 162, 163, 337; belief in, a characteristic of humanism, 220, 221; common, thwarted of late, 323. *See also* Man

Humayun, Mogul emperor (1508–1556), 321

humble connections, advantage of, 209

humour, sense of: the "saving grace", 230; a hoary nostrum, 240

Huxley, Aldous (1894–1963): *Grey Eminence*, 269

Hyderabad, 285; F.'s happiness in, 317; university at, 321

"I will purge..." and similar phrases, 36, 45

Ibsen, Henrik (1828–1906): subject of entry in commonplace book, 183; *Per Gynt*, 258, 282

ideals: F.'s distrust of, 45; willingness to drop a couple to oblige a friend, commended by Butler, 214; in politics, Cavafy bored by, 237; and brutality, 247. *See also* causes

idleness: of Shakers, commended, 334

illness: and crime, in *Erewhon*, 214; Proust and, 216–17; in Virginia Woolf and others, 240–1

imagination: entailed in tolerance, 45; our only guide into the world created by words, 86; the creative, 180

immortality: not to be won by talking, 230

incompetence: need to get rid of feeling of, 291

India: F.'s visit to, in 1945 (when the "old gentleman" whose illness aroused the colonel's indignation at Delhi was Hermon Ould, *q.v.*), 54, 315–23; William Arnold and, 190–2; Iqbal and, 282–3; Masood and, 285–7; books about, 297; Americans bored over, 329; inscription on a gateway in, 341; Moslem buildings in, 354

India Office: *Marine Records, 570a* (*Antelope's* logbook, December 1791 to June 1793) and *570c* (pay records), 305

Indian languages, 318, 320

Indian literature, 297, 320. *See also* Iqbal

Indians claiming descent from Sun, 19

individual, the (individuals): does not exist, 9–10; a divine achievement, 55–6; versus the community or State, 56–7, 66; impossible to abolish, 73, 363; or to grade, 117; F.'s quest for, in America, 327, 328

industrialism, 292; simplicity and, 204; Edward Carpenter and, 206; effect of, on writers and others, 267–8; unforeseen by Voltaire, 336

influence: exerted by books which one feels one could almost have written, 215
informality: growth of, 270–1
information: contrasted with atmosphere (must be accurate, should be signed), 77–80, 86; irrelevant to literature, 84
Inglis, Sir Robert (1786–1855): on Henry Thornton, 185, 186
insanity, *see* madness
inspired breathlessness, 242
instinct: superior to reason, 35
institutionalism: the snag in, 300
insurance: replacing charity, 268; soddening effect of, 293
intellect, the: not everything, but dangerous to insult, 41; Soviet regimentation of, 224; Virginia Woolf and, 247. *See also* reason
intellectuals: versus scientists, 58
intelligence: poetic and prose varieties, 198
internationalism (super-nationalism): Goethe ripe for, 37; Rolland and, 229; a cert, 294; Sir Mirza Ismail and, 320
inventions, *see* scientific research
inventiveness, *see* Man
Iqbal, Mohammed (1875–1938), 282–4, 320
Ireland, Northern: Forrest Reid and, 264
Isherwood, Christopher (1904–), 248; *Mr Norris Changes Trains*, 271. *See also Ascent of F6; Dog beneath the Skin*
Islam: Iqbal and, 282–3; and the sense of peace, 354–5
Ismail, Sir Mirza (1883–1959), 319, 320
isolation: subject of entry in commonplace book, 184
Italy: Renaissance, 88, 90; D'Annunzio and, 230, 232

Jacopone da Tod: (1230–1306): quoted (as also, following F., by W. H. Auden in "Kairos and Logos"), 72, 90
Jaipur: conference in, 315, 318–20
James I (1566–1625), 82; made a mess, 90
James, Henry (1843–1916), 103, 104; as psychologist, 79; Forrest Reid and, 264; *Portrait of a Lady*, 364
James, Mrs (F.'s great-grand-mother), 17
Jebb, John, Bishop of Limerick (1775–1833), 181–4
Jerusalem, the New, 206
Jew-consciousness, *see* antisemitism
Jewish gifts to the world, 216
Jocasta (incestuous mother of Oedipus in Greek myth), 258
John, King (1167?–1216), 353
John Company, *see* East India Company
Johnson, Samuel (1709–84), 271; goes to Brighton instead of Stratford (as guest of the Thrales, and probably not as a calculated slight on the Jubilee), 155; quoted by Bishop Jebb, 184
Jones, the boy, 274
Jonson, Ben (1572–1637), 154
Jourdain, M. (Molière's *Le Bourgeois Gentilhomme*), 270
journalism: big opportunity of, 107. *See also* newspapers
journalists: their tendency to call artists uppish, 91. *See also* middlemen
Joyce, James (1882–1941), 267, 269, 272; *Ulysses*, 273
Julian the Apostate (332–63; as Emperor, tried with scant success to oust Christianity), 235
justice: economic, versus personal freedom, 56; Virginia Woolf's

and fury"), 105; *Merchant of Venice* quoted ("naughty world"), 29; *Midsummer Night's Dream* quoted ("Following darkness"), 265; *Othello*, 151, 153, 177; *Richard II* quoted ("death of kings"), 103; *Richard III*, 170; *Timon of Athens*, 153

Shakti Yogins, 26

Shaw, George Bernard (1856–1950): on Haydn, 109–10; possible allusion to *You Never Can Tell* ("you think . . ."), 269; and T. E. Lawrence, 341

Sheffield, 205

Sheffield, John Holroyd, 1st Earl of (1735–1821), 158, 160

Shelburne, William Petty, 2nd Earl of (1737–1805), 168

Shelley, Percy Bysshe (1792–1822), 206; on imagination (Preface to *The Cenci*), 86; on poets (*Defence of Poetry*), 91

Shostakovich, Dmitry (1906–), 106

Shrapnel, Colonel Henry (inventor of the Shrapnel shell; 1761–1842), 199

silliness: as a check to silliness, 14

Simnel, Lambert (*fl.* 1487–1525), 148–9

simplicity: Tolstoy's belief in, 201, 204

simplification: temptation of, 24

sinner, the: comprehensible to the modern mind, 185

"Sir Patrick Spens", 77, 79, 81

sister: disgrace of having a, 12

Sistine Chapel, Rome, 90

Skelton, John ("Poet Laureate"—a title meaning much less than F. appears to suppose; *c.* 1460–1529), 133–49

"Skittles" (Catherine Walters, a fashionable courtesan; 1839–1920), 288

Slater, Montagu (1902–), 177, 179

slavery, *see* Wilberforce

"Slumber did my spirit seal, A" (Wordsworth), 79

small: right and wrong ways of being made to feel, 212

smartness, *see* fashion

Smetana, Bedřich (1824–84), 38

Smith, Sydney (1771–1845), 46

sneering: and planning, 55; guffaws being organized into sneers, 100; cannot belittle art, 219; at modern poetry, 281

"So, we'll go no more a roving" (Byron), 79

social conscience: man's dalliance with idea of, 9

socialism: Edward Carpenter's, 206–7; Beatrice Webb's, 208–9

society: its duty to its members, 94; including the artist, 94–8. *See also* community, the; State, the

Solon (Athenian law-giver; *c.* 638–558 B.C.): on happiness, 336

Sophocles (*c.* 496–406 B.C.), 103, 104; pessimism of, 69; *Antigone*, 29, 90, 215 (is F.'s central faith); *Oedipus*, 258

soul, the: in Nazi propaganda, 35, 37; cannot be purged by charity, 187–8

"sound and fury" (*Macbeth*), 105

South Africa: F. in (1929), 324–6

"Southey's sister", i.e, his future sister-in-law, Sara Fricker, whom Coleridge married, 77

Soviet Union, *see* Russia

speech: linked with love, peace, light, 30

Spencer, Bernard (1909–63), quoted, 279

"Spens, Sir Patrick", 77, 79, 81

spiders' threads thrown back into the past, 183

spiritual retreat, need for a, 25
spontaneity: no place for, in modern war, 29; hated by Nazis, 34; possessed by working class, formerly by aristocracy, 293
sport: and nationalism, 60
sportsman: albatross-shooter a, 81
Sprott, W. J. H. (Professor of, successively, Philosophy and Psychology at Nottingham; 1897–1971): dedication to, ii
Stalin, Joseph (1879–1953), 59
stamp-collecting, 297
Stanley, Oliver (1896–1950): cliché-box of, 272
Stanley of Alderley, Lady (1807–1895), 300
stars, relief afforded by: old style, 89; new style, 262
State, the: sacrifices to, 9; Nazi worship of, 34, 41; Milton and, 51; versus the individual, 66. *See also* community, the; society
Steegman, John (1899–1966): *Cambridge*, 343–7
Stein, Gertrude (1874–1946), 269
Stephen, Adrian (1883–1948): *The Dreadnought Hoax*, 239
Stephen, Sir Leslie (Virginia Woolf's father; 1832–1904), 205, 250
Stevenage: a meteorite town, 57
Stevenson, Robert Louis (1850–1894), 83
stock exchange, the aesthetic, 105
stone: is like grass, 247
"stone-dead hath no fellow" (3rd Earl of Essex, recommending the execution of Strafford; as reported by Clarendon in his *History of the Great Rebellion*), 329–30
"Stop": an example of pure information, 77–80

Strachey, Lytton (1880–1932), 266, 272, 274, 277; *Queen Victoria*, 273–6
Strasbourg: Voltaire at, 337
Stratford-on-Avon: Jubilee of 1769, 154–6
Stravinsky, Igor (1882–1971): a typical reaction to, 100
street-watchings (systematic observations of demonstrations, marches etc., aimed at providing objective reports on the behaviour of police and demonstrators), 48
strength: Antigone's preferred to Carlylean heroes', 215
strong, the: stupidity of, 68
Struther, Jan (1901–53): *Mrs Miniver*, 291–4
study: only a serious form of gossip, 84
style: order in which words are arranged, 80–1; Mrs Miniver and, 292
subconscious, the: bucket let down into, 82–3, 111; and modern literature, 268–70. *See also* personality
Sun: attitude of descendants of, 19
super-nationalism, *see* internationalism
Sweden, 353
Sweerts, Michael (1624–64): *A Family Group* (now attributed to Michiel Nouts), 129
Swift, Jonathan (1667–1745): *Gulliver's Travels*, 213, 313; influenced F. negatively, 215
Swinburne, Algernon Charles (1837–1909): "Hertha" quoted ("beloved Republic"), 11, 67, 68
Swinnerton, Frank (1884–), 276
Sykes family, 17
sympathy: no longer enough, 65

ANNOTATED INDEX

Tacitus (*c.* 56–120), 295
Tagore, Rabindranath (1861–1941), 282, 283, 284, 321
Tasso, Torquato (1544–95): *Gerusalemme Liberata*, 106
taste, good: belief in, a characteristic of humanism, 220–1; Forrest Reid's natural, 264. *See also* culture
Tchaikovsky, Peter (1840–93): Second Piano Concerto, 115; Fourth Symphony, 124
témoignage, *see* Baudelaire
Templewood,Lord,*see* Hoare, Sir S.
Tennyson, Alfred, Lord (1809–1892): and Palace of Art, 241
Terry, Sir Richard (1865–1938), 99–100
Themistocles (Athenian leader during Persian wars; *c.* 528–462 B.C.), 237
Thornton, Henry (F.'s great-grandfather; 1760–1815; the election verse was recalled by his daughter Marianne in her "Recollections", now, like his diary, in Cambridge University Library), 182, 185–9.
Thornton, Marianne (F.'s great-aunt; 1797–1887), 187
"Three Blind Mice", 119–20
Thucydides (*c.* 460–400 B.C.), 295
Times, The, 61, 91, 100, 225, 271, 292; *Atlas*, 297
tins: pros and cons of eating out of, 340
Titian (*c.* 1488–1576): *Entombment*, 127
Todi, Jacopone da, *see* Jacopone
tolerance: necessity of, 43–6; no longer enough, 65; Lamb's and Stevenson's, 83; cultural, 104; Voltaire's belief in, 162; Samuel Butler's belief in, 214; Rose Macaulay's, 267; symbolized by London Library, 299

Tolstoy, Leo (1828–1910): his belief in simplicity, 201, 204; compared with Proust, 216, 218, 219; with Rolland, 226; S. R. Masood and, 286; *The Cossacks*, 201–2, 204; *The Death of Ivan Ilyitch*, 201, 202–3, 204; *The Kreutzer Sonata*, 123; *The Three Hermits*, 201, 203–4, 369; *War and Peace*, 152; one of F.'s three great books, 212
Toma, Admiral, 70
tongues: holding of, 28–30
Tovey, Sir Donald (1875–1940), 109, 124
Toynbee, Arnold (1889–): *A Study of History*, 43, 269
Tradesmen's Entrance: necessity of retaining a, 293
tradition: the life of, 57; cultural, 102
tragedy: appropriate response to, 21; the European, contrasting reactions to, 220–3
trams: need for accurate information about, 77–8
Treacle Tommy, 289
trees: in America, 327, 328; at Abinger, 353, 355–6
Trevelyan, R. C. (1872–1951): "Virginia Woolf" (*Abinger Chronicle*, April 1941), 240
Trollope, Anthony (1815–82), 296
trousers: fate of a pair of, 325–6
truth: two kinds of, 81, 84; concern for, felt by Voltaire, 162, 163; by Gide, 221, 225; by Virginia Woolf, 241, 248; by Lytton Strachey, 274
twentieth century: its disillusionment, 10; its "challenge", 54–8. *See also* modern mind, the: nineteen-thirties; nineteen-twenties
tyrants: becoming the norm, 10; seldom listen to sages, 27. *See also* dictators

405

uncle, a huntin' *see* Forster, W.

unconscious, *see* subconscious

unhappiness: in childhood, dangerous effects of, 163

unimportant and unpractical people: relative far-sightedness of, 22

United States, *see* America

university education: disposes one to overwork "but", 118; distrusted by Edward Carpenter, 206; conception of, must include generosity, 347

unpleasantness: the right to shirk, 59

unseen, the: Quakers' sense of, Clapham Sect's indifference to, 188

uselessness: of literature, in varying degrees, 79–80; privileges of, 86

U.S.S.R., *see* Russia

Vahid, S. A.: translations of Iqbal, 282–4

Valassopoulo, George: translations of Cavafy, 233, 236

Valkyries: symbols of courage and intelligence, 68

van Gogh, Vincent (1853–90), 4–5 (where the remarks allegedly written on "the white walls of his cell" evidently represent messages conveyed to F. by the paintings on the walls of his "half-dozen rooms" at the Exhibition—although "Sorrow is better than *laughter*" is Ecclesiastes 7:3, and is quoted, accurately and in English, by van Gogh in a letter to his brother Theo written in the autumn of 1876), 6, 7, 36, 126

variety: hated by Nazis, 34, 36; mistaken for weakness, 53; admitted by democracy, 67; bores some people, 70; inescapable, 73

Vaughan Williams, Ralph (1872–1958), 144

vegetation: worship of, foreseen, 356

Velasco, Isabel de, 128

Velasquez (1599–1660), 103, 104; *Las Meninas*, 128

Verdi, Giuseppe (1813–91): *Otello*, 177, 367

Victoria, Queen (1819–1901), 275–6

Victorian age: summarized, 54–5; apparent permanence of, 196, 248; satirized by Samuel Butler, 212–14; solemnity of, 273. *See also* nineteenth century

village life: in Dorset, 199; in Gloucestershire, 291

violence, *see* force

Virgil (70–19 B.C.), 114; and the holders of tongues, 29; *Aeneid*, 33; quoted (6:462; "a land rugged and forlorn" in Page's translation), 335

"Visit to a Gnani, A" (section of Edward Carpenter's *From Adam's Peak to Elephanta*), 207

Voltaire (1694–1778), 260; and Frederick the Great, 162–5; one of two people F. would name to speak for Europe at the Last Judgement, 162–3; preferred to Macchiavelli, 215; and Ferney, 335–8; allusion to "écrasez l'infâme", 337; summarized, 337. *See also* Keate

Wagner, Richard (1813–83), 21, 22; Beachcomber on, 110; his use of C sharp, 120; he never let the fancy roam (allusion to Keats, *q.v.*), 122–3; and Coriolanus Overture, 124; *Nibelung's Ring*, 68; *Tristan and Isolde*, 367

Addendum

The couplet on page 345 is, it seems, a garbled version of

> Alas! for the South, her books have grown fewer—
> She never was much given to literature.

—as given in a volume entitled *Purely Original Verse. Complete Works, and a Number of New Productions*, by J. Gordon Coogler (1865–1901), published at Columbia, South Carolina, with two title-pages dated 1897 and 1901 respectively. Coogler's Introduction quotes freely from reviews of earlier volumes; one review refers to him as "the Sir Edward Arnold of Columbia"— meaning, probably, Sir Edwin Arnold (1832–1904, author of a portentous blank-verse poem *The Light of Asia*), though on the evidence of this couplet William McGonegall seems more appropriate. I am grateful to Professor George W. Williams of Duke University for nailing, and his colleague Professor Carl Anderson for mailing, the source of this "quotation".